SÂR DUBNOTAL

vs.
Jack the Ripper

SÂR DUBNOTAL

vs.
Jack the Ripper

From The Memoirs of Sâr Dubnotal
adapted by
Brian Stableford

A Black Coat Press Book

Acknowledgements: We are indebted to Alain Rozemblum and Marc Madouraud.

English adaptation and introduction Copyright © 2009 by Brian Stableford.
Cover illustration by Gino Starace.

Visit our website at www.blackcoatpress.com

Table of Contents

Introduction

This collection comprises five linked novellas taken from a popular part-work series published in Paris in 1909-10 by A. Eichler, featuring the "occult detective" Sâr Dubnotal. The series eventually ran to 20 issues, most of which were independent stories, but the sequence that ran from No. 7 to No. 11 recovered a villain briefly featured in No. 1, *Le Manoir hanté de Crec'h-ar-Vran* ("The Haunted Manor of Crec'h-ar-Vran"), and described a series of phases in an ongoing battle between that villain, identified in the title of No. 7 as *Tserpchikopf, le sanglant hypnotiseur* ("Tserpchikopf, the Bloody Hypnotist"), and the multitalented hero.[1]

The present collection omits No. 8, *La Piste astrale* [The Astral Trail], of which no copy could be located, but the substance of that episode is summarized in the following one, *L'Ecartelée de Montmartre* ("The Quartered Woman of Montmartre") and the omission makes little difference to the overall story line, which reaches its climax in *Jack l'éventreur* ("Jack the Ripper"), and then proceeds to a curious epilogue in *Haine postume* ("Posthumous Hatred"). All of the original items are now very rare; these translations have been made from photocopies supplied by the periodicals section of the Bibliothèque Nationale.

The original publications were unsigned and their authorship is unknown; the suggestion that they might have been the work of the prolific Norbert Sevestre, although widely

---

[1] A complete bibliography of the Sâr Dubnotal series is included in *Shadowmen: Heroes and Villains of French Pulp Fiction*, Black Coat Press (ISBN 978-0-9740711-3-8).

quoted, is unsupported by any documentary evidence. It is perhaps understandable why no one was eager to claim them, as they were obviously dictated in a hurry by someone who does not appeared to have had sufficient imaginative stamina to sustain his competence through the requisite wordage of each episode, never planned his plots in advance and never did second drafts. This is by no means an ideal method for the production of mystery stories, which require tight plotting if they are to be fully effective, but it was a standard method of literary production at the time, when cheap fiction for semi-literate readers was pumped out in vast quantities in a highly competitive market. Although it was not an environment con-ducive to literary quality, that feverish market was a selective regime that encouraged various kinds of innovative mutation, and it is that aspect of the fiction produced in that era which remains interesting today.

This particular series of novellas is historically interest-ing because of the contribution it made to the evolution of "superheroes" in early French pulp fiction. The development of the character of Sâr Dubnotal fitted into a brief early inter-val in the much more gradual development by Jean de La Hire of the character of the Nyctalope, several of whose exploits are featured in other Black Coat Press volumes.[2] Nowadays, of course, there is a standard pattern that writers use to explain the "origins" of superheroes—which is to say, explaining how they came to possess their extraordinary abilities—but La Hire and the author of Sâr Dubnotal had no such ready-made tem-plate available, and had to improvise, having no idea what readers might be prepared to find plausible. While La Hire floundered and prevaricated, however—eventually offering several quite distinct accounts of the identity and history of the Nyctalope—the author of Sâr Dubnotal gladly took advantage of the only rhetorical framework that was readily available to

---

[2] *The Nyctalope vs. Lucifer* (ISBN 978-1-932983-98-2), *The Nyctalope on Mars* (ISBN 978-1-934543-46-7) and *Enter the Nyctalope* (ISBN 978-1-934543-99-3).

him: the literary mythos of the occult revival, spiced up with a little jargon borrowed from Friedrich Nietzsche.

That decision gave the character of Sâr Dubnotal an imaginary back-story stretching back beyond the limits of history, and an actual literary ancestry stretching back more than half a century. The convolutions of that back-story and literary ancestry are remarkably complicated, and they provide a striking illustration of Oscar Wilde's dictum that life imitates art far more frequently (and far more insistently) than art imitates life—to which, one might add the remark, in this particular context, that life generally exhibits execrably bad taste when it comes to choosing which works of art to imitate. This is, of course, not in the least surprising; the same psychological factors that make the clichés and naiveties of pulp fiction attractive and exciting, despite its faults, are responsible for the eagerness of so many people to import them into their lives. Habitual readers are, in general, less vulnerable to that tendency than adherents of urban legendry and advertising, who obtain their clichés and naiveties from more brutal sources, but the fringes of literacy—where such garish works of fiction as the exploits of Sâr Dubnotal exist and thrive—inevitably reveal actual patterns of hopeful and fearful illusion far more obviously than the various pinnacles of literary endeavor in which careful and considered works flourish.

The ultimate origins of "occult science" lie in a tension that developed in the world dominated by the Roman Empire between rival schools of philosophy developed from Greek antecedents, when a broad orthodoxy whose core lay in the works of Aristotle was opposed by dissenters whose thought was "neo-Pythagorean" or "neo-Platonic." The latter schools of thought tended to be fervently interested in a supposed mystical harmony underlying the world of appearances, contained in hidden networks of connection that were analogical rather than straightforwardly causal.

That intellectual tension was recovered, and further sharpened, in the Renaissance, when the old Aristotelian orthodoxy was cleverly integrated into Christian thought by Thomas Aquinas. One of the side-effects of that integration was that the rival schools of neo-Pythagorean and neo-Platonic thought acquired a vague satanic taint, although the suggestion that they were morally suspect was always vigorously denied by their adherents. The defensiveness that Renaissance neo-Pythagoreans and neo-Platonists were forced to adopt greatly encouraged a tendency to obfuscation and mystification already innate within those schools of thought, illustrated by the extraordinarily elaborate jargon that became attached to the fundamentally neo-Platonic field of alchemy. Mysticism became a significant topic in its own right, sprawling across the boundaries of church doctrine in an ungainly fashion.

The revivification and mystification of the neo-Pythagorean and neo-Platonic traditions in Renaissance Europe inevitably absorbed other holistic and mystical traditions that similarly claimed descent from antiquity, most notably the Jewish Kabbalah. This ever-expanding synthesis eventually came to be called "the Hermetic tradition," because of its alleged origins in the works of the legendary Hermes Trismegistus, to whom a passing reference had been made by Saint Augustine in *De Civitate Dei*. Two significant documents relating to this supposed tradition began to circulate in manuscript in the 15th century, a copy of one of which—the *Corpus Hermeticum*—was acquired by Cosimo de Medici in 1460 and given to the neo-Platonist scholar Marsilio Ficino. Ficino's version of the *Corpus*, together with his commentary and extrapolations of its claims, was widely circulated; its admirers included Rodrigo Borgia, who became Pope Alexander VI, and Giordano Bruno, one of the most prominent advocates of the heliocentric theory of cosmology.

The idea of the Hermetic tradition was remarkably flexible, and its elasticity was seized upon by such determined innovators as Paracelsus, who became the first of a new breed of inventive occultists bent on usurping ancient authority and claiming its nebulous weight for their own ideas. The *Corpus Hermeticum* was exposed as a fraud in 1614 by Isaac Casaubon, who traced many of its sources and identified some of its anachronisms, but Casaubon's skepticism had little effect. Time had, in any case, moved on; the same year saw the emergence of a new and spectacularly successful mystical mythology cast in the Paracelsian mold. The new occult philosophy made its debut in a pamphlet generally known as the *Fama Fraternitus*, which offered a brief biography of a magician named Christian Rosenkreutz [Christian Rosy-Cross]; it was followed by the *Confessio Frateritas* (1615), which described his magical initiation, and then by the allegorical *Chymische Hochzeit Christiani Rosenkreuz* (1616; tr. as *The Heretick Romance; or, the Chymical Wedding*). The third of these items was signed by Johann Valentin Andreae—who was later to publish the Utopian romance *Christianopolis* (1619)—and who may well have written all three.

The "Rosicrucian" pamphlets excited an enormous amount of attention as would-be members searched high and low for the mysterious Brotherhood of the Rosy-Cross, but no such organization actually existed and contemporary attempts to fill the breach were conspicuously half-hearted. That evident absence, however, only encouraged subsequent readers of the pamphlets and their abundant spinoff to suggest that the Rosicrucians were simply too well-hidden to be easily found, and they became increasingly popular as a literary device. It is a Rosicrucian who provides the "philosophical microscope" used to observe Mercury in the Chevalier de Béthune's *Relation du monde de Mercure* (1750), and his kindred hovered in the background of much subsequent French imaginative fiction, including the philosophical components of Honoré de Balzac's celebration of the *Comédie Humaine*, which also made much of the works of the mystic Emmanuel Swedenborg. Such references remained esoteric, however, until the Rosicrucian myth achieved a crucial breakthrough to popularity in Edward Bulwer-Lytton's *Zanoni* (1842).

Bulwer-Lytton, who later became Baron Lytton of Knebworth, had a lifelong interest in mysticism and magic—his library, preserved at Knebworth, still includes the texts he

11

used in his research. That interest had already been displayed in his fiction in *Asmodeus at Large* (1833), *Godolphin* (1833) and the best-selling historical novel *The Last Days of Pompeii* (1834), but *Zanoni* proved far more influential, especially in establishing a crucial literary dyad: on the one hand, the eponymous master of mystical science, who seems to be immortal and to posses various magical powers, but remains essentially enigmatic within the text; and on the other, a young aspirant who is desperate to be initiated into his secrets, despite the fact that such initiation is a hazardous business for the unworthy, whose innocence, curiosity and ambition add up a useful narrative viewpoint with which readers may identify. A similar relationship is reprised, in even more melodramatic terms, in Bulwer-Lytton's later novel *A Strange Story* (1862), by which time the influence of *Zanoni* had spread far and wide—and was by no means confined to literary work.

In France, the man who took Bulwer-Lytton's example most conspicuously to heart was a failed *littérateur* named Alphonse-Louis Constant, who decided that, if he could not succeeded as a mystical artist, he might do better as an artful mystic. He became interested in the esoteric discipline of "Martinism," founded by the 18th century mystic Martinez de Pasqually (1727-1774), which had previously attracted the attention and support of such literary men as Jacques Cazotte. Having decided to revive and continue the lapsed Martinist tradition, Constant adopted the pseudonym "Eliphas Lévi" and began to pass himself off as a pseudo-Rosicrucian mage, concocting two highly influential works that passed themselves off as non-fiction, although they were almost entirely products of his own imagination: *Dogme et rituel de la haute magie* (1854-56; tr. as *The Doctrine and Ritual of Transcendental Magic*) and *Histoire de la magie* (1859; tr. as *The History of Magic*). They became the principal source of all subsequent handbooks of "high magic" and supposed histories of magic.

The publication of Lévi's scholarly fantasies coincided with the rapid spread of Spiritualism, an American-originated craze that generated a new religion, in which "mediums" claimed to be able to contact the dead and communicate with them, initially by means of encoded "raps" and "table-turning," and later by means of spirit manifestations composed of "ectoplasm." Although the originators of the craze, the Fox sisters, eventually confessed to fraud, and many other celebrity mediums were exposed as deceptive conjurers, the movement proved unstoppable, evidently answering a deeply-felt need that many people had to believe in an afterlife and obtain various kinds of reassurance therefrom. The phenomena that mediums appeared to produce in their "séances" posed a stark challenge to 19th century science, which generated a long series of more-or-less organized "investigations" by scientists of every stripe—many of whom proved far easier to dupe than stage magicians, who understood how the tricks were worked but had a professional interest in not revealing their secrets.

The English physicist William Crookes was one of the most prestigious investigators who were converted to belief in Spiritualism, and the subsequent zeal led him to become an ardent propagandist for the movement in the 1870s. His support generated tremendous controversy; a report that he published in the *Quarterly Journal of Science* in 1874 was widely reprinted and translated, and became a key inspiration for the foundation of a Society for Psychic Research in 1882. In France, the astronomer and prolific popularizer of science Camille Flammarion became an exceedingly ardent spiritualist, initially associated with a domestic movement founded by Hippolyte Rivail, a.k.a. "Allan Kardec."

The séances that Flammarion hosted in Paris between the 1860s and the 1920s attracted the involvement of such celebrities as the actor Victorien Sardou, the scientist Gustave Le Bon and the writers Victor Hugo and Arthur Conan Doyle, as well as many of the famous mediums of the day, including Eusapia Palladino. In America, meanwhile, the investigation of fraudulent mediums became a key element in the early development of private detective agencies, as described in Allan Pinkerton's documentary account of *The Spiritualists and the Detectives* (1877). By the time Eusapia Palladino undertook a lavishly-publicized tour of the USA in 1909, there were so many skeptics determined to debunk the movement that she was caught cheating at virtually every performance she gave, but it made no difference to the credulity of believers.

As described in the introduction to the Black Coat Press edition of Jules Lermina's *Panic in Paris*,[3] a key development in the Parisian occult revival occurred when that writer's daughter married one of the *bouquinistes* who kept stalls on the banks of the Seine, Henri Chacornac. Lermina financed the shop that Charornac subsequently opened at No. 11, Quai Saint-Michel in 1884 under the title Librairie Générale des Science Occultes, which became very successful, not merely as a commercial enterprise, but as a meeting-place and focal point of the Parisian "occult community." Another important focal point, also formulated in 1884, was the Parisian branch of Madame Blavatsky's Theosophical Society, which recruited members on a considerable scale. Both institutions catered for a much broader range of occult interests than were sanctioned by the relatively narrow parameters of Spiritualist faith, pandering to the kind of holistic generality that had generated such hopefully all-inclusive documents as the *Corpus Hermeticum* and the *Fama Fraternitatis*.

Henri Chacornac's most avid and ambitious customers included two medical students at the University of Paris, Gérard Encausse and Augustin Chaboseau; a Hungarian-descended Lorrainean aristocrat named Stanislaus de Guaita and two of his protégés, Joseph Péladan and Albert Jounet; and the would-be historians of the occult Jules Bois and Edouard Schuré. The shop's clientele also included many literary men whose interest in occult matters was more purely artistic, including numerous Parnassian poets and several of the writers who would soon inspire or take up central positions within the nascent Decadent Movement.

Encausse, who used the signature Papus—allegedly meaning "Physician" and borrowed from a document called

---

[3] ISBN 978-1-934543-83-2.

the "Nuctemeron of Apollonius of Tyana," faked by Eliphas Lévi—joined the Parisian branch of the Theosophical Society shortly after its formation, but left in a matter of months to found his own Hermetic society, the Ordre Kabbalistique de la Rose-Croix, in collaboration with Guaita and Péladan. Guaita was a literary man who had published three volumes of poetry before undergoing an abrupt "conversion" when the Decadent writer Catulle Mendès advised him to read Eliphas Lévi. Péladan had become interested in Catholic Mysticism early in the 1870s, and was also enthusiastic about homeopathy, a medical system which relied very heavily on neo-Platonic affinities; he had come to Paris in 1882 to embark on a literary career, initially as an art critic, and had become friendly with the proto-Decadent writer and philosopher of Dandyism Jules Barbey d'Aurevilly before Guaita became his substitute patron. Péladan's first novel, *Le Vice Suprême*, was published in 1884, launching a moderately successful career, but he had already conceived a desire to take Barbey's theory of Dandyism to the next level and remake himself as a Rosicrucian Magus, and that remained his primary aim.

The alliance between Papus, Guaita and Péladan, which also included Chaboseau, Jounet and the writer Paul Adam, did not last long, because Péladan—not a man given to sharing authority—soon split from his former colleagues to form his own neo-Rosicrucian Order, which went on to enjoy tremendous success, completely eclipsing its forerunner. Péladan had already extended his baptismal name to Joséphin, but soon decided that even that was not sufficiently grandiose, and changed it to Mérodach, a name borrowed from ancient Sumeria; he borrowed the title of "Sâr," which had allegedly been used by a caste of priest-magicians, from the same source.

Encausse, Guaita and Chaboseau decided to concentrate on their own revamped version of Martinism, although Encausse subsequently went on to join the Parisian branch of the Order of the Golden Dawn and numerous other organizations, while Guaita was content to remain an individual eccentric, sustained in lofty isolation by his independent means. Péladan effortlessly outshone his former associates, partly because he integrated his career as a moderately popular novelist into his career as a lifestyle fantasist, but mainly because he was so much more strident; his self-aggrandizement was great enough to win him especially detailed consideration in Max Nordau's full frontal attack on the Decadent Movement, the Occult Revival and all that they seemed to symbolize, *Entartung* (1893; tr. as *Degeneration*).

Péladan was by no means the only influential figure in *fin-de-siècle* Paris to combine lifestyle fantasy with a literary career, and the literary men who patronized Henri Chacornac's bookshop and accepted the influence of his wares often found themselves acquiring a reputation as mystics or magicians, even when they made no effort to cultivate such images. The writers who deliberately cultivated the overlap included Bois and Schuré, both of whom made considerable use of fiction in popularizing their ideas—although Bois' literary work had a much wider range—but the greatest impact by far was made by a literary work was that contrived by Joris-Karl Huysmans' account of fashionable Satanism, *Là-Bas* (1891), in which several notable lifestyle fantasists appear, in disguised form, as characters—including Remy de Gourmont's mistress, Berthe Courrière, who served as Huysmans' guide to the "occult underworld" while he was researching the book. The most celebrated English quasi-Rosicrucian organization, the Order of the Golden Dawn, included many members who combined careers in literature with lifestyle fantasy in varying proportions, most notably W. B. Yeats, Arthur Machen, Algernon Blackwood, A. E. Waite and Aleister Crowley.

Like Encausse, many of the writers who combined occult and literary interests were involved, if only briefly or peripherally, with the Theosophical Society whose central ideological document was Madame Blavatsky's *The Secret Doctrine: The Synthesis of Science, Religion, and Philosophy* (1888). Not content with a Léviesque history of magic, Blavatsky invented a highly imaginative account of the entire past and future evolution of humankind, featuring seven "root races" (two of which had yet to materialize) associated with various primordial continents, including Hyperborea, Lemuria and Atlantis. Theosophical ideas spawned an entire subgenre of literary fantasy, overflowing abundantly into popular pulp fiction, where they made a significant mark on early "sword and sorcery" fiction by Robert E. Howard and his contemporaries. The most successful writer of quasi-Theosophical occult fiction was Marie Corelli, who became the best-selling writer in the English language during the *fin-de-siècle*, with such works as *A Romance of Two Worlds* (1886), *Ardath* (1889) and *The Soul of Lilith* (1892).

It was against this historical backcloth that "occult detective fiction" developed—perhaps inevitably. Initially, as in Allan Pinkerton's documentary account, literary detectives were intent on discovering rational explanations for seemingly-supernatural events, elucidating mysteries and exposing frauds; Sherlock Holmes never had any truck with supernatural explanations, despite the fact that his creator became a devout Spiritualist, because it would have betrayed the logic of his deductive endeavors, and most of his clones followed his example. L. T. Meade and Robert Eustace produced a series of stories for *Cassell's Magazine* in 1897 whose hero is characterized as *A Master of Mysteries* (book version 1898), and who specialized in using deductive logic to reveal the mundane truth behind seemingly-supernatural apparitions. It was not long, however, before the credulous got into the act, introducing a new species of mystery whose solutions were frankly supernatural, and whose investigation therefore required a new kind of special expertise.

Two other genteel collaborators, Hesketh Pritchard and his mother Kate, who wrote as "E. and H. Heron," produced a series for *Pearson's Magazine* in 1898-9 featuring Flaxman Low, explicitly described as a "psychic detective," that was presumably designed as an ideological reply to Meade and Eustace. Allen Upward produced a similar series for the *Royal Magazine* in 1905-06, but the writer who made the crucial breakthrough in this kind of fiction, raising it to a much higher level of popularity as well as literary and metaphysical sophistication was ex-Theosophist and ex-Golden Dawn member Algernon Blackwood, who produced a series of novellas collected as *John Silence, Physician Extraordinary* (1908).

It was Blackwood's collection, which was heavily advertised and sold very well, that provided the template for future ventures. The most significant of those future ventures included a series by William Hope Hodgson collected as *Carnacki the Ghost-Finder* (1913); a series by Aleister Crowley, initially published in 1917-18 under the pseudonym Edward Kelly and belatedly collected as *The Scrutinies of Simon Iff* (1987); a series by Crowley's former associate Violet Firth, who used the pseudonym Dion Fortune for her prolific adventures in lifestyle fantasy, collected as *The Secrets of Dr. Taverner* (1926); and a series launched by the self-professed psychic Margaret Lawrence in *Number Seven Queer Street* (1945).[4] The exploits of Sâr Dubnotal constituted the first such series to appear in France.

It is highly improbably that the author of Sâr Dubnotal had read the adventures of Flaxman Low or John Silence, but he probably knew of their existence. Whether he came up with the idea of developing a French rival, or whether he was commissioned to do so by Eichler, there is no way of knowing, but he does not give the impression of being well-informed in matters of occult theory and might well have relied on hearsay and newspaper reportage for his "research." The proximal inspiration is more likely to have derived from the publicity surrounding Eusapia Palladino's American tour than from any literary source.

The Eastern components of the protagonist's character are lifted from Theosophy and his title is appropriated from Péladan, but other aspects of the series' fundamental imaginative apparatus are more difficult to track to their sources; the jargon used is highly idiosyncratic, and it is not easy to figure

---

[4] There was also *Ozmar the Mystic* (1896) by Emeric Hulme-Beaman.

out why, for instance, the author prefers "*télépsychique*" [telepsychic] to the more conventional *télépathique* [telepathic] when describing thought transmission, although a case could be made out for his usage being the more appropriate. The most significant items of jargon contained in the series, on the grounds of their incessant repetition, are the Greek-derived *psychognosie* [psychognosis] and *psychagogue*, which exists in English as well as French. Both terms have fallen into disuse since 1909, but were bandied about quite freely during the occult revival, and provide interesting examples of terms over the use of which occultists and proto-psychologists squabbled, each attributing different meanings to them.

Psychognosie is probably best-known nowadays by virtue its adaptation into German by the philosopher Franz Bentano, who used it as a suggested label for "descriptive psychology," a kind of proto-Behaviorism that attempted to build an exact empirical science on the observable manifestations of psychology. Webster's definition of the equivalent English term—"Any penetrating study of the psyche, especially as concerned with the individual character"—also favors the context of psychology rather than occult theory, but does not actually exclude the mystical twist that Theosophists and other occult revivalists would have added to it.

On-line dictionaries tend to define "psychagogue" as "necromancer," giving Webster's as their authority, but Webster's originally gave a quite different and much more accurate account of the term's derivation and meaning. Unlike "psychognosis," which is a modern synthesis from Greek roots, psychagogue is derived directly from the Greek *psychagogos*, which referred to a conductor of souls to the Underworld—a role often attributed to Hermes, who thus acquired the term as an epithet. Like psychognosis, it was avidly re-appropriated by 19th century psychologists, for whom "psychagogy" became a species of psychotherapy not unlike what is nowadays called "life coaching." The author of the novella series, however, obviously construes "guidance of the soul" in an intermediate sense, appropriate to the business of "Sârs" rather than that of divine messengers or psychiatrists.

Interestingly, the author of the novella series characterizes Sâr Dubnotal's intermediate status between the human and the divine as that of a *surhomme*, which would be translatable as "superman" had he not taken care to attribute it specifically to Friedrich Nietzsche, thus representing it as a translation of *übermensch* [overman]. Although Nietzsche's concept has been much misrepresented, largely because of its perverted adaptation into Nazi philosophy, Nietzsche thought of the superiority of overmen primarily in terms of artistic creativity rather than violent swagger or occult ability, but the choice of that label as a descriptor of a Theosophically-defined "psychagogue" is an interesting one, as much because it illustrates the limits of the author's borrowing from Theosophy and its kindred systems as for what it adds by way of complication.

It is entirely possible, of course, that the impression that the author of Sâr Dubnotal did not know much about occult theory is merely an impression, and that the paucity of his references is explicable in terms of a desire not to burden the reader, but some of the passing references he does make in these translated stories seem to be dubious in their accuracy, and he seems much more comfortable when he is relating items of Breton folklore—more specifically, items of the folklore of Finistère, on the southern coast of which one of the series' standard settings, Trez-Hir beach, is located. This does not necessarily mean that the author was a Breton, but it does suggest that he might have been in the habit of spending his holidays in Finistère. If he did, his holiday reading probably did not include the works of Eliphas Lévi, Madame Blavatsky, Jules Bois or Joséphin Péladan, although the Sâr Dubnotal series might have been richer in bizarre narrative décor or interesting food for thought if it had.

It is not obvious that the exploits of Sâr Dubnotal would actually have benefited from the kind of intense and complex metaphysical speculation that saturates Blackwood's John Silence stories, which—despite their success—could not have been of much interest to ordinary readers. We now know that when William Hope Hodgson involved Carnacki with such earnest arcane material in "The Hog," he could not find a contemporary market for the story, which was only published posthumously. The Sâr Dubnotal series would, however, be much better than it is if all it lacked was a pseudo-scholarly interest in occult matters. Unfortunately, its intellectual deficiencies go far beyond that.

All detective stories pose a fundamental challenge to their writers, in that it is very difficult for a writer plausibly to depict a character of unusual intelligence and erudite expertise. No character can really possess more intelligence or knowledge than his author, and those who seem to do so are enabled to pull off the trick because an author can take a lot longer to think about his plots than a reader takes to consume his stories, and can research them as carefully as he pleases. Such careful thought and research enable a writer to construct elaborate patterns of misdirection and feign enormous erudition, and also take advantage of his own second thoughts—or even third, fourth and fifth thoughts—in constructing what are allegedly his character's immediate intuitions and deductions. Much, if not all, of that advantage is sacrificed if an author is content to publish his first drafts, and if the author is not very bright or knowledgeable to start with, his chances of contriving a convincing depiction of an intelligent and erudite detective are likely to be slim. The margin of his failure is bound to seem even greater if he represents his protagonist not merely as an exceptionally clever human being, but as a person possessed of arcane knowledge and powers that make him a literal "overman."

As the reader of this collection will quickly realize, the author's perpetual insistence that Sâr Dubnotal is a man of unusual insight and intelligence are not at all borne out by his actual performances; not only will the reader out-guess "the Great Psychagogue" at every turn (assisted, admittedly, but the fact that the omniscient narrative voice keeps feeding him tidbits of information that would be better left unspecified), but he will eventually be given evidence that even the Master's pet curlew is brighter than the Master himself. The fact that Sâr Dubnotal can use occult means of obtaining information when necessary—although he and the author share a very odd notion of what constitutes necessity—merely serves to add to his evident deficiencies as a gatherer of evidence and employer of deductive logic. The vast majority of his successes during his dogged pursuit of the arch-villain are derived from fortunate coincidences rather than from the methodical application of logic, or even from the evocation of his woefully-inconsistent and oddly-impotent occult powers.

These faults probably stem from mere carelessness and incompetence on the author's part, but they do serve to highlight one of the fundamental difficulties of superhero fiction, which is that melodrama tends to work best when a hero is a manifest underdog fighting against the odds. When it is the villain who holds all the narrative trump cards—as, for instance, Sax Rohmer's insidious Dr. Fu Manchu does in his ongoing conflict with the mundane agents of Scotland Yard—whereas the hero has to rely entirely on native wit, pluck and moral determination, the victories of good over evil are all the sweeter and all the more welcome. It is intrinsically difficult to extract much suspense from a situation in which an invulnerable hero, with all kinds of magic at his disposal, is confronted with a mere thug, however much moral satisfaction there may be in punishing the thug in question for his transgressions. The authors chronicling the adventures of the comic book Superman were eventually to spend more than half a century figuring out bizarrely ingenious ways around that problem, with considerable success, but the author of Sâr Dubnotal ran straight into it, utterly unprepared, and it is hardly surprising that he could not cope with it.

By the same token, superhero fiction is also exceptionally prone to the problem of "melodramatic inflation," which requires the hero of a series to meet increasingly greater threats if his later adventures are not to seem feebler than their predecessors. Not only do superheroes require super-villains to fight, but those super-villains must continually increase their threat-level, collectively if not individually. Where the same villain is employed repeatedly, as in the present series, the character inevitably requires continual "enhancement" of some kind; either his power must increase or the evil nature of his deeds must be exaggerated—or, for preference, both.

Even for a writer disposed to planning his work beforehand and making full use of his second, third and fourth thoughts, that can be a challenging task. Again, it is a problem for which the author of Sâr Dubnotal evidently made little preparation, although he did try manfully to cope with it, using a narrative method that had been popular in French fiction for more than a century, having been pioneered by and named after the Marquis de Sade. Unfortunately (or maybe not) the standards of decency applicable to French popular fiction in 1909 prevented him from making quite as much use of the strategy as he might have wished in crediting ever-more-hideous crimes to his villain, and he never succeeded in offering a plausible explanation of why the villain had taken to spicing up his crimes with such gratuitous sadism.

These faults are bound to make the adventures of Sâr Dubnotal a rather frustrating experience for the modern reader, who is used to much slicker performances in dealing with the relevant problems, even from the lowliest of literary hacks, but the main interest of the stories assembled here lies in their lack of polish, and their awkwardness in confronting problems of narrative construction that were new at the time. Progress is the accumulated legacy of trial and error, and if we never look at the failed experiments, we cannot fully appreciate the triumphs of the successful ones.

What follows is what the unknown author of the novella series actually wrote, rendered into English that reads as smoothly as I can contrive without being manifestly inaccurate. Perhaps the unknown author should have done things differently, or not written the series at all, but he did write it, and he was at least trying to do something new, and different.

His attempt to achieve that goal is not without its own intrinsic fascination as a literary and historical artifact.

Brian Stableford

SÂR DUBNOTAL

Chaque fascicule contient un récit complet.

THE HAUNTED MANOR OF CREC'H-AR-VRAN

I: A Tragic Vacation

At 10 p.m. on August 8, 1889, an event as terrible as it was mysterious brought panic to the placid population of the Breton seaside resort of Trez-Hir.

At one of the windows of the old manor of Crec'h-ar-Vran, which overlooked the beach, two human shadows—both women in night-dresses—abruptly appeared. They uttered cries of fright and gesticulated like madwomen. Suddenly, they climbed over the balcony and hurled themselves into space from the height of the second floor.

One would have thought that they would be killed instantly. By a miracle, that did not happen. Falling on their feet in the courtyard of the château, they were not long delayed in reappearing on the edge of the cliff on the crest of which the edifice was situated.

A terrible storm was rumbling in the sky, which lightning-flashes split incessantly. By their light, the two poor creatures were seen running frantically along the cliff-top. One of them, unfortunately, lost her balance, rebounded from ledge to ledge, and ended up falling on to the strand, where she lay inanimate…

To explain what happened, it is necessary to go back in time.

An hour before the frightful scene that we have just described, the resort of Trez-Hir was as tranquil as usual. Already, though, the evening was charged with electric effluvia. There was not a breath of wind. The bathers on vacation in

Trez-Hir sought in vain for a hint of breeze at the water's edge. A strange suggestion of tragedy overhung the end of that summer day.

On the rocks, to one side, the eel-fishers were waiting for the tide to go out. Women old and young, with their hooked implements at their feet, they seemed to be experiencing the same mysterious anguish, and were chatting in low voices. Brief lightning-flashes sometimes split the darkness, unmasking the grim silhouette of the old feudal manor of Crec'h-ar-Vran, squatting like an enormous sphinx at the very top of the cliff on the western headland of Trez-Hir. Involuntarily, it was toward that somber cube of granite and ivy that the Breton women turned their gazes. The inexplicable oppression they felt came as much from there as from the heavy atmosphere.

There was no suggestion of any human presence there—and Crec'h-ar-Vran had, in fact, been unoccupied for five years.

Suddenly, one of the fisherwomen uttered any exclamation full of anguish: "My God!"

"What? What is it, Géno?" demanded the other women, already shivering all over.

A few bathers, hearing the cry, were hurrying forward. They mingled with the fisherwomen and interrogated old Géno in her turn—but the latter's teeth continued to chatter, and she seemed incapable of proffering a single syllable or making any movement. Her arm, extended obliquely above the triple or quadruple rampart of heads imprisoning her, was pointing to the silhouette of the accursed château on the cliff—the fantastic and disquieting dwelling that had not been visited in five years, but two of whose windows, that evening, had just been abruptly illuminated.

All eyes having followed the direction of Géno's arm, a chorus of terrified exclamations erupted, at least among the Breton women. "My God!" they repeated, following the example of their companion and making the sign of the cross repeatedly, as if to ward off imminent peril. "My God!"

The bathers also looked at the château, but they could not see anything to justify the emotion of the women. One of them, who answered to the bellicose name of César Sabrejolle, even tried to make a joke of it.

"Well, what?" he said, ironically. "Is that all? I think you're trying to put one over us, old Géno!"

The fact is that, at first sight, the spectacle of those lights at the windows of Crec'h-ar-Vran was not at all extraordinary for people who did not know the manor's history. It was not the same for the Breton women, who knew that history, and who certainly did not think of it as a joking matter. Old Géno, therefore, reacted sharply to the man's impertinence.

"Put one over on you?" she cried. "I must have too much energy, my dear Monsieur. Instead of jeering you'd do better to follow our example and say a prayer for the Souls who are returning up there."

At these words, a fearful and approving murmur ran through the ranks of the Breton women, who were huddling close together like a flock of sheep at the approach of a wolf.

The strong-minded César shrugged his shoulders—and Gaston and Maxime, his close friends, imitated him.

To be sure, during the month they had been on vacation in Trez-Hir, recuperating in the new and peaceful bathing-station on the Armorican coast, glad to escape the hubbub of Paris—its noise, its dust, its exhausting feverish activity, its machinery of costly and taxing pleasures—and enchanted to find themselves here among friends, in the resort of Trez-Hir, far from any railway station, only reachable by coach, the three inseparable companions had heard vague mention of the manor of Crec'h-ar-Vran, which was reputed to be haunted.

At certain hours on dark nights, the people of the region claimed that its walls and windows—specifically, the two that were now lit up—were crowned with sinister flames that disappeared and reappeared repeatedly. This frightful apparition was always presaged by noises as disturbing as they were strange, whose echoes were audible, weakly but distinctly, at the foot of the promontory. Sometimes, it was like the drumming of hailstones on slate roofs, sometimes like violent blows struck on the walls, sometimes like the dry click of a door opening or closing.

La Souriman, a poor village-woman, more feared than respected because of her medical knowledge and the relations she was said to entertain with the Korrigans, or goblins—whose thick-set and deformed bodies, grimacing faces and furtive mannerisms her own person vaguely recalled—told anyone who wanted to listen that the revenant was not a myth, and that she had seen it with her own eyes, lying in ambush on the stroke of ten at the window in question, and that it was incontestably a Soul in torment, for it was draped in a shroud. Furthermore, did not Fri-Dû, the Le Boëcs' guard-dog, howl in distress at the precise moment when the revenant appeared?

Our bathers, however, had scarcely paid any heed to what they called stupid fairy tales and silly nonsense, only worthy of belief, at the most, by Breton-speakers—a race of neurotics, they said, disdainfully, who reeked of superstition and alcohol. Tennis, croquet, the flirtations of the beautiful Madame X*** and the swimwear of the sparkling Madame Y*** left them little time to think about the gloomy manor—whose sole purpose, in their eyes, was to add a touch of romance to the landscape.

For his part, César Sabrejolle had certainly thought of going to take a closer look at that "rampart of local superstition," as he put it, but it was not easy to get access to the manor. The sandy beach of Trez-Hir, extends between two granite promontories, measures a kilometer in length. Situated on the heath that overlooks the sea, the village of Kerambellec, to which Trez-Hir is administratively linked, is mid-way between these two promontories, which are formidable heaps of rocks more-or-less glued together by a layer of earth too thin and too poor, and especially too fully-impregnated with salt to give birth to anything but lichens, heather and gorse.

As the crow flies, Kerambellec is scarcely 800 meters distant from the Château de Crec'h-ar-Vran, but to reach that eagle's nest, similar to the eyries of Rhenish burgraves, one must take a goat-path that winds in zigzag fashion up the sheer slopes of the cliff, as if suspended there. And what a path! Men cannot go up it facing forwards, and the slightest false step would be fatal to anyone reckless enough to venture there without a guide. At each abrupt turn, the eye plunges into gulfs opening like hatchet-blows amid the cyclopean rocks.

In the times when Crec'h-ar-Vran was inhabited, a solid fence of iron mesh ran along the edge of that path, protecting pedestrians against fatal falls, but since that time the fence, eaten away by rust and broken by the sea-winds, has given way in more than one place. In these conditions, the climb became truly perilous, and it required all the experience and agility of Père Le Boëc, the titular caretaker of the manor, to come and go therefrom—as he did nearly every day, in all weathers, to obtain provisions in Kerambellec. But that was not the main reason why the compatriots of that excellent man admired his bravery, and that of his wife Soizic; it was because they both lived contentedly up there, where no one in the parish would have dared to spend a single night.

The fear that the manor inspired in the entire population was such that, except for la Souriman, there was not a Christian soul who would visit the Le Boëcs. Even la Souriman only climbed up rarely, and never stayed there very long. Nor would she go except for a specific purpose, attracted by large glasses of rum and the generous tips given to her by the caretaker's wife, whose varicose veins she treated.

In sum, César Sabrejolle, in view of the difficulties of the path, had given up on visiting the château, and he would have taken no more notice of it than usual if Géno's cry had not excited his curiosity and that of his friends.

Meanwhile, the threat of the storm increased; dull rolls of thunder now accompanied the lightning flashes that slit the darkness.

"We'd better go to bed," said Maxime.

"Are you tired?" asked Gaston.

"No, but the cataracts of the sky are about to open, and I don't like to take my baths fully-dressed."

"Let's wait a little longer," said the heroic César Sabre-jolle. "We'll look like cowards if we run away now. These Breton women will imagine that it's the lights of Crec'h-ar-Vran that have scared us away. As if, after Comte, Reclus, Berthelot and Renan,[5] anyone at the end of the present century could still believe in haunted houses, revenants and will-o'-the-wisps!" He suddenly slapped his forehead, though, and exclaimed: "I've got it! Of course! Yes, I have the key to the puzzle—everything has become crystal clear, as if wiped by a cloth. Oh, what idiots we are!"

"Tell us, then, if you can explain the singular occurrence," said Gaston, his lips pursed.

"All right! Oh, idiot that you are, my poor Gaston—for you told us yourself, this afternoon, that the manor of Crec'h-ar-Vran had been let to three English people."

"What the Devil am I thinking?" Gaston conceded. "They were a striking sight, those English folk! Striking enough for me to take the trouble to ask the coach-driver what their names were."

"And what were they?" asked Maxime.

"Mr. and Mrs. Hastings—a young couple—and Miss Barbara Longmore, the lady's sister."

"Oh, Barbara!" sniggered César. "So it's the flame of your candle that has frightened the honest fisherwomen of Kerambellec so much!"

Maxime and Gaston joined in with their leader's hearty laughter. Whether because the humor of the joke escaped them, or because they were unsatisfied by an explanation of that sort, however, the Breton women did not crack a smile.

---

[5] The philosopher Auguste Comte, the geographer Elisée Reclus, the chemist Marcellin Berthelot and the historian Ernest Renan were among the leading French skeptics of the 19th century; their best-known works sounded loud clarion calls in favor of a rigorously scientific (or "positive," in Comte's terminology) world-view.

Even old Géno muttered between the stumps of her to-bacco-blackened teeth: "Is there any reason to laugh like that, even if there are English people up there? Come on, Messieurs! If these goddams aren't devils or magicians, it won't take long for them to regret what they've done."

"Can one fall into such depths of credulity?" murmured Maxime.

"And animal stupidity!" Gaston added.

"I beg your pardon?" queried Géno, who was rather bad-tempered, and had vaguely heard what they said.

"Nothing, nothing, my good woman" Maxime hastened to reply. "We weren't talking about you."

"We were talking about the pope," César sniggered.

While they talked, despite the slightly aggressive tone that the conversation had taken on, the bathers and fisherwomen continued to keep watch on the haughty feudal dwelling, whose rude contours were illuminated by the lightning-flashes. From the beach, the manor's outbuildings were invisible, including the isolated lodge occupied by the Le Boëcs. As only two windows were a-glow, like lidless eyes, the black and sullen mass of Crec'h-ar-Vran resembled a monster on the lookout for prey.

"By the way, that reminds me of a good story of *psychognosis*, as they say nowadays," said César, laughing more heartily. "One evening when a phantom tried to frighten me, I grabbed my gun and shot it in the backside. The effect was magical. My phantom started braying like an ass and ran off at a gallop. It was a neighbor who had disguised himself as a ghost. Fortunately for him, my shotgun was only loaded with rock salt—but I swear that the fellow didn't scratch his backside for quite…"

A livid streak of lightning, followed after a brief interval by a formidable roll of thunder, cut him short just as a new group of people approached. This group was composed of three men who had been intriguing the inhabitants of the village and the bathers on the beach for several days. The most remarkable of them—as much because of his height and the virile beauty of his features, whose expression was noble, grave and singularly energetic, all at the same time, as by virtue of his sumptuously picturesque semi-Oriental and semi-European costume—called himself Severus el Tebib.

Was that strange name really his own? That was a question that sprang to mind, but remained unanswered. Physically, there was no indication of the nationality, or even the race, of the man who called himself by that name. Was he French, Asian or Arab? It was impossible to tell. The harmonious but firm oval of his face was elongated by the triangle of curly brown beard. His eyebrows, similarly brown, arched across a forehead whose height and convexity revealed a superior intelligence, while his straight moustache, of a shade intermediate between blond an chestnut, formed a silky stripe above lips that were neither thin nor plump, nor pinched, nor sensual: the beautiful lips of a vigorous, sound and healthy man.

The most astonishing and admirable thing about that marvelous representative of a unknown race, however, was his eyes: two large eyes of a greenish color, which really were those mirrors of the soul of which poets speak, for they reflected the highest qualities of heart and mind that a man can possess. Astonishingly mobile, they continually changed expression, and the flame that illuminated them, sometimes softly and sometimes fiercely, seemed to emit a mysterious subtle fluid that penetrated into the most secret recesses of one's being.

Severus el Tebib wore puffy white silk trousers embroidered in gold thread in the Hindu fashion, a large cashmere sash and fur slippers. A waistcoat and a satin-lined frock-coat, a white short with a stiff collar, a black cravat pinned by a sapphire carved in the form of a skull and as large as a hazel-nut, completed a strangely disparate costume, which did no harm to the imposing nobility of his bearing.

For a week, Severus el Tebib had been living in a house built for him on the model of an Indian "bungalow," which we shall soon have occasion to describe. That dwelling stood on the eastern promontory of the Trez-Hir resort, about a mile away from, and almost directly opposite, the manor of Crec'h-ar-Vran. He had only made brief appearances on the beach. Where had he come from? Who was he? Why had he settled in this remote corner of Brittany? So many enigmas.

As for the two people who accompanied him this evening, let us be content for the moment to say that one was a young man of 25, of similarly uncertain nationality, although he was dressed entirely in the French manner, and the other was a gigantic Hindu servant.

Severus, who preceded his companions, had approached the crowd formed by the Breton women and the bathers, and had caught César Sabrejolle's last few words. Had those words struck a disagreeable note in his ears? His pupils, at any rate, took on a rapid tawny gleam. "Monsieur," he said, in the purest French accent, "Would you be kind enough to tell me the reason for this assembly, and, if you don't mind, why you are speaking in such scornful tones about psychognosis?"

This question was asked so courteously that César, initially nonplussed, soon recovered his normal aplomb and recounted everything that he knew about the manor of Crec'h-ar-Vran, the superstitions of the Breton women, and the arrival of the British family at the château.

Severus raised his eyes toward the lighted windows, and his companions did likewise. "That's strange," he murmured.

"What's strange about it?" asked César Sabrejolle in his turn. "What, Monsieur! Do you perhaps share the superstition of these wretched Bretons?"

"Please let us leave superstition to one side, Monsieur," Severus replied, dryly. "You mentioned psychognosis just now. Do you know what it is?"

"What?" said César.

"Psychognosis," Severus repeated, "is the Science of Souls, or Spirits, in their manifestations and relationships with the material world if not in their very essence—which is God's secret."

"And you believe, personally, in this Science of Souls?"

"I believe that the divine power is infinite."

"Like human credulity!" César retorted, sarcastically.

"I could reply that mocking that of which one is ignorant is not an indication of great intelligence. Denial is easy! When a fact embarrasses you or disturbs you, what is more comfortable that closing your eyes? One can then say, in all conscience, 'I don't see anything!'"

"That's still better," César said, becoming more heated, "than letting oneself be swindled by spiritualists, kabbalists, occultists and other charlatans of the same stripe."

Severus smiled condescendingly. "Not belonging personally to any of those sects, I am not qualified to defend them. Moreover, I don't disagree that there are some among those who lay claim to psychic knowledge, as there are everywhere else, false savants—charlatans, to employ your expression. Tricksters and fakers are the worst enemies of all science. They, and their sacrilegious practices, are the people who bring discredit upon psychognosis and retard its progress. Come, Monsieur, you will never be as hard as I am myself on the exploiters of the Invisible and the Mysterious!"

Without waiting for César's response, Severus el Tebib turned to old Géno. "Do you truly believe that the manor is haunted?" he asked.

"It *is* haunted, my good sir!" Géno said, putting her hands together. "Five years ago, the old Comte de Tréguilly died, only a few days before the death of Vicomte Jean, his son, the inheritor of his name and his titles, and since that double decease, the manor is no longer habitable. The proof is that Madame la Comtesse was unable to stay there after the death of Monsieur Jean, her husband, and that the Le Boëcs, brave as they are, dare not leave their lodge after 10 p.m."

"It's at 10 p.m. that the phenomena begin to manifest themselves?"

"Yes, Monsieur."

"Come on!" Sabrejolle put in, unwilling to conceded defeat. "The Le Boëcs presumably have an interest in putting these rumors about, to ensure that they have the manor to themselves and to discourage strangers from coming to live there."

"My God!" cried the Breton woman, scandalized. "How can you say such horrible things about the Le Boëcs, who are the most honest Christians in the land!"

"In that case, there's a young woman in the neighborhood who's neurotic without knowing it. In all supposedly haunted houses, or in their vicinity, one always observes the presence of an adolescent girl whose nervous system has been subject to certain alterations."

"There are no dwellings within a radius of eight hundred meters," Géno observed, whose attention was attracted to the storm, which, without decisively bursting, was slowly shedding its effluvia upon the plateau of Kerambellec. From a fuliginous obscurity, the sky suddenly passed into a blinding clarity, and the accursed château, thus alternately masked and unmasked, was animated by a grim and mysterious life.

Severus consulted his watch in the glare of a lightning-flash.

"9:45 p.m.," he said to César. "In a quarter of an hour, Monsieur, we shall see who is right—these women or you."

"How's that?" said César, astonished.

"You'll soon find out. But first, let's get closer to the promontory; the tenants of the château might need our help."

The skeptic gladly agreed to the proposition, which he saw as a means of winning an easy victory over his opponent. His friends followed him. The Breton women, however, drew away across the sandbanks exposed by the ebb-tide, for the time had come for them to go in search of the sand-eels that serve as bait for the fishermen of the Breton coast. They muttered a forceful *De profundis* as they went, to give them courage.

The strangers reached the base of the promontory, where they stopped abruptly in response to a gesture from Severus. The first stroke of ten was sounding in the village church and, coincident with the distant ringing of the bell, the long howl of a dog that scents death passing by went up from the courtyard of the manor.

César Sabrejolle and his friends began to lose their self-confidence.

As the bell continued to ring in the darkness, the dog's howling became more lugubrious.

Strangely, the two lights in the manor were suddenly extinguished, and two human screams, cries of distress, punctuated by the voices of the storm, mingled with the sinister plaints of the guard-dog.

The Breton women, already distant on the sands, were gripped by fearful panic. Abandoning their fishing expedition, they ran toward the village as fast as their legs could carry them. César Sabrejolle would gladly have done likewise, and it was not without difficulty that he succeeded in mastering himself, aided by his vanity. "We were talking about trickery, Monsieur," he said to Severus. "I think that some is being served up to us."

"That's quite possible," his interlocutor replied. "But do you recall what Shakespeare's Hamlet said? *There are more things in Heaven and Earth, Horatio, than are dreamt of in your philosophy!*"

As if to prove him right, a terrible bolt of lightning cleaved the darkness. The entire atmosphere lit up; the electrical detonations multiplied, only leaving brief intervals between them, in the course of which their salvos reverberated noisily in the clefts in the cliff. The people could no longer hear themselves speak. To complete the misfortune, the clouds burst and a deluge of rain fell in furious floods upon the strand.

At the same time, the screams in the manor redoubled their intensity, so sharp and so desperate that they further increased the Aeschylean horror of that tragic night. Two fearful female voices were recognizable by their timbre, which one male voice was trying in vain to calm.

It was then that the heart-rending scene that we described at the beginning of the chapter unfolded, by the light of one last lightning-flash. Severus and his companions aw the body of a woman in a night-dress tumble over the edge of the cliff, whirl around in the air and roll on the sand at their feet, like a great white bird.

II. A New Tenant

At noon the next day, beneath a warm Sun that made the blue waters of Trez-Hir bay sparkle, two men headed toward the manor of Crec'h-ar-Vran. They had crossed the entire length of the beach, leaving the church and the scattered houses of Kerambellec far to their right. One of the two men was Severus el Tebib; the other was the young man who had been with him the previous evening. Before setting forth on the steep and narrow path that led to the château, Severus invited his companion to stand beside him on a rock.

The young man obeyed. He offered, at first glance, a striking contrast to the imposing Severus. His navy blue suit, his Panama hat and his yellow shoes gave him the typical appearance of a fashionable bather at a seaside resort. Almost as tall as Severus el Tebib, although less powerfully built, he was lithe and muscular without being athletic. His long blond hair was curly at the temples; he had the soft skin and beardless face of an adolescent, but his eyes were almost as changeable, as troubling and as impregnated with magnetism as those of his companion.

"So," said Severus, after a moment, reflection, "the English people have gone. I was too busy to see them this morning—and besides, I entrusted that matter to you and I'm depending on you."

"Yes, Master," the young man replied, respectfully. "Miss Barbara, who fell from the cliff onto the sand, whom you picked up and cared for, and saved from death, was transported to Morlaix this morning. She's still very weak, but the terror she experienced probably shook her more than the fall.

In any case, thanks to you, her recovery is assured, and the Hastings asked me to present to you once more the expression of their profound gratitude."

"I only did my duty, Rudolph," Severus said. "I understand why the Hastings did not want to stay in Trez-Hir any longer; I only regret that their haste in leaving a place that can only recall tragic memories for them has prevented me from questioning them as I would have wished. Do you know what caused the two women to panic?"

"Our investigators began their inquiry as soon as possible, Master, but it's still far from complete, and I can only repeat to you the little that they told me."

"I'm listening, Rudolph."

"It seems," the young man said, "that it was simply because its location pleased them, and the rental terms appeared very reasonable, that the Hastings rented the manor of Crec'h-ar-Vran. They knew absolutely nothing about the evil rumors concerning the dwelling; the caretakers, the old Le Boëcs, had been careful not to breathe a word, and they came straight to the château, without stopping off in Kerambellec."

"I would have preferred to be dealing with skeptics of the same species as little Monsieur Sabrejolle, whose pitiful flight yesterday, as the drama reached its climax, made us smile. If the English had come to lodge there in a spirit of bravado, I certainly wouldn't be displeased that their incredulity had attracted an unforgettable lesson."

"You think, then, Master, that we can definitely set aside the hypothesis of a trick?"

"I think so—for on what would that hypothesis be founded? The tricksters can't be the Le Boëcs; if they had any interest in putting off prospective tenants, they would have begun by telling the English people that the manor is haunted, in order to frighten them in advance and thus ensure the success of their wretched scheme."

"But the tricksters might be people from Kerambellec?" Rudolph suggested.

"No, since the manor is only accessible by this perilous route, which no one dares to risk. Besides, I can't see any motive that would drive someone to enact such a criminal farce."

"So your opinion is formed, Master?"

"Not yet. Are you forgetting, Rudolph, the guarantees with which I have to surround myself in such circumstances?"

"Oh, no! I'm not forgetting anything," the young man murmured, dully. "Oh, Master, when shall we be rid of this host of pseudo-psychagogues and fake mediums whose worthless conjuring-tricks so often stop us as we are about to cross the sacred threshold of Mystery?"

"Unmasking them, frustrating them and, if necessary, punishing them, gives me moral satisfaction," Severus said, gravely. "Do we not have, in any case, sufficient opportunities to decipher enigmas not to attach more importance than necessary to the practices of these charlatans?"

"That's true, Master."

"We shall, therefore, take all the usual precautions," Severus decided. "I know what my duty is, and you can take it for granted that I shall not fail in it—but continue your story, my friend."

"I'll finish it, Master. The English family had been installed in the manor for a few hours. They had dined together, and then had retired to two neighboring rooms overlooking the bay—the ones whose windows we saw lit up yesterday evening. At 10 p.m., as they were going to bed, having locked the doors to the corridor and left the door connecting their two rooms ajar, Miss Barbara, frightened by the howling of the dog Fri-Dû, called out to her sister, who came running. At the same moment, the two women let out a terrible scream, which attracted Mr. Hasting. Under an irresistible pressure, the door to the corridor—which, I repeat, had been locked—had just opened wide. No one was visible, however!

"Mr. Hasting, who is by no means resolute, thought that his sister-in-law had forgotten to turn they key, although she believed that she had done so. He went to close the door, without making further enquiries, when the candle set on the

41

night-stand was snuffed out by a powerful draught, which went through Miss Barbara's room and into the other. There it similarly put out the light and opened the other door to the corridor, which had been locked and bolted—whence came the mad terror of the women and the leap through the window, and then their hectic flight, which was almost fatal for one of them."

"Yes," murmured Severus, "The phenomenon is quite characteristic. Here is a field of activity that seems to open up to us, to occupy the time of our vacation in this charming resort of Trez-Hir, where I shall maintain my *pied-à-terre* as a new base of operations. Let's go up to the manor, Rudolph."

"I'll follow you, Master."

A few minutes of rapid ascent led the two men, who seemed equally resistant to vertigo and fatigue, to the summit of the promontory. It formed a trapezoid platform that might have been three hundred meters across at its greatest breadth and scarcely fifty at its least. The manor stood at the extremity of this plateau, of which its foundations occupied the entire tip. A rather large courtyard separated it from the caretakers' lodge, built behind a cast-iron gate barring the pathway.

When they arrived at this gate, the strangers were welcomed by the barking of a dog whose kennel was adjacent to the lodge. A placard hung from the gate bearing the inscription: *TO LET OR FOR SALE: SEE THE CARETAKERS.*

Severus prepared to ring, but the dog's barking saved him the trouble. Forewarned of the approach of visitors by the faithful animal, an old man dressed in patched trousers, a woolen pullover, a beret and a pair of clogs—the very picture of a retired seaman—came out of the lodge. He approached the gate and looked the strangers over briefly before opening up.

"This property is to let?" Severus asked, negligently.

"Or for sale, Monsieur, as you see," said the old man, pointing at the notice.

"You are the concierge?"

"The caretaker, Monsieur," the old man corrected, politely, touching his beret and passing the wad of tobacco he was chewing from one side of his mouth to the other. "Yves Le Boëc at your service, ex-able seaman in the Fleet, invalided out without a pension, for temporary infirmity."

"May we visit the château?" asked Severus.

"If it's to buy or rent it, yes. Otherwise, be off with you!"

"My intention is to rent it, if the property pleases me," said Severus, quickly. "But with whom do I have to deal, in that case?"

"Oh, with me, Monsieur. In that regard, I have the full authority of Madame la Comtesse de Tréguilly.

At that moment, Soizic came to join her husband, along with another old woman even more wizened and mummified, but singularly alert for her age, whose little grey eyes, sunk into their orbital caverns, sparkled with malice.

"Excuse me," said Le Boëc. "This is Soizic, Monsieur, my lawful wife, the mother of three children, all of whom I've lost. And this old lady is a bone-setter from Kerambellec, who sometimes comes to treat my wife, and whom they call la Souriman."

The two strangers bowed as courteously as if they had been dealing with the Comtesse de Tréguilly in person.

"These Messieurs want to rent," said Père Le Boëc to his wife. "Run and fetch the keys, Soizic."

Soizic limped away, for she was not longer in the first flush of youth, and la Souriman's remedies did not appear to have had much effect on her afflicted legs.

Several minutes went by; Soizic did not return. "Where have you put your keys?" she shouted, eventually, from the threshold of the house. "I can't put my hands on them."

"It would have astonished me if you'd found them," said Le Boëc, disdainfully. "Oh, my God, these women! What a trial!" And he hastened toward the lodge.

La Souriman immediately approached Severus. "No, Monsieur it's a joke, isn't it? You don't really want to rent Crec'h-ar-Vran?"

"Why not?"

The old woman reached out a hand.

"Give me charity, my good Monsieur, and I won't lie to you by as much as a syllable."

Severus took a *louis* from his pocket. "I'm listening."

"Well, Monsieur," said la Souriman, in a low voice, "the manor is haunted. It has a revenant, if you prefer. I've seen it, so I can tell you about it. Don't rent the manor, if you value your life—or the same will happen to you that happened to the English folk who were here yesterday, and whom I didn't have a chance to warn, to their misfortune."

"You haven't told me anything that I don't already know," said Severus coldly—but he held out the *louis* to the old woman, saying: "Take it anyway."

La Souriman made the gold coin vanish into the depths of her skirt with a grateful smile, and joy opened her toothless mouth wide. "God bless you, my good Monsieur! But please don't tell the Le Boëcs that I've said anything to you. The poor folk are obliged to keep quiet themselves, or else Madame le Comtesse would send them away. She's angry enough already that the property isn't bringing anything in."

"Very well," said Severus. "I won't say anything." And he dismissed the bone-setter with a gesture. She set off along the path to the village.

"Rudolph," Severus said, then, "we're going to inspect Crec'h-ar-Vran and its outbuildings from top to bottom, and assure ourselves that it doesn't contain any suspect hiding-place in which someone might conceal themselves after night-fall. Go see if the Le Boëcs have found their keys and tell the man to bring a rake."

"A rake, Master?"

"Yes, I'll need one."

Leaving Soizic in charge of the lodge, Père Le Boëc, who had finally unearthed his bunch of keys and fetched the required implement, let his guests toward the entrance to the manor. While they walked Severus and Rudolph, disdaining the magical spectacle of the bay and Trez-Hir beach stretched out at their feet, concentrated their attention on the somber Gothic edifice, entirely cloaked in ivy, which had the ability to terrify all the fisherwomen, and even the fishermen, of the region.

Square and massive, flanked by a tower at each corner, pierced by two rows of windows as deep and narrow as loopholes, the 600-year-old building, which had been ruined and restored several times over, really did have something frightful about it. There was only one access door. There had once been three others in the lateral faces and at the rear, but they had been walled up a long time ago. The one that remained, opening in the façade, was of well-proven solidity and was formidably garnished with locks and bolts.

"You can leave the rake outside," Severus said to the caretaker before going in.

The three men went inside in Indian file, into a vestibule so gloomy that Père Le Boëc had to light the taper that he had been careful to bring.

First they visited four large cold, dark and bare rooms on the ground floor, fitted out as an office, a kitchen, a laundry room and a wine-cellar.

In the passage, Severus and Rudolph tapped the walls with their toes or the tips of their canes, cocking their ears to judge the nature of the sounds they produced. Their ploy began to intrigue Père Le Boëc, who could not hide his anxiety when the former said to him point-blank: "By the way, old chap, you haven't yet explained why the English family who were your tenants yesterday decamped so abruptly?"

"Oh, they were crazy!" muttered the old man. "If one were to believe everything one were told! Didn't they imagine hearing footsteps in their rooms, and feeling draughts in their faces? It made their blood run cold. The ladies started howling like the damned. They didn't even take the trouble to put on their skirts, and threw themselves out of the windows at the risk of broken bones. Finally, they took themselves off. I took their luggage to Kerambellec his morning. *Bon voyage!*"

Severus frowned slightly. "Do you think these English folk were as crazy as you'd like me to believe? Weren't the noises they heard and the draughts they felt real? Tell me frankly!"

"My word, Monsieur," said Le Boëc, becoming even more ill-at-ease. "I don't quite know how to answer you. I wasn't there, so I can't swear to anything."

"All right," said Severus, not insisting—but when the old caretaker set off up the staircase that led to the upper floors, he whispered in Rudolph's ear: "This man is evidently above suspicion. Far from trying to frighten visitors away from the château, he only has one thought: to inspire confidence in them in order to keep them as tenants."

The visit—one might almost say the investigation—was scrupulously continued. The rooms on the first floor, including a dining-room, two drawing-rooms, one large and one small, and a study, furnished in the Renaissance style, were carefully examined by the two mysterious individuals, who then asked to see those on the second floor.

Yves Le Boëc appeared to defer to this latter desire a little less willingly.

Four rooms, disposed in pairs on either side of a broad corridor, looked out over the front and the rear of the manor. The old man went into the latter two frankly enough, but when the moment came to pass on to the others, which the English trio had occupied and whose lighted windows had provoked so much comment the night before, he hesitated. He blushed, went pale, twisted his beret between his fingers, and finished up declaring: "Oh those—there's nothing much in there; they're in a mess. The English people must have slept there, and Soizic hasn't tidied up since."

"Open them anyway," said Severus.

Le Boëc did so, regretfully, and stood aside to let the visitors go in, without following them.

The latter cast an eye over the two connecting rooms. There did not seem to be anything unusual about them. Severus observed, however, that the beds were made and the sheets tucked in. He gazed for some time at two portraits hanging in one of the rooms. One depicted a septuagenarian and the other a man of 40 or 45; they bore a striking resemblance to one another, in spite of the age-difference.

"Comtes Hector and Jean de Tréguilly," Rudolph read from the frames.

"Who made the beds?" asked Severus, turning toward the corridor where Le Boëc as waiting.

"The Englishwomen, Monsieur."

"Your wife didn't help them?"

"Well, Monsieur, to tell you the truth, no. She hasn't set foot in this room, and won't do so any time soon. In Brittany, we have our own ideas about the dead—and as it's here that Comtes Hector and Jean died…"

"That's a precious item of information," Severus whispered to Rudolph. In a louder voice, as he and his companion returned to the corridor, he went on: "Very well, Monsieur Yves, Now let's take a quick look at the attics, the cellars and the outbuildings. I'd also very much like to see the château's burial crypt, if it has one."

"It's at the far side of the courtyard, Monsieur, behind the domestic offices. I'll take you there shortly."

The investigations continued. The two visitors left no corner unexplored, and the observations they made must have been satisfactory, for Severus said to the young man: "Our presentiment was not mistaken, Rudolph. The phenomenon can be explained. I know it—I feel it."

"And your instinct is infallible, Master," Rudolph relied, in a tone of unfeigned admiration.

Having emerged from the main building, the door of which Le Boëc closed, they headed for the Tréguilly burial-vault under the guidance of the caretaker. Severus merely cast a glance over the little edifice. "That's enough," he said. "Get your rake, Monsieur Yves, and rake the courtyard within a radius of two meters from the manor and the crypt. Obliterate every trace of footprints; the surface of the sand must be completely smooth. When you've done that, we'll meet you in your lodge, where we'll conclude the tenancy agreement."

"You'll take it, then?" exclaimed the caretaker, all the more joyous because he had not expected such a satisfactory conclusion.

"Yes," Severus replied. "Hurry up!"

A quarter of an hour later, Père Le Boëc gave his visitors a duly-formulated receipt, which made them tenants of Crec'h-ar-Vran for a period of six months, for the sum of 2000 francs. Severus had not even haggled over the price.

The old man could not believe his eyes or his ears. Never had such a bounty fallen from the sky since the death of the Comtes. He was not entirely certain that he was not dreaming—but no, the strangers were men of flesh and blood, and the 2000 francs, paid in advance, were held in his hand in the form of a wad of banknotes, plus five *louis* for a *denier à Dieu*—who surely had his own share in the windfall.[6]

"Is the sand raked?" Severus asked, one last time.

"Yes, Monsieur."

"Good. See you soon, old chap!"

"Are you moving in today, then?" asked Le Boëc.

"*Moving in* isn't the right expression, but I'll spend the night at the manor."

"Alone?" stammered the old man, going very pale.

"Alone," said Severus, calmly. "It's 2 p.m. I'll ring the bell at the gate at 8 p.m."

And then he left with his companions, leaving Père Le Boëc well-and-truly flabbergasted.

III. A Difficult Inquiry

"My dear disciple," said Severus, while Rudolph and he were going back down to the beach, "I hope that our investiga-

---

[6] "*Denier à Dieu*" [literally, "a penny for God"] is a French legal term, referring to a token payment given as evidence that a contract has been made.

tors have lost no time in carrying forward their little inquiry concerning the Comtes de Tréguilly. Let's hurry back to the bungalow to hear their report. I only have a few hours to spare, since I've promised to return to Crec'h-ar-Vran this evening and I'm genuinely in a hurry to get things done."

"The affair interests you to that degree, Master?"

"I would not call myself Sâr Dubnotal the Psychagogue, and would not be the Mystery-lover that I am, if I did not hasten to pick up his trail that Providence has thrown our way."

The stranger had pronounced these words simply, without any sort of emphasis, and Rudolph had listen to them without a flicker of reaction. These two men were undoubtedly inaccessible to human emotion and, as handsome as gods, possessed a marmoreal impassivity. Nevertheless, and observer would have been struck by the enthusiastically admiring gaze with which Rudolph looked at the man he called his "Master," and who, emerging from the incognito in which we have so far seen him maintained, had just announced his real name and title: Sâr Dubnotal the Psychagogue, who, in the increasingly numerous milieux in which psychic problems excite minds, was already nicknamed the Conquistador of the Invisible, and the Napoleon of the Immaterial!

Although Rudolph had learned from the example of his Master to armor himself with an imperturbably phlegmatic attitude, he had not yet succeeded in completely suppressing the surges of pride that overtook his brain when he saw his paltry self called to share the existence, gather information for, and perhaps to continue the career of that prodigious being, to whom Nietzsche would have unhesitatingly accorded the title of *übermensch*.[7]

---

[7] I have translated the original text's *surhomme* as *übermensch* here because that is the term that Friedrich Nietzsche actually used, but in subsequent instances I have rendered it into English as "overman," that being a better translation, in my judgment, than the more frequently employed "superman," which

To tell the truth, however bizarre the fact might seem, Rudolph actually knew very little about that career. He knew nothing about Sâr Dubnotal's origins, just as he was ignorant of his own.

Twenty years before, Rudolph had been nothing but a little Bohemian in the power of a band of gypsies wandering around Western Europe. Those gypsies had treated him as their own child, but there was no doubt that he belonged to a different race, for his blond curls, delicate complexion and pale eyes were singularly different from theirs. The criminal gang, who lived by plunder, in whom the spirit of adventure and independence and the primitive love of wide horizons and dusty roads sometimes led to Germany, sometimes to France and sometimes to Italy, must have stolen him at an age that is memory was incapable of retrieving.

One day, chance had brought the gypsies and Sâr Dubnotal into contact. The grace and lively intelligence of the child had made a considerable impact on the mysterious person who, on payment of a large sum, had obtained permission from the Bohemians to take him away.

Where did he taken him? Into what strange dreamlands, into the midst of what extraordinary populations? Of that distant epoch, spent in Asia, Rudolph only retained a dim memory. He had been too young to have much consciousness of the new and marvelous life that opened up before him, thanks to his guardian.

Then, as now, Sâr Dubnotal had been in the prime of his beauty and strength, in the healthy maturity of age. The 20 years that had gone by since then had not hollowed out a single wrinkle on his vast brow, nor blanched a single hair on his temples. That persistent youth, on which the ravages of time seemed to have no effect, was no longer a subject of astonishment for Rudolph, since he knew that Sâr Dubnotal, after long years spent in the observation of nature, exchanging in-

---

has taken on very different implications as a result of its widespread use in science fiction and comic books.

formation with sages steeped in tradition, and in the deciphering of lapidary hieroglyphics and antique papyri, had discovered secrets glimpsed by the alchemists of the Middle Ages, and was able to prolong his youth and his life beyond the limits that the passions, ignorance and diseases imposed on the existence of other mortals.

Under that direction, Rudolph had extracted in a few demi-decades the entire sum of human knowledge. He had pushed on further, going from the known into the unknown, and crossing, in the Master's footsteps, the redoubtable threshold that separates terrestrial life from that other life which is improperly called death. He was not unaware, however, that there still remained much to learn, for science is infinite, since it is divine in origin, and Sâr Dubnotal, one of the best pupils he was, but by no means the only one, did not hide from his disciples that he would only communicate to them a little of what he had learned himself, and that little only to those he judged worthy of receiving his secrets.

It was in Asia, particularly in Chaldea and the Indies, that these neophytes had been initiated by the Grand Master— and now, still guided by him, they had the entire universe for their field of experience: in addition to the miserable planet on which human *larvae* swarmed,[8] the immense and resplendent domain that is called, according to circumstance, the Void, the Ether or the Empyrean, and which Sâr Dubnotal preferred to designate as Celestial or Interastral Space.

Three o'clock was chiming when the Great Psychagogue, who, in order to conserve his incognito during his sojourn in Trez-Hir, had adopted the pseudonym of Severus el Tebib—which is to say, "the Doctor"—arrived home with Rudolph.[9]

---

[8] Although the term *larves* [larvae] might be misconstrued here, subsequent uses of the term make it clear that the author is referring to a kind of ghost.

[9] "El Tebib" [the Physician] was an epithet routinely bestowed in Arab countries upon Western explorers who demonstrated

The bungalow, a faithful copy of rich Hindu dwellings, was much easier to access than the manor of Crec'h-ar-Vran, for it was located at the base of the promontory and opened on to the beach itself. A tall hedge blocked its approach and permitted the Master's numerous following of pupils and servants to spend the greater part of their time on the veranda, without fear of prying eyes.

Severus gave a few instructions to the gigantic Hindu who had come to open the door and who bowed down with humble reverence, and then withdrew, still in company with Rudolph, his favorite disciple, into the part of the bungalow reserved for his personal use.

The immense room that he entered presented the strange appearance of a cross between a chemist's laboratory and the lumber-room of some rich and eclectic collector. Magnificent Dakkhat wall-hangings draped the arched windows, filtering the daylight and only giving way to a gentle half-light between walls ornamented with mosaics decorated with capricious arabesques.

When the eye had grown accustomed to that semi-darkness, it initially distinguished an immense table laden with bizarre objects: enormous retorts, alembics of every shape, test-tubes of all sizes, long-necked flasks, microscopes, measuring-compasses, scalpels and writing-pads. Around this table, set against the lateral walls of the room, display-cases supported the most curious and rare specimens of tropical flora and fauna. At the back of the room, on the shelves of a colossal bookcase, thousands of manuscripts and volumes with ancient bindings were aligned. A learned librarian would have been impressed to see the famous *Necronomicon* sitting next to a well-thumbed copy of the *Saaamaaa Manuscript*. Here and there, bunches of flowers sprouted from large vases in

---

conspicuous medical skills, most notably the Scottish botanist and naval physician Walter Dudney, who was one of the more successful followers of Mungo Park in furthering early 19th century African exploration.

sculpted copper, which were sustained by bamboo baskets. The skeletons of prehistoric animals hung down from the paneled ceiling, the disquieting carcass of an ichthyosaurus bumping into the steel-wired jaw of a diplodocus. The sweet perfume of incense rose up from a censer set in a corner.

As Sâr Dubnotal let himself fall on to a pouf, a patter of tiny feet glided over the thick carpet, while a sound of wings became audible behind him. Two Siamese cats with lustrous fur leapt up on to his knees and three birds, surging forth from invisible perches, settled on his shoulders: a black hen whose beak was surrounded by red wattles, a one-eyed and crooked-legged curlew, and a golden-eyed owl.

The Great Psychagogue gently caressed all these pet animals and called them by their names, which had the effect of exciting their pleasure, for they purred, clucked and hooted competitively. This concert woke up a sort of large rattlesnake, which seemed torpid, and which slowly loosened its coils, which were wound around the arms of a chandelier, slowly and rhythmically swaying its frightful flattened head above that of the Master, then suddenly knotted a scaly cravat about his neck. Far from being alarmed, Sâr Dubnotal stroked the reptile, whose forked tongue flickered in and out of its mouth.

At that moment, a young man came into the laboratory, after having knocked, and the Psychagogue said to him: "Well, Otto?"

The newcomer bowed very deeply before relying: "What can I tell you, Master? Frank, Fréjus and I have questioned all the good people of Kerambellec one after another without being able to extract the slightest information from them regarding the manor or the Tréguilly family. If only we had been allowed to have recourse to more powerful methods—but you only tolerate their employment when ordinary means have been exhausted."

"I have my reasons for that," said Sâr Dubnotal. "It's a matter of avoiding any needless expenditure of fluid. The source of that force is not inexhaustible, and God knows," he concluded gravely, "how much trouble one has to go to in order to renew it."

"How shall we procure the necessary information, then?" Rudolph asked.

"Since these Bretons won't yield to persuasion, I'll be obliged to take other measures," replied the Great Psychagogue, sending Otto away with a nod of his head, "but I prefer only to use them myself." He disengaged himself from his favorite animals and went to the door with Rudolph. "Our investigators are excellent detectives, whose flair and skill often spares me a great deal of work, but—like everyone else—they sometimes come back empty-handed, and then I have to go into the field myself."

"And nothing escapes you, Master!" said the young enthusiast.

"Don't exaggerate, my friend! My powers are human, and therefore limited, and I don't always get what I want."

"I've not seen that often, thus far," said Rudolph, with a smile.

While talking, the Master and the pupil had left the bungalow and taken the road to Kerambellec. There were no bathers to be seen on the beach. Not at all proud of their behavior on the previous evening, César Sabrejolle and his friends, who formed almost the whole of the little colony at the bathing station, had stayed in their lodgings.

On arriving in the square in front of the church, Sâr Dubnotal perceived a few fisherwomen. Intending to question them, he advanced toward them, but they took fright and dispersed as he approached, like a flock of seagulls.

"Otto was right," the Master said to Rudolph. "The people of Kerambellec don't give much away, although they're scarcely savages. Let's try to find one on his own."

They continued on their way, and encountered a middle-aged man—a solid Breton seaman. Rudolph spoke to him, and he consented to stop—but as soon as the Great Psychagogue pronounced the name of the haunted manor, the mariner's features darkened and he shook his head. "I can't say any-thing," he declared.

"You can't or you don't want to?"

The man made no reply.

Sâr Dubnotal frowned, and his admirable eyes, darting a sudden gleam, looked straight into those of the seaman. The Breton, however, did not weaken under that powerful gaze. He was content to lower his eyelids, and repeated categorically that he had nothing to say.

Sâr Dubnotal affected to be satisfied. "That seaman isn't hypnotizable," he said to his disciple after drawing away. "Not everyone, as you know, is subject to the influence of the flu-id—as Charcot understood very well, hypnotism is, first and foremost, a neurosis.[10] It's necessary to find a less resistant subject."

The two psychagogues consulted several other inhabi-tants of Kerambellec one by one, but the rapid examination to which Sâr Dubnotal subjected them suggested that it would be futile to attempt any experiment upon them. In order to be easily obtained, the hypnotic trance, in the course of which the entranced individual behaves like a somnambulist submissive to the will of the hypnotizer, requires an unhealthy predisposi-tion that was lacking in these robust fellows, who were accus-tomed to be stubborn, never losing their self-composure in the fury of the wind and waves.

Sâr Dubnotal began to fear that he would not be able to complete his inquiry successfully—but when they encountered la Souriman a few 100 meters further on, the Great Psychago-gue understood at first glance that he had finally found the

---

[10] Jean-Martin Charcot (1825-1893), who pioneered the psy-chotherapeutic use of hypnosis in treating "hysterical" pa-tients, did not make any such allegation—not, at least, in such brutal terms. The "magnetic fluid" hypothesized by Franz Mesmer had been largely discarded as an explanatory device by hypnotists, and the concept of *névrose* [neurosis] belongs to a different conceptual framework.

subject for which he was searching. Frail in appearance, la Souriman was no more than a bag of nerves. Being three-quarters drunk besides, she was admirably suited by her pathological state to serve the Master's purpose.

The pretended witch advanced to meet Sâr Dubnotal of her own accord. She recalled the *louis d'or* she had received a little while before, and hoped for a further windfall that would render her legless. Sâr Dubnotal put his hand in his pocket, and the old woman's hope was immediately transformed into the joy of realized desire. With her hopes thus fulfilled, she was in the best possible state to be put into a magnetic trance. The Psychagogue's eyes became flamboyant, emitting invisible effluvia; his hands sketched two or three of those mysterious gestures that are known as "passes."

Fluttering her eyelids like a fascinated bird, la Souriman had neither the time nor the will-power to escape from the subtle but overwhelming influence of the fluid. Her body became motionless, and in her rigid and blanched face, on which large drops of sweat formed, there was no longer any movement save for her lips.

"Woman Souriman," Sâr Dubnotal articulated, in an imperious tone, "I order you to reply frankly to all the questions that are about to be asked of you."

The bone-setter paled even further and shivered from head to toe. "I am at your orders, Monsieur," she said, in a hoarse and jerky voice.

"Good. Tell me what you know about the manor of Crec'h-ar-Vran."

"It's very, very old," the hypnotized woman replied, automatically. "Long abandoned to the crows, it was restored in 1839 by Comte Hector de Tréguilly, who had just lost his young wife and who shut himself away, in despair, with his only son, Vicomte Jean, who was then only a few months old."

"Has the manor been the theater of any notable event since then?" asked the Master Psychagogue.

"Until 1880, no. From that year on, by contrast, it has generated a great deal of gossip among the people of Kerambellec."

"The people of Kerambellec have become exceedingly discreet, it seems, Repeat what they say, woman Souriman."

"It's a long story."

"Repeat it."

The bone-setter's reluctance evaporated. The fluid, increasing its effect upon her, rendered her as loquacious as might be wished.

"In 1880," she said, "Jean de Tréguilly, who had married, became a widower in his turn. He had but one son, so the family was reduced to three men belonging to three successive generations: Comte Hector, aged 65 years, his son Jean, the Vicomte, in his 40s, and his grandson Albert, who was then in his 15th year.

"Instead of imitating Comte Hector and faithfully preserving the cult of his first wife, Jean de Tréguilly, after several months as a widower, manifested the intention of getting married again to a certain Azilis Le Floch, a person of the lowest class, the daughter of convicted criminal, a clockmaker in Kerambellec. He had apparently been bewitched by the seventeen-year-old Azilis—her beautiful green eyes, her enticing smile and her magnificent hair—for nothing could change his mind: neither the prayers of the old Comte, nor the severe and disrespectful criticisms of young Albert, whose blood boiled at the thought of having such a stepmother.

"The most regrettable thing was Monsieur Le Floch's past. Extremely skilful in his craft, Le Floch could as easily put his talent to profitable use in picking a lock as in constructing a clock capable of working for a hundred years. The gendarmes in Morlaix paid him frequent visits, as a consequence of which his judiciary record was enriched by several convictions. The young and beautiful Azilis was not above reproach herself. Even so, the marriage took place in 1881.

"Contrary to what might have been feared, once Azilis was a Vicomtesse, she showed herself to be entirely worthy of the high position that she occupied. She accepted the rebukes of her stepson, Albert, and the scenes that he made, in a Christian manner. Her husband, to whom she gave two daughters in two years, never had anything for which to reproach her.

"Then, in 1883, Albert, who was decidedly incorrigible and who had gone so far as to accuse his stepmother of being an adventuress and a loose woman, was asked by Jean de Tréguilly, his father, to leave Crec'h-ar-Vran. Too proud to dispute the order or to admit that he was in the wrong, the young man packed his bags, obtained authorization to realize the personal fortune that had been left to him by his mother, and left for America.

"Justly indignant at his conduct, his father made no secret of his determination to disinherit him, and the sole resource that remained to Albert was to create an honorable position in a new fatherland, but his efforts failed. He lost his entire fortune in misguided speculations. No one knows what would have become of him had not his father—who had effectively disinherited him in his will, only leaving him the small fraction of which the law did not permit him to be dispossessed—been gripped by pity or remorse and manifested the intention of reversing his earlier decision. He sent a sum of money to Albert to allow him to pay his debts, with instructions to return to France immediately, promising him a complete pardon. Lady Azilis raised no objection to this, although the alteration of her husband's testamentary dispositions would have been very prejudicial to her children and herself.

"Albert was expected at Crec'h-ar-Vran in a matter of months, and the Vicomte had already informed his notary, when he was prevented from putting his intentions into immediate effect by the sudden death of his own father, old Comte Hector, who had been confined to bed by paralysis for some time. Lady Azilis, who had not left the duty of caring for him to anyone else, was deeply affected by his death, to the point at which she suffered a brief illness, which obliged her husband to a further delay in the regulation of his affairs. The latter's heath was not very brilliant itself; he complained of headaches and insomnia, which he combated with the aid of massive doses of chloral.

"One day, Lady Azilis had to absent herself in order to make various purchases in Morlaix, which obliged her to spend the night in that town. She had not yet got out of bed when she received a telegram from Père Le Boëc, the caretaker of Crec'h-ar-Vran, at the hotel where she was staying. Comte Jean, apparently struck down by an embolism, had been found dead in his bed that very morning!"

La Souriman stopped, out of breath. Her respiration was halting and her eyelids were fluttering. Sâr Dubnotal let her catch her breath, and then gave her an order to continue her story. Having become the passive instrument of his will, she resumed immediately.

"The young woman's grief on finding dead the spouse she had left, if not in perfect health, at least full of life, was heart-rending, all the more so because her stepson would probably hold her responsible for this new misfortune.

"In fact, when he arrived at the château, Albert failed in all his duties. He did not respect his stepmother's mourning. Financial interest alone seemed to have brought him back to France. When he found that his father had not had time to modify his will, and that the greater part of his fortune would go to the children of his second marriage, he became terribly angry. He cursed the dead man and heaped gross insults upon he unfortunate widow, accusing her of exercising undue influence on the inheritance and worse. That made any compromise impossible. Lady Azilis, who would probably have been prepared to come to some arrangement, took refuge in her pride as a woman and an outraged mother.

"The new Comte de Tréguilly could do nothing but retake the road to exile. That was what he did; the last news that was heard of him was that he had joined the American army, in which he had attained the rank of lieutenant…"

La Souriman fell silent.

Sâr Dubnotal, launching further effluvia at the entranced subject, asked sharply: "Do you know why the Comtesse left

Crec'h-ar-Vran? Is it because she too believes it to be haunted?"

"It appears that she experienced a terrible disturbance not long after her husband's burial. She never offered any explanation on this point, but in Kerambellec we're convinced that the disturbance was caused by the revenant that frightened the English people so much yesterday evening."

"Since when, exactly has the phenomenon been manifest? Was the Comtesse the first to experience it?"

"There is no agreement as to that," said la Souriman. "Some say yes, others no. It's even claimed that Comte Jean did not die of an embolism, but of fright."

"Because he too saw the revenant?"

"Yes—but for myself I doubt it."

"Are there still former domestic servants of the château in Kerambellec?" Sâr Dubnotal asked.

"None, apart from the Le Boëcs, who don't know any more than I do. The maids, the cook and the valets went to Paris with the Comtesse. Everyone agrees, though, in saying that the manor wasn't haunted before the death of Comte Hector de Tréguilly. As regards Comte Jean, I've always thought that the physicians were right and that he really did die of an embolism, not of fright—but I can't swear to anything…"

Sâr Dubnotal understood that la Souriman had told him everything she could, and that he would not get another interesting syllable out of her. So, passing his thumbs over her forehead and eyelids, he hastened to bring her out of her tiring trance.

"My God!" stammered the bone-setter, as she woke up. Unable to understand why she felt ill, she darted a suspicious glance at the strangers, and left without demanding her money.

Sâr Dubnotal thought about the old woman's final words. "It's regrettable that the key point can't be elucidated," he said, after a pause, "for if the manor is haunted, it can only be by the spirit of one of the two Comtes, and it's necessary to know which."

At that moment, Otto rejoined the Master, still annoyed by his lack of success. "How do you know they aren't both haunting it?" he exclaimed.

"It's easy to see, my friend, that you're a member of my research team and not my college of disciples," Sâr Dubnotal replied, smiling. "Look at Rudolph. No such question has ever sprung to his lips."

"Indeed," said Rudolph. "It would be exceedingly strange if the two Comtes, who led an honest and retiring existence, had both been condemned to that ordeal of culpable souls. One of them, perhaps—God alone reads the depths of consciences, and it might be that a man who is universally taken to be an honest man down here has been a frightful rogue deep down, or, at least, that he has some particularly reprehensible action with which to reproach himself. Every sin is expiated in the Beyond…"

The Great Psychagogue placidly relayed the bone-setter's story to Otto.

"Well," said the investigator, "I'll willingly take the side of those who attribute the death of Comte Jean to a disturbance caused by the sight of some phantom. In which case that phantom—that revenant, as they call it—can only be old Comte Hector. Before his death, Crec'h-ar-Vran wasn't haunted. You were told, Master, that when the old Comte shut himself up in the château, he had just lost his wife. Who knows how she died?"

"Who knows, indeed?" said Sâr Dubnotal, thoughtfully. "The majority of human beings do not know themselves, so how can they know others? The Beyond is the realm of surprises. Before attaining the degree of perfection in which souls are nothing but Benevolence and Beauty, they must endure tribulations, however meritorious the lives they led on this Earth might have seemed in the feeble judgment of mortals." He turned toward the distant feudal dwelling and said, in an authoritative manner: "Enough idle talk! This evening, I shall know for sure whether or not Crec'h-ar-Vran received the visits of a spirit, and, if so, I hope to be in a position to tell you

tomorrow, my friends, who that spirit is and what is tormenting it."

IV. Alone in the Face of the Mystery

"My God, Yves! Do you think that Monsieur Severus
will dare to sleep alone in Crec'h-ar-Vran?" Soizic Le Boëc
asked her husband as she saw the daylight fading.

"He still says so, and it's my opinion that he won't
change his mind. Have you taken a good look at him, Soizic?
What eyes!"

"Just as long as he isn't the Devil!" said the old woman,
shivering.

"Shut up!" her husband said, rudely. "Would the Devil
have handed over 2000 francs, plus five handsome *louis* as a
denier à Dieu, to rent the house, to which he can come whenever he pleases?"

Soizic made no reply, but five minutes later, on hearing
Fri-Dû barking and the bell at the gate ringing, she murmured:
"Speak of the Devil, and you see the tip of his tail."

The Great Psychagogue was, indeed, alone. Even his disciple Rudolph was not with him. He offered his hand casually
to the caretaker, who had never encountered such urbanity as
that of his rich and imposing tenant, and said: "Monsieur
Yves, before going to sleep in the manor, whose keys you will
be pleased to give me, I'd like you to give me some information. If my memory serves me right, you told me a little while
ago that the rooms the English people took were those in
which your masters Hector and Jean de Tréguilly died. Well,
would you tell me in which of those rooms the old Comte
died?"

"The more distant," Le Boëc replied, with some hesitation. "The one that Mr. and Mrs. Hasting occupied."

"Then Comte Jean must have died in the other?"

"Yes, Monsieur, the one that Miss Barbara Longmore was in yesterday evening, at the time of the…accident. Oh, if they had only listened to me, none of that would have happened. I told them, as I've told you, Monsieur, to sleep somewhere else—anywhere they liked, since there's no lack of bedrooms in the château, thank God, except those two rooms. Believe it or not—meaning no offence—it was exactly those two rooms that they took!"

"I'm not at all surprised," said Sâr Dubnotal, in an imperceptibly ironic tone. "The English, more than anyone else, have a taste for forbidden fruit. But to get back to our own business, there are one or two more questions, Monsieur Yves. Has the Comtesse ever returned to the manor since the death of her father-in-law and her husband?"

"Never! Oh, certainly not!" said Père Le Boëc, whose tongue as beginning to loosen now that the tenancy agreement was signed and he had pocketed, in addition to the *denier à Dieu*, the full price of the rental. "Come back, her? Mercy! She nearly died of fright the only time she dared to go back into her husband's room. It was at 10 p.m. one evening. Suddenly, I heard screaming—and what screams! And then Fri-Dû started howling—and what howls! Oh, I remember it—I'm certain I'll remember it forever! It appeared that a spirit had blown out her candle—yes, and given her a couple of slaps, Monsieur!"

Sâr Dubnotal resumed a slight smile of satisfaction. "Has she at least been seen in Kerambellec, where her father, I believe, worked as a clockmaker?"

"Never, Monsieur. The people of the village, especially La Souriman, wouldn't have hesitated to tell us if anyone had seen her. No, no, she's had enough of this neighborhood, after all these stories, her widowhood and the abominable things that her stepson Albert said about her. Anyway, what would bring her back to Kerambellec? The clockmaker Le Floch—a notorious scoundrel, just between the two of us—broke his mainspring a long time ago; besides which, the Comtesse

63

wasn't proud of being his daughter and didn't ever want to see him again."

"How long is it since this Le Floch died?"

"Three years, Monsieur. Le Floch evidently wasn't worth much, but all the same, he deserved better than to end up like that. Instead of letting him perish like a filthy old wolf in that hole in the cliff where he went to earth in his final years, the Comtesse should have remembered that he was her father, and had him hospitalized in some regional asylum."

"Perhaps she didn't know the extremity to which he'd been reduced?" Sâr Dubnotal suggested.

"Go on! I told her ten times, Monsieur—and the parish priest and the schoolmaster too. Nothing came of it. Le Floch, however, seemed to have mended his ways toward the end. He never ceased muttering *mea culpas*. Truly, he touched us with his lamentable tone, and his eyes questing for the alms of forgiveness. No one can convince me that he wasn't sincere. He'd repented his sins; they probably weighed heavily on his conscience. Perhaps, too, he wasn't entirely in his right mind. Otherwise, I can't explain why, when Fri-Dû, who had got into the habit, started barking at 10 p.m. every night, he joined in the concert too, howling like a lost soul. By thunder! I'm no more chicken than then next man, but it was enough, some nights, to make one hand in one's resignation!"

"In that case," said Sâr Dubnotal, "why haven't you left Crec'h-ar-Vran?"

"Why? Why? I often ask myself the same question, Monsieur. It's just that we're attached, my Soizic and me, to these great rocks on which we've lived for so many years, perched between the sky and the sea, where we've loved one another and raised our three poor little ones, whom the Virgin has in her holy care! Then again, it's easy to say, but where would we go at our age? Where could we find work, shelter, a crust of bread? No, Monsieur, so long one is young, the ship may sail! So long as he has blood and muscles, a man can run around—but once past the cape of 60, he has to lay down his arms and retreat into his shell, like a periwinkle!"

64

"Undoubtedly," Sâr Dubnotal agreed. "But what about these continuing troubles?"

"One gets used them, gradually, like everything else. Oh, in the beginning, to be sure, we got the wind up, Soizic and me, when Fri-Dû started wailing like a Christian at 10 p.m. every evening, and we heard the gates opening and closing at the end of the courtyard, without being able to see anything in the darkness, and the windows clattering, and I don't know what frightful music of rattling and groaning coming through the walls of the manor."

"Couldn't some trickster have got into the place without your knowledge?"

"To be frank, that's the first question I asked myself. Yes, I said to myself, just like Soizic and you, someone's having you on, old Yves. You need to see which way the wind is blowing and get your hands on the scoundrel who's amusing himself by scaring you to death. Prepare to come about! Well, I'd only forgotten one thing, which was to put a rudder on my brig. No—I'd lost the compass! How could the scoundrel have hoisted himself up there? Tack as much as you like around the courtyard, Monsieur. See for yourself whether a squirrel could scale those sheer walls. There's only the one path, and it's barred by the gate, whose bell sounds if anyone tries to open it.

"Besides, people in these parts don't play that sort of game. Bretons don't like to treat anything that concerns religion lightly, or joke about the dead, whose poor souls populate the heath and the strand—for lack, mostly, of having had a word with the curé or his deputy before drinking one last draught from the big cup." Père Le Boëc launched a jet of brown-tinted saliva as he turned toward the manor, which was tinted purple by the dusk, then shook his head and went in: "No, no, The plain and simple truth—and I don't mind telling you, since it doesn't seem to frighten you at all—is that Crec'h-ar-Vran is haunted, and the people of Kerambellec are quite right to call it the Accursed Manor.

"We know something about that, my wife and I—and after 10 p.m., Monsieur, you won't get us out of our lodge for an empire. We're just glad that the revenants never take it into their heads to set a course in our direction. The one thing that reassures us is that we have a clear conscience. With that, one can sleep at any time."

"Thank you for the information, Monsieur Yves," said Sâr Dubnotal, in his grave and placid voice.

"At least take advantage of it, and, if you're going sleep in the château, don't install yourself in the second room..."

"Have no fear," Sâr Dubnotal replied, evasively. With that, he wished the caretaker good night, took the keys and walked slowly toward the manor.

It was still light enough for Sâr Dubnotal to take a walk around the château before going inside. Leaning over the ground raked by Père Le Boëc, he seemed to be looking for a trail that did not exist. "No footprints in the sand," he murmured. "That precaution was superfluous, but I don't regret having taken it. I'm sure now that no one has entered the manor since then."

When the door was open he took a small electric torch from his coat and switched it on. A luminous beam sprang forth into the corridor. He closed and locked the door, shot the bolts, then placed a heavy table behind the oak battens and piled on benches that he had fetched from the office.

After that, to settle his conscience, he immediately proceeded to a scrupulous domiciliary inspection, which led him from the cellars, which were intolerably mephitic because the ventilation-shafts were sealed off, via the rooms on the ground floor and the two upper floors—save for the two "accursed rooms," which he reserved until later—to the attics, where he made sure that the skylights were firmly shut.

The windows all had their shutters closed, with the exception of the ones on the second floor that the Keepsakes had opened to air their apartment.

Visibly satisfied with the results of his new investigation, Sâr Dubnotal deliberately went into Come Jean de Tréguilly's bedroom, previously occupied by Miss Barbara Longmore, carefully bolted the door, set his electric torch down on a table in the middle of the room and lit the candle in a candlestick on the mantelpiece—after which he extinguished the torch and put to back in his pocket.

At that moment, a wall-clock above the mantelpiece, made in the Henri II style but of relatively recent manufacture, chimed nine. The mantelpiece was facing the bed, set between the door to the corridor and that of the next room: Comte Hector's bedroom.

"That's odd," said Sâr Dubnotal, moving closer. "How is that wall-clock still going after so many years? Did Miss Barbara take it into her head to wind it?"

The Master climbed up on a chair to examine the clock more closely and his eyes fell upon the name of the maker engraved in the wood: *Le Floch, Clockmaker, Kerambellec.*

"I understand!" he murmured. "That village artisan, I've been told, had a rare skill. He made this clock for his daughter, the Comtesse de Tréguilly, and he equipped it with a movement capable of operating for many years without it requiring to be wound."

With this point elucidated to his evident satisfaction, the Psychagogue surveyed the room with a keen gaze, looking under the table, the chest of drawers and the bed in the alcove, whose mattress he turned over—in fact, everywhere. He sounded the walls, the ceiling, the floor and the chimney. He looked behind the portraits of the two Comtes and another portrait of a young woman, in whom he immediately recognized, by the description that had been given to him, the Comtesse de Tréguilly, née Azilis Le Floch.

"She's very beautiful," he said, simply.

Passing into the next room, with the lighted candlestick in one hand and his cane in the other, he proceeded to examine it in exactly the same fashion, without making any interesting discovery. Then he closed the shutters of both windows and, going back into the first room, barricaded the communicating door, pushing an armchair up against it. He placed the candlestick on a table and, after having closed the metal flue-curtain, which was in the side wall opposite the partition wall between the two bedrooms, Sâr Dubnotal sat down in the arm-chair obstructing the communicating door.

One after another, he took from his pockets a golden casket, a flat-sided crystal bottle with a silver stopper and a little book bound in crocodile skin. "Let's renew our strength," he murmured, "and then we'll read a few pages of this treatise on Spagyrics."[11]

From the golden casket he took three or four white tablets, which he swallowed. Then, lifting the unstopped bottle to his lips, he took a few sips of a reddish elixir.

"The suppression of vulgar aliments, whose digestion and assimilation wears away the workings of the organism, is agreeable to me as it is profitable," the Master remarked, as if speaking aside. Thus reassured that he had made a substantial meal, he opened his book and absorbed himself in erudite reading, but not without raising his head from time to time to consult the face of the clock.

Half past nine sounded.

"Another 30 minutes to wait!" he said

Sâr Dubnotal read in silence until 9:55 p.m., and then closed his book and sat up watchfully. "Nothing yet! Another four minutes…three…two…one…. Ah! Finally!"

As he pronounced this exclamation, an incident occurred that did not have the capacity to trouble the Master, but which would certainly have given gooseflesh to any other man placed in his situation and called, like him, to witness the most

---

[11] The text gives the book's title as *Traité des Spagirites*, followers of Spagyrics sometimes being described as "Spagyrites." The term was coined by Paracelsus to mean alchemy applied for medical purposes, although now that Paracelsian "chemical medicine" is no longer seen—as it was in his own day—as a rival of herbal medicine, the word is frequently used by herbalists to describe some of their own production methods.

mysterious and harrowing phenomena that it is possible to imagine.

Suddenly, as the wall-clock sounded the last chime of 10 p.m., a desperate howling, which came from Fri-Dû's kennel, disturbed the nocturnal silence. At the same time, Sâr Dubnotal's cocked ear caught the click of a door-catch. It will be recalled that the Master had taken care to barricade all the doors, especially the main entrance on the ground floor—but it was the main entrance that had just closed with a click. As the clock completed the clear notes of its chime, furtive, almost indistinct footsteps, climbed the staircase one step at a time—and the guard-dog in the courtyard uttered the most lamentable howls.

Lying back in his armchair, alone in the face of the Mystery, the Great Psychagogue listened. At that critical moment, there was not the slightest tremor in his noble visage. His eyes fixed upon the door, he sat motionless, waiting impassively.

After climbing the stairway, the footsteps approached along the corridor, and stopped on the other side of the door. For four or five seconds nothing more was audible but a dull, hoarse moaning—a sort of stifled plaint.

The dog and the wall-clock had both fallen silent, and the moaning was coming not from the courtyard but from the corridor, scarcely ten paces from the place where the Master was sitting.

Fri-Dû suddenly resumed barking. And this is what Sâr Dubnotal saw:

The key that he had left in Comte Jean's bedroom door turned slowly in the lock, even though it was inside and could not be operated from the corridor. Then the two bolts, pulled by an invisible hand, withdrew from their sockets, and the door turned on its hinges.

No one was standing in the frame of that wide open door—and yet, there must have been someone there, for the carpet was pressed down by footsteps similar to those that Sâr Dubnotal had heard so feebly on the stairs and in the corridor a short while before.

The door, moreover, closed again almost immediately, and was locked and bolted before Sâr Dubnotal's very eyes. The latter could not be alone any longer.

The only witness to this fantastic scene, which the majority of mortals would have been unable to bear without fainting or temporarily losing their reason, still did not budge from his seat, and he lost none of his prodigious self-composure.

It was obvious to this superhuman man, if one may put it thus, no longer felt the instinctive thrill of fear in his flesh, and that nothing that set a chill the best-tempered hearts could succeed in disturbing his. Sâr Dubnotal was not, however, at the end of the frightful experience.

After a few seconds of tragic silence, the dog Fri-Dû, in the depths of the courtyard, resumed howling in mortal distress, and the stiff and rhythmic footsteps of the revenant seemed to advance toward the table, while a glacial draught passed over the candlestick, extinguishing the flame, and came to strike Sâr Dubnotal in the face.

An opaque obscurity instantly overwhelmed the room, and to the horror of that abrupt darkness was added an inexplicable noise of items of furniture falling over and bumping into one another.

Sâr Dubnotal finally emerged from his immobility. His right hand slipped into his jacket pocket and drew out his secret torch, which he switched on. A beam of electric light cut a dazzling cone through the darkness, initially setting an aureole about the portrait of the Comtesse, whose features seemed to become animated by an expression of indescribable alarm. Then the Master, using the torch-beam like a searchlight, examined all four corners of the room in turn.

There was no one there! There was absolutely nothing. Apart from Sâr Dubnotal, there was no living being there—no visible one, at least.

Something no less marvelous was that the furniture was all in place, and the room was perfectly tidy.

Had Sâr Dubnotal been the victim of a hallucination?

No, for his attention was immediately attracted by the unusual friction of a large oaken prayer-stool upholstered in velvet, next to the bed. The Master aimed the beam of his torch in that direction, and he saw that the velvet was depressed, as if beneath the weight of an invisible body.

He was about to make an even more remarkable observation.

An ivory crucifix hanging on the wall behind the bed became detached from its nail and, sustained in mid-air by a mysterious force, came to place itself above the bedclothes, at the same height as the shelf of the prayer-stool, where it remained motionless.

Immediately, a frightful, heart-rending plaint, a cry of despair, went up from the seemingly-unoccupied seat, whose wood creaked as if it were about to split.

Outside, the dog was still howling.

The sea breeze, which had risen, battered the wall of the manor with sudden and violent gusts, as if it were rushing to attack the feudal dwelling with an unrelenting sequence of assaults. Was it trying to bury beneath its granite ruins the bold individual who had dared to go there to sound the mysteries of death?

Sâr Dubnotal waited for a few more seconds without moving. The plaint was succeeded by an almost imperceptible murmur of prayer, punctuated by dolorous sighs, each a sort of lugubrious "*mea culpa.*"

The Psychagogue waited for this prayer to finish, and then, softly and in an infinitely compassionate tone, asked: "is that you, Comte Hector de Tréguilly?"

There was no response, save for the sound of footsteps moving across the carpet.

He was about to repeat his question when his armchair, pulled and shaken in every direction, was nearly wrenched out from under him. At the same time, he felt the contact of an icy hand, which tried to take his torch away from him.

Without getting excited, Sâr Dubnotal—who had probably been expecting some such attempt—got up, seized the immaterial fingers in his own, and cried, forcefully: "Comte Jean de Tréguilly, is that you?"

The effect of this bold gesture and this new question was prodigious.

The hand that Sâr Dubnotal was holding was torn away so violently that the shock almost knocked him down; there was a loud scream and a frightful confusion. The portrait of the Comtesse came out of its frame and took off like a wind-borne leaf, while those of the two Comtes shook furiously. The key grated, the bolts slid back, the door opened and closed again with a gust of wind, and Sâr Dubnotal heard the sound of frantic running along the corridor and down the staircase.

As if by enchantment, Fri-Dû stopped barking, and everything fell back into the enormous silence of the night.

Sâr Dubnotal struck a match, re-lit the candle, and ran his gaze around the room.

It was in the same state as it had been in before 10 p.m.—but no! Something was missing.

The crucifix had resumed its place on the wall; the table had stood up of its own accord, along with the candlestick; the armchair was solidly wedged against the communicating door; but—a strange and almost incredible thing that gave the Great Psychagogue much pause for thought—the frame of the portrait of Azilis Le Floch, Comtesse de Tréguilly, remained empty. *The canvas had, inexplicably, disappeared.*

V. The Recalcitrant Spirit

"Rudolph, the mystery is more impenetrable than I thought. I expected to clear it up tonight, but, on the contrary, I've seen it thicken—and this business, I see now, will put my power to a stern proof."

"Oh, Master," the young disciple protested, ardently, "Are there still enigmas for you?"

True science does not proceed without modesty, and Sâr Dubnotal was a true scientist. "Certainly my friend," he replied. "For me, as for all humans, Celestial Space is populated with secrets, although Science sometimes permits me to decipher a few of them…"

"Your nocturnal sentry-duty…?"

"Went well."

"The spirit…?"

"Really exists, and that point is settled. Monsieur César Sabrejolle should have accompanied me; it would have been enough to shake his skepticism."

"Sabrejolle's merely a braggart," said Rudolph. "The weight of the Mystery would crush him like a fly. But he's a fool wrapped up in cunning, and he'd rather deny than go to see, as they say."

"Whatever he is," said Sâr Dubnotal, "the manor is haunted. Can you guess by whom?"

"By the spirit of old Comte Hector?"

"Not at all, and that's exactly what put me off the track. In sum, Otto's deductions seemed quite judicious to me. That gentleman's sudden retreat to this grim Breton manor could as easily be explained by remorse as by grief. We had grounds to suspect that the Soul in pain was his. But no; I'm certain that it is, in fact, that of Comte Jean. La Souriman's story, whose sincerity we cannot suspect, represented him to us as a slightly weak man, overly besotted with the young and beautiful Azilis, but essentially excellent. What might the sin be that obliges his Soul to return to wander the place where it abandoned his body? The problem is established, but we don't yet have any clue that would help us to solve it. Yesterday, when he heard me pronounce his name, the spirit took flight—and the strangest thing of all was that he took the portrait of Azilis with him, leaving the frame behind. I searched for the canvas all over the château, without being able to find it…"

This conversation between the Master Psychagogue and Rudolph was taking place in the courtyard of the manor on the day after the memorable night on which the phenomena described in the previous chapter had been produced. Sâr Dubnotal had given orders on the previous day for his disciple to rejoin him at Crec'h-ar-Vran with Annunciata Gianetti, an Italian woman—a compatriot of Eusapia Palladino and just as celebrated—whom he liked to employ as a medium.

The word "medium" is etymologically neutral. There are male mediums and female mediums. Female mediums are the more numerous and also the best, although they have a regrettable tendency to fraud. Under hypnotic influence, they fall into a nervous state in which their personality is divided into two.

Several species of mediums are known, and there is no lack of opportunity for us to see them operate, according to their nature and various specialties. Annunciata Gianetti, who looked to be in her early 20s, was an extremely impressionable medium who enjoyed to a rare degree—one that was even dangerous to her health and sanity—the faculty of entering into communication with the Immaterial, while voluntarily allowing the will of her hypnotizer to substitute itself entirely for her own.

Sâr Dubnotal wanted to take advantage of la Gianetti's precious faculty to obtain responses from the violent and turbulent spirit of the manor, which had been so recalcitrant when the Psychagogue had attempted to interrogate it himself. We should add that he was not sure that the experiment would succeed, for, by the very fact that they are free of any terrestrial attachment, Souls cannot be constrained to subject themselves to submission by the human will. It is voluntarily that they sometimes accept to manifest themselves to the living in order to guide them, enlighten them or reveal to them certain profound truths—or, entirely to the contrary, to dupe them and frighten them.

Annunciata was standing a few paces away from the two men. Short, slender and nervous, she was dressed in the Italian fashion, in a striped skirt, with her bosom partly concealed beneath a large cashmere headscarf knotted in front. Her head, protected by that picturesque Neapolitan headgear, was ornamented by opulent black hair, disposed in heavy plaits and virginal bandeaux, which only allowed a pale triangle of flesh to be seen at her forehead. She was very beautiful, but the gaze of her dark eyes was habitually bleak, as if their gleam were turned inwards. It was easily imaginable that the woman's thoughts were often absent, and that she looked at her surroundings, if not without seeing them, at least without taking any interest in them.

"In the final analysis, Rudolph," Sâr Dubnotal went on, after a brief silence devoted to reflection, "it's necessary that everything should be clarified. When I undertake a task, I don't abandon it at the first obstacle. I want to know, and I intend to find out, what grave sin Comte Jean committed on this Earth, and why his spirit chose the moment when I was in the mortuary room to remove the canvas the Comtesse's portrait—for I'm convinced that that's the key to the puzzle. Come on, Rudolph, and you too, Annunciata! We're going down into the crypt."

Followed by la Gianetti, the Master and his pupil head toward the sepulcher of the Comtes de Tréguilly—which was, as we have said, situated behind the manor.

From the threshold of their lodge, Yves and Soizic Le Boëc watched them with a mixture of dread and amazement. Half an hour earlier, when Rudolph, accompanied by the Italian woman, had rung the bell at the gate and asked the caretaker to let him come in to rejoin the Master, the ex-able seaman of the Fleet, who had not yet seen his tenant reappear, had exclaimed: "Your Master! Pray for him, my dear Monsieur! Since yesterday he has given us no sign of life; his light went out at 10 p.m., and the Holy Virgin is my witness that I know no more than that."

"We've arranged to meet him," Rudolph had relied, simply, who had gone to knock on the door of the manor while Père Le Boëc muttered: "Good! My God, if he's washed up by the waves, there'll be a holy fuss!" His feelings can be imagined, and those of his wife, when they both observed five minutes later that the stranger, who had emerged safe and sound from the manor at the first summons, seemed to be in perfectly good health. Their surprise only increased when they saw him, after a brief conversation, taking the newcomers with him in the direction of the crypt.

"He must have the Devil in him, or I'm no more than a second-class gunner," the old man concluded, gesturing to his wife to go back indoors. "There's some unholy disorder underlying all this, you mark my words!"

The brave Père Le Boëc did not mean this literally, but, if he had been able to witness the fantastic scene of which the funeral crypt of the Comtes de Tréguilly was about to be the theater, he would doubtless have come round conclusively to the opinion of Soizic, for whom the strange tenant and a certain individual with horns and cloven hooves were one and the same.

After having tried two or three keys from the bunch confided to him by the caretaker in the enormous padlock securing the iron bars, Sâr Dubnotal was able to open the barred gate of the crypt. It was as black as the inside of an oven.

A stairway of 30 steps descended underground, ending in a cavern about five meters wide and six deep, in which one could not distinguish the floor from above, so thick was the ambient shadow. To the right and the left of a central aisle the sepulchers of the noble family were aligned.

Comte Hector had had the rest of his ancestors—who had been buried in the communal cemetery in Kerambellec— exhumed in order to transfer them here. Their tombs, five in number, occupied the left-hand row. He and his son Jean lay to the right, where three graves recovered by their stones still remained unoccupied.

For five years, no one had dared cross the threshold of the funereal monument. In Kerambellec, they trembled at the mere idea of being in the vicinity of that crypt, from which the phantom emerged every night to terrorize the living.

The gravedigger who had buried the last Comtes had died shortly after them, and, if the Comtesse de Tréguilly had wanted, for one reason or another, to have their remains removed from the vault, she would not have found anyone in the parish, or within a considerable radius, to undertake the work.

The Great Psychagogue did not hesitate to venture into that lugubrious subterranean vault. He went down first, illuminating it by means of his electric torch. Abruptly inundated with light, the crypt took on a redoubtable appearance, with its massive walls of bare granite, which resembled gravestones.

The steps resounded in a sinister manner beneath Sâr Dubnotal's footsteps. Rudolph, the bearer of a heavy satchel slung over his shoulder, came next, and la Gianetti brought up the rear.

The three strangers stopped in the central aisle, in front of Comte Jean de Tréguilly's sepulcher; his name was engraved on its marble lid.

Although the sacred place in which they were standing inspired a profound respect in them, that respect was not associated with any dread. Was it not with the most laudable of intentions that the three strangers had come to trouble the peace of the dead men who were lying there?

"Out of deference, I would have preferred to undertake the evocation in my bungalow," Sâr Dubnotal explained, "but I fear that the experiment might have failed, in which case I would have been obliged to have recourse to a more delicate method of obtaining information, which could only be applied here."

Meanwhile, Rudolph was rummaging in his satchel. He took out a small black wand, which he gave to the Italian woman. There was a minute or two of silence, and of self-composure. The Master Psychagogue and his disciple were contemplating Jean de Tréguilly's tomb.

"Gianetti," said Sâr Dubnotal, afterwards, stressing each syllable and fixing his magnetic eyes on his subject's strange pupils, "I instruct you to ask the spirit of the Comte to manifest itself to you."

The medium, becoming paler than a bed-sheet, fluttered her eyelids. A great spasm ran through her stiffened body; her features convulsed; her taut nerves vibrated as if to break, and pale white foam moistened the corners of her discolored lips.

"Go on!" said Sâr Dubnotal.

Annunciata's arm appeared to stretch out, as if moved by a spring, and, tapping lightly and curtly three times on the marble slab with her wand, the medium pronounced in a blank voice: "Comte Jean de Tréguilly, would you do me the great favor of entering into communication with me?"

Silence reigned once more, solemn and profound.

Eventually, a dull knock coming from inside the tomb replied to the three blows struck on the stone by the medium's wand, then two more raps, spaced out and distinctive. La Gianetti, on hearing them, appeared to be prey to a mysterious influence, foreign to that of Sâr Dubnotal, and subject to a nervous crisis that left her standing up, but stiff and inert, as if she were a victim of catalepsy.

Seeing that the invoked spirit, instead of lending itself to la Gianetti's desire, was manifesting the intention of possessing her—which is to say, of making use of her corporeal instrument—and that it had plunged her into a sort of coma as a first step, the Great Psychagogue forestalled the danger. Furrowing his brows as if to condense all his force and transmit a part of it to his subject, he passed his hand back and forth in front of Annunciata's forehead. She gradually emerged from the trance and ended up darting a frightened gaze around her.

"Where am I? What am I doing?" she stammered, with a cold sweat on her temples and her pupils dilated with horror and fear.

The Master continued to lavish mysterious touches upon her, which gradually seemed to calm her down. "Don't worry!" he said to her. "Repeat your invitation. But be careful, Annunciata—the spirit you're invoking is not well-disposed toward us. Be extremely prudent and diplomatic."

La Gianetti obeyed, regretfully. She was obviously reluctant to recommence and experiment that put a painful stress on her nerves and put her very life in danger—but Sâr Dubnotal knew that he was capable of averting the peril, however great it might be, and his imperious will subdued that of the medium.

This time the drumming that resounded beneath the slab clearly indicated that congenial communication with the spirit had finally been established. The dead man had responded to the medium's summons and was interrogating her, without seeking to harm her.

"Translate his question, Annunciata," instructed Sâr Dubnotal.

"He's asking me what you want."

"Reply that you'd like to know why he haunts Crec'h-ar-Vran and why he took away his wife's portrait."

The subject, increasingly docile, carried out the Master's orders mentally.

Immediately, the subterranean drumming resumed.

"The spirit declares that I'm excessively curious, and that all he will consent to do for me is to resume concrete form temporarily."

"Accept!" said Sâr Dubnotal, swiftly.

The Italian young woman struck the slab with her wand. It oscillated slightly, lifting up alternately to either side; these oscillations soon gained in amplitude. Then something happened that was extraordinary enough even to obliterate skepticism as solidly established as that of Monsieur César Sabrejolle. Detaching itself entirely from its setting, the heavy granite block was lifted gently into the air and floated at a man's height, apparently giving the lie to the most elementary principles of weight and equilibrium, seemingly without any support.

Immediately afterwards, the coffin creaked and opened up, and from its gaping maw sprang a sort of mist: a light whitish vapor that rose up like incense-smoke toward the vault of the cave.

The temperature of the crypt dropped instantly.

Sâr Dubnotal and Rudolph shivered, in spite of the thickness of their garments, but their companion, despite being more lightly clad, did not appear be suffering from the unusual

79

chill. She remained stiff and insensible, while the mist, gradually condensing, took on the shape and form of a phantom.

The phantom's features, indistinct at first, became increasingly clear, and the Master Psychagogue eventually recognized the face of Comte Jean de Tréguilly, whose portrait he had studied the previous evening in the mortuary chamber. He and Rudolph both started in surprise, however, on remarking that the spirit seemed to be troubled, and held the posterior part of his skull between his hands, which were crossed over behind his head.

"What does that signify, Master?" the disciple murmured. "Why that posture? One would think that the apparition did not want us to see the nape of his neck."

Sâr Dubnotal leaned toward the medium's ear and whispered to her, in a voice as faint as a breath: "Annunciata, entreat the spirit to tell you what is worrying him, and what the significance is of that posture."

La Gianetti repeated the question in a loud voice.

The result was disastrous.

A cry, more horrible than a death-rattle, vibrated within the narrow space; the phantom disappeared into the cloud from which it had emerged, the cloud dissipated in its turn and the slab fell back with a crash over the gaping coffin.

Rudolph looked at his master for a moment without speaking. There was a bizarre, disturbing noise at the top of the staircase, as if chains were grating and rattling against the wrought-iron bars. One might have thought that a locksmith were hastening to padlock the gate that formed the entrance to the crypt, as if to bury the three guilty strangers alive for having violated the peace of that sepulcher. Shaken by an involuntary tremor of anguish and dread, the young man went pale and asked: "Can you hear that, Master?"

Quite calmly, Sâr Dubnotal continued listening. "Someone's locking us in," he murmured.

"Who?"

"Go and see."

Rudolph went up the 30 steps four at a time.

"Oh!" he cried, not trying to hide his anxiety.

From the depths of the crypt, Sâr Dubnotal asked: "What is it?"

"The gate's locked, Master! The chain is wrapped around the bars and the padlock is sealed."

"Try to open it," said the Psychagogue, calmly.

Rudolph gripped the bars with both hands and shook the grille violently. He could not see anyone on the other side of it. The grille, however, was solid enough to withstand any such proof. It resisted.

"Impossible!" Rudolph shouted. "The padlock chain won't permit it."

"Wait!" replied Sâr Dubnotal. He came up. Through the interstices of the bars, his gaze plunged into the sunlit courtyard of the manor. "You didn't see Père Le Boëc?" he queried.

"No."

"Nor his wife?"

"No one! Do you suspect the caretakers of Crec'h-ar-Vran of being the authors of this practical joke?"

"I don't know what to think," confessed the Great Psychagogue, shaking the bars in his turn. The Le Boëcs are alone in the manor. If a human hand padlocked the gate, it can only have been than of Yves or Soizic."

The iron door still did not give way.

"Should I call Père Le Boëc?" asked Rudolph.

"Your voice won't carry as far as his lodge," the Master replied. "Better to pass your arm through the bars to reach the padlock. Do you have the key?"

"Yes," said Rudolph, plunging his hand into the pocket of his jacket." Immediately, though, he added: "That's odd. I was sure I'd put the key there…"

One by one, the disciple emptied all his pockets. To his extreme surprise, though, he could not find the key.

"You don't have it about your person, by any chance, Master?" he asked.

"Me? You know full well that I haven't."

81

"I can't find it."

"You've searched hard?"

"Everywhere!"

Sâr Dubnotal had lost none of his astonishing self-composure. "I see what's going on," he said. "Let's go back down into the crypt, Rudolph."

"What? You're not going to try to get out of here?"

"We have plenty of time," the Psychagogue replied, coolly. "Let's finish our work first."

"But hasn't the spirit gone into hiding, Master?"

"Exactly—I'm all more determined to discover its secret."

"And you think we'll be able to leave this burial-place easily?"

Sâr Dubnotal's serene and confident smile reassured the young man. "Oh, yes. I understand everything now. It was needless to suspect the Le Boëcs, who have nothing to do with our incarceration—which is temporary, as proved by the disappearance of the key."

"Who do you suspect, then, Master?"

"The spirit of Comte Jean," the Master replied, simply. "The recalcitrant and antisocial Soul."

"Ah!" said Rudolph. "I see it all. The Comte wanted to imprison us to punish us for out audacity, didn't he?"

"Yes," said the Great Psychagogue.

The situation of the two men and their companion Annunciata, immured in the crypt by the Soul whose repose they were troubling, was so unexpected and frightening that Rudolph felt himself invaded by superstitious dread once again. He was familiar with the formidable power of immaterial beings, and even though Sâr Dubnotal was no less powerful, he wondered whether the Master or the spirit would triumph.

The Great Psychagogue went back down the stairway, followed by Rudolph.

"Comte Jean does not know that all the walls and iron bars in the world cannot keep me captive against my will," Sâr Dubnotal said, returning to the side of the tomb. "Even so, our task is becoming increasingly arduous, and it's as well that I told you to bring your satchel, Rudolph. We shall be obliged to retrace our steps methodically in order to discover all or part of the secret of this dead man, who obviously has powerful reasons for manifesting such hostility. That precautionary gesture of hiding the nape of his neck intrigues me, as it intrigued you. Provided that the decomposition of cadaver does not make it impossible, we can take molds from it!"

Thus recalled to his duty, Rudolph stopped tormenting himself. "The Comte's body is probably embalmed," he said.

"I hope so. Annunciata, lift that slab."

Levitation, or lifting and moving objects at a distance solely by the force of the psychic fluid—a phenomenon proven a thousand times, but still controversial today—was child's play for Sâr Dubnotal's admirable medium. In effect, the psychic fluid acts on all objects as a magnet acts upon iron filings or amber on pieces of paper, and la Gianetti was literally impregnated with it. That was why Sâr Dubnotal had no fear of being kept captive in the vault. In cases of hindrance, he had no need of pincers or picks to open the grille or stove in partition walls. His medium would suffice: a human lever moved by his will and animated by a virtually irresistible force.

Extending her hands, agitated by a convulsive tremor, the young woman lightly touched the capstone, which lifted into the air again and went to settle on the neighboring tomb.

"The coffin next!" said Sâr Dubnotal. "Bring it into the aisle."

The fluid did it work again. A heavy oaken coffin, lifted up in the same manner, settled at the feet of the two men. The lid, whose screws were corroded by rust, was easily detached, and Rudolph leaned forward to set aside the shroud. "We can take imprints!" he exclaimed. "Look, Master—the corpse is mummified!"

The body of Comte Jean de Tréguilly was, in fact, in a state of perfect conservation. If not for the closed eyelids and the waxy texture of the epidermis, one might have believed that the man—who had been buried for many years—was only asleep. Clumps of hair and beard sill framed the face, imprinted with the solemn serenity of death. The lips were slightly open, revealing white and firmly-rooted teeth. Nothing came away when Sâr Dubnotal, having leaned over the bier in his turn, carefully turned the cadaver over in order to examine the other side.

"His carnal envelope is marvelously well-preserved," he said. "Take a mold of the hands, Rudolph."

The young man, full of respect for the relic but inaccessible to the mixture of repulsion and fear that the sight of a cadaver caused most people to experience, took a large ball of virginal wax from his satchel, kneaded it and made several flat cakes. He placed one of them over the palm of the dead man's right hand and, by means of a skilful and regular pressure, obtained an exact impression of the hand's lines in the wax.

Directing the light of his torch upon the proof thus obtained, Sâr Dubnotal—for whom cheiromancy, like all the other divinatory arts, held no secrets—studied it with minute attention.

"That's curious," he said, as his examination advanced. "The disposition of the lines of Comte Jean's hand confirms the information we've already been given about him. The head line, which is rather sketchy, and the heart line, which is, by contrast, very clear, indicate that the man was both weak and virtuous. If he has sinned, it wasn't because of lack of reflection or out of ignorance. He must have committed a sin; he has certainly not committed a crime. The Mound of Venus, which is abnormally developed, leads me to believe that his love for his wife blinded him. The lifeline, which is abruptly interrupted, explains his premature death, which a certain sign allows me to attribute, not to natural causes—like that embolism of which there was mention—but to an accident. Fear, at any rate, was not involved in it. Oh. If I'm not mistaken, we've made a sensational discovery, Rudolph!"

The Great Psychagogue redoubled his attention, then continued: "I see! There was a crime—a diabolically clever crime, leaving no trace, calculated to mislead the physicians and the law. Comte Jean de Tréguilly was murdered, and probably died in a state of sin. That suffices to explain why his spirit haunts this place. Evoke it again, Annunciata. Interrogate it; try to find out who killed him and the motive for that abominable crime, which remained unsuspected and unpunished."

The medium did as she was told, but even though she brought all of her power into play, her efforts remained sterile. Evidently irritated by the violation of his sepulcher, Comte Jean would not respond to any summons.

Sâr Dubnotal had, of course, anticipated this regrettable complication. "Whether the Comte's spirit likes it or not," he said, calmly, "I shall unravel this tangled plot. Let's proceed methodically, Rudolph. The evident reluctance of the dead man to enter into communication with us, and his attempt to frighten us by locking the door of the crypt, prove that he has some interest in not divulging the name of the criminal whose victim he is. Is that because the criminal is a family member?"

Rudolph shook his head. "Don't forget, Master, that his family only comprised: firstly, the Comtesse, who was in Morlaix when the death occurred and who seems to be above suspicion; secondly, the clockmaker Le Floch, whose reputation, scarcely enviable as it was, was not that of a murderer, and who never came to the château in any case; thirdly, Vicomte Albert, similarly absent, whose return from America only took place some days afterwards; and fourthly, the children of the second marriage, both of whom were then too young."

"Yes, I know that very well, Rudolph. Appearances are certainly against that assumption; however, until I have proof to the contrary, I shall hold to my hypothesis. I can't suspect the Le Boëcs, or any other domestic, of having committed the crime, for if that were the case, Comte Jean's spirit would not be mulish and hostile, but would help us to unmask the murderer."

The Great Psychagogue reflected momentarily, and went on: "The more I think about it, the more importance I attach to

85

the phantom's gesture of trying to hide the nape of its neck from us. If you will, my friend, we shall examine the cadaver more closely and also take a mold of the occipital region."

The two men leaned over again. With great precaution, Rudolph parted the dead man's hair and was about to apply a flat block of wax to the base of the skull when he uttered an exclamation: "Ah! Look, Master—there!" His index-finger indicated a brownish dot at the base of the dead man's neck.

Sâr Dubnotal directed his keen gaze thereupon, and a more ardent gleam appeared in his black pupils. "Don't touch anything, Rudolph!" he said. "Simply move that wisp of hair, and don't move again."

The disciple obeyed, while his master selected a fine scalpel and a delicate pair of forceps from an instrument case taken from his satchel.

Anatomy and surgery had no secrets for Sâr Dubnotal. With a marvelous dexterity he opened up the cadaver's desiccated flesh, making use of the tip of his scalpel. Then he took up the forceps and, to Rudolph's great surprise, ended up extracting a narrow steel spike about five centimeters long, corroded by rust. He dipped the spike into a liquid in a phial; almost immediately, the steel recovered its original polish and gleam.

There was a long, heavy silence that lasted five or six seconds. The spike had passed from Sâr Dubnotal's hands to those of his disciple.

"What do you think of that, Rudolph?"

The young man turned the object over in his fingers repeatedly. "It's the tip of a clockmaker's needle," he said. "One of those long needles that such artisans use to test the delicate workings of watches."

"Yes," said the Great Psychagogue, tranquilly.

Rudolph looked at his master. "Ah!" he said. "So, was it Le Floch?"

"It's a little too soon for accusations," Sâr Dubnotal replied, "but there's certainly an initial presumption against him. There's every chance that the needle came from his workshop—and what Père Le Boëc told me about his miserable life and his virtually accursed death would almost confirm that presumption, if…"

"If?" the young man queried.

"If the spirit of Comte Jean were less uncooperative and we did not already know that Le Floch never set foot in Crec'h-ar-Vran."

"We still have the proof that Jean de Tréguilly was murdered," Rudolph remarked. "Here's the murder weapon. The question now is to discover exactly how it was used."

"A difficult question to resolve," said Sâr Dubnotal. "It's necessary to set aside the hypothesis of the culpability of Le Floch, since it's established that the man was never admitted into the Comte's intimate presence. It's true that he could have made an accomplice of the murderer and furnished him with the needle…"

"But how could the crime have been committed, Master?"

"That's what I'm asking myself."

"So the mystery, in your view, remains complete?"

"Complete, and more troubling than ever."

"How shall we pierce it, Master?"

"I don't know yet, but I shall not give up until clarification is achieved and justice is done."

"Why not interrogate the spirit of Le Floch?"

"I've thought of that, but first I want to look at the mortuary chamber again. Perhaps we'll find something there that will enlighten us as to the manner in which this needle perforated Comte Jean's neck while he slept. He was found in the morning—let us bear this detail in mind—dead in his bed, as if he had been struck dead. No trace of violence was discovered, otherwise suspicions would certainly have been aroused against his staff, particularly Père Le Boëc. That's explicable, since it was the needle that caused his abrupt death by perforating the nape of his neck. On the other hand, the Comte abused chloral; it's a narcotic that induces very heavy sleep. The murderer might well have profited from that circumstance

87

to commit his murder in peace. But who was that murderer? How was he able to introduce himself into the room in which the Comte was sleeping? These two points escape us, and they're of the highest importance." The Master paused then concluded: "As to the motive for the crime, I might have an idea about that."

He made use of Rudolph's hands, and those of la Gianetti—still very shaken by her psychic efforts—to close the coffin again and put everything back in place.

Two minutes later, all three left the funeral crypt of the Comtes de Tréguilly with the greatest ease imaginable; to do that, Sâr Dubnotal did not even need to make use of the good offices of his medium to open the gate by means of levitation. The spirit of Comte Jean, finally understanding the power the Psychagogue had at his disposal, had apparently changed his mind. Rudolph had found the key to the crypt again, in the depths of his pocket—and in any case, the gate was wide open.

VI. In Which Science Serves the Ends of Justice

Père Le Boëc was raking the courtyard of the manor when Sâr Dubnotal and his assistants reappeared. Having wondered, with as much surprise as alarm, what the strangers were doing in the funeral crypt, he had made use of the first available pretext to get closer to them.

Sâr Dubnotal pretended not to have understood the real reason for his devoted application to duty. "Ah, there you are, Monsieur Yves!" he said. "That's lucky! I needed to talk to you."

The ex-able seaman raised his beret, blushing slightly, ashamed of being caught in a flagrant indiscretion, and hastened to reply: "At your service, Monsieur Severus."

The Master Psychagogue got straight to the point. "Come on," he said, "gather your memories, my man, and above all be frank, if you want to conserve my esteem and ensure the tranquility of your old age. Did Madame la Comtesse always live on good terms with her husband? Did any difference of opinion ever arise between them? Do you recall ever having seen them argue, even once?"

Slightly alarmed by this preamble, the old man collected himself, scratched his head and affirmed: "No, never."

"Think hard."

"Of course!" Le Boëc suddenly exclaimed. "Yes, you're right, damn it! Yes, yes, there was something once—a cloud in the blue sky of their marriage, as they say."

"What cloud?"

"Here it is. Monsieur Jean, who was only the Vicomte then, had met someone on the beach: a bather, a Russian, I think, named Prince Tserchkoff, or something similar. He had invited that braggart to pay him a visit at the manor—but it appears that the Prince started paying court to the Vicomtesse. Monsieur Jean caught him at it, made a scene with Madame and kicked the Cossack out."

"And that happened…?"

"My word, two or three months, at the most, before Monsieur Jean's death."

Exactly when he decided to revise his will and to reconcile himself with his son Albert, remarked Sâr Dubnotal, silently. *Perhaps the flirtation between that Tserchkoff and Azilis enlightened him as to the Vicomtesse's true sentiments*. Aloud he said: "Thank you, my friend. Are you coming, Rudolph, Annunciata?"

All three went back into the manor, where a further surprise awaited Rudolph.

On their arrival in Comte Jean de Tréguilly's mortuary chamber, he and Sâr Dubnotal immediately looked in the direction of the Comtesse's portrait. The canvas that had disappeared so inexplicably had been no less inexplicably replaced in its frame! Young and pretty enough to bring a saint to damnation, Azilis de Tréguilly seemed to be gazing ironically at the Great Psychagogue.

"What?" said the stupefied disciple. "The portrait has come back, Master!"

Instead of being astonished by this new sortilege, the latter took on an expression of satisfaction. "Let's congratulate ourselves, my friend," he replied. "I told you that I had an idea, but that idea was not in accord with the disappearance of the canvas. Now, I'm almost sure of myself." Standing in front of the portrait, he extended his arm with an energetic gesture. "The victim will be avenged," he pronounced. "The guilty party, whoever he or she might be, will be punished!"

Rudolph contemplated him in silence, while la Gianetti, indifferent as usual, sat down in an armchair.

Sâr Dubnotal reflected for a few moments, then went over to the bed. It was an old Renaissance bed, of the four-poster sort, with helical columns. Without hesitations, evidently knowing what he was doing, the Master picked the pillow, removed its pillow-case, and turned it over and around in every direction.

"Aha!" he said, suddenly. "I think I have it. What's the significance of this mended tear, beneath which I can feel something hard?"

Rudolph hurried forward. In the middle of the pillow was the trace of a fairly large straight rip, which had been carefully sewn up.

"Undo the repair!" Sâr Dubnotal ordered his disciple.

The young man used his knife to do the job more rapidly, and discovered among the feathers a little cubic box made of thin wood, and six centimeters square.

"Don't you understand?" said Sâr Dubnotal, taking the object from his hands and examining it closely. "This box explains how the needle was able to perforate the Comte's neck while he slept, stupefied by chloral!"

"I confess, Master..."

Arming himself with a knife. Sâr Dubnotal prized off the lid of the box. That lid was pierced by a tiny hole. He asked for the steel spike found in the cadaver's neck, and passed it through the hole. "It fits exactly," he murmured. Then he showed Rudolph the interior of the box.

There was a delicate and complicated piece of clockwork therein: a marvelous spring-loaded mechanism. That spring, initially coiled in the depths of the box, unwound, extended and filled the whole. A delicate silver plate was fixed at its extremity and a droplet of wax attacked to that plate almost stopped up a tiny hole into which the head of the needle fitted perfectly.

"It's quite simple," Sâr Dubnotal went on. "See how ingenious the mechanism is, Rudolph. When the spring is wound and the box is closed, the machine is harmless; the point of the needle hardly touches the hole in the lid. But suppose that the spring, mounted in advance and fitted with an automatic trigger, were abruptly released at a fixed time. Suppose that the box had been hidden in the pillow with diabolical skill, in such a way that the Comte, whose habits were certainly known to the author of the crime, was fatally led to place the nape of his neck in the very hollow of the pillow in which a repair had been made. What would happen? When the spring was activated, the needle, violently projected through the lid, was forcefully driven between two vertebrae into the sleeper's spinal cord. It ruptured the ganglia and death was immediate.

"The following morning, the physician summoned could do no more than certify the death, attributing it to the most probable cause. The needle, profoundly embedded in the nape, escaped his superficial investigations all the more easily because it did not provoke any bloodshed. The double thickness of the fabric of the pillow and the pillow-case completely masked the box hidden in the feathers."

"But who carried out this monstrous crime, Master?"

"Now is the time to summon the spirit of Le Floch," Sâr Dubnotal replied. "I don't think he committed the crime himself, but, given his professional skill, I haven't the slightest doubt that this piece of clockwork came out of his workshop."

"He must, therefore, have been the murderer's accomplice?"

91

"The knowing accomplice, yes," replied Sâr Dubnotal, "for the fabricator of the device must have known what it was intended to do."

Calling to la Gianetti, who started as if she had woken up abruptly, Sâr Dubnotal told her what he wanted her to do, instructing her to concentrate all the fluid with which she was saturated, to make the clockmaker's spirit amenable and persuade it to respond, by means of raps on the room's occasional table, to all his questions.

The medium removed the table-cloth, took up her wand, and commenced the mental evocation.

The spirit of Le Floch did not show the same reluctance as that of the Comte to enter into communication with her. Precipitate knocking resounded under the table.

"Ask him, Annunciata, whether he recognizes this box?"

"Yes," replied the medium, after a moment. "He tells me that he made it with his own hands five years ago, and that is why he is condemned to a long expiation."

"Would he care to specify," said Sâr Dubnotal, "the exact purpose of this dangerous device?"

The medium transmitted the question; the reply came almost immediately: "To take a human life."

"That of Comte Jean de Tréguilly?"

"Yes." The confession was made after a few seconds of hesitation.

"Good," said Sâr Dubnotal. "Now, Annunciata, ask the spirit of Le Floch if he was the one who placed the box inside the pillow?"

"No, it wasn't him!" said the medium, precipitately, faithfully interpreting for the spirit. "He swears that it wasn't him."

"Who was it, then?" There was a hint of sarcasm in Sâr Dubnotal's masculine voice.

La Gianetti, frightfully pale, with her eyes rolled back and her entire body quivering, interrogated the table—but the table no longer rendered anything but incoherent sounds.

"He's stuttering," panted the medium, exhausted by the prolonged tension of her fragile nerves. "He says that he doesn't know, that he can't remember, that he can't offer any explanation of that point."

"He's lying!" thundered Sâr Dubnotal. "But I excuse his scruples, and if he won't talk, I shall." The Great Psychagogue turned back to the portrait of Azilis, and, while the exhausted medium collapsed in an armchair, he slowly pronounced, syllable by syllable: "The person who placed the box in the pillow, who is responsible before God and before men for the death of Comte Jean de Tréguilly, is that woman, the Comtesse de Tréguilly, the former Azilis Le Floch."

At this solemn declaration, Rudolph, in spite of his phlegmatic temperament, felt a chill run through his veins. "Is it possible, Master?" he exclaimed.

"It is. Listen to me, Rudolph, and you'll see how everything fits together and becomes clear. Since I launched myself upon this astral trail, I have not cased to concentrate all my will-power, and all my deductive skill, on unraveling the weave and following the conductive thread of the mystery. I confess that contradictory evidence put me off the track for some time—but all's well that ends well, and my doubts have given way to firm certainty."

He took a deep breath and continued: "Doesn't the Comtesse's guilt explain everything? I can read the truth like an open book, I tell you, Rudolph. I see, as clearly as I see you, this Azilis Le Floch, a hypocritical and perverse creature, winning the heart and then the hand of the unfortunate Vicomte by means of her charms and her cunning. Having become his wife, she assumed all the qualities that she did not have; she feigned virtue and disinterest with diabolical artistry.

"Unfortunately for her, young Albert de Tréguilly, alerted by his instinct, guessed the truth. Incapable of mastering himself, though, too inexperienced to combat such a capable actress, he fell into the trap she laid for him: he lost his head, complained, and did not measure his words. To all his insults, the unscrupulous woman replied with a feigned gen-

93

tleness that deceived Comte Jean and ended up making him ill-disposed toward his son. The final scene completed the misunderstanding; the rascally woman achieved her objective, which was to get rid of Albert and have him disinherited by his father, to her own profit and that of her children—and the poor boy, banished from the hereditary manor, took the road to exile.

"Azilis, from that moment on, thought the game was won. Why, though, did she allow herself to be taken by surprise one day, in a compromising situation with a friend of her foolish spouse? The latter, foolish as he was, began to reflect and to wonder whether his dear Azilis was really the honest and modest matron that he imagined. By the same token, he thought about his elder son, that Albert whom he had sent away, deprived of all that part of his heritage of which the law permitted him to dispose, and almost cursed! Remorse took hold of him. He decided to revise his will and recall his son.

"Azilis made no objection; she was too clever for that— but she arranged things so skillfully, and set events in train so neatly that her husband could not detect her plan. Albert, however, was on his way; he might reappear at Crec'h-ar-Vran at any moment. There was no time to lose. From then on, the death of Comte Hector, who might have spoken in favor of his grandson, and that of Comte Jean, who had manifested analogous tendencies, were decided in her mind. Both must disappear before Albert returned—and both did, indeed, disappear.

"Azilis began by getting rid of Comte Hector. What could be easier? Old, impotent and crippled, was not the old man at her mercy? I can see her, Rudolph, murdering that poor man by degrees, all the while seeming to be caring for him with daughterly devotion. I can see her making up harmful tisanes, exposing him to abrupt changes of temperature, hastening his end, which is too long delayed, with the pressure of a pillow.

"The turn of the new Comte now! The task is more arduous, but you know how Azilis surmounted the difficulties.

The complicity of her father, whom she paid handsomely for his trouble—atypically, for avarice is as fundamental to her character as hypocrisy—furnished her with a mysterious and terrible weapon.

"Carefully contrived, the spring in the box could remain coiled for many hours, even an entire day, before being triggered. No more was required for the villainess to procure herself an alibi. She knew that her husband, perhaps at her instigation, took large doses of chloral, whereupon he lay down on his back and fall instantly into a leaden sleep. To place the box inside the pillow, after having carefully sowed up the tear, and then go to Morlaix in order to create a alibi and return home the following day in tears, as if she had not expected the fatal denouement, were the only precautions Azilis had to take.

"Her plan succeeded. Albert did not even want to accept the feeble indemnity that she offered him, out of prudence, and almost all of the Tréguilly fortune has passed to the children of the second marriage. You may believe, Rudolph, that that guilty party thinks herself perfectly safe, especially since Le Floch has rendered up his soul."

"But why, if that is the case, did the spirit of Comte Jean refuse to denounce her?" Rudolph asked, mechanically.

"To avoid a scandal, because he continues to love his wife in the other world as he lived her on the planet, with an infinite, exclusive and redemptive love. And also, finally, to avoid the spilled blood pouring over the children of his second marriage—on two innocents who were not involved in their mother's crimes."

"That's very honorable—but in that case, why is he haunting Crec'h-ar-Vran?"

"The Comte's spirit has not attained a state of perfection," said Sâr Dubnotal, simply. "His blind passion for his wife made him commit errors that he has been expiating for five years, and which he will probably be expiating for some time yet. He defied the will of Comte Hector, who was hostile to his misalliance with Azilis, although he was already too decrepit to oppose it effectively, and he was guilty, above all, of serious wrongs with respect to his son Albert. Don't forget, Rudolph, that he is paying for all that in the other world. A culpable spirit is submitted to a punishment proportional to the gravity of its terrestrial faults. Purgatory is not a vain word!"

"One last observation, Master," the disciple said, respectfully. "What about the stolen portrait?"

"Put back in its place this morning?" Sâr Dubnotal completed. "In truth, Rudolph, the incident perplexed me at first. I've reflected since then, and I've explained it as a fit of bad temper on the part of the Comte, when he observed my presence in the mortuary chamber. He wanted to shield his wife from my inquiry, and if he brought back the canvas promptly, it was because he saw that it was contrary to his aim—that my curiosity had been further excited and had been directed thereby to his wife.

"As for the box, Azilis would certainly have wanted to remove it from the pillow, but—as we know from Yves Le Boëc's story—the apparition of her husband gave her such a fright that she has never dared to return to that room, into which she only ventured by night in order to make all evidence of her crime disappear."

Epilogue

The following day, Sâr Dubnotal left Kerambellec, accompanied only by his gigantic Hindu servant. He was taken by carriage to Morlaix, from which he went to Paris by railway.

He had had no difficulty obtaining the address of the Comtesse de Tréguilly. Yves Le Boëc had given it to him without protest, and it was in the Bottin directory any case.

Still flanked by the Hindu, Sâr Dubnotal presented himself at Azilis' home early one morning, in order to be sure of finding her in. He found her in the midst of feverish matrimonial preparations.

After having waited patiently for a number of years, Azilis was about to regularize her union with Prince Tserpchikopf—not Tserchkoff, as Père Le Boëc had said, his tongue not being very sure when it came to foreign names.

When the two singular visitors—who had insisted on seeing her, claiming that it was a serious and pressing personal matter—were introduced into her presence, Azilis, gripped by a somber presentiment, went pale and became unsteady.

Sâr Dubnotal did not give her time to collect herself. His eyes sparkling with wrath, he stood before her like a judge and said to her, point-blank: "Azilis Le Floch, Comtesse de Tréguilly, I know that you have murdered your father-in-law and your husband, in order to take possession of their fortune, a part of which should have returned to your son-in-law. What have you to say in your defense?"

"Forgive me!" said the miserable and perverse creature, hoarsely, falling to her knees without even thinking of denying that formal accusation. "I have, indeed, committed many sins and many crimes, Monsieur, but I repent of them, and it's at your feet that I'm begging for your mercy."

The Psychagogue did not let her stop until she had completed her confession. Scarcely had she finished than she fainted, out of shame and fear.

When she came to her senses, she was obliged, in a formal written declaration, to abandon all her personal rights to the Comte's inheritance. Sâr Dubnotal took responsibility for transmitting the benefit of these rights to the person to whom they legitimately reverted, Lieutenant Albert de Tréguilly of the American Navy, by means known to him.

The future of the two children of the second marriage remained assured by another clause in the document, for the execution of which the Great Psychagogue also took responsibility.

By means of these concessions, Azilis imagined that she would be rid of Sâr Dubnotal, in whom she saw no one but an agent of her son-in-law Albert. She was not long delayed in realizing how great her error was. With a gaze charged with

97

scorn and menace, the Master Psychagogue plunged her into the depths of fear again.

"I could deliver you to human justice," he told her. "I shall not do so, because the sanctions at its disposal, including the scaffold, are insufficiently efficacious, and because I wish to respect the posthumous wishes of the late Comte de Tréguilly. But you shall not marry Prince Tserpchikopf, whose role in this affair I shall, moreover, elucidate, and you shall not play any further part in the raising of your children. I intend that they should be brought up in an honest milieu, and that they should have other examples before their eyes than yours."

At these words, Azilis straightened up like a viper pushed to excess, and fell prey to a fit of rage that revealed her true nature. "By what right do you insult me in my own home?" she cried—and, extending her audacity, she added: "Must I call my servants and I have you thrown out?"

Sâr Dubnotal contented himself with pointing out his own athletic companion. "If your servants value their lives, they certainly will not come to trouble us, for I shall not tolerate their intervention. Don't shout so loudly, therefore, Madame, and get ready to come with me."

"Who are you, to treat me thus?" Azilis stammered.

"The Master's tall stature seemed to grow even further, and the majesty of his severe face ended up terrorizing the wretched creature. "I am your Destiny!" he said. "Henceforth, you belong to me. It is now 9 a.m. At noon you shall set forth, in the care of my Hindu servant, Naïni."

"Great God! And where do you intend to take me?"

"Toward expiation!" the Master Psychagogue said, simply.

Azilis released a heart-rending sob. "What! You won't even allow me to bid adieu to Prince Tserpchikopf?"

"No, not under any pretext. You have been implacable in crime; I shall be likewise in punishment. Besides, if the Prince has, as I believe, been your accomplice, you shall soon have an opportunity to see him again, elsewhere."

Crushed, the guilty woman lowered her head.

At the appointed hour, and in spite of her supplications, her tears and her resistance, she was obliged to leave Paris under the guard of the formidable Argus that Sâr Dubnotal had given her. If she tried to rebel or to flee, Naïni had orders to denounce her immediately to the authorities. She knew what her fate would inevitably be in that case, and she seemed to resign herself to submit to the will of the mysterious man who had come to reproach her for her crimes.

Justice was done; from that moment on, the manor of Crec'h-ar-Vran ceased to receive the phantom's nocturnal visits.

Azilis Le Floch, Comtesse de Tréguilly, only accepted the verdict of her judge with her lips, however. Profoundly deceptive, she bore rage in her heart, along with ideas of revenge, the reckless desire to recover her liberty and to get back to Prince Tserpchikopf, the man for love of whom she had sacrificed two others—and without turning another page just now in the marvelous and authentic Memoirs of Sâr Dubnotal, the Great Psychagogue, we can inform the reader that Azilis succeeded in taking flight and escaping her fate—temporarily, at least—with the complicity of her Russian fiancé.

A struggle has been going on ever since between Sâr Dubnotal and that criminal couple—a fierce struggle, whose extraordinary vicissitudes we might perhaps recount on another occasion. The imagination of novelists has never surpassed the prodigious interest of those exciting episodes, which bring all the passions into play and in which the sincerity of the narrative throws into sharp relief the prodigiously fantastic and often unsuspected aspect of the events of real life.

SÂR DUBNOTAL

«Peut psychologique" charlatanís rugit Sâr Dubnotal «Je puis donc te demasquer enfin!"

TSERPCHIKOPF, THE BLOODY HYPNOTIST

I. Tserpchikopf, the Bloody Hypnotist

One morning in late August 1889, Sâr Dubnotal, the Great Psychagogue, was opening his voluminous post in the study of the magnificent bungalow, or Hindu chalet, that he had had constructed in the Breton seaside resort of Trez-Hir to serve as both a peaceful retreat and a base of operations in the missions of justice and redressing of wrongs to which he had resolved to dedicate his science and his marvelous powers.

One of his exotic domestics—he had engaged almost all his staff in the Indies—had just respectfully deposited on the table in front of him an immense silver tray laden with telegrams, letters and newspapers. Seated in a rocking-chair in a corner of the vast room, furnished in the Oriental style—which served both as his chemistry laboratory and his writing study, but to which the mosaic tiling, the walls hung with rich silks and arched windows lent a character of exotic originality—Sâr Dubnotal ran his eyes rapidly over the correspondence, which was from all over the world and was written in 20 different languages.

First he attacked the dispatches that emanated from the investigators and emissaries that he maintained at his own expense in the majority of the great cities of two continents. The Grandmaster of Psychognosis did not, in fact, neglect any natural means of obtaining information, and wanted to keep directly in touch with everything that was happening on the planet's surface. The marvelous faculty that had allowed him to discover hidden truths and decipher the most obscure enigmas, by means of a scientific method that he had invented and of which he remained the uncontested and incontestable master, did not prevent him from having recourse to the methods dear to the great detectives. By means of the relationships that he maintained with the astral world, with the aid of his mediums, he could extend his enquiries as far as the domain of the invisible, but he was not a man to abuse the formidable power that God had permitted him to acquire, and he was scrupulous in not interrogating the Beyond too frequently.

When Sâr Dubnotal had taken account of each of the dispatches laid out on the tray, he passed it, fully opened, to a young man who was standing by his side.

This remarkably handsome young man, slender but strong, with a high forehead and eyes bathed in a flame of genius, and an expression that was serious and honest, but also energetic, was none other than Rudolph, the Master's favorite disciple.

Rudolph read in his turn, took note of interesting items of information, put to one side the documents that it was necessary to keep and threw the rest into a wicker basket. He did not leave the responsibility of burning the contents of that basket after the session to anyone else.

"Decidedly," murmured the Great Psychagogue, opening the envelope of the final telegram and parading a distracted gaze over the sheet of paper, on which only a few banal lines were traced, "the mail has brought me nothing today. I haven't even received the dispatch from Naïni that I was expecting, which I instructed him to send me as soon as he arrived in Marseilles."

"It will reach you in a little while, Master," Rudolph replied. "It's not yet overdue."

"Perhaps so," said Sâr Dubnotal, who seemed worried. Something was obviously bothering him. This was shortly after the events described in our first chapter, whose sequel we promised to give the reader—who will recall that Naïni, from whom Sâr Dubnotal was expecting news, occupied a trusted position among his numerous personal staff.

Originating from the banks of the Ganges, Naïni was possessed of gigantic statue and Herculean strength. In his youth, he had been in the service of a despotic and cruel rajah who had maltreated him odiously, so he was all the more appreciative of the generosity and spirit of justice of Sâr Dubnotal, to whom he was as devoted as a spaniel. He manifested a punctual and military obedience, without allowing himself to be stopped by any obstacle, whenever he acted to accomplish his master's will.

"The mission that I've given Naïni is very difficult," the Great Psychagogue went on. "It's not certain that he'll be able to carry it out."

"Didn't the Comtesse de Tréguilly accept his guardianship and go with him of her own free will?" asked Rudolph.

"How proud is that perverse woman, my friend? Do you recall the diabolical refinements of cunning and cruelty with which she contrived the deaths of her father-in-law, Comte Hector, and her husband, Comte Jean, in order to secure a fortune that should only have gone to her in part, legally?"

"Do you believe, Master, that it was only by virtue of greed that that young and pretty woman, the mother of two delightful daughters bearing the noble name of Tréguilly, rendered herself culpable of those odious deeds?"

The Great Psychagogue shrugged his shoulders imperceptibly. "That was, at least, one of the motives she obeyed," he replied. "I've no need to remind you what happened—you know the story of the haunted manor of Crec'h-ar-Vran and you assisted me when I discovered the traces and the irrefutable proofs of the crime. You've kept up to date, since then, with the reparative measures I've taken to put young Comte Albert de Tréguilly in possession of his fortune again, and you're not unaware that I obtained the consent of the criminal, by menacing her with human justice, to disappear for a time that I considered suitable and to lead a life of repentance in a place known to me alone. You can also understand that the cupidity of the clockmaker's daughter who became the Comtesse de Tréguilly was not the sole cause to which it is necessary to impute her rascally deeds. Azilis de Tréguilly had made the acquaintance of a supposed Russian boyar, Prince Tserpchikopf, and she wanted to be a widow in order to be free to marry him."

"Perhaps it was that enigmatic individual who drove her to the crime, Master."

"I'm not far from thinking that," said the Great Psychagogue, with a wrathful gleam in his eyes, "and now that the Comtesse has been separated from his influence, my first concern will be to clarify this new enigma.

"Who is this Tserpchikopf? What was his fundamental intention in becoming the lover of Azilis and inciting her to dispose of her husband? Did he really love her, or was it the Tréguilly fortune with which he fell in love? In brief, are we dealing with a man led astray by passion, or a vulgar malefactor and dangerous knight of industry to whom Azilis herself would have ended up falling victim, after having served as his instrument? That's what it's important to find out, Rudolph, and that's what will employ our activity for some time.

"I'm anxious, nonetheless, that I haven't received the telegram that Naïni should have sent me from Marseilles before taking the steamship with the Comtesse. So long as she hasn't left France, the machinations of this Tserpchikopf are to be feared like the fangs of a wild beast that has already gripped its prey."

"Truly, Master, you're right," said Rudolph, after a few moments' reflection. "Naïni's silence is inexplicable, and I fear now that some misfortune might have overtaken him."

"I fear so too," said the Great Psychagogue, getting up from his rocking chair and pacing back and forth across the room.

"Have your investigators not attempted to discover the residence of the supposed Russian prince, Master? They surely ought to be able to follow him and prevent him from meeting up with Azilis?"

"That is what they're supposed to do, according to my instructions," said Sâr Dubnotal. "I've put all three of them into the field, and I'm impatiently awaiting their return."

By a curious coincidence, the Great Pychagogue had scarcely finished speaking when someone knocked on the door and Otto, Frank and Fréjus, the three researchers, presented themselves to offer the Master an account of the results of their investigations.

"Well, my friends," he asked them anxiously. "Have you discovered Tserpchikopf's domicile?"

"Yes, Master," replied Fréjus, a sharp and lively little Frenchman. "We didn't have any trouble getting that information from the Comtesse's concierge. While in Paris, Prince Tserpchikopf occupied a furnished apartment in the Boulevard Voltaire."

"Occupied, you say. Has he moved, then?"

"That's exactly the snag, Master," Fréjus replied. "When we presented ourselves in the Boulevard Voltaire and asked for the Prince in order to say a few words to him in private—pfft! The bird was no longer in the aviary."

"His concierges?"

"Were unable to tell us anything, Master."

"Unable, or unwilling?"

"Oh, their good will wasn't in question," Frank put in, swiftly. He was an athletic Englishman, an ex-detective of junior rank at Scotland Yard. "They would have liked nothing better than to tell us if they could, for it appears that Tserpchikopf decamped covertly, without paying their wages!"

"Yes," said Otto, the German, "the good people were taken in by the fellow's grand manners, and are ruing it today. Tserpchikopf has behaved toward them like the common pickpocket he must be."

"And you haven't succeeded in picking up his trail?" inquired Sâr Dubnotal, in a manner that was both ironic and anxious.

The three agents lowered their heads. Clever as they were, they had come back to Trez-Hir empty-handed. Their most active attempts to discover the so-called boyar had come to nothing. Tserpchikopf had become undiscoverable. Had he left Paris? That was probable, but not having received orders to go any further afield than the city, the investigators had thought they ought to come and render an account of the futility of their enquiries and ask for new instructions.

"It's been three days since Naïni and the Comtesse set off," murmured Sâr Dubnotal. "Today is Thursday and they should have arrived in Marseilles on Monday evening. The telegram should have reached me some time ago, unless some accident has occurred." He addressed himself to the investigators, saying: "When did Tserpchikopf leave the Boulevard Voltaire?"

"Three days ago," replied Fréjus. "Monday last. It seems that on that day, at about 6 p.m., Tserpchikopf received a visit from someone, and it was then that he made arrangements to gather his effects, pack his trunks and decamp under the concierges' very noses."

Rudolph could not suppress a scornful gesture. "Why did they let him go?" he asked.

"Oh, they were completely taken in," Frank replied. "Tserpchikopf gives the impression of having more than one trick up his sleeve, and he had no difficulty in deceiving their vigilance. He sent the man on an errand and stayed chatting with his wife in the lodge while his domestic and the individual Fréjus just mentioned rapidly took his luggage out."

"And the concierge didn't see through the trick?" said the Great Psychagogue, astonished. "She didn't see any of the coming and going with packages?"

"Yes and no, Master. No, at first, because Tserpchikopf absorbed all her attention with his discourse. He told her that his steward in Russia had told him that he had sent the revenues from his properties and he asked her to make up her bill. One of the movers dropped a case on the stairs, though, and she wanted to know what had caused the noise so she came out of the lodge…"

"Did Tserpchikopf try to stop her?"

"The brave woman didn't say that, Master," Otto speci-
fied. "The fact is that, as she headed for the door, she was
overtaken by a sort of fainting fit, which made her collapse
unconscious on the floor. Imagine her surprise on finding,
when she came round, that her tenant had disappeared!"

"It was then that her suspicions began to awaken," Fréjus
went on. "She had never before been subject to such a fainting
fit, which had come upon her so suddenly, and she thought
that Tserpchikopf might have played some dirty trick on her.
She remembered that, just as she was about to leave, the Russian had looked at her strangely. 'The Prince's eyes glowed
like braziers,' she told us—and she couldn't bear that fierce
gleam."

"That's information of the highest importance," the
Great Psychagogue said to Rudolph. "That detail opens up
horizons that I had certainly not envisaged." He went on:
"Continue your report, Fréjus."

The Frenchman, intrigued by his Master's reflection,
continued swiftly: "When her husband returned, the concierge
told him what had happened. She affirmed that Tserpchikopf
had put a spell on her and had taken advantage of her prolonged faint to make off. The concierge thought at first that his
wife's mind was wandering, but when he went up to the
boyar's apartment to give him the various objects that he had
been sent to buy, he found the place empty and realized that
his worthy spouse had not been the victim of a hallucination.
The disorder that reigned in the rooms dispelled all doubt in
that regard."

"Has his wife experienced any visual and auditory
trouble since then?" asked Sâr Dubnotal.

"Yes, Master," Otto said, "and she's fully convinced that
someone has put a spell on her, as our friend Fréjus says. She
still sees the Slav's phosphorescent pupils gleaming in front of
her, and it takes away her appetite for food and drink."

The Great Psychagogue stopped pacing back and forth.
"The woman is only half-deceived," he said, gravely. "Tserp-

chikopf hasn't put a spell on her, but, unless I'm much mistaken, he's hypnotized her."

"Hypnotized?" exclaimed the investigators.

"Yes, my lads. Hypnotized by means of his gaze alone—which indicates an uncommon magnetic power in the man, who might perhaps be a redoubtable adversary for us."

"It seems increasingly likely that Naïni has got on the wrong side of him," Rudolph remarked.

"I believe so," said Sâr Dubnotal, coldly. "Tserpchikopf's precipitate departure closely followed that of the Comtesse and the Hindu. The individual who came to the Prince's lodgings undoubtedly brought him news of Azilis' capture, and he must have got under way immediately to render aid to his accomplice. In that case, my boys, Naïni has had a strong opponent to deal with, and his silence, although it no longer surprises me, makes me even more anxious. His physical strength wouldn't be any use to him against a hypnotist."

"Unless he was resistant to the magnetic effluvia," said Rudolph.

"That's true, and your observation reassures me slightly, my friend, for Naïni isn't easy to hypnotize—as I've had occasion to observe. But as Frank has said, Tserpchikopf must have more than one trick up his sleeve, and the Hindu, in spite of his prudence and his zeal, must have been fooled by one of them."

Sâr Dubnotal dismissed his investigators, asking them to send in one of his mediums, the Italian woman Annunciata Gianetti. To his disciple, he said: "Rudolph, you know how I hesitate to use what the vulgar call 'supernatural' means to obtain information. This time, however, I shall make use of them, since other methods have produced nothing. What has become of Azilis and Naïni? I need to know, and the time I would lose in going to Marseilles to open inquiries on the spot I can put to better use here."

"What are you going to do, Master?" his disciple asked.

Becoming singularly grave, Sâr Dubnotal replied: "I'm going to consult my friend Ranijesti, at a distance, Rudolph. I hope, with his help, to dissipate the mystery hanging over the voyage of Azilis and my Hindu servant."

II. The Evocation

At that moment, someone knocked on the study door.

"Come in!" said Sâr Dubnotal.

The door opened and a woman dressed in the Italian fashion came into the room.

Brunette, thin and nervous, the Italian woman was so perpetually distraught that, despite being very attractive, she only projected a gaze of bleak indifference before her as she entered.

The Great Psychagogue did not give her time to sit down. "Rudolph," he said, "fetch the satchel and follow me to the Green Room with Annunciata."

The "Green Room" was so called because of the uniform shade of its furnishings and its walls. Contiguous with the study, it was much less bright than the latter because of the thick curtains that masked its windows. The furniture was rather rudimentary: a few armchairs, a large sofa, a round table, and a small table with a writing-desk were all that it comprised.

Sâr Dubnotal went into the Green Room and sat down on an armchair, while the medium went to lie languidly on the sofa. "Close the door and draw the curtains," the Great Psychagogue said to Rudolph.

The young man obeyed and the room, already gloomy in itself, was overwhelmed by a strange darkness comparable to that reigning in depths of the sea that are never penetrated by the light of day. It was not black darkness, in which everything is confounded in an impenetrable cloud the color of soot; the two psychagogues could vaguely distinguish the contours of objects, and La Gianetti's supine silhouette, recumbent through a sort of emerald green fog, but they would not have

109

been able to reads a newspaper, even by placing it very close to their eyes, and they were divining rather than seeing the round table and the medium.

"Switch on the electric lamp, Rudolph," Sâr Dubnotal said.

After groping in the leather satchel that he was carrying, the disciple took out a torch equipped with a reflector, operated the switch and projected a beam of bright yellow light into the green penumbra. Parading that golden beam from one end of the room to the other, Rudolph searched the four corners one by one, and then brought the luminous beam to rest on the Italian woman's pale face.

Annunciata appeared to be asleep. Her eyelids were closed, and not a single fiber of her body was quivering.

Sâr Dubnotal examined her attentively, and murmured in a satisfied manner: "The medium is in good condition, Rudolph. I hope that we'll succeed." Then, with his imperious gaze fixed on the Italian, he said in a louder voice: "Annunciata, are you ready to enter into communication with the double that I indicate to you?"

"Yes, Master," the medium replied, in a monotonous and weary tone.

"Good!"

Without delay, Sâr Dubnotal and Rudolph put on large green dressing-gowns that had been hanging in a wardrobe. Annunciata did the same, and took the little wand that Rudolph held out to her in her right hand.

The disciple immediately switched off the torch, while Sâr Dubnotal said: "Annunciata, I would like you to put me in communication with the yogi Ranijesti."

This yogi, or Hindu mage, had once studied psychognosis in company with Sâr Dubnotal. Profoundly versed in that science, Ranijesti had had himself immured alive, without rice or water, in a cellar in Benares, in order that he might enjoy in advance, by a temporary suspension of animation, the bliss associated with a higher degree of nirvana. As is well known, such actions are frequent among yogis, who contrive to sus-

110

pend their vital functions and can safely remain for several months, or even several months in succession, in that intermediary state between being and non-being.

Before descending into the anticipated tomb, Ranijesti had promised Sâr Dubnotal to enlighten him by means of his insights any time the Master Psychagogue found himself embarrassed by a psychic problem. Whenever Sâr Dubnotal invoked him, his emanation—his double—would respond to him in one form or another. Ranijesti had also offered to watch over him and those that were dear to him—in brief, to serve him as a tutelary spirit and an occult protector. Sâr Dubnotal had often contacted him through the intermediary of one of his mediums, and Ranijesti had never failed yet in his terrestrial engagements.

Annunciata Gianetti approached the round table and the three taps that she struck on the wood with the end of her wand resounded distinctly in the silence. After the last, she let herself fall back at full length on the sofa, where she remained motionless.

There was a brief pause. Nothing responded as yet to the mysterious summons of the medium—who had become inert, as if unconscious.

Finally, next to Annunciata's prostrate body—so close to it that one might have imagined that it emanated from her—a light mist arose and formed an ovoid cloud, which drew away from the medium and took up a position between the table and the ceiling. The pale and blurred figure of a scarcely-materialized individual was not long delayed in emerging from the middle of that cloud, which became less vaporous by degrees and took on the aspect of an aura. It was a handsome old man dressed in oriental costume, coiffed in a Hindu turban, whose noble face was illuminated by a flame of ecstasy and genius.

"Ranijesti!" murmured Sâr Dubnotal, his eyes fixed on the astonishing apparition.

Oppressed by a respectful dread, Rudolph stammered: "He's smiling at you, Master!"

"Because he recognizes me too," said Sâr Dubnotal.

The two men watched the apparition become increasingly precise. It was the projection of the wise yogi immured alive in Benares—his astral double, if you will—that was standing before them, patient, tranquil and sympathetic, seemingly waiting for someone to start questioning him.

"Annunciata," Sâr Dubnotal hasted to resume, "ask my friend Ranijesti if he will consent to enter into direct communication with me."

The medium stirred on her couch. Her arm extended toward the table, and with her wand she sounded a sequence of dull and rapid raps on the wood.

Then something extraordinary happened. The Hindu's double, the fluid old man standing before the two psychagogues like an etheric statue articulated, weakly by distinctly: "Speak, Sâr Dubnotal! I am here to reply to your questions."

At these words, Annunciata uttered a strident scream, rolled from the divan on to the floor of the room and stopped moving, while Rudolph, increasingly excited, felt his heart beat wildly within his breast. Accustomed as he was to these evocation scenes, the young disciple of the grandmaster of psychognosis experienced an impression of anxiety and malaise in confrontation with Ranijesti's double.

Sâr Dubnotal, by contrast, maintained his self-composure. Taking the words of Augustus in Corneille's *Cinna* out of context, he might have said: "I am master of myself as well as the universe"—including that which is secret from and invisible to men. [12]

---

[12] In Pierre Corneille's *Cinna* (1641) the embittered Cinna leads a plot against the Roman Emperor Augustus; when it is betrayed, the world-weary emperor—who would like nothing better than to abdicate—demonstrates his moral superiority by resisting the impulse to have the conspirators executed (hence the quoted line) and thus offers a fine example to future ages. Although the play was based on a real incident, the actual historical example offered by Augustus' reign, as Corneille knew

With all the acuity of his shining eyes, the overman looked at Ranijesti. In a calm voice, he said: "May God's blessing always be upon you, in the terrestrial world and inter-rastral space! I regret extracting you from the contemplative bliss of nirvana once again, but grave anxieties are besieging me. Do you know my Hindu Naïni?"

"Yes," the yogi's double replied, softly. "I know him and hold him in esteem, for he is a fine servant, docile and totally devoted to his master. Has some misfortune overtaken him?"

"That is what I desire to know," said the Great Psycha-gogue. I have had no news of him for three days, and I am anxious. I had instructed him to take Comtesse Azilis de Tréguilly to a place of retreat, in order that she might redeem herself, so far as possible, by penitence and repentance, for two abominable crimes that she committed for love of a Russian named Tserpchikopf, who must be her accomplice.

"Naïni had been instructed to take ship with the woman at Marseilles. I have not received the telegram that he should have sent me, and I am wondering whether Azilis might have got rid him with the aid of her accomplice, who left Paris shortly after her—in order to rejoin her, I suspect."

The phantom's features contracted visibly. "It is not easy to elucidate the mystery," he said. "I do not know the Com-tesse or Tserpchikopf—but wait, my brother Psychagogue! I shall attempt, at least, to extract you from cruel uncertainty by revealing to you what has become of Naïni."

"I shall wait as long as necessary," said Sâr Dubnotal.

"The wait will not be long," murmured the double, whose vaporous form began to pale, "but I shall not reappear in this aspect, materialized in your evocation room. Prepare the slate—that is what will transmit my response."

---

perfectly well, was far more ambiguous—as was that of Louis XIII, the French king at the time the play was written, whose posthumous reputation was tainted by his long acceptance of the guidance of Cardinal Richelieu.

"Thank you, noble yogi!" said Sâr Dubnotal, in a grave and penetrating tone.

Slowly, the apparition faded away. The lines of the phantasmal face blurred; the fluidic body ceased to be distinct, and was soon no more than a grey cloud suspended in the air, which drew nearer to the medium.

When that light vapor had dissipated in its turn, Rudolph switched on the electric torch in response to an order from his master. With the Great Psychagogue's aid, he replaced the Italian woman on the divan. Annunciata, shaken by a nervous tremor, darted a wild glance at the two men, then seemed to fall back into her trance—a trance so profound that it resembled a faint. Sure that her condition did not present any real danger for the moment, they were already occupied with other things.

Rudolph placed a bronze hand-bell on the table, along with a large slate and a piece of chalk. Then he made a tour of the room, as if to make sure that everything there was in order, and came back to sit next to Sâr Dubnotal. After consulting his watch, he switched off the luminous beam of the torch.

"What time is it?" murmured the overman.

"8:30 a.m."

Half an hour went by, as long as a day for the young disciple, who was impatient to know Ranijesti's response, but briefer than a minute for Sâr Dubnotal, who was plunged in profound meditation.

"Finally" sighed the disciple, all of a sudden.

The hand-bell, seized by an invisible hand, had just left the table and, although it was invisible, was heard tinkling in the depths of the room, with a regular and silvery ring. This light carillon, which drew Sâr Dubnotal abruptly from his reverie, was succeeded by the rapid scratching of the chalk moving over the slate.

When that scratching ceased in the darkness of the Green Room, Sâr Dubnotal got to his feet with a single movement. "Thank you again! A thousand thanks, Ranijesti!" he said, while Rudolph ran to the window and parted the thick curtains.

Darkness gave way to daylight within the room.

Approaching the table, the Master Psychagogue leaned over the slate. It was covered with Hindi characters traced in chalk. And this is what Sâr Dubnotal was able to read:

The autopsy of his body is due to take place this very day, at 3 p.m. Prevent that operation, Sâr Dubnotal, for your servant is, in reality, not dead. Ranijesti.

III. The Catastrophe of Express 213

Sâr Dubnotal left nothing to chance. Inured to all the vicissitudes of life, he was always ready to face the worst eventualities. For long years he had lived as an anchorite in his rich properties in India, and devoted all his time to his learned studies. It was only after having penetrated the abstruse secrets of the physical and psychic science, and having become—before he had been given the title—the Grandmaster of Psychognosis that he had reappeared in human society, where he had been called to play the noblest, the most admirable and the most mysterious role imaginable.

As his Memoirs explain—Memoirs that we are, so to speak, merely transcribing here—he had understood that this society is far from being perfect, and that it was his duty to employ his exceptional power in the service of the weak and the oppressed. To do that, it was necessary for him to conform to the conditions of modern life. In our era of excessive progress, he who does not run is left behind, but that did not inconvenience him, for his spirit had outdistanced everyone else by far. Even so, the telegraph, the telephone and the railway—automobilism had not yet heard mention of him—were marvelous instruments in his service. Frequently obliged to travel, to move from one city to another, or from one country to another, he did not require more than a few moments to get

115

under way. His luggage was reduced to two or three suitcases packed in advance with items that were strictly indispensable.

Scarcely a quarter of an hour after reading Ranijesti's communication, Sâr Dubnotal, having rapidly given the necessary instructions, took his place with Rudolph, Annunciata and his three investigators in a carriage harnessed to two good horses, driven by his coachman Joseph. "It's 9:30 a.m.," Sâr Dubnotal said to the latter. "We have to catch the Morlaix express to Paris, which leaves at 10:45 a.m."

"It's a long way from Trez-Hir to Morlaix," Joseph replied. "Fourteen kilometers!"

"Break the horses, if necessary," the Great Psychagogue said, dryly. "A man's life is at stake. It's also necessary to stop at the Post Office to send two telegrams."

While the carriage rolled along at top speed, Sâr Dubnotal drafted the two telegrams to which he had alluded on a notepad.

The first was composed thus:

Court of Marseilles. To the Investigating Magistrate in charge of the Naïni case.

Monsieur, I am the master of the Hindu Naïni, deceased in Marseilles in circumstances of which I am still unaware. If my telegram reaches you in time, please delay the autopsy of the body until my arrival; that will avoid an irreparable disaster.

In order that you should not think that this is a hoax, I add that Naïni has a small scar on the ring-finger of his left hand. Verify that. I am departing for Marseilles immediately, and hope to present myself at the court tomorrow morning. Salutations.

Severus el Tebib.

This telegram, signed with the master's customary pseudonym, was entrusted to Otto, as was the second telegram—which, addressed to a Parisian correspondent of Sâr Dubnotal, asked the latter to charter a special train at the Gare de Lyon, to depart for Marseilles at 9 p.m. precisely.

As the carriage passed the Post Office in Morlaix, where they soon arrived, Otto jumped out, after promising to rejoin the overman at the station as soon as possible.

"There's not a minute to lose," Sâr Dubnotal explained to his assistants. "I hope that I shall be able, by calling upon the resources of science, to reanimate my poor Hindu, who must be in a state of catalepsy—but if the autopsy has taken place, my intervention will become futile."

It is a deplorable prejudice, universally spread, that what are known as *rigor mortis* and cadaverous chill, along with the cessation of respiratory function, are certain signs of death in any circumstances. Often, the physician summoned to a supposed dead man contents himself with feeling for a pulse and holding a mirror to the lips. If he perceives no pulsation, contact with the inert body procures a glacial sensation and no mist forms on the glass of the mirror, the professional concludes therefrom that death has already done its work, and calmly gives permission for burial—and yet everyone knows that we do not only have a body, but also a soul. It is because we fail to take rational account of this fact that so many unfortunates are condemned to the horrors of premature burial and the atrocious agony of living interment.

It is, without doubt, extremely difficult to reanimate a person fallen into an absolute form of coma, but "difficult" does not signify "impossible," and Sâr Dubnotal had solved the problem. Just as he possessed a water of rejuvenation capable of prolonging youth and life, so he had discovered another mysterious elixir, a few drops of which were sufficient to reanimate the pseudo-dead.

This apparent resurrection could only take place of course, if no vital organ had been too profoundly injured. Such was the case with Naïni, according to the consulted yogi. The vital issue was, therefore, to prevent the autopsy, which would have killed the good servant irremediably by dissecting his body.

Leaping from the carriage, the Master, his disciple Rudolph, his medium Annunciata Gianetti and his two aides

117

Frank and Fréjus—who were not long delayed in being rejoined by the breathless Otto—plunged into Morlaix station. They were just in time; they had already heard the roar of the Brest-Paris express, which arrived at Morlaix at 10:42 a.m. and departed again at 10:45 a.m. Sâr Dubnotal and his followers installed themselves in a first class carriage.

The discovery of the practical crystallization of carbon, or the artificial fabrication of diamonds, and the exploitation of rich pearl-fisheries in Ceylon had permitted the Psychagogue to amass a colossal fortune. Sâr Dubnotal was one of the few billionaires in the world, who could, as revealed by statisticians with strong arithmetical support, dispense two million francs a month—more than 70,000 a day; exactly 3000 an hour—without any impoverishment! In matters of money, the Master Psychagogue was never stingy. He only prized his fortune for the ease of execution it gave him and the good that it permitted him to do.

The journey to Paris went by without incident. Our heroes crossed the capital in a carriage and reached the Gare de Lyon at 8:30 p.m. Sâr Dubnotal's correspondent had received the telegram and taken the necessary steps; a special express designated for the wealthy foreigner was under pressure. At 8:45 p.m., the Great Psychagogue and his entourage installed themselves in the comfortable seats of a P-L-M sleeping-car. Express 213 departed at exactly 9 p.m.

Sâr Dubnotal and his companions, thinking only of the objective of their journey, had not noticed the behavior of an individual with a criminal face who had stared at them in turn with a strange insistence, and who had paid particular attention to Sâr Dubnotal

"It's really him! It can only be him!" this suspicious character had muttered—and he had run to the station telegraph office, sent a telegram, and then disappeared.

At that moment, Express 213 was already eating up the distance. It had passed the fortifications and was puffing, roaring and whistling through the darkness of the countryside.

To go from Paris to Marseilles required ten hours of traveling by express train in those days, but Sâr Dubnotal, by courtesy of a regal gratification, had obtained an assurance from his engineer that they would reach the great Phocean city by 5 a.m.

The weather had turned to rain. The torrential downpour lashed the widows of the train obliquely as it traveled at a speed of 120 kilometers an hour. After darting vague glances through the obscured windows, the Great Psychagogue's aides and disciple lay down in their couchettes to go to sleep. Sâr Dubnotal did not follow their example. He was deep in thought.

What was he thinking about? What could he be thinking about, except the singular affair into which he had just thrown himself with his usual ardor and determination, renouncing all the healthy and restful distractions that he had enjoyed on the Channel coast? The affair, it is true, promised to be passably strange.

Assuming that Sâr Dubnotal succeeded in reanimating the Hindu, it was not at all certain that the latter would be able to clarify the matter of the accident or murder attempt of which he had been the victim. Personally, the Great Psychagogue rejected the hypothesis of a death, or an apparent death, due to natural causes. It was infinitely more probable that the valiant servant, who was in good health and possessed of a robust constitution, had been the victim of Azilis' criminal machinations, as Comtes Hector and Jean de Tréguilly had been before him.

Was not the skill of that creature demonic? Moreover, she certainly had an accomplice.

The more Sâr Dubnotal meditated upon the possible role of the so-called Russian boyar, the more persuaded he was that Tserpchikopf had been involved in all of Azilis' crimes. Azilis was naturally perverse and unscrupulous—she was a purely sensual and deeply amoral creature—but it was doubtful that she would have thought of getting rid of her father-in-law and husband on her own. Was not Tserpchikopf, if not the hand that had carried out that double tragedy, at least the brain that had conceived it? The Great Psychagogue was convinced of it.

What was this Tserpchikopf, then? An impostor, evidently, who shamelessly dressed himself up with the noblest of titles. Doubtless also a malefactor on a grand scale—one of those chevaliers of crime whose bloody exploits had thrilled the world for a long time without anyone knowing who was responsible for them.

The professionals of that black-clad criminal aristocracy hold formidable trumps in their hand, and assure themselves of impunity much more easily than is believed. The best detectives can do almost nothing against them. These bandits have an admirably-organized counter-police, which almost always warns them in time, not to mention the indiscretions of the press, which are often sufficient to put them on their guard.

It is a sad admission to make, but the law hardly ever captures anyone but conscripts in that terrible army. The others, the veterans and the chiefs, slip through the meshes of the nets that are drawn around them as if they were playing a game. The truth is that in France, at least, more than half the crimes committed go unpunished. No one knows, and probably never will know, who commits them. Anyone who examines the chronicles of criminality will see that this is no exaggeration.

Was Tserpchikopf one of those redoubtable evildoers, who would later be described as the Apaches of the greater world, swarming not merely in Paris but in all the important cities of Europe and America?

I must find out! thought Sâr Dubnotal. *I will find out!*

Meanwhile, the express was still heading southwards at full steam. One by one, it passed through the stations of Laroche, Dijon, Mâcon, Lyon, Valence and Grenoble.

At 4 a.m., it went through Avignon station like a streak of lightning. That one being only about 20 leagues distant from Marseilles, Sâr Dubnotal reckoned that they would arrive on time.

A frightful catastrophe abruptly ruined that expectation.

As the train approached a bridge extended over a tributary of the Rhône, Sâr Dubnotal had an obscure presentiment of imminent danger. He felt anxious and troubled. He was not asleep, but he had closed his eyes in order to look within more easily. And all of a sudden, confirming that presentiment, an apparition appeared, visible to his closed eyes, perfectly distinct and recognizable as Ranijesti's double.

The yogi's face was distraught, and his lips were moving convulsively. "*Beware, Sâr Dubnotal!*" he murmured. "*The train is about to be derailed!*"

The Great Psychagogue opened his eyes.

The apparition had vanished—but Sâr Dubnotal could not have been mistaken. He had received a warning from his tutelary spirit—a warning that he was not permitted to mistrust.

"Look out!" he cried in his turn, shaking his sleep-numbed companions. "Listen, for the love of God! Hold on to the luggage-racks and lift up your legs on your couchettes!"

He had scarcely finished speaking when a terrible detonation deafened them all.

At the same moment, the express, which had just moved on to the bridge, leapt sideways, left the track, and fell back on to the apron of the bridge. With a frightful racket of dislocated wheels and twisted, broken and ripped metalwork, as its walls tore apart and its windows shattered, it went over the parapet and plunged head first into the river—which was not very wide, to be sure, but was steeply-banked, torrential and deep...

IV. A Murky Affair

One day and one night before Sâr Dubnotal set out for Marseilles in the circumstances described, a strange and inexplicable drama that was to have enormous repercussions had taken place in one of the best hotels of the great Phocean city.

It was even 1 a.m. and Firmin, one of the domestics in the Royal Palace—such is the name of the establishment, situated on the Cours Belzunce—was going from room to room to put himself at the disposal of travelers, to polish their shoes and offer them chocolate, tea or coffee, when, having arrived at the door of room number 5, he observed that it was ajar.

Number 5 had been occupied, since the previous evening, by a Hindu who had presented himself at the hotel in company with a young white woman, and who had been entered in the establishment's register under the simple name of Naïni. As for his companion, she had omitted to inscribe her name, as the law demands; assuming that she was the legitimate wife of the Hindu, however, the manager at the Royal Palace had not thought it necessary to insist that she fulfilled that formality.

The Hindu had reserved a private room for her: number 6, next door to number 5. A communicating door permitted direct passage from one room to the next, without there being any need to use the corridor to which they both gave out.

Thinking that the Hindu had already got up, Firmin knocked on the slightly-open door and then opened it wide. Immediately, a cry of fright sprang from his lips.

Naïni was lying inanimate on the rug beside the bed. He had not taken off any of his clothes; his turban was still wound around his head.

The first impulse of the domestic was to hurl himself into number 6 to summon the Hindu's companion. The communicating door was closed and locked, but because the key was on the side of number 5, Firmin—whose appeals went unanswered—did not hesitate to open it.

To his amazement, he found that the room was empty. The woman had disappeared, mysteriously. That disappearance, however, could not have taken place more than a few hours ago, for the unmade bed was still warm where the feet would be placed, as Firmin observed when he removed the eiderdown.

What put the lid on the honest fellow's perplexity, however, was the observation that the door from that room to the corridor was hermetically sealed. Two bolts inside were shot home and the door was double-locked with the key. The woman could not have gone out that way.

Had she gone through her companion's room? Firmin did not go so far as to ask himself that. In a panic, he ran back to Naïni's inert body and, having observed that the Hindu was no longer breathing, threw himself into the corridor and went down the stairs for at a time in order to warn the hotel's manager.

The manager, distressed by the news, hurried up to number 5 with Firmin. The observations he made told them nothing new. He found the Hindu in the same position and, having sounded his chest, declared that death had done its work, for the heart was no longer beating, the extremities were cold and no breath was emerging from the discolored lips.

But to what could that sudden death be attributed? Was it a natural death, a crime or suicide? The woman's disappearance opened the door to the most sinister hypotheses.

If there had been a crime, however, a few traces of the misdeed ought to have remained—but the manager could see nothing to indicate that the Hindu's room had been the theater of a scene of violence. The most perfect order reigned in the room. No trace of blood had stained the dead man's effects, the carpet or the bedclothes.

The most bizarre thing was that, unlike the woman's bed, the Hindu's had not been unmade. Evidently, Naïni had not gone to bed, and whatever had caused his death had occurred just as he was about to get undressed.

"In my opinion," said the manager, "the man has not been murdered, but has succumbed to the rupture of an aneurism."

"Do you think so?" asked Firmin, timidly. "How, then, do you explain the disappearance of his companion?"

"In the most natural way imaginable," said the manager, after a few moments of reflection. "The communicating door must have been closed by the Hindu yesterday evening. His companion had gone to bed early, and when he collapsed, falling abruptly unconscious, she was sleeping peacefully. She would not have heard the body fall, but she might have woken up in the middle of the night, and, needing to talk to her companion, come into his room..."

"But the communicating door was locked!" exclaimed Firmin.

"No," replied the manager. "At that time, it was simply closed, and the woman had no difficulty opening it. How do you think she got out of number 6, if not that way?"

"I don't know."

"There's a window," said the manager, "but you're not unaware that that window overlooks the hotel's interior courtyard, and the height at which it opens, is absolutely opposed to any attempt of that sort. No, no, Firmin, just let me finish, and you'll understand everything. I told you that the woman, for some reason that escapes me for the moment, but which I hope to discover soon, needed to see her companion in the middle of the night. She went in to his room, and it was then that she saw him lying beside the bed. Terror—a mad, irrational terror—took hold of her and drive her to flee. She probably feared that she might be held responsible for the death of her companion and, without considering that her flight might reinforce the suspicion, had no thought but to get out of the hotel. Yes, yes, that's certainly what happened, and we must hope that the death won't cause us too much annoyance."

Firmin, however, did not seem convinced. "It's possible, Monsieur, and I wish it might be true with all my heart, for the sake of the Palace, but..."

"What?"

"Your explanation leaves many points unclarified."

"Which?"

"Firstly, why did the woman take the precaution of going out via number 5, after having locked the communicating door?"

124

"I see that as merely further evidence of the extreme anxiety into which our client was plunged following the terrifying discovery."

"All right! But it remains to be discovered how she was able to leave the hotel."

"She would have asked the concierge to let her out," said the manager.

"That surprises me," murmured Firmin. "If the concierge had lifted the bar for that woman, he would have told us so this morning."

"That might, however, have been an omission on his part. We'll go see. Let's go down and ask him."

"You aren't going to make a closer examination of the body first?"

"I shall certainly refrain from doing so. It's necessary to alert the police without delay, and we don't have the right to disturb anything whatsoever before the arrival of the Commissaire."

The two men ran to the concierge's lodge, who was astonished to learn about the drama and, strangely enough, affirmed that he had not let anyone out during the night.

"You're sure of that, Marius?" he manager queried, profoundly disappointed. "You didn't open the door for anyone?"

"No one, Monsieur."

"That's extraordinary," the manager said. "In that case, how was the woman able to leave the hotel?"

"She hasn't left," said the concierge. "Otherwise, I'd have known."

"What time did you open the door for the first time?"

"6 a.m., as usual."

"And you claim that our client hasn't gone out, before or after?"

"I'm prepared to swear, Monsieur. I do my duty conscientiously, as you know, and I defy anyone to come in or go out without my knowing. I haven't opened up to anyone during the night, because no one came to my lodge to ask me to lift the bar, and no one has gone through the door since 6 a.m.

but the normal suppliers. No client of the Palace has gone out as yet."

"I thought so," said Firmin. "Couldn't the woman have hidden in another room?"

"Yes, in the hotel common rooms," said the manager. "Yes, that remains to be seen. But it's impossible, my friends, for me to put off involving the law. It's necessary to inform the Commissaire immediately, in order to discharge our responsibility. Run to the police station, Firmin. In the meantime, I'll make a search of the hotel with your colleagues, and Marius will make sure that no guest leaves the hotel without my permission."

"What about the scandal, Monsieur?"

"We'll try to avoid it. I'd like to think that the Commissaire will conduct his inquiry with all due discretion, and besides, my conviction hasn't changed; it can't be a criminal matter. A respectable establishment like ours has nothing in common with cut-throats, and this Naïni did not seem to be a man who would allow himself to be killed easily. Did you see him, Firmin? What an athlete!"

"Yes," said the domestic. He seemed to be a sturdy fellow, with his six feet six inches of height, his formidable build and his muscles of bronze. But that doesn't alter the fact that he's kicked the bucket, Monsieur, and until there's proof to the contrary, my opinion is that the young lady who accompanied him wasn't entirely uninvolved in that demise."

"Think what you like," the manager replied, irritatedly, "but in the name of Heaven, Firmin, keep your thoughts to yourself! If the hypothesis of a murder becomes established, it'll be the ruination of us all."

"Have no fear, Monsieur; I can hold my tongue when necessary—I'll be as mute as a carp."

With that solemn promise, the domestic departed at a run, while Marius, with excessive precaution, closed the establishment's coaching entrance and his superior, gathering together the entire staff of the palace, undertook a methodical search for the dead man's mysterious companion.

Unfortunately, the search produced no result. Neither in the hotel's cellars nor in its attics, nor in its unoccupied rooms, was any trace of the unknown woman found. Marius became increasingly categorical, however, swearing by his great gods that the woman could not have left unceremoniously, unless…

"Unless?" queried the manager, having returned from his futile expedition.

"Unless she was Proserpine in person, Monsieur, the wife of Beelzebub, the princess of Hell, and vanished in a puff of smoke."

At this point, the local Commissaire arrived, escorted by his secretary and two or three officers in plain clothes. The manager rapidly explained what had happened, and insisted on the certainty that the death could only have had natural causes."

The functionary contented himself with replying: "Take us to the body."

The manager hastened to defer to this order and went up to number 5, followed by the entire group. The Commissaire, signaling to his men to wait by the door, went over to Naïni's body on his own.

"Damn!" he said. "What a fine man he was! And you think that such an athlete could have succumbed to a ruptured aneurism, Monsieur?"

"Of course, Monsieur le Commissaire. There's no other explanation of his sudden death, since the young woman who was accompanying him certainly couldn't have put an end to him."

"By violence, undoubtedly not," the policeman replied, sententiously, "but by trickery?"

"If there had been a crime, the room wouldn't be in such good order."

"That depends." And the policeman began to sound the Hindu's chest in his turn. "My word," he said, after a few moments, "whether was a crime or not, that man has nonetheless passed strangely from life to death, and I doubt that the medical examiner will easily give permission for burial. One of my men will go find him. While we await his arrival, we'll pursue our enquiries. You haven't disturbed anything in the room, Monsieur?"

"Nothing."

"Or in the woman's?"

"Nothing at all."

"Good—but let's see, didn't the Hindu have any luggage?"

"No, Monsieur le Commissaire," said Firmin. "He only had a traveling bag, which he held in his hand."

"Where is the bag?"

The domestic looked round rapidly. "There, on the side-table."

A tan leather bag was indeed posed on the item of furniture designated by Firmin. The policeman went over to the table, and then started. The bag was quite empty! "There's nothing in it," he said.

Firmin was about to protest, knowing full well that the bag had been full the previous evening, for he had seen Naïni open it and take out certain papers, but a half-imperious and half-pleading wink from the manager suddenly reminded him of the promise he had made to be as discreet as a carp, in order not to compromise the Palace's good reputation.

"Nothing!" the Commissaire went on. "No papers, no money. We may assume, I think, that the Hindu has been robbed."

"Oh, Monsieur le Commissaire," replied the manager, in a reproachful tone tinged with deference, "the Palace is too respectable an establishment for you to believe a word of what you just said. The fact that the bag is empty doesn't prove anything. Many travelers arrive here with trunks and cases that don't contain anything."

The policeman made no reply. Returning to the body, he set about rummaging through the Hindu's pockets. "Well, then!" he exclaimed, immediately. "Was this Naïni as poor as Job?"

"Why?" inquired the increasingly anxious manager.

"Because his pockets are also empty, of course. Not a *sou*!"

"That's strange," said the manager of the Palace, reluctantly.

"Certainly!" said the policeman. "And you'll agree, Monsieur, that even if there was no murder—which I'd like to believe, in spite of everything—the hypothesis of a theft is becoming increasingly probable. Would the Hindu have come here if he were devoid of any resources?"

The manager was not yet ready to give in. "Perhaps," he said. "Leaving without paying the bill is as common in hotels as it is in restaurants. It might be that this Monsieur Naïni, used to a certain comfort and desirous of putting an end to his life, chose the Palace to carry out his plan."

"And the woman, Monsieur? What part do you think the woman played in all that? No, there's something other than a simple suicide behind this, believe me. Besides, the physician will tell us whether has put an end to his days or whether a criminal hand was involved in it. Whatever has happened, it would be as well to find the dead man's companion as quickly as possible. You made a grave mistake in not recording the woman's name in your register."

"How could I have suspected what would happen?" the poor man said.

The Commissaire shrugged his shoulders. "That's not the point, Monsieur. It's necessary to follow the rules, that's all."

"Believe me, I regret it."

"I don't doubt it, but regrets are superfluous. Have you, at least, done what you can to discover the fugitive?"

"Yes—my staff and I have searched the hotel from top to bottom."

"With no result?"

"Alas!"

"And you affirm, nevertheless, that the woman could not have left the hotel overnight?"

"The concierge guarantees it."

"Well, this is the most mysterious and murkiest affair that I've ever had to deal with," murmured the policeman. "I'm eager to see what the Investigating Magistrate will make of it, when he's commissioned to solve the puzzle."

The arrival of the medical examiner diverted the functionary's reflections. That professional, having undressed Naïni, examined every facet of the body. To his extreme surprise, he discovered nothing suspicious. Not only was the Hindu's cold and rigid cadaver devoid of any trace of injury or lesion that might have caused death, but it did not present the discolored appearance that the bodies of individuals who have fallen victim to a heart attack or a ruptured blood vessel usually take on.

"No diagnosis is possible in these conditions," said the doctor. "Only an autopsy of the corpse will enlighten me."

"Might Naïni have been the victim of poisoning?" interrogated the policemen.

"It's quite possible, but I repeat that an autopsy is the only thing that can clarify that point. I might add that I'm not inclined to favor your hypothesis, Monsieur le Commissaire, for I don't know of any poison that would leave a cadaver in such a perfect state of preservation."

The manager was exultant. "I'm sure that the cause of death was natural," he said.

"Everything indicates that," said the doctor, "but, to my great regret, I can only issue a burial permit after an autopsy. Inform the Investigating Magistrate, Monsieur le Commissaire. I shall maintain myself at his disposal."

"Understood, Doctor," said the policeman—and he sent one of his men to the Magistrate's residence.

Chapter 5. Countermand

When Severus el Tebib's telegram had been handed to him and he had read it, Monsieur Philémon Chêneboy, the

Investigating Magistrate responsible for the Naïni affair, was left powerfully intrigued and perplexed.

It was 2 p.m., and the zealous Magistrate, who had had the Hindu's body transported to the morgue the day before, was about to witness the autopsy—which, as Sâr Dubnotal had learned by mysterious means, was scheduled to take place that same afternoon at 3 p.m. His first impulse had been to pay no heed to the opinion of his unknown correspondent and to go to the morgue with his clerk, but while his carriage was rolling toward the funereal edifice he had the leisure to re-read the telegram several times, six words of which made a particular impression on him: "That will avoid an irreparable disaster."

To what disaster might Monsieur Severus el Tebib be making allusion? Monsieur Chêneboy asked himself that in vain, but the very fact that he could not find a satisfactory explanation excited his anxiety and his curiosity all the more. He also asked himself many other questions. Who was this Severus el Tebib? By what right did he seek to interfere with the operation of French law? He called himself the man's master; no man is another's master, strictly speaking, at least in our democratic country, but even if he were, how could that entitle him to interfere with a legally-ordained autopsy?

All these questions, which were weighing upon his mind, caused the old Magistrate to purse his clean-shaven lips resentfully. In the course of his already-long career, Monsieur Chêneboy could not recall having encountered an analogous case; he searched for a precedent but found none.

"I don't understand it," he said, ingenuously, to Clovis Barbasson, his clerk. "This affair is already obscure enough, I itself; I'm extremely annoyed by this newly-emerged complication."

"Do you still think that the Hindu found dead at the Royal Palace was the victim of a crime, Monsieur?" the clerk inquired, respectfully.

"No! That is to say, I don't know anything," admitted Monsieur Chêneboy. "All this seems very puzzling to me. Why didn't the Hindu enter the name of the young woman who was accompanying him in the hotel register? Why was the woman, who appears to have been of French nationality, with him? Why has she disappeared, without all the police enquiries being able to find her?" The Investigating Magistrate reflected momentarily. "If only the medical examiner knew what had caused the Hindu's death," he went on. "But no, his science has been thrown into complete confusion, and he had to refuse permission for burial."

"I know," said Barbasson. "The body doesn't exhibit any external lesion."

"None."

"And the staff of the hotel reject the hypothesis of a murder completely, isn't that so, Monsieur?"

"That's to be expected. They have no interest in admitting that their establishment might have been the theater of a drama. Besides, my friend, they have quite rightly pointed out that the execution of such a crime was materially impossible. The Hindu, nearly seven feet tall, would not have let himself be killed without putting up a vigorous resistance, even if the murderers were ten against one, given that a gunshot would have woken everyone up."

"The disappearance of the unknown woman who was accompanying him is most strange," murmured Barbasson.

"Certainly. The concierge affirms that she could not have left the hotel, and that gives much food for thought. There might, however be an explanation—the same one that the manager of the Palace suggested. If the woman had followed the Hindu to the hotel at the hazard of some adventure, and the chance acquaintance had died suddenly during the night, one could easily believe that the fear of attracting the suspicion of the law might have driven her to decamp furtively."

"Undoubtedly, Monsieur—but remember that Naïni and she were occupying two adjoining rooms rather than the same one. The Hindu was found dead on the rug beside his bed in room number 5, whose door was not locked. On the other hand, the communicating door between the two rooms was locked with a double turn, as was the door from number six to the corridor."

"What a mess!" complained Monsieur Chêneboy. "The most extraordinary thing of all is that no money, jewels, or documents of any sort were found in the dead man's bag."

"Even if there was no murder, it certainly seems that there was a theft," remarked the clerk. "And if there was a theft, Monsieur, the young woman who fled so mysteriously from the Royal Palace was probably involved in it."

"I repeat, Barbasson, that I'm truly baffled," declared Monsieur Chêneboy, resentfully. "The autopsy of the body might perhaps cast some light on the mystery; but it's necessary that everything turns against us, and that this Monsieur Severus—may the Devil take him!—should send me this accursed telegram!"

"Quite so!" said Barbasson. "What special interest can he have in stopping the procedure?"

"I've asked myself that," said the Magistrate, "and I've also asked myself whether, in spite of the protestations of the sender, the said telegram might have been sent by some practical joker."

"It's not my place to give you advice, Monsieur, but if I were in your shoes, it seems to me that I'd ignore it and proceed with the autopsy anyway."

"I'll certainly do that if Naïni's cadaver doesn't have the scar on the left ring-finger that Monsieur Severus mentions—but in the contrary case, that will prove that he gentleman really does know the Hindu, and I won't hide from you, Barbasson, that I'd prefer to await his arrival."

"Very well!" said the clerk. "Let's stick to that, Monsieur. The existence or non-existence of the identifying mark will determine your decision."

Ten minutes later, the Magistrate, slightly reassured, went into the morgue. The medical examiners were waiting for him beside the body, which was extended on a marble slab in the refrigerated room.

Naïni seemed to be quite dead. His gigantic ebon corpse, entirely naked, presented the very image of eternal rest. Fixed in complete immobility, it was as cold as the slab on which it was lying.

Monsieur Chêneboy, slightly intimidated by the cadaver's colossal proportions, scarcely replied to the doctors' greetings. With the famous telegram in his hand, he approached the slab as if he were doing so reluctantly.

Already armed with his scalpel, the chief medical officer asked: "May I begin, Monsieur?"

"Wait a minute," stammered Monsieur Chêneboy. "I want to see his finger...there!" And he leaned over Naïni's left hand, which was hanging down, icy and inert. "Oh!" he cried, immediately. "The scar!"

Nonplussed, and wondering whether the excellent Monsieur Chêneboy had gone mad, the doctors looked at one another. He handed them the telegram and wiped the sweat from his forehead.

"What do you think of that, Messieurs?" he asked. "You see, the scar on the left ring-finger exists. Monsieur Severus el Tebib has not deceived me, and, in all conscience, I really think that it would be better to defer to his wishes and wait for him to arrive before proceeding with the autopsy."

The physicians took on the resentful expression of a dog from which one has just snatched a bone, but, out of respect for the Magistrate, they gave in without saying a word.

"That's agreed, Messieurs," added Monsieur Chêneboy, for whom the decision became irrevocable. "Since Monsieur Severus isn't due to arrive until tomorrow morning, we'll wait until then. The body hasn't yet started to decompose?"

"No," replied the chief medical officer. "It can be preserved almost indefinitely in this refrigerator."

"Until tomorrow, then, Messieurs. We'll meet here at 2 p.m., to give Monsieur Severus time to present himself at my office in the morning."

Dismissing his clerk, the Magistrate headed for his own residence alone, more perplexed than ever, if that were possible, but certainly less anxious. The mysterious phrase in the telegram—"that will avoid an irreparable disaster"—would not have given him a moment's respite if he had ignored the plea of Severus el Tebib. It would have seemed to him that the disaster were threatening him, and he would have had frightful nightmares all night long.

Egotism evidently has its beneficial side.

If Monsieur Chêneboy had, in fact, been a little less careful of his precious tranquility of mind, poor Naïni would have been delivered to the doctors' scalpels, and all hope of reanimating him—if the resurrection had a chance to proceed—would have vanished.

The Magistrate waited for the next day with confidence, and slept soundly. He had no inkling of the fact that, while he was asleep, train 213, which was bringing Severus el Tebib, was rushing to its doom!

VI. The Rescue

In response to the shout uttered by Sâr Dubnotal a few second before train 213 left the track, his companions, without seeking to understand what was happening, had no thought but to obey him. They suspended themselves by their hands from the luggage racks and lifted their legs up into their couchettes. As they did so, the first impact occurred. It was terrible.

Rudolph, Annunciata and the three investigators thought their last hour had come, and uttered screams of distress that mingled with the formidable bang with which the train's derailment was accompanied. It was as if a bomb had exploded beneath the very wheels of the express.

With a chaotic leap, the engine and the tender plunged into the torrent. As for Sâr Dubnotal's carriage, it was trapped by the parapet, and remained there, in a balance so precarious that the slightest shock might have been sufficient to tip the carriage over the edge of the bridge and into the abyss.

Torn away from their couchettes and hurled into one another, the Psychagogue's companions shouted for help. La Gianetti especially, seized by a nervous crisis, uttered heart-rending screams that disturbed the already much-shaken self-composure of the men. Only Sâr Dubnotal remained master of himself.

The lights in the carriage went out abruptly. By the grey and uncertain light of the nascent dawn, the Great Psychagogue looked for Rudolph's precious satchel, which contained, among other instruments, an electric torch. It had rolled out of the luggage-rack under one of the seats. Creeping on his hands and knees, in order that no false movement might displace the precariously-perched carriage's center of gravity, Sâr Dubnotal succeeded in recovering it. It seemed to be intact. He opened it by forcing the lock and took out the electric torch, which he switched on. He was then able to appreciate the full horror of the situation.

"My friends," he said, with the utmost self-composure, "don't be afraid. We're in an awkward situation, but we'll get out of it, believe me."

Subjugated by his admirable calmness, his companions—including Annunciata—stopped screaming. Huddled in a group in one corner of the steeply-inclined carriage, they looked at one another with frightened eyes. Their clothes were in tatters; their hands and their faces, cut by shards of glass, were streaming with blood.

Beneath his feet, Sâr Dubnotal felt the floor of the carriage oscillating in a disturbing fashion. Evidently, the enormous mass only had a weak point of support.

How could they get out of that inextricable tangle of wood and iron?

"Everyone keep quite still!" the Master ordered, forcefully. And with infinite precaution, he crawled toward the door on the side of the carriage where the track was. That door, torn from its hinges, left an opening sufficient to let a man through—except that the carriage's steep inclination toward the river made getting out difficult. The Great Psychagogue could only count on his own resources, though, to get himself and his companions out of trouble.

Tensing his nerves of steel, he slid through the opening, and then let himself fall gently on to the track, calling an instruction to the others not to move.

Feeble cries coming from the other side of the bridge attracted his attention. He went forward and, in the half-light, caught sight of the engineer, who was calling for help. The shock of the impact had thrown him between the rails, but the fall—which could have been fatal—had only stunned him without injuring him badly.

In the blink of an eye Sâr Dubnotal was beside him. "Get up, my friend," he said to him, having rapidly sounded his chest and taken account of the fact that his condition was not serious. "I need you to help me rescue my companions."

Comforted by the encouragements that had been lavished upon him, the man finally recognized that he was more afraid than hurt and stopped groaning. He sat up, rubbed his painful limbs and asked, anxiously: "What can we do, Monsieur? What can we do?"

"Arles isn't far away?"

"Scarcely three kilometers, Monsieur. Oh, it's frightful! Have you seen my driver?"

"No," Sâr Dubnotal replied. "I'll go look for him, but I fear that he must have been precipitated into the torrent with the locomotive."

"Poor fellow!" stammered the engineer, with a sob in his throat. "Oh, what frightful bad luck! What a blow for his wife and children!"

"Come on, come on!" said the Great Psychagogue, gently. "I'll attend to him and his family, I tell you. Can you walk."

"Yes, Monsieur."

"Are you capable of running all the way to Arles?"

"I'll try."

"Run, then," said Sâr Dubnotal, "and send us a relief train right away—the station-master will put one together."

The engineer limped away.

Sâr Dubnotal made a rapid examination of the vicinity while his assistants, still imprisoned in the carriage, resigned themselves to wait in their awkward and critical position. Sâr Dubnotal wanted to know what had caused the catastrophe, and thought that he might discover it more easily if he were alone. In his opinion, it was a matter of a criminal outrage. He recalled quite clearly that the derailment had been accompanied by a loud bang, like that produced by an anarchist device—a bomb or a petard.

He searched the track at the place where the locomotive had left the rails. "Ah!" he cried. "I wasn't mistaken!" The truth had just appeared to him, suddenly; the traces of a recent explosion were still manifest there. A guilty hand had prepared and determined the catastrophe. That explosion, produced by a bomb whose debris and shrapnel were still strewn among the sleepers, has twisted the steel rails, torn away the rivets and opened a large crevasse in the very fabric of the bridge.

"If the blast of the powder hadn't been concentrated in an upward direction, the whole bridge would have collapsed into the river," the psychagogue murmured. "Who could be responsible for this monstrous outrage? Is it my life he wanted to take? The madman! It's almost as if he had put a rope around his neck. Whoever he is, I'll prove to him that one cannot attack me with impunity!"

Continuing his investigations, Sâr Dubnotal observed, by leaning over the half-destroyed parapet, that the engine and the tender had been caught and rolled over by the waters of the torrent, and that it was necessary to abandon any hope of saving the driver.

He died at his post, and he's left a widow and orphans, whose material existence the train company will ensure, the Great Psychagogue thought. *I'll make sure that the interests of the poor folk are safeguarded, and I'll give them a pension myself—but my primary concern will be to avenge the victims of this monstrous murder attempt!*

An hour went by, interminable for the prisoners in the sleeping-car, whom Sâr Dubnotal comforted as best he could—but he did not want any of them to attempt to jump on to the track as he had done, for it was the weight of the group they formed in the rear that was maintaining the equilibrium of the carriage, and if that weight were diminished, even by a little, the enormous carriage was certain to tumble into the torrent.

Finally, a dull roar announced the arrival of the relief train. The engineer had found a train at Arles and the station-master had immediately sent the engine and one carriage to the scene of the accident. The rescue crew, encouraged and supervised by Sâr Dubnotal in person, worked wonders. After an hour of titanic effort, the valiant employees of the P-L-M succeeded in righting the stricken carriage, and the travelers emerged from it without sustaining any further damage.

Sâr Dubnotal dressed their slight wounds and they all felt well enough to resume their journey. The psychagogue rewarded the devotion of the rescue crew appropriately. There was no possibility of raising the engine that had fallen into the torrent without special cranes, so they all climbed on to the relief train, which immediately set off to retrace its path.

The Master was more determined than ever to reach Marseilles before the autopsy of his Hindu servant. In his opinion, the murder attempt that had caused the catastrophe of train 213 had been directed against him, or rather against his journey.

Someone obviously wants to stop me mounting an investigation, he thought. *The people who sought to undo Naïni are no strangers to this criminal attempt. Even so, I can't explain how they were able to anticipate my coming in sufficient time to prepare it.*

On seeing the Master deep in grim mediation, his disciple, his investigators and his medium dared not say a word.

Finally, Sâr Dubnotal appeared to recover all his serenity. "Well, my friends," he said, almost gaily. "We've had a narrow escape while we slept, haven't we?"

139

"The rest of us certainly have," Rudolph replied, "but you, Master, can't have anything to fear from death?"

The ice was broken; they chatted. The valor of those men, inured to danger, made light of such adventures, and when Sâr Dubnotal made them party to his suspicions, none of them thought any longer of anything but exacting vengeance upon the wretches who had plotted their destruction in a cowardly fashion.

VII. A Miracle That Wasn't One

The relief train had to stop in Arles, where it had been formed. It reached the town at 7 a.m. There, Sâr Dubnotal and his followers took an express departing for Marseilles, where they disembarked at 8:30 a.m. In sum, the derailment of the express had only cost them an insignificant loss of time. Provided that the Hindu's autopsy had not taken place the day before, Sâr Dubnotal, certain that it would not take place before 10 a.m., still hoped to be able to prevent it.

The first thing that the Psychagogue and his companions wanted to do was to buy garments to replace the ones they were wearing—which, being torn and stained with blood and mud, scarcely gave them a respectable appearance—at the clothing store nearest to the station. Annunciata had a large shawl, with which she could wrap herself up decently in the meantime.

This indispensable metamorphosis only took a few minutes. As soon as it was complete, the group split up. Frank and Fréjus took a cab to the Royal Palace, with the aim of catching up with the Commissaire's investigation into the Naïni affair, on their master's behalf. Sâr Dubnotal, Rudolph and la Gianetti went to see the Investigating Magistrate, whose address was given to them by the first policeman they encountered. As for Otto, he had the macabre pleasure of being immediately dispatched to the morgue to inform any interested parties of the arrival of Monsieur Severus, in case that the latter did not find the Magistrate at home.

At that early hour, however, the Magistrate was indeed still at home.

On the way, Sâr Dubnotal bought a few newspapers that mentioned the Naïni affair. He was able to read them in Monsieur Chêneboy's reception-room, after having sent him as card bearing the name of Severus el Tebib—for the Magistrate had not yet finished dressing. He was not long delayed, though, in receiving his visitors.

The Great Psychagogue introduced Rudolph and Annunciata as his friends, and said: "I hope, Monsieur, that you have been able to grant my request and postpone my servant's autopsy."

"Indeed," said Monsieur Chêneboy, "but I confess that I can't understand why you have made that request."

Sâr Dubnotal put on a slight smile. "It's quite simple, Monsieur. Why did I make the request? Simply because Naïni might not be dead."

At this unexpected reply, Monsieur Chêneboy shivered, and pushed back his armchair. An extreme anxiety was legible in his little grey eyes, whose gaze alternately between his three visitors. He tugged at the white hair of his side-whiskers nervously. He was obviously wondering whether these people were in their right minds, or whether they were making fun of him.

"I understand your surprise, Monsieur," Sâr Dubnotal went on, placidly, "but might not the physicians be mistaken, and the supposed dead man merely asleep?"

"Asleep!" exclaimed Monsieur Chêneboy, raising his arms to the heavens, "Asleep! A man that does not move, is not breathing, is as cold as marble and whose rigidity is absolute? Come on, you're joking!"

"Not at all, Monsieur. It was quite intentionally that I employed the word 'asleep,' which you will understand more easily than a long scientific explanation of the doubts I retain as to the reality of my servant's demise. Suppose, for instance,

141

that Naïni had been subjected to a cataleptic crisis; do you deny that lethargic unconsciousness might give the illusion of death?"

"Oh!" said the Magistrate, going very pale. "Yes, I understand now. Catalepsy! The man might have fallen into a cataleptic state!"

"Take note that I'm not affirming anything, Monsieur. I said 'suppose,' and, to be frank, I should add that I'm convinced that it's nothing of the sort. My servant has never been subject to that sort of morbid fit of unconsciousness. Admirably constituted, as you have doubtless been able to observe for yourself, he is built to live for 100 years—but if you want to know my opinion, he has been the victim of a crime."

"What crime?" stammered Monsieur Chêneboy, who had lost his bearings completely.

"Monsieur," said Sâr Dubnotal, gravely, "your time is too precious for me to think of abusing your benevolence. I shall therefore spare you interminable explanations. As the proverb says, it's at the foot of the wall that one sees the mason; I therefore propose that we go to the morgue together immediately, where I hope to prove to you that Naïni is still alive."

"Of course! If you can establish that proof, and the man returns to life, I shall proclaim the miracle, and you will assuredly be the most extraordinary thaumaturge that I have ever had the opportunity to admire!"

"Let's go, then, Monsieur."

"Can we not put off the experiment until this afternoon?"

"Are you busy this morning?"

"No," said the Magistrate, hesitantly, "but you'll understand, Monsieur Severus, that I'd prefer the medical examiners to be there, in order to fulfill my responsibility, and I only asked them to reconvene at 2 p.m."

"Very well," Sâr Dubnotal agreed. "We'll meet at the morgue at 2 p.m., Monsieur." And he took his leave of the respectable Magistrate.

At the appointed hour, Sâr Dubnotal, still flanked by la Gianetti and Rudolph—who was carrying his precious satchel slung over his shoulder—presented himself at the morgue.

Otto was waiting at the door of the funereal establishment. "I've been able to see Naïni's body," he whispered in the Great Psychagogue's ear. "It's very well preserved."

"Good," replied Sâr Dubnotal. "Go rejoin your comrades and assist in their investigation."

Monsieur Chêneboy and the two doctors were waiting for Monsieur Severus in the refrigerated room. The doctors gave the three newcomers a rather hostile welcome. The Magistrate had explained the project that the Hindu's master was about to undertake to them as best he could, but they judged it insane. So far as they were concerned, Naïni's death was so evident that they could not understand why Monsieur Chêneboy had lent any credence to the nonsensical assertions of Monsieur Severus.

"I haven't lent any credence to it," the Magistrate had replied, timidly, "but we can still wait and see. I can assure you, Messieurs, that Monsieur Severus's assertion astonished me, but he seems to me to be a remarkable man."

"Perhaps he's a sorcerer," the Chief Medical Examiner had sniggered, simultaneously amused and furious at Monsieur Chêneboy's naivety.

At this point, Sâr Dubnotal and his companions came in, and the doctors resumed their sullen expressions.

The Great Psychagogue bowed to the three men, made a sign to Rudolph and la Gianetti to follow him, and went to the slab on which the Hindu was lying.

"Messieurs," he said, addressing himself to the doctors. "You are, it seems, absolutely convinced that death has done its work and that there is nothing left to do but bury this man. I am obliged to tell you that you are mistaken. Naïni, totally inert and deprived of the appearances of life as he is, will soon be thanking me for saving him from your scalpels."

"Madness" cried the Chief Medical Examiner, indignant that that unknown should accuse him of incompetence in public.

Sâr Dubnotal shrugged his shoulders. "Monsieur," he asked the Magistrate, "may I commence the experiment that will permit you to draw a comparison between the noble science of these... doctors and my humble professional capacities?"

The Magistrate had no time to reply. Beside himself, the senior physician cried: "Are you a doctor too, then? In that case, prove it. Since you take such a haughty tone with us, Monsieur, would you care to produce your university diploma? You know that it's prohibited to exercise our profession in France without having carried out substantial studies and obtained the relevant certifications. Monsieur, if this individual cannot prove that he belongs to the Faculty, I formally forbid him to touch the body with so much as his little finger."

Coldly, Sâr Dubnotal took a large document from his portfolio and handed it to Monsieur Chêneboy. It was a doctoral diploma in medicine in the name of Severus el Tebib. A few years before, the psychagogue had submitted his thesis and passed his examinations with flying colors, in order that he might be permitted to laugh at the bureaucratic niceties of anyone who opposed him.

On seeing the diploma, the Chief Medical Examiner could not hide his chagrin.

"Enough idle discussion!" said Sâr Dubnotal. "Let's get on with it. Rudolph, fetch some napkins and a warm linen sheet—and open your satchel! Annunciata, I believe that your intervention will not be necessary, this time."

Indeed, Sâr Dubnotal, working by himself, turned the Hindu's rigid body over, placed his ear between the shoulder-blades, and remained still, holding his breath.

"Everything's all right!" he said, as he straightened up. From Rudolph's satchel, he took a bottle filled with a special oil, with which he anointed Naïni's back; then, taking hold of a napkin, he rubbed the moistened areas vigorously. After that, he turned the body over again, used a spatula to separate the Hindu's clenched jaws, and introduced into his throat the contents of a crystal phial, which he shook from time to time.

Up to this point, his measures had had no effect, and the medical examiners, who had been momentarily disconcerted, were beginning to recover their aplomb and laugh at their colleague's sterile efforts when something occurred that was so extraordinary that they were struck dumb. The amiable Investigating Magistrate could not retain a cry of fright.

The supposed dead man had just opened his eyes!

The bewilderment of the witnesses lasted longer than Naïni required to sit up straight on the slab, jump down to the floor and envelop himself in the sheet that Rudolph hastened to hold out to him.

"Where am I?" he stammered. "What happened?"

"Well, Messieurs?" Sâr Dubnotal inquired ironically, turning to the doctors.

The latter were too stupefied to respond, but Monsieur Chêneboy, shaking with excitement, did it for them. "Monsieur Severus, you are certainly the cleverest man in the world, and these gentlemen certainly regret having cast aspersions on your marvelous professional ability. You have accomplished a veritable miracle, and I give you my word that this extraordinary cure will be the subject of a communication to the Faculty of Medicine in Paris!"

Sâr Dubnotal was no longer listening. Rudolph had gone in quest of a cab and, followed by the Italian woman and the Hindu, muffled by his sheet, the Great Psychagogue was already heading for the door.

Chapter VIII. Singular Complications

While Sâr Dubnotal was at the home of the Investigating Magistrate, Frank and Fréjus had been actively occupied in their personal mission. They had, as we have said, been taken to the Royal Palace.

The vast and comfortable hotel in the Cours Belzunce was still in a state of excitement. A swarm of detectives and journalists were striving to glean new information from the staff and to unravel the murky plot of the Naïni affair. Photographers were taking snapshot after snapshot.

The representatives of the police and the press were wasting their time, though; the mystery remained just as impenetrable as it had been the day before, and the day before that. No one knew what had happened to Azilis de Tréguilly—and no one had even been able to discover her identity. When people referred to the Hindu's companion, they were reduced to calling her "the unknown woman" or "the stranger." His trail remained impossible to pick up. It was even impossible to offer a plausible explanation of the woman's disappearance, as the hotel's concierge stubbornly continued to affirm that she could not have gone through the doorway without his knowledge.

In order to facilitate their task, Fréjus and Frank passed themselves off as reporters in quest of sensational news, and, without seeming to touch upon the subject, set about questioning all the Royal Palace's domestics, who cold only confirm the concierge's assertions. However, the interview with Firmin, the valet who had discovered by Hindu's "body," appeared to give some satisfaction to Frank and Fréjus.

"Come on, Firmin, summon up your memories," Frank said to him, "and answer our questions clearly."

"There's a *louis* in it for you!" added the cunning Fréjus, swiftly.

Hooked by that superb fee and flattered to be the object of the two reporters' solicitations, Firmin forgot the errand on which the manager had sent him. "At your service, Messieurs," he said.

"Who was on duty when the Hindu and his companion arrived at the hotel?" inquired Frank.

"I was, Monsieur."

"Marvelous. At what time did the two of them retire to their respective rooms on the eve of the drama?"

"Let's see—they arrived at the Palace at about 8 p.m. and were served dinner in room number 5, occupied by Monsieur Naïni. The lady scarcely touched her plate. She seemed to be ill, and hardly said anything. Monsieur Naïni, by contrast, ate heartily. At 10 p.m., I cleared the table. When I returned to my duties, it was 11 p.m. The lady had gone up to her room and Monsieur Naïni was smoking a cigar at the entrance to his. I asked them both if they needed anything, and when they said no, I didn't persist."

"Do you know whether the communicating door was still open at that time?"

"Yes, Monsieur—it was ajar."

"But the following morning, it was found locked?"

"Yes, Monsieur."

"On which side was the key?"

"On the Hindu's side."

"You're sure?"

"Certain."

"That morning, was the door from Naïni's room to the corridor closed?"

"Closed, yes, but not locked or bolted. That's why, when I presented myself to offer the Monsieur my services, I was able to enter without difficulty. Imagine my fright on finding him lying fully dressed at the foot of the bed, stone dead!"

"And the exterior door of the other room?"

"That one was doubly locked and bolted, Monsieur."

"That's odd," Frank murmured. "Had the unknown woman gone to bed?"

"Probably, since her bed was unmade."

"Nothing was found in the rooms?"

"Nothing but a little leather valise belonging to the Hindu—and that was completely empty."

"What about the dead man's effects?"

"Nothing there either," the valet said. "Not so much as *that!*" he clicked his thumbnail against the teeth of his upper jaw. "No, not a *sou* or a single piece of paper. Nothing at all!"

"No watch? No cigar-case?"

"Nothing, I tell you—on the strength of which, the Commissaire de Police has insinuated that someone must have robbed the Hindu."

"Do you, personally, think he was murdered, Firmin?"

"No, Monsieur—but, like the Commissaire, I believe he was robbed."

"Let's go over it again," said Frank. "You say that you served the couple's supper. Did anyone help you?"

"No one."

"What did their meal comprise?"

"A plate of curried rice, cold chicken and a salad with hard-boiled eggs, all washed down with hot tea."

"What did the woman eat?"

"Very little, as I told you. A slice of chicken, two salad leaves and a banana."

"She didn't touch the rice?"

"No."

"Did she have anything to drink?"

"Yes—one or two cups of tea."

"Who poured the tea?"

"The Hindu."

"Might the woman have been able to put some sort of powder in the plate of curry that her companion ate?"

"I can guarantee that she didn't, Monsieur. I offered her the bowl first, and she thanked me but shook her head. Then I passed it to Monsieur Naïni, who served himself, and I took it away immediately to put it down by the door."

"Odd!" Frank repeated.

"One more question, Firmin," said Fréjus. Did you bring all the dishes from the pantry in one go?"

"Yes, Monsieur."

"Who gave them to you?"

"The *maître d'hôtel*."

"And you brought them directly from the pantry to the room?"

"Very nearly, Monsieur. As I went up the stairs, one of our clients, a commercial traveler, asked me to come and light the candle in his room. It had gone out and he had no matches. In order to oblige him, I had to put the tray down on sideboard on the first-floor landing, where numbers 5 and 6 are, and go up to the second floor, where the traveler was lodged."

"Was, you say. He's gone, then?"

"Yes, at noon the day before yesterday."

"The day when the body was discovered?"

"Exactly."

"Why did he leave?"

"He complained about the noise caused by the drama, the visit from the police, and God knows what else. To hear him, our hotel was nothing but an ill-famed dive, a den of thieves in which one risked being knocked down and robbed. 'I shan't stay here another minute,' he declared, when the Magistrate had gone."

"Had he interrogated him?"

"Briefly, yes, Monsieur, like the other guests—but he didn't know anything, hadn't seen or heard anything, and produced papers attesting to his perfect honorability."

"What was his name?"

"Monsieur Schönprink, a Belgian salesman."

"When you went up to his room to relight his candle, did he go with you?"

"No, Monsieur. He went to the lavatory, which is at the end of the corridor on the first floor, and didn't come up until afterwards, when I'd picked up my tray."

"Very good, Firmin," said Fréjus, placidly. "That doesn't tell us anything much, but here's what I promise you, all the same." And he slipped a *louis* into the happy valet's hand, while adding in a casual manner: "Do you happen to know which hotel this Monsieur Schönprink went to, who valued his security and tranquility so highly?"

"Yes—he went to the Hôtel du Globe on the Cannebière, where he'll be ten times as exposed and disturbed as here, the old grouch! Clients like that, of whom there are always too many, are welcome to get out! It's isn't me who'll regret it. Can you imagine that he didn't even give a tip to the coachman or the groom, who took his trunks—enormous trunks, Monsieur, as large and deep as carriages, and heavy, I can tell you! There was one so heavy that it needed three of us to bring it down from the second floor!"

"Thank you, Firmin," said Frank and Fréjus, laughing as they went out into the street. There, however, their faces darkened, and with common accord they took to their heels at top speed, after having asked for directions to the Hôtel du Globe.

"Monsieur Schönprink?" they asked the manager of that establishment, at which they arrived in the blink of an eye.

"Departed."

"What?"

"Departed yesterday at noon, Messieurs."

"For?"

"I don't know, but I don't think he'll be long delayed in returning, for he left his luggage here."

"Good—we'll come back," said Fréjus, swiftly, dragging his friend outside. As they drew away, Fréjus continued: "Listen, Frank, I believe we're on the track. The behavior of this Schönprink seems to me to be highly suspicious. We have to clarify his role. Let's go rejoin the Master and tell him what we've learned. I won't be surprised if he's of the same mind."

"What do you think, exactly?"

"That this Schönprink was in cahoots with Azilis, of course. Assume that, and everything's explained."

"How?"

"My poor Frank, you've gone down in my estimation. Long live the Sûreté, damn it! It will sink Scotland Yard! Yes, old chap, you've only seen the light at the end of the tunnel, while I've begun to recognize it."

"Explain it then, you insufferable braggart!"

"Braggart! Ah, you'll see whether I'm bragging, whether I have the key to the puzzle! Schönprink? Well, Schönprink, is none other than Tserpchikopf, I'll wager! Made up, disguised and in possession of false papers, the boyar must have followed Naïni and Azilis, perhaps taking the very same train to Marseilles. He checked into the Palace after them, having communicated secretly with the Hindu's prisoner, either by the intermediary of an accomplice in Paris, or directly, on the train.

"Once their plan was formulated, the two scoundrels had little trouble putting it into action. Tserpchikopf, profiting from Firmin's temporary absence, had only to sprinkle the curried rice with some compound designed to poison the Hindu without leaving suspect traces—that's why Naïni's body has no trace of injury. Azilis, having not touched the dish, could not have been inconvenienced by it. The drug must only have taken effect two hours after ingestion.

"When she heard the body fall, Azilis, who had pretended to go to sleep, didn't dare get up straight away, and that's why her bed was still warm in the morning. But when nothing stirred in number 5 she was reassured, went into the Hindu's room through the communicating door—which was still open—closed it behind her with a key, stripped the body of everything that might facilitate identification and rejoined Tserpchikopf on the second floor, after having put out the light and closed the door of number 6 after her.

"The following day, after the departure of the Commissaire—who, instead of interrogating the Palace's clients, must have thought it better to visit their rooms one by one—the Russian decamped, taking Azilis with him in one of those voluminous trunks. Do you understand now why no one saw her leave the hotel? If the police had been more perspicacious, the disappearance of the guest in number 6 would have ceased to be mysterious."

Frank shook his colleague's hand warmly "By Jove, yes—you're right, Fréjus! For once, I've allowed myself to be beaten."

"For once?" exclaimed the Frenchman, jovially. "Ha ha! It's neither the first time nor the last!"

At that moment, it was 3 p.m. Sâr Dubnotal had arranged to meet his investigators at 4 p.m. Frank and Fréjus went to the main Post Office, where they were to meet him. On the way they ran into Otto, who was brought up to date. He shared the conviction of his comrades, and congratulated Fréjus in his turn.

The Great Psychagogue was punctual, even though he had been forced to take Naïni to the clerk at the Palais de Justice, where his clothes had been deposited, after leaving the morgue. It was not without difficulty that he got the seals lifted, but when the frail clerk saw the gigantic Hindu showing signs of impatience, he hastened to say that, as a gracious concession, Monsieur Naïni would be allowed to dispense with the usual formalities.

The Hindu did not seem to be feeling any ill-effects from his strange and macabre adventure. Along with his life, Sâr Dubnotal's elixir had given him back his usual impassivity. Interrogated by his Master, however, he had been unable to give him any information that could cast light of the drama at the Royal Palace.

During the journey from Paris to Marseilles, Azilis had not given him any cause for concern. He had been shut up with her in a reserved compartment, from which he only permitted her to go out in order to go to the lavatory, when he had followed her as far as the door. He had not noticed her exchange a single word with any other passenger on the train. The Comtesse had not appeared any more restive at the Hotel. Apparently resigned to her fate, she had allowed herself to be taken to her room, accepted dinner in Naïni's company and had gone to bed at about 10 p.m.

In order to take every precaution, the Hindu had taken way the key to the door from her room to the corridor and left the communicating door ajar. Intending to stay on watch all night, he had lit a cigar and was savoring it like a connoisseur when a strange malaise had abruptly overtaken him. All that he could remember thereafter was collapsing in a heap beside the bed. His amazement had been extreme when he awoke in the morgue and saw himself surrounded by Sâr Dubnotal, Rudolph, Annunciata and three unknown men.

His lethargy, complete and prolonged, had only left the impression of a brief nap, and when he leaned the details of the affair from the Great Psychagogue's lips—the discovery of his inanimate body by the valet Firmin, the inexplicable disappearance of his companion, the loss of his money, his papers and his watch—he rubbed his eyes, thinking that he was dreaming.

After imparting this information, Sâr Dubnotal had hastened to meet his investigators in order to discover the results of their enquiries. The two groups met up at the Post Office. In order that no indiscreet ear should catch a word of their conversation, the Great Psychagogue interrogated his aides in Hindi and asked them to reply in the same language, which they all spoke fluently.

Fréjus made his report and had the great joy of observing that Sâr Dubnotal, like Frank and Otto, agreed with him.

"Your deductions do honor to your sagacity, Fréjus," the Master told him. "Evidently, they're correct. I'm only astonished that the police Commissaire and the Investigating Magistrate didn't suspect Schönprink. If that man and Tserpchikopf are really one and the same, as is almost certain, the Russian is an extremely cunning, bold and redoubtable adversary—one of the most arrant blackguards that I've ever encountered.

"Thanks to Fréjus, my dear friends, we've just taken a large stride toward the truth; but we'd be wrong to congratulate ourselves too much, for our troubles aren't at an end and we'll have many more obstacles to get over before putting our hands on the collar of the pretended boyar and getting Azilis back. I'm sure, in fact, that they've left Marseilles permanently, in spite of what Schönprink, alias Tserpchikopf, told the manager of the Hôtel du Globe. Schönprink will never set foot in that establishment again. The trunks he has abandoned doubtless only contain items of no value, perhaps stones, newspapers or old clothes intended to give them weight.

"On the other hand, I've told you that I'm convinced that the murder attempt directed against us was perpetrated by the same people who wanted to get rid of Naïni. Tserpchikopf and Azilis would, therefore, be its authors—but in that case, it's necessary to admit the existence of one or several accomplices, whose existence we have not suspected until now. Given that, we can take one more forward step on the right track. Did the manager of the Hôtel du Globe tell you whether Schönprink was accompanied by a woman at the moment of his departure, Fréjus?"

"No; unfortunately, I didn't think to ask him, Master."

"It doesn't matter, for no doubt remains in my mind on that subject. Schönprink, or rather Tserpchikopf, took Azilis out in one of his trunks. During the day, when the comings-and goings permitted her to pass unnoticed, Azilis must have left the new hotel surreptitiously. Tserpchikopf must have met up with her in the city and they must both have taken an evening train to Avignon or the next station. At midnight at the latest, they could have been at one or other of those stations, from which they could have made their way on foot to the bridge where the catastrophe took place. As our train was not due to pass over the bridge until 4 a.m., they had all the time they needed to deposit the device with which they were equipped on the railway line. In order to do that, however, they must have been forewarned of our arrival, and that's where things get murky again."

Sâr Dubnotal reflected, and appeared to come to a sudden decision. "Wait for me here," he said to his aides. "I need to talk to the receptionist at the Post Office."

Two minutes later, the Great Psychagogue was in private conference with the functionary. When he emerged from the office, Sâr held the duplicate of a telegram in his hand, while the pale and tremulous receptionist, who had large drops of sweat on his temples, shook his head as he watched him draw away.

What had happened between the two men? How had the Great Psychagogue succeeded in persuading the functionary to reveal a professional secret to him? No one ever found out.

Sâr Dubnotal showed the dispatch to his disciple and his aides. It had been sent from the Gare de Lyon in Paris. Dated the previous evening, at nine thirty, it bore these strange words:

Schönprink, commercial traveler, Poste Restante, Marseilles.

Devil just took special basket nine-five.
Pion.[13]

"What!" exclaimed Rudolph, Otto, Frank and Fréjus, with one voice. "What is this new charade?"

"I'm asking myself he same thing," murmured Sâr Dubnotal. "But this telegram proves to us that Tserpchikopf does have an accomplice, and that the accomplice is in Paris. It's through the intermediary of this person who signs himself '*Pion*' that Azilis was able to warn the Russian, I'm sure of it. Who is this *Pion*? We'll find out in due course, and that will be the moment to devote all your flair to my service, Otto, Frank and Fréjus…

"For the moment, it's a matter of deciphering this coded message, for I think the key to the mystery that still envelops the catastrophe of express 213 is there. Come on, my friends—this dispatch means something. What?"

No one replied.

"Let's assume that 'Devil' means me," suggested Sâr Dubnotal, with a slight smile, and that 'basket' signifies train. What does that give us? 'Severus has just taken special train nine-five.'"

"Oh!" exclaimed his companions, in chorus.

"Take note that the supposition is only partly satisfactory, for the 'nine-five' remained to be explained."

---

[13] The word "Devil" is given in English, not as "*Diable.*" I have left "Pion" [Pawn] in French here, as it appears to be being used as a proper name.

155

"Perhaps it should be translated as 95," hazarded Frank.

"I've thought of that, but the number doesn't correspond to that of express 213."

Again the psychagogue's aides remained silent. None of them understood the final term in the puzzle.

Suddenly, Sâr Dubnotal slapped his forehead. "I've got it!" he said. "Everything's as clear as day. 'Nine-five' signifies 9 p.m. and 5 a.m. Our train left Paris at 9 p.m. and was due to reach Marseilles at 5 a.m. The so-called *Pion* thus alerted Schönprink—which is to say, Tserpchikopf—to the exact time of our arrival. Tserpchikopf, I found out during my conversation with the receptionist, has come to the Post Office frequently asking whether he had anything for him in the name of Schönprink. The original of this dispatch was given to him at ten p.m. The last train for Avignon leaves at 10:30 p.m.; he took it with Azilis. We know the rest."

"Scotland Yard, eh?" Fréjus said to Frank, maliciously. "Still sunk, no?"

"What about you, then?" the Englishman retorted, tit-for-tat.

"Boys," Sâr Dubnotal put in, gravely, "there's no point in squabbling yet again about the merits of your respective police forces. In a few days' time, you'll be able to compete in ardor and skill, for we're all going back to Paris and you'll immediately set out on campaign to winkle out the signatory of thus dispatch as soon as possible. I warn you that it won't be easy. *Pion* is certainly just a pseudonym, and we don't know anything about the individual: real name, sex, age, address. We must, however, find him at any cost. He's the only means we have of getting back on the trail of the Russian and Azilis. The authors of the outrage against express 213 and the poisoning of Naïni will certainly not have neglected any precaution to put us off the track. We might spend months trying to find out where they're hidden, while *Pion* lives in Paris and suspects nothing.

"Come on, my children, let's go!"

An hour later, the Great Psychagogue's entire company was speeding toward the capital with him.

The next day, Sâr Dubnotal's investigators began their search.

One by one, they beat all the quarters of Paris in search of Tserpchikopf's enigmatic accomplice—but in vain. The days went by without their being able to discover the slightest clue.

Sâr Dubnotal, Rudolph, Annunciata and Naïni had returned to Trez-Hir, where they waited impatiently for the results of these laborious enquiries, but absolutely nothing came of them. *Pion* remained undiscoverable, and Tserpchikopf and Azilis seemed to have vanished in a puff of smoke.

The grandmaster of psychognosis was, however, anxious to conclude the matter. One night, forsaking his bedroom, he shut himself up in a little round room surmounted by a dome, which topped a turret elevated above the bungalow at an angle, which served as his observatory. The next morning, Rudolph, needing his instructions, found him in his study in front of a large sheet of paper full of figures and bizarre diagrams, like those seen in horoscopes.

Without looking up from his calculations, Sâr Dubnotal sent his disciple away with a curt but benevolent word. When he appeared at the communal table for the midday meal, everyone saw by the serenity of his forehead and the clarity of his gaze that no anxiety or indecision remained in his mind.

As soon as they had returned to the bungalow, he had examined Naïni and analyzed his blood, in order to try to recover some trace of the mysterious poison that had struck the Hindu down without provoking the decomposition of his tissues. The experiment had been crowned with success. He found a few traces of antiar,[14] the toxic sap of a tropical plant,

---

[14] The original text has "upas antiar," emphasizing that antiar is a resinous gum derived from the upas tree (*Antiaris toxicaria*), which was once used by indigenes of the East Indies to poison arrow-heads. The narrative is more than usually inco-

which he apparently knew much better than the medical examiners of Marseilles. Thus, Fréjus' hypothesis was confirmed. Tserpchikopf had indeed sent away the valet Firmin in order to pour two or three drops of that infernal drug—whose secret is known only to the Malays—into the rice dish, which Azilis had been warned not to touch.

The possession of a phial of antiar made the Russian an even more redoubtable enemy than had been supposed, and Sâr Dubnotal considered it more than ever to be his duty to track down the pitiless master criminal.

At the end of September, the Great Psychagogue, Rudolph and Annunciata returned to Paris. In the meantime, a magnificent steam yacht had arrived at a mooring in Trez-Hir Bay. It belonged to Sâr Dubnotal, who had summoned it from Colombo, where it had been docked. Aboard the *Derviche*—as the yacht was called—a numerous crew awaited the Great Psychagogue's instructions, who only gave them after the night spent in his observatory—which is to say, at the moment of his own departure. He seemed perfectly sure of his course of action.

As he left the bungalow with his usual entourage to take the express from Morlaix to Paris, he said to the gigantic Hindu: "This time, Naïni, you shall not have the pleasure of keeping company with the Comtesse de Tréguilly—nor, in consequence, the disappointment of seeing her slip through your fingers. In a week's time, she will embark on the *Derviche*, on

---

herent at this point, and there is a substantial gap on the page where the chapter ends—which would not normally be tolerated in such publications, in which text tended to be exactly fitted to the available space by cutting or stretching at the typesetting stage. As the reader will observe, the narrative thread is abandoned here, to be picked up at a very different point. It is possible that another writer took over from the original author, rather ineptly, in order to finish the story, but it is also possible that the latter had simply run out of inspiration when he dictated this particular passage.

which I certainly hope that her villainous boyar will also take a berth. I've consulted the stars, Naïni, and they have told me that Tserpchikopf and Azilis will not escape my justice indefinitely, if I set forth on campaign. With all the resources at my disposal, I can defy the rogues to keep me in check any longer."

IX. The False Mage

Five days after Sâr Dubnotal's departure for Paris, where he only stopped off briefly, a music-hall in Victoria Street in London was besieged from 6 p.m. on by an enormous crowd, whose members had come to see a performance of magic that was due to begin at 8 p.m. precisely.

For some time, the London press had been making much mention of the presence in the metropolis of a famous yogi, or Hindu mage. This yogi called himself Luckvrak the Enchanter, and it was said that extraordinary phenomena were produced under his influence, such as the spontaneous germination of plants, the evocation of a specter, the ascent of an individual into the air, and the creation of living creatures, particularly goldfish.

The manager of the music-hall in Victoria Street had engaged him especially for the evening, to carry out his experiments in public. The curiosity that the announcement of such a spectacle had aroused in the population of the great city is easily imaginable. Credulous or skeptical, everyone wanted to see the mage Luckvrak at work. Wagers were made for or against the sincerity of the promised experiments. People interested in the occult sciences—and God knows that there are as many such people in England as anywhere else!—willingly accepted that sincerity in advance.

At that time, Sâr Dubnotal had not yet thought of writing his Memoirs, and psychognosis was little known, but the experiments made by the London Dialectical Society under the

159

presidency of the knowledgeable naturalist John Lubbock[15] had clearly established the existence of a mysterious force that manifests itself with intelligence through the intermediary of mediums. The illustrious physicist William Crookes had repeated these experiments in 1874, their results proving that the phenomena really do exist, and cannot be denied by any honest witness.

In brief, the whole of scientific, literary and worldly London had taken an interest in the announcement of the performance, and well before the time that the curtain was due to go up, the management of the music-hall had to close the doors, the hall being full to overflowing. The session began amid a profound gathering of spectators, crammed into the galleries and on the steps of the amphitheater.

As the curtain went up, the mage Luckvrak, a man of middle age, came to the front of the stage to greet the audience and introduce his medium, a beautiful young woman whose seductive smile and harmonious figure, clad in an elegant white silk costume, excited general admiration.

"I shall reward you as best I can by carrying out as many experiments as possible, and I hope that you will be convinced of the reality of my supernatural power. I am not a Hindu, as my name and my title of yogi might lead you to believe. Born in America to slave parents I have, however, lived for a long

---

[15] Sir John Lubbock, Baron Avebury (1834-1913), was a successful banker and Liberal politician as well as a natural philosopher, whose strong interest in human and insect evolution—especially mental evolution—was encouraged by his friendship with Charles Darwin. The citation relates to the fact that in 1869 he accepted the presidency of the first formal scientific inquiry mounted in Britain to investigate the phenomena allegedly produced by Spiritualist mediums; the committee's eventual report was actually conscientiously ambivalent, stating that no firm proof had been obtained of the reality of the phenomena, but suggesting that they were sufficiently interesting to warrant further research.

time in the Indies, where I was initiated into the secret practices of Brahmins and fakirs. As for my companion, Dolorosa, she is Dutch by birth. I met her by chance in Rotterdam and, her psychic abilities having made a considerable impact on me, I recruited her as a medium. Now that you know us, Ladies and Gentlemen, we shall put an end to your visible impatience by immediately commencing the first item on the program."

In the middle of the stage there was a heavy round oak table covered by a cloth. Beside that table there was a smaller table bearing a put full of earth and a plate full of grains of wheat. A little further away there was a bucket of water and an armchair. Luckvrak made Dolorosa sit down in the armchair and announced: "First, Ladies and Gentleman, I shall hypnotize the medium and suggest that she do all that the spectators might care to indicate to me in a low voice."

So saying, the mage executed a few rapid passes and stared intently into the eyes of his subject, who came to her feet automatically and remained upright, as stiff and pale as a corpse.

"There!" said Luckvrak. "I shall descend into the hall to put myself at the disposal of the honorable society.

Jumping down from the stage, he went to the back of the theater, whispered in the ear of a spectator, received a response in the same manner without the nearest neighbors being able to hear a single word of the exchange, turned toward the stage and fixed his gaze on Dolorosa.

Immediately, the young woman took a few steps forward and, adopting the gracious manner of a lady invited to dance, threw herself into a hectic waltz.

"Ladies and Gentlemen," Luckvrak cried then, "would you care to ask this gentleman, whom I do not have the honor of knowing, whether he asked me to make my subject waltz?"

"It's true!" said the spectator. "I'm amazed!"

The mage repeated this curious experiment several times, with different individuals, varying the instruction, and the success was complete every time. Without having any need to articulate a single word, without even moving his lips, he transmitted his thoughts to the young woman, who executed his mute instructions in a mechanical fashion.

As there were still skeptics in the hall, Luckvrak went further. He offered to hypnotize one of the spectators—any of them, provided that the person was nervous and impressionable.

Miss Dora Dutton, a dramatic artiste well known to and beloved by the public, happened to be in the hall. She met the requisite conditions and offered to serve as the operator's subject.

Luckvrak succeeded in repeating with her everything that he had done with Dolorosa. One facetious spectator having asked the mage to make her steal a watch from a member of the audience, Miss Dutton moved like an automaton toward an old and serious gentleman with a long white beard sitting in the first row, reached into his waistcoat pocket and lifted out his chronometer with a dexterity that would have done honor to a professional pickpocket.

There being no possible suspicion of the actress being in connivance with the mage, the auditorium resounded with frenzied cheers. The old man and a young man sitting beside him were the only ones not to applaud, although the former, leaning toward the other, said to him in a voice as soft as a breath: "No doubt is permissible, indeed. That man is a powerful hypnotist!"

Miss Dutton, liberated from the suggestion that weighed upon her, returned to her seat, blushing, in the midst of cries of "Bravo!" and the sympathetic laughter of the spectators. Then Luckvrak, calling for silence with a significant gesture, put on a capacious white robe thrown over the back of the armchair and went on: "Ladies and Gentlemen, we shall now pass on to demonstrations of magic, properly speaking."

He summoned Dolorosa, went with her to the bucket, and asked the nearest spectators to come and make sure that the bucket only contained pure water. The old man with the white beard and his young companion were among a number of people who came up on stage.

When they had all returned to their seats, Luckvrak said: "Dolorosa, make life appear out of nothing: populate the water in this bucket with little fish!"

He had scarcely finished speaking when the water began to seethe, and goldfish were seen wriggling therein.

Carried away by enthusiasm, the members of the audience stamped their feet and applauded frantically, while Luckvrak took off his white robe and replaced it on the back of the armchair. Meanwhile, far from joining in with the acclamation, the old man and the young man exchanged a rapid glance, and the elder said to the younger: "This time, we have him. Oh, the impostor!"

Luckvrak was triumphant. Modestly, he declared that they had not seen anything yet, but that he was about to do things that were even more extraordinary—and he was as good as his word.

The table, from which he had removed the cloth, began to rotate, and then rose several centimeters into the air. It fell back only to rise up again, without the operator appearing to touch it.

The latter then placed the put full of earth on the table, threw a grain of wheat into the pot and said: "Dolorosa, make the plant emerge from the seed!"

Instantly, a green stem pierced the earth, grew, thickened and produced an ear of wheat.

This time the enthusiasm of the hall knew no bounds, and deafening ovations were coming from all sides when the old man with the white beard was seen to stand up to his full height, tear off his beard—which was fake, and covered up another, shorter one of the sleekest black—threw off his overcoat and, metamorphosed and rejuvenated, singularly imposing, with his large green eyes flashing, leapt up on to the stage followed by his young companion.

It was Sâr Dubnotal and Rudolph!

"False psychagogue! Charlatan!" cried Sâr Dubnotal, in a thunderous voice. "So I can finally unmask you!"

These words, pronounced in Russian, were addressed to the mage, whose features revealed a singular mixture of shame and rage. With his arms folded across his broad chest, Sâr Dubnotal looked him up and down with sovereign arrogance, while Rudolph stared no less fixedly at Dolorosa—who, abruptly extracted from the hypnotic trance, was standing up in an attitude of extreme terror.

Luckvrak recoiled, and tried to flee; an imperious gesture from Sâr Dubnotal stopped him dead.

"If you take one more step, Tserpchikopf, I shall deliver you to the law! Ah, bloody hypnotist, whose crimes have remained unpunished, you didn't expect this epilogue, did you?"

Meanwhile, the spectators, nonplussed at first, were gradually getting excited again. Because none of them understood Russian, they had only heard meaningless words that made them think that the old man was out of his mind. Taking the mage's side, they clamored for the intervention of the policemen who were posted at the back of the auditorium, and the latter ran toward Sâr Dubnotal, who was universally considered to be a spoilsport.

Quite calm before the storm that he had provoked, the Grandmaster of Psychognosis did not want it to burst. "Constables," he said, this time in excellent English, "please excuse my intervention. This pretended yogi is nothing but a charlatan. He is worse still; a criminal; a murderer." Turning to the false mage, he added: "Dare to deny it, Tserpchikopf!"

Terrorized, Tserpchikopf remained silent.

In spite of this silence, which was equivalent to a confession, the policeman hesitated to apprehend him.

Sâr Dubnotal took advantage of that moment of indecision to take possession of the mage's white robe. He reached into it and took out a long tube and a rubber bulb that had been concealed within it. "I say nothing that I cannot prove," he went on. "Look at this apparatus, constables! It was with this that your pretended mage delivered the goldfish into the bucket. He squeezed the bulb as he leaned over the bucket, and the goldfish emerged from the tube and fell into the water."

The audience literally held its breath. Sâr Dubnotal continued: "As for that table, it's rigged. Secret mechanisms can move it around without the occult intervention of that woman, who has, believe me, never been a medium in her life. The phenomenon of the ear of wheat? Equally fake. Fixed in the thickness of the table, a steel sheath, moved by a mechanism and containing the stem, pierced the pot, and that's why everyone thought they saw the plant germinate."

Sâr Dubnotal fixed Tserpchikopf, who was trembling like a leaf, with his thunderous stare. "Science can only suffer from the unworthy actions of these mountebanks of occultism," he said, "and that is why I have a duty to unmask them publicly. I shall not stop there with Luckvrak, whose real name is Tserpchikopf, the probable author of a great may crimes and the certain author of an attempted murder committed in Marseilles against the person of my servant Naïni. Anyone who goes to the French consulate can inform himself as to that! Constables, I am Tserpchikopf's accuser, and I require his arrest."

At these words—which, by their tone of noble sincerity, compelled general conviction—the anger of the crowd, as changeable in its impulses as the sea, turned against the false mage and his companion. In spite of the policemen, the stage was attacked.

Rudolph and Sâr Dubnotal, taken by surprise, were only able to protect Azilis, whom they hurriedly dragged outside.

A few moments later, when Sâr Dubnotal—who had confided Azilis to Rudolph's care—arrived in a cab at Chelsea police station, where he intended to make his formal complaint against Tserpchikopf, he had the painful surprise of discovering that the scoundrel had succeeded in escaping on the way.

The policemen, who had had a great deal of trouble preventing the spectators from lynching him, had put him in a carriage, but the sergeant and the constable who were to accompany him had neglected to put him in handcuffs, and he profited from this omission to subject them to magnetic passes, whose effect was so powerful and so immediate that the two men, plunged into a hypnotic trance, found themselves at his mercy.

That escape was all the more regrettable because, in order to pick up the Slav's trail, Sâr Dubnotal had been obliged to use all the resources of his science.

At least, he still had Azilis. As we know, in a spirit of mercy, and also in order not to dishonor the name of Tréguilly, the Great Psychagogue had decided not to deliver the Comtesse into the hands of the law. He did not take the trouble to make the miserable creature confess to the poisoning of Naïni and the derailment of express 213.

She was embarked the following day on the *Derviche*, which was waiting, moored downstream of the Tower of London, in accordance with the Master's exact instructions, and which bore the guilty woman away to a place designated by the psychagogue for her expiation and repentance.

It still remained for him to find Tserpchikopf, the bloody hypnotist, and his enigmatic accomplice *Pion*. He resolved to do everything possible to achieve that. The reader will learn more in our next chapter about many vicissitudes, as tragic as they were mysterious, that the long campaign undertaken by the master psychagogue passed through.

SâR DUBNOTAL

Chaque fascicule contient un récit complet.

Aussitôt, un corps humain apparut, noirâtre, sur le fond pâle de l'écran de toile.

THE QUARTERED WOMAN OF MONTMARTRE

I. A Sensational Crime

On January 15, 1890, the popular and populous quarter of Montmartre was the theater of a monstrous crime that disturbed Paris and the whole of France. [16]

One morning, at about 6 a.m.—which is to say, before daybreak—a female bread-porter named Louise Plache, who was going to deliver merchandise to clients in the Avenue de Clichy, made a terrifying discovery.

She was about to ring the bell of number 357, as she did every morning, when the door to the vestibule opened wide in front of her. An individual emerged, bumping into the porter on the sidewalk, and fled along the avenue, which was dark and deserted at that hour.

At the time, the woman did not think of pursuing the individual, even though she had a presentiment that he had just done something nasty. Perhaps he was a burglar, perhaps something worse. Overcoming her anxiety, she went into the house to call the concierge and make her party to her fears.

The vestibule was unlit. She went on, feeling her way as far the lodge and rapped on the window, calling: "Madame Gosselin! Madame Gosselin!" The concierge did not reply.

---

[16] The term I have translated as "quartered woman," *écartelée*, is normally used in heraldry, with reference to coats of arms that are divided into quarters, rather than to a "quartered" body (as in "hanged, drawn and quartered") so there is a hint of *double entendre* about this title that does not translate.

Louise Plache renewed her appeals, but they had no more success than before. Alarmed by the persistent silence, she ran outside to look for a *sergent de ville*. A few houses further on, she encountered agent 1654 of the 18th arrondissement. She asked him to follow her quickly. So far as she was concerned, there was no longer any doubt that Madame Gosselin, the concierge at number 357, had been murdered by the man who had bumped into her on the sidewalk a few minutes earlier.

Agent 1654 was unconvinced by the pessimistic suppositions of Louise Plache, and secretly thought them fanciful. Even so, he ran all the way, and on reaching number 357 he took an electric torch from his pocket, switched it on, and then went resolutely into the vestibule, followed by the bread-porter.

Simultaneous cries of horror escaped from both their mouths. By the feeble light of the torch, they had just perceived, at the end of the corridor, a woman in a night-dress attached by the wrists to the cage of an elevator, while her feet were secured lower down to the columns of the shaft.

The cage, suspended about two meters above the ground, had, in ascending to that height, literally torn the young unfortunate woman apart. Her limbs, atrociously stretched, were partly detached from her trunk, releasing streams of blood.

Agent 1654 and Louise Plache had barely glanced at the cadaver. The spectacle was so horrible that, in spite of his courage, even the *sergent de ville* could not help recoiling to the doorway. There, he recovered his self-composure somewhat.

As the victim was showing no sign of life, it seemed that the best thing to do was to return to the station to alert his superiors.

Half an hour later, the Commissaire, his secretary and several of agent 1654's colleagues arrived on the scene. Until then, it was believed that the woman quartered by the lift was Madame Gosselin, the concierge. The woman in question, a childless widow, was the sole occupant of the lodge of number

357, and as she had not responded to the appeals of Louis Plache, the hypothesis appeared perfectly reasonable.

It was, however, mistaken.

The initial inquiries of the police established that the quartered woman was one of the house's tenants. For about six months, she had occupied a small apartment on the ground floor.

As for poor Madame Gosselin, she was also found dead, but at home. The murderer had got into her lodge through a window to the courtyard and had stabbed her. Her bloody body was lying on the rug beside the bed-alcove in which she slept.

The tenant's corpse was detached from the cage of the elevator, with great difficulty. It was observed that she had been gagged beforehand by the murderer. No trace was found on her body of any wounds other than those caused by the operation of the elevator. The unfortunate woman had evidently been torn apart while alive. That took to the horror to its limit.

The Sûreté, once alerted, opened an inquiry in collaboration with the Investigating Magistrate charged with the tragic affair. Certain details were obtained regarding the tenant.

Her name was Annie Stephenson—at least, that was the name under which she had rented a vacant apartment in number 357 six months before. She was apparently English, and had lost her parents shortly before. The latter having left her a tidy sum, she had come to France to live on its income. She was a pretty blonde, whose black clothes heightened her rosy beauty.

Like the majority of Englishwomen living abroad, she had rather independent ways, but did not depart in any way from the rules of decorum. Her fellow tenants knew nothing to her detriment and held her in high esteem, in spite of her slightly haughty reserve. She was not married and contented herself with the services of a housemaid who came to her home every morning.

Her apartment consisted of four rooms: a drawing-room overlooking the Avenue de Clichy, a bedroom overlooking the house's interior courtyard; a large bathroom; and a small kitchen, which also served as a dining room. The apartment communicated directly with the large vestibule by means of a door that opened almost directly opposite that of the lodge. In order to go into her apartment Miss Stephenson was obliged to go past the lodge, but she had no need to use either the staircase or the elevator.

The drawing-room window was only about a meter and a half above the sidewalk. The murderer might, therefore, have slipped into the Englishwoman's apartment that way—but the solid shutters with which the window was fitted showed no trace of effraction. By contrast, the bedroom window—which, let us repeat, overlooked the courtyard, was found ajar, as was the entrance door to the vestibule.

From these various observations, it was concluded that the murderer must have got into the house from the rear, after climbing over a low wall, which bordered the courtyard on that side. Once in the courtyard, he had got into the lodge through the window and had stabbed the unfortunate Madame Gosselin. Then, after returning to the courtyard, he had been able to force Miss Stephenson's bedroom window and take her by surprise as she slept, without any fear that the noise would wake up the concierge.

Up to that pint, the inquiry furnished quite satisfactory elements of information. The Magistrate and the Sûreté inspectors were thus able to explain how, after gagging his victim, the guilty party has been able to drag her into the vestibule, attach her to the cage and the framework of the elevator, and set the apparatus in motion in such a fashion as to quarter the unfortunate woman, without fear of any troublesome interruption.

It even explained how the wretch had succeeded in taking flight so easily. Doubtless he had profited from this passage through the lodge to pull the cord and open the large door to the vestibule; in that way, if he were surprised, he could be outside with a single bound.

But what was the motive for the crime?

Why those monstrous refinements of cruelty toward one of the victims?

That was the enigma that remained insoluble.

There had been no theft. No object of value was missing from the concierge's lodge, and all the evidence suggested that the murder had only killed that poor woman in order to carry out his hideous crime at his ease. There was nothing suggestive of a burglary in Annie's apartment either. The young woman's money and jewelry were found in her writing-desk; the murderer had opened the drawer without emptying it. On the other hand, no papers belonging to the Englishwoman were found—not a letter, not a card, not the slightest personal document. Nothing!

The strangest thing of all was that in the kitchen, where Annie was in the habit of taking her meals, the preparations for an excellent dinner for two people were found. On the table, two places were already made up with plates of cold meat, a stuffed partridge, pastries, two bottles of fine wine, one of them champagne, a bottle of Chartreuse and—a heat-rending detail—a superb bouquet of white roses!

Who should the diners have been? Annie for one, undoubtedly—but the other? Had the young woman been expecting someone the evening before, who had not been able to come?

The housemaid was questioned. She did not know anything about it—and she was amazed to see the table set. Until then she had considered Miss Stephenson to be a very sober person, who never ate so well and only drank milk or tea. On the other hand, it was her job, as housemaid, to do the shopping for her employer, and she had not bought any partridge, pastries, wine or chartreuse—nor had she bought the bouquet placed on the table.

An impenetrable mystery, therefore, surrounded the tragedy in Montmartre.

Was it a passionate vendetta, or the work of some mo-nomaniac?

To decide between the two hypotheses and find a solu-tion, it would have been necessary to check and complete the meager information obtained in relation to Miss Annie Ste-phenson, the victim, at any rate, of one of the most barbaric murders that the judiciary annals had recorded for a long time. However, the young woman had no relatives or friends in Par-is, and there was no means, in the absence of papers of any sort, of finding any that she might have had in England.

That same day, the bodies of the concierge and the En-glishwoman were transported to the morgue for autopsy, and the evening newspapers began to spread the news of the crime in special editions. At the same time, they announced that the agents of the law would proceed the following day to autopsy the victims—an operation whose outcome was anxiously awaited, for it was important to know for sure which of the two women had been the first to die, even though there was every reason to believe that it had been Madame Gosselin.

Essentially, the agents of the law wanted first of all to re-construct the scene of the crime, thus to follow the murderer, so to speak, step by step in his nocturnal comings and goings, and, by means of that imaginary and retrospective tracking, to try to discover the motive that had impelled him.

No one had any suspicion of the extraordinary events that were to unfold the following night, and would impede the action of the law completely.

II. The Amazing Adventure of the Night Watchman

Until recently, as our readers will know, it was customa-ry to exhibit the cadavers of people whose identity had not been established in a vast glass cage in the morgue; the crowd filed in front of that cage and made its observations, of which professional ears carefully took note in order to make use of them—as was often appropriate—in the interests of justice.

Although there was no certainty of the identity of Miss Annie Stephenson, however, the authorities decided to make an exception to the rule in her case, in order to avoid an influx of curiosity-seekers. In order to shield them from public curiosity, the morgue director had the bodies of the Englishwoman and the concierge deposited on a large slab in a refrigerated room. For decency's sake, if not for precautionary reasons, they were hidden beneath sheets, for they were frightful to behold—especially that of the unfortunate young woman whose limbs had been partly detached from her torso.

After the closure of the establishment, which took place at nightfall, the director and his employees retired. Leaving the night-watchman, Père Berton, installed in what he called his "guardroom." The man had long become used to the spectacle of death. He had, in fact, fought in the Crimean War and in Italy, taking part in the siege of Sebastopol and the battles of Magenta and Solferino, during which Russians, Englishmen, Italians, Austrians and Frenchmen had fallen in their thousands in glorious mêlées. The constant proximity of a few "maccabees," as he called the cadavers in the morgue, was, therefore, nothing to frighten him, and he congratulated himself for having found an employment for his old age that doubled the income of his modest military pension.[17]

He had always considered this employment as a sinecure. "Nothing to do but fold my arms and smoke my pipe!" he was accustomed to telling his friends—and he indulged in wordplay of a rather dubious sort with regard to the good character of his "inmates," who never importuned him with their recriminations or argued with him, sleeping soundly in their

---

[17] The siege of Sebastopol took place in 1854-55, and the battles of Magenta and Solferino were both fought in 1859. The fact that "*macchabées*" [maccabees] is a slang term for dead bodies in French presumably derives from the story of the seven Maccabee martyrs recounted in the Biblical apocrypha.

own icy room while he drowsed comfortably next to the nice fire that he took care to light in his "guardroom."

"Berton," the director had said to him, before leaving that evening, "I recommend that you maintain the most absolute discretion. All Paris has been upset by the news of the drama in the Avenue de Clichy, and a veritable army of reporters has already entered the campaign. Among these journalists, as you know, there are tactless individuals of the worst sort, who stick their noses in everywhere and too often meddle in things that don't concern them. Beware of them, Berton! I wouldn't be surprised if one of those fellows pays you a visit tonight. Today, I've already had to kick out a few today, who wanted to see the victims at any price and take photographs of them, in spite of the strict orders of the Prefecture—so you can expect them to return to the job, and must, in consequence, be prepared."

"What shall I do?" asked the old veteran.

"It's quite simple. Barricade the door carefully and don't open up for anyone. Once inside, those fellows are certainly capable of violating the prohibition and taking flashlight photographs in spite of your presence."

"I'd like to see them try!" muttered the ex-grenadier, putting on a terrible frown. "A thousand million bullets! Let them come—they'll get a nice welcome!"

"It's not a matter of renewing your exploits at Sebastopol, old man! Content yourself with playing the role of the besieged this time. Leave the journalists at the door, but don't tell them anything if they want to interview you."

"Understood, Mon Capitaine…I mean, Monsieur. I'll crouch in my den and leave the journalists outside."

Knowing that he could count on his night-watchman, the director did not labor the point, and Père Berton, left alone in the morgue, got ready to follow his superior's instructions to the letter. He carefully locked and bolted the door, made sure that the shutters over the windows were firmly closed, and then, having unhooked the muffled lantern that he used to make his rounds, retired to his "guardroom," where a good fire was burning.

"Umph!" he said, slumping voluptuously into a wicker armchair, with his feet on the andirons and his pipe in his mouth. "This is very nice. I'd certainly have liked a fire like this in the trenches at Sebastopol. It was bitter by night at the bottom of those damned snow-filled holes! We had no need of refrigeration apparatus to preserve the maccabees! Believe me they were frozen before they were dead! It wasn't soldiers who fell but men of ice!" And he started laughing noisily, delighted with the macabre comparison that he had just drawn.

Several hours went by in the greatest tranquility. Contrary to what the supervisor had feared, no reporters came knocking on the door of the morgue in the course of the evening. Reassured on this point, Père Berton through a few logs into the fireplace and got ready to take a nap. His "inmates" has no need of him, he assumed, and he was not obliged to spend the entire night under arms. That had been necessary, of course, in 1855 or 1859, when the Russians and Austrians had taken pleasure in attacking the French lines under cover of darkness. A thousand million bullets! Woe betide the sentinel who fell asleep! If the cold didn't freeze him alive, he would have been woken up by some huge devil of a Slav or a Teuton, who would have reminded him of his duty, without saying a word, with a single thrust of a bayonet.

Here, though, Père Berton was safe. At least, that was what he firmly believed, and, once he had wrapped himself up in an old cape—a relic of his campaigns—it did not take him long to close his eyes and start snoring like an organ-pipe.

It might have been 1 a.m., and the watchman was sleeping like a baby, when a suspicious noise coming from the refrigerated room snatched him out of his rule-breaking slumber. One might have thought that the noise had been made by a corpse falling to the ground.

"What's that?" he asked himself, rubbing his eyes. "Am I dreaming, or has one of my inmates not felt secure on the slab and wanted to try out the floor?"

177

He cocked an ear and, still hearing the noise in the neighboring room without being able to make out exactly what it was, thought at first that the director's anticipation had been realized, and that an audacious journalist had taken advantage of his nap to force an entry into the morgue.

"A thousand million bullets!" he muttered, arming himself with a cudgel and his lantern. "If the journalists have taken the position by surprise, it's a matter of taking it back by force. Come on, grenadiers! Up and at 'em!"

Nevertheless, Père Berton thought it best to be prudent before engaging in hostilities. He was a good 65 years old and although he was singularly spry and determined for his age, he might perhaps have been the underdog in a hand-to-hand combat with a young and vigorous adversary. Hiding the light of his lantern under his cape, he gently cracked open the door of his room, which opened into a corridor. From there he darted a rapid glance at the entrance door. To his great surprise, he observed that it was shut. Had he been mistaken? Had no one come into the morgue?

The same noise, however, was still audible in the refrigerated room. One might have thought that someone was inspecting the cadavers, turning them over on their slabs.

Who was that sinister visitor? And how could he have got into the building?

In spite of his bravery, Père Berton began to be a little bit frightened. This was a puzzle to which he could not find the key, unless...

Ah! Yes, damn it, that's it! Why didn't I think of it sooner!

Often, in cold weather, in the middle of the night, legions of water-rats climbed out of the Seine and rushed to attack the morgue, attracted by the odor of the corpses. Père Berton had been obliged to repel assaults of that kind on more than one occasion. The rodents were so audacious that he had come to dread that he might not be able to put them to flight on his own, and he had asked the supervisor several times if he might have the collaboration of a cat or a fox-terrier—but the head of the establishment thought that the presence of a domestic animal in that funereal residence might perhaps give rise to criticism, justified or otherwise, and he had not wanted to grant the old warden's request. The latter, therefore, had nothing but his stick with which to defend himself against the rodents. That was little enough, given the number, boldness and ferocity of the assailants, driven to the hunt by hunger—but Père Bertron had seen many others. He always fell upon the enemy valiantly, and dispersed the vermin with cudgel-blows, kicks and thumps.

"Just you wait, you brigands!" he cried, hurling himself toward the door of the refrigerated room "I'll teach you to respect my inmates!"

He shoved the door open and lifted up his lantern to illuminate the room. Imagine how amazed and alarmed he was when, instead of a horde of rats, he saw a man in front of him, also carrying a hooded lantern and dragging a large canvas sack. So far as Père Breton could tell, in his disturbed state, the man was tall and broad-shouldered, dressed in a long black overcoat and a soft, broad-brimmed hat akin to a sombrero.

The rim of the sombrero was pulled down in front over a black velvet mask, which hid the man's face, only allowing the sight, through the eyeholes, of two gleaming quasi-feline pupils.

The strange nocturnal visitor was standing beside the slab on which the sad remains of Madame Gosselin and Annie Stephenson had been laid. On seeing the night-watchman come in, he turned round abruptly, and fixed Berton with a savage stare, which revealed even more anger than disappointment.

The night-watchman observed that one of the two bodies had fallen on to the floor—but that was nearly all he was able to observe, for he was immediately gripped by an indefinable anxiety: a sort of giddiness, which became more intense the longer he looked at the individual standing in front of him. That man's two flamboyant pupils literally fascinated him; from then on he almost lost consciousness of what was hap-

179

pening, and sensed his will-power melting and slipping away...

He ought to have seized the intruder by the collar, or at least called for help, but, strangely enough, not a sound emerged from his throat and he felt incapable of taking a step forward. His club and his lantern slipped from his hands and rolled on the ground.

The masked man's sardonic laughter accompanied the commencement of his defeat. "Who are you?" he asked Berton, afterwards.

The latter immediately recovered the power of speech, but it was not to shout threats or imprecations, as one might have imagined. Meekly, he replied: "I'm the night-watchman, Monsieur."

"What are you doing in this room? Why have you disturbed me?"

"My duty..."

"Eh!" said the unknown. "I laugh at you duty! Come here."

Drawn and pale, Berton went toward the masked man with the jerky gait of an automaton.

"I could made you regret your indiscretion bitterly," the enigmatic individual went on, his eyes continuing to emit rapid flashes through the holes of the mask, "but I'll take pity on your great age and content myself with obliging you to give me a hand." He pointed to the cadaver that had fallen on the floor. "That's the corpse of Miss Annie Stephenson, isn't it?" he asked.

"Yes," said the ex-grenadier, mechanically.

"Well, you're going to help me put it in this sack."

"Why?"

"No questions," said the unknown man, brutally, fixing his fascinating gaze upon the poor old man. "Obey me, or I'll be forced to resort to other methods."

The hero of Sebastopol and Solferino did not understand what was happening to him. In any other circumstances, he would have leapt at the throat of such a rogue and would rather have chopped him into little pieces than obey him—but he no longer felt that he was the same man. Since those eyes had taken him captive with the fire of their sharp gaze, it was as if all his energy had evaporated. He could not even think of rebelling, and murmured humbly: "I'm at your disposal, Monsieur."

Again the masked individual laughed in a sinister manner. "Very well! But let's make haste, for time's pressing." Having said that, he crouched down and, without taking his eyes off Berton, ordered him to put the unfortunate Annie's corpse into the sack, which he was holding open.

The night-watchman, completely subjugated by the unknown man's mysterious ascendancy, carried out the order without protest.

"Good!" said the man in the mask. "Tie up the sack now, then help me to load it on to my shoulders."

Berton hoisted the funereal parcel on to his interlocutor's robust shoulders. The latter did not give way under the heavy burden.

"Old man," that individual went on, "What's happened here remains between us, eh? Go and open the front door for me, for it's time to leave. Afterwards, close the door carefully, and the shutters on the rear window, through which I got in. Finally, return to the guard-room and don't budge again until tomorrow morning."

"Yes, Monsieur," the old watchman replied, with stupefying docility.

Immediately, the man headed for the door, which Berton had just opened by a crack. Before venturing outside, he started a suspicious glance through the crack. There was no one on the Pont Notre-Dame, where—as everyone knows—the morgue is situated. The nocturnal silence was only troubled by the distant rumble of an approaching fiacre.

The man went out under the establishment's peristyle and, hiding in the dense shadow of a column without setting down his burden, signaled to the watchman to go away. Immediately, Berton closed, locked and bolted the door, then secured the shutters on the window forced by the astonishing burglar, and went back to his guard-room.

He was just in time. A bizarre numbness overwhelmed the old man's limbs. His head became as heavy as a lump of lead and he tottered like a drunk. He experienced an irresistible desire to sleep, and was scarcely seated in his armchair than he fell into a profound slumber.

How long would that strange lethargy have lasted? Several more hours, perhaps—but a loud drumming that suddenly sounded on the main door woke him up with a start. It was broad daylight in the guard-room.

Alarmed, Berton came to his feet in a single movement, cast a stupefied glance around him, and saw that the hands of the wall-clock stood at 8 a.m.

What had come over him, to make him sleep like a log and forget that the employees of the establishment started work at 7:30 a.m.? What would Monsieur le Directeur—who often presented himself at the same time as the staff and never much later—think of him?

The most bizarre thing about the old watchman's adventure was that he retained no memory of it. He had a vague recollection of a certain masked individual whose eyes shone like furnaces, but he thought that it was merely the residue of some frightful nightmare.

"One might think that I'd been on the spree, damn it!" he grumbled, hastening to go turn the key of the exterior door and draw the bolts. "What will they think of me?"

He did not have to wait long to find out.

The four or five employees of the morgue, and the director himself, had been languishing outside for half an hour, and were beginning to lose patience. They had been knocking at the door and the window-shutters, and shouting for Berton as loudly as they could, but Berton had shown no sign of life. Had he died suddenly at his post? At his age, that was certainly possible, and the exceedingly anxious director had ended up sending for a locksmith, who had just arrived with the tools necessary to force the closed door. He was about to set to work when Berton's sudden awakening saved him the trouble. The door opened abruptly, and the old watchman appeared, pale and trembling, to stare at the crowd that was already assembled under the peristyle.

As one can imagine, all these comings and goings, all the loud shouting and all the blows struck upon the door and the shutters had not failed to attract the attention of passers-by, and, as there is never any shortage of jokers I such assemblies, witty gibes were heard, which Père Berton would have been pleased to make himself in ordinary circumstances.

"Bah!" said one. "The maccabees have barricaded themselves in so that they can get a little peace!"

"No," replied another, "you're wrong, friend—the morgue has closed because of a bereavement."

And everyone laughed, except for the director, who was extremely annoyed by the misadventure. So, when he saw Berton safe and sound, he started abusing him. "Well, have you gone deaf or mad? I'd like to know why you didn't come to open up for us right away? We've been kicking our heels outside the door for half an hour! It's shameful!"

Père Berton did not know what to say. "Forgive me, Monsieur le Directeur," he stammered. "I've been taken ill, I think. I must have fainted…"

"Get away with you! Does an old veteran like you get taken ill like a little girl?"

"A thousand million bullets, no! But with respect, Monsieur…"

"Come on, tell us the truth! You've had too much to drink, haven't you?"

At this insinuation by his boss, the old man took on such an expression of outraged dignity that laughter broke out again on all sides.

"Too much to drink? Me?"

"Yes, you, damn it!"

"I never drink, Monsieur."

"What, then?"

"What do you want me to say, since I don't have the slightest understanding of what has happened to me?"

The old man's going soft in the head, the director thought, privately. "That's all right," he said, dryly. "Let's not say anything more about it. But make sure that it doesn't happen again, Père Breton, or I'll be obliged to let you go." And he went into the morgue, preceded by the old watchman, who was exceedingly crestfallen, and followed by the employees, who were laughing up their sleeves.

The director certainly had no inkling of the discomfiture that awaited him in the refrigerated room, to which he went without further delay in order to begin preparations, with his staff, for the autopsy of the bodies of Annie Stephenson and the concierge. On perceiving the disappearance of the former cadaver, the director could not suppress an exclamation.

"Berton! Berton!" he shouted. "In the name of Heaven, what happened last night? Answer me! Tell us the truth, whatever it might be! I want to know what has become of that cadaver!"

In response to this order from his superior, it seemed that a glimmer of light began to dawn in the watchman's memory. Shards of memory came back to him, which, when brought together, ended up forming an almost-complete weave—although the fabric still had many holes in it. When Berton had filled in the lacunae, however, his story was too fantastic to be credited by the director, so the latter soon formed the conviction that the watchman had either lost his mind or was lying brazenly.

At any rate, Miss Stephenson's corpse had vanished. It could not have flown away on its own, so someone must have broken into the morgue. Besides, the watchman did not deny that—what was inadmissible was that he had not even tried to stop that break-in and the bold theft that had followed it,

"I repeat, Monsieur," stammered Berton, "that it was as if the individual's gaze turned me to stone."

"Idiot!" the director retorted, dryly. "Someone must alert the police immediately. I've had enough of your nonsense,

Berton! Do you really think that you can get away with this? Well, we'll see!"

A crowd had gathered in the public hall. Its members could not guess the reason for the argument, but the director's outbursts, the alarm of the staff and the unusual hustle and bustle was sufficient indication that something serious had occurred, and they were hoping to find out what it was. A few words pronounced by an employee put the curious on the right track. A body had disappeared! The night-watchman was suspected of complicity in the macabre theft, organized and perpetrated by unknown malefactors with an unknown purpose.

The rumor had scarcely got started when official confirmation of a sort was obtained. Forgetting the presence of the idlers, the director of the morgue, who had accompanied the employee charged with alerting the police to the door, while giving him instructions, turned round toward Berton and shouted, in a paroxysm of over-excitement: "Where is that body? I want to know where it is. Oh, you'll have to explain yourself, my good man, and it won't be sufficient to allege, as you just have, that the malefactor who got into the morgue last night petrified you!"

The last words had scarcely been pronounced than a man detached himself from the front row of the crowd. "I beg your pardon, Monsieur le Directeur," he said, as he came forward, "but would you permit me to say a few words to you?"

The director turned on his heels and looked at the man who had just spoken to him in a hostile fashion. He was all set to snap at him angrily, and opened his mouth to do exactly that, but the nobility of his interlocutor's features, his gravity, his distinction, and perhaps also the originality of his costume—which comprised a simple black frock-coat, white trousers and a Hindu turban—modified his attitude. He bowed and said politely: "Speak, Monsieur—I'm listening."

"I don't know Monsieur Berton," the stranger said, "and I have no particular reason to interest myself in him. It seems to me, however, that you're mistaken in holding him responsible for the disappearance of one of the cadavers consigned to his care. The story that he has told you is an exact expression of the truth."

"You know the truth, then?"

"Yes," said the stranger, gravely. "I've guessed it, at least in part, from the words that you spoke just now. Once again, Berton must be absolved of all blame."

"Why?"

"Because he has been hypnotized."

III. Sâr Dubnotal at the Crime Scene

The reader will have understood that the man in the turban was none other than Sâr Dubnotal, the Great Psychagogue. How did he happen to be on the Pont Notre-Dame at that precise moment?

Before replying to that question, it is necessary for us to go back in time a little way, for everything in the astonishing chain of events in which that extraordinary man was about to become involved was connected, and it was not chance alone that had brought him to the morgue that morning.

At the time when our story began, the Master was living in Paris under his pseudonym, Severus el Tebib. An affair of the greatest importance had obliged him to quit the Breton seaside resort of Trez-Hir, where he spent his leisure time, and take up residence in the Champs-Elysées, in a superb building that he had acquired there.

As a consequence of extremely curious circumstances, of which mention has been made in previous chapters, Sâr Dubnotal had learned of the existence of a gang of thieves and cutthroats called the Chessmen,[18] whose leader, or King, was a fake Russian boyar by the name of Tserpchikopf.

---

[18] I would normally have left *Bande des Echecs* [Gang of Chessmen] in French, as it is a proper name, but that would have created a problem with respect to the designation of the

Tserpchikopf had succeeded in liberating his accomplice, Azilis de Tréguilly—who had been arrested by Sâr Dubnotal following the double murder of her father-in-law and husband, which she had committed—but the Great Psychagogue had picked up the trail of the fugitives in London, where one of them was posing as a celebrated yogi, or Hindu mage, and the other as his assistant. Azilis had been captured, but Tserpchikopf had succeeded in escaping, and it was not long afterwards that the Great Psychagogue had acquired the certainty that the blackguard was the head of the Chessmen.

In addition to its King—who was, as we have said, Tserpchikopf—that gang comprised a Queen, two Fools, or lieutenants, two Knights, or emissaries, and Pawns, or auxiliaries numbered one to eight. They had lairs, called Castles, including the White Castle, the Blue Castle and the Red Castle. The gang's name—the Chessmen—as well as the other terms that it borrowed from the game dear to Palamedes,[19] was explained by the pretension it had to hold the police in check. The rallying cry of these bandits was, in fact, "Check and mate!" and the members of the association had the em-

---

pieces, the names of which I have translated from now on into English, even though there are no "*Fous*" [Fools, or jesters] in English chess sets (which prefer Bishops). The policy generates one minor difficulty with respect to the colored *Tours* [Castles], when one such designation is subsequently used as a house name, in which context it seemed more appropriate to leave it in French. The *Pion* of Part II was evidently revealed in the missing episode to be merely one of eight Pawns.

[19] The origins of chess are unknown, but the auctioneer James Christie (1730-1803) invented a story that it was invented by the Greek hero Palamedes to while away the time during the siege of Troy. Legend had credited Palamedes with various other inventions, but he is not featured in Homer because he had already been killed (thanks to the treachery of his jealous rival Odysseus) before the action of the *Iliad* begins.

blems of their titles tattooed on their right arms: King, Queen, Fool, Knight and Pawn.

Otto, Frank and Fréjus, the Master's three secret agents, had received orders to search for Tserpchikopf. With the aid of a few clues that the Master had transmitted to them, they had been fortunate enough to discover one of the bandits, Gustave Panloude, known as Pawn One. When Panloude went to Tunis, the three investigators thought that he was going to meet the King and had followed him, in the hope of killing two birds with one stone. Alerted telegraphically, Sâr Dubnotal had followed the, one day behind, with his young disciple Rudolph and one of his best mediums, the Italian woman Annunciata Gianetti.

Gustave Panloude had been captured by the Master in person, but once again, the ungraspable Tserpchikopf had succeeded in fleeing, after having magnetized Otto, Frank and Fréjus and attempted to have Sâr Dubnotal killed by the three unfortunates, who had become passive instruments of his will.[20]

The following day, seeing that there was nothing left for them to do in Tunis, the Master Psychagogue and his followers had re-embarked for Marseilles, taking Gustave Panloude with them. Sâr Dubnotal had taken care to hypnotize his captive, from whom he counted on extracting precious information about the Chessmen and their King, but an unexpected complication disrupted this plan and forced the Great Psychagogue to turn his attention away from Tserpchikopf much sooner than he had expected.

On the eve of the disappearance of Annie Stephenson's cadaver, on the same day as the drama in the Avenue de Clichy, at about 11 a.m.—which is to say, before the evening papers had reported the new atrocity—a man had presented

---

[20] This is a summary of the events of *La Piste astrale* [The Astral Trail], which takes place between the previous chapter and this chapter, of which no copy could be located.

himself at the house in the Champs-Elysées and asked to see Fréjus, the Master's French sleuth, urgently.

That man was an inspector in the Parisian Sûreté. Closely linked to Fréjus in the days when the latter had belonged to the famous detective brigade, he had never entirely lost contact with him. The two friends had continued to correspond; Topinard—as the inspector was called—knew why Fréjus had handed in his resignation and why he had entered Sâr Dubnotal's employment. They both had the greatest confidence in one another.

Several times before, Topinard had come to find his former colleague in order to ask for his help in some difficult inquiry. With the authorization of his master, Fréjus—and sometimes Frank and Otto too—had thus had occasion to lend a hand to the secret police of Paris. What was more, Sâr Dubnotal had occasionally got involved, whereupon the murkiest, most enigmatic and most disconcerting cases had not been long delayed in becoming as clear as daylight. With the sole aim of making himself useful to society and serving the ends of justice, the Master never hesitated to enter the lists.

As soon as Topinard was introduced to Fréjus' presence he threw his arms around him. "Ah, you old rogue," he said, "what luck that you're free! But are you, really?"

"That depends, Fréjus replied, shaking his comrade's hand. "What is it about?"

"An astounding affair, old friend! A crime such as has Paris has probably never seen before, which is destined to go down in posterity." With the enthusiasm of a professional besotted with his trade, the inspector swiftly gave Fréjus the details of the discovery of the double tragedy in Montmartre. "Can you imagine," he concluded, "that the chief of the Sûreté has given me the special responsibility of finding the guilty party? This morning, immediately after being alerted, my boss and I went to the crime scene. We've made a few interesting observations, and we're due to go back out there this afternoon—but everything leads me to believe that this affair will be very difficult to disentangle, and I thought of asking for your help."

"You're very kind," said Fréjus, smiling. "I accept, on one condition—which is that my master has no objection."

"Go and ask him, and…"

"And?"

"If possible, interest him in the affair. When he's involved, everything goes as smoothly as if it were on wheels."

"You never said a truer word, old Top, for the Master knows no obstacles—the ideal pneumatic tire, eh? Except, you see, that he's already on the track of a sort of Slav who is all past and present criminals rolled into one, and I fear that he'll be reluctant to undertake another investigation."

"Talk to him anyway," said the inspector. "We'll soon see."

To Topinard's extreme satisfaction, Fréjus reported a favorable result. "The Master's on board," he said. "I repeated your story, which didn't leave him indifferent. He's already given orders in this regard, and it isn't me alone but the entire brigade that is setting off on campaign. Except that the Master is insistent on witnessing this afternoon's judiciary procedures, and it's necessary that the head of the Sûreté and the Investigating Magistrate raise no objection to his presence."

"My boss," Topinard said, "is too well aware of the services that yours has already rendered us not to accept his assistance gratefully. I'll let him know. As for the Investigating Magistrate, there's no need to take him into our confidence; we'll pass you and your boss off as inspectors."

On that, the two friends separated, having arranged a rendezvous at the crime scene for half past one.

Sâr Dubnotal dressed a little less characteristically than he usually did, and, solely accompanied by Fréjus, went to number 357, Avenue de Clichy, at the appointed time. Topinard was waiting for them. He introduced the Great Psychagogue to the head of the Sûreté, who welcomed him very warmly, but did not seek to conceal the difficulties of the enterprise.

"I've been told that your method of investigation is somewhat supernatural," he said, "and I know that you have often succeeded in cases where my best sleuths have been stumped...but that's all right by me; I'm curious to see how you'll tackle the affair this time."

Sâr Dubnotal contented himself with replying that he would leave the other gentlemen to open the inquiry and would only intervene if they were unsuccessful. Effectively, he left the Investigating Magistrate and the policemen to do their jobs, made no verbal observations, and only took a few notes. At the end of the session, the officers of the law were little further forward than before. To tell the truth, they were not expecting the inquiry to make any considerable progress until the autopsy of the two cadavers had allowed them to verify their initial deductions.

"Well, Monsieur Severus?" asked the head of the Sûreté. "What do you think of it all?"

"Not a great deal, as yet," Sâr Dubnotal replied, simply. "It seems to me, however, that you're expecting too much of the autopsy."

"What do you mean?"

"In my opinion, the autopsy, like the reconstitution of the crime scene, won't take you a single step closer to the truth. As the murder of the concierge was surely only a precautionary measure taken by the murderer to get rid of an inconvenient witness, I don't see why it's necessary to inflict the posthumous torture of dissection on the unfortunate woman's body. If I were in your shoes, I'd have recourse to a very different method of information."

"Which consists of...?"

Sâr Dubnotal smiled and avoided the question. "For the time being, let's stick to the observations we've just made. One thing seems certain to me, and that is that the murderer knew Annie Stephenson—if that is actually the victim's name."

"What leads you to doubt it?" asked the head of the Sûreté.

Again, the Master Psychagogue avoided answering. "I'll go further," he said. "I believe that Miss Stephenson—let's continue to call her by that name until we're better informed—was waiting yesterday evening for the visit of the man who killed her, that the dinner preparations were made with him in mind, and that the man did not enter the house, as you suppose, at the back of the courtyard but through the front window that opens on to the avenue, with the consent and help of his victim. I will add that it must have happened very late in the evening, after the closure of the vestibule door, and, of course, without the knowledge of the concierge and the tenants…"

"What!" exclaimed the head of the Sûreté. "You think that an honorable young person like Miss Stephenson would not be afraid to admit anyone whatsoever into her home, at such an hour and in such scabrous circumstances?"

"I didn't say 'anyone whatsoever.' " the Great Psychagogue remarked. "I believe that I said, on the contrary, that the victim knew the murderer."

"Mere supposition!" objected the policeman, unable to help himself.

"Undoubtedly, but one that is valuable, for it gives us the key to the mystery."

"The key to the mystery?"

"Why yes, my dear Monsieur! I reject absolutely the hypothesis of a vulgar crime motivated by theft. No more can I believe in a crime of passion. My conviction is that we're in the presence of a vengeance slaked in particularly atrocious circumstances by someone known to Miss Stephenson—an acquaintance that no one ever saw at number 357, and whom the young woman did not want to receive in her home overtly, whether because she feared malicious gossip or because the visitor had expressed his own desire to pass unnoticed."

"And it's on that basis that you will support the personal inquiry that you will conduct in parallel to ours, Monsieur Severus?"

The Master Psychagogue nodded his head. "It is on that basis...but let's see, Monsieur le Chef de la Sûreté, what time will the autopsy be carried out tomorrow morning?"

"Between 8 and 8:30 a.m."

"May I be present, even though I don't expect anything much to come of it?"

"Certainly."

"Thank you," said Sâr Dubnotal. "I'll be there on time."

The Great Psychagogue had kept his word—which explains, with nothing further to add, his presence in the funereal establishment at such an early hour and the intervention that had ensued.

IV. Where is the Cadaver?

Sâr Dubnotal's declaration had produced a sharp movement of curiosity in the crowd, and the director himself was unable to suppress a shudder.

"Hypnotized?" he exclaimed. "You think that someone hypnotized Berton?"

"I'm sure of it," replied the Master, who was accompanied by Rudolph and Fréjus.

"That's amazing!" murmured the director. "Great God what a business! What will the Magistrate and the medical examiners think of me?"

"Have those gentlemen not arrived yet?" asked the Master.

"No, but they won't be long. Look, there are their carriages now, if I'm not mistaken."

Indeed, two fiacres had just stopped in front of the morgue. The head of the Sûreté, Inspector Topinard, the Investigating Magistrate and two other individuals—who were the medical examiners charged with carrying out the autopsy—rapidly got out.

193

The poor director was so embarrassed that Sâr Dubnotal took pity on him. "I came to attend to autopsy," he said. "Let me explain the incident to these gentlemen, and I'll guarantee that none of them will think of criticizing your conduct."

So saying, the Master Psychagogue went to the head of the Sûreté and told him about the disappearance if Annie Stephenson's body.

"That's all we needed!" said the policeman, overwhelmed by bewilderment. "Wasn't this business murky enough already? How shall we ever sort it out?"

"We shall sort it out with patience, and by redoubling our activity," affirmed Sâr Dubnotal.

"Possibly—but Paris will be stupefied when the news gets around. Was Père Breton telling the truth? Was he really unable to oppose the theft of the body?"

"There can be no doubt about that," Sâr Dubnotal replied. "Besides, there's nothing easier than verifying his assertions."

"Hmm! Nothing easier..."

"Let's go into the morgue," said the Master. "Trust me—the demonstration will be all the more convincing if I make it before your eyes and those of the Investigating Magistrate and the medical examiners."

The entire company went inside the establishment, leaving the idlers behind in the public hall. Then Sâr Dubnotal summoned Père Breton, who was still distraught about his misadventure. Without any preamble, he directed the magnetic flame that sprang from his own eyes into the night-watchman's, and said to him abruptly: "Berton, you're going to go to sleep and relive the scene of the theft."

Already plunged into the second state, as initiates call it—which is to say, into a hypno-somnambulistic trance—the old watchman was no longer his own man. He was dispossessed of his will and ready to submit to that of the operator who wanted to make him repeat all the events and actions of which the morgue had been the theater during the night.

"There!" Sâr Dubnotal went on. "You've returned to the moment of the drama. Go on!"

What happened then was prodigious. Like an automaton, Père Breton set off toward the guard-room, sat down in his armchair, and seemed to lapse into a sound sleep. Suddenly, he stood up, cocked an ear, armed himself with his cudgel and his lantern, went back into the corridor, darted a prudent glance toward the entrance door and advanced on tiptoe toward the refrigerated room. In brief, he reproduced all his movements of the previous night exactly.

He did not content himself with behaving in the same fashion; he repeated the same words. He recommenced the same monologue about the rats that invaded the morgue in cold weather and attacked he cadavers, about asking the supervisor for a cat or a dog and being refused. By way of conclusion, he precipitated himself into the refrigerated room, appeared suddenly to see the man in the mask again, and mimed the entire scene of the encounter so marvelously that the Investigating Magistrate, the head of the Sûreté and the medical examiners were completely satisfied.

"There's no doubt about it—Berton is telling the truth," the director himself conceded.

"I'm convinced too," said the head of the Sûreté. "Unfortunately, we're no further forward; we have no more idea than we had before why the malefactor got in here and stole the cadaver, or what he did with it."

"We shall try to elucidate that matter," said Sâr Dubnotal, after having released Berton from his dangerous hypnotic trance. "In any case, Messieurs you are obliged to renounce the autopsy of Miss Stephenson's body…"

"And to stamp our feet on the spot," groaned the head of the Sûreté.

"Not at all—let's get moving!" said Sâr Dubnotal, in a tone that was perhaps not devoid of irony. "Let's pick up the trail—we must recover the stolen body, at all costs."

"That's easy to say," said the policeman, resentfully.

Sâr Dubnotal did not persist, and took his leave, taking Rudolph and Fréjus with him. The three men headed for the Champs-Elysées.

That same evening, a gigantic question mark was displayed in all the newspapers, whose successive editions were snatched by a crowd avid for details.

Where is the body? Find Annie's body!

Was there a connection between the two successive outrages to which the young Englishwoman had been the victim? Could the frightful crime in Montmartre and the unspeakable profanation of the morgue be attributed to the same malefactor? The entire press wanted to know.

For long days, the newspapers did not entertain their readers, so to speak, with anything but the mysterious affair.

The inquiries made by the agents of the law regarding Annie Stephenson's past made no progress. In England, it had been impossible to discover the slightest clue to assist in clarifying that past. Numerous families bore the name of Stephenson, but none of them was morning the disappearance of one of its members. The fact that the victim had represented herself as an orphan and had come to settle in France did not necessarily mean that she had no relatives in her country of origin, and it was strange that not a single blood relation, friend or former acquaintance of Annie Stephenson came forward to the English authorities to furnish information about the young woman.

Given the material impossibility of verifying her identity, all suppositions were permissible, and people ended up believing that the young Englishwoman had not told the truth about herself to her landlord and her neighbors. Perhaps she had thought it necessary to conceal herself under an assumed name, and was not really called Annie Stephenson. If that were the case, the policemen's task became singularly arduous.

Since the cadaver's disappearance, however, Sâr Dubnotal's hypothesis imputing the crime to an acquaintance of Miss Stephenson's had gained acceptance. Evidently, someone had had an interest in getting rid of the young woman. The somber enigma of the morgue remained to be elucidated, to be sure, but had not the murderer, by stealing the body, wanted to prevent it being identified? That was quite probable. While the identity of a murder victim remains unknown, there is every chance that the guilty party will escape justice.

None of that, however, explained why Miss Stephenson's murder had been committed with such savagery. That was something that confounded the finest sleuths in the Sûreté, a disconcerting fact that stood in contradiction to every hypothesis on which they were tempted to settle. If the murderer had been determined to prevent the identification of the cadaver, why had he amused himself—if that was the right word—by inflicting that barbaric torture on his victim? Why had he not simply stabbed her, as he had done with Madame Gosselin, and then disfigured the body by slashing the face? He could even have cut off the head and taken it with him. That would have been easier than going to the morgue to steal the entire cadaver.

Truly, no one knew what to think, and public opinion, stirred up by the atrocity of the crime and excited by the succession of mysteries, complained bitterly about what it called the culpable incapacity of the police. The reproach was undeserved, though; the police had done and were continuing to do their duty.

The bed of the Seine had been dragged from the Pont Notre-Dame to the Auteuil viaduct; if the cadaver had been thrown into the river, as some people supposed, the patient and repeated soundings would certainly have discovered it. Such was not the case, and it was necessary to conclude that the Vampire of the Morgue—as the macabre abductor was dubbed—had not got rid of his burden by throwing it in the water.

Throughout Paris, there was horror and terror in every heart. Certain details were recalled that brought tears to the most unfeeling eyes. Where had the bouquet of white roses found in Annie Stephenson's dining room come from? What beloved and spoiled guest had the poor young woman been expecting to welcome on the very eve of her terrible death?

The inspectors of the Sûreté established definitely that the Englishwoman had bought the wines, the Chartreuse, the stuffed partridge and the various *hors-d'oeuvres* that had made up the menu of the feast in person, for they had found the addresses of the suppliers, who remembered having sold all those excellent things to a young woman whose description exactly matched that of the dead woman.

On the other hand, it was impossible to discover the source of the virginal bouquet, in order to ascertain whether Annie Stephenson had bought it herself, or whether someone else had given it to her. One newspaper having suggested that the bouquet might have been brought to the victim by the murderer, there was not a fiancée in Paris who did not nurture, deep down, frightful apprehensions when she welcomed the elect of her heart. Fear is contagious, and many women in love could already see themselves hanging from the cage of an imaginary elevator!

V. The Accursed Villa

Meanwhile, by virtue of an unexpected change of mind that left his entourage greatly astonished and intrigued, Sâr Dubnotal no longer seemed prepared to take more than a mediocre interest in the extraordinary case.

Several times, Inspector Topinard presented himself at the house to ask Fréjus how the Master's enquires were going, and the response never varied.

"I don't understand it at all," Fréjus said. "One might think that he had completely lost interest in his investigation. My comrades and I don't know what to make of it, or why, instead of launching us in pursuit of the man in the mask, he's put us back on the trail of Tserpchikopf."

"Really?"

"Yes. You know, Top, old chap. The boss gets ideas like that. One hardly ever knows what's he's really thinking."

The fact is that Sâr Dubnotal was no longer occupied, at least apparently, with anything but the Chessmen. Gustave Panloude, having been subjected to preliminary hypnosis, had furnished him with some curious indications. He had learned by that means that the gang, cleverly organized for burglaries, armed robberies, kidnappings, blackmail and forgery, had recently lost more than one member. Imprudent moves, sometimes committed by a Fool and sometimes by a Pawn, had cost it dear, and, thanks to these imprudent moves, the Sûreté had been able to discover the gang's three lairs, one by one: the White, Red and Black Castles. The inspectors, however, thought that they were only dealing with simple thieves, and did not even suspect the existence of such an interesting organization. The Fools, Knights and Pawns caught red-handed in murder or theft never betrayed their accomplices. Subservient to the will of their King, who was a powerful hypnotist, they only made insignificant admissions. The Chessmen had been gradually destroyed, without his existence being divulged, nor that of the Queen. Neither of them was in the hands of the authorities.

Gustave Panloude also explained to Sâr Dubnotal that, after the arrest of Azilis de Tréguilly, Tserpchikopf had decided to leave Paris and take the theater of his exploits elsewhere. In Tunis, to which he had gone first, he had hoped to get into the Bardo palace and steel the jewels from the Bey's crown, but the capture of Pawn One, who was to have helped him in that bold plan, and whose trunks contained their perfected burglar's tools, had robbed him of any chance of success.

The Great Psychagogue also interrogated Gustave Panloude on the subject of the Chessmen' Queen. All that the former bandit could tell him was that the woman in question, who was young and beautiful, very intelligent and well-educated, had quarreled with Tserpchikopf.

"Do you know what the quarrel was about?" asked Sâr Dubnotal.

"No," replied the repentant malefactor, "but my guess is that Tserpchikopf intended to dethrone the Queen and replace her with Azilis."

"That's a plausible explanation," the Master remarked. "To get back to the Queen, though, it seems to me that you ought to be able to give me a little more information about her."

Panloude shook his head. "No," he said. "We mere Pawns don't know anything about the origins, the name or the private life of that enigmatic creature. Like the King, she speaks several languages fluently, and can play the role of a Russian, a Swede, a German or an Englishwoman equally well, or even a Circassian or an Andalusian. She can make herself up perfectly, and I don't recall having seen her look the same twice running. Her hair changes from golden blonde one day to brunette the next, or chestnut or jet black. With the aid of kohl, red pencil and rice-powder she undergoes a complete metamorphosis. Special corsets and clever padding give her a slender or opulent beauty at will."

"So, Panloude, you couldn't be sure of recognizing her if you happened to meet her?"

"No, Monsieur. To be sure of her identity, it would be necessary to examine her right arm, where Tserpchikopf, an expert tattooist, designed the emblem of her title: a queen from a chess set.

This information, as is evident, was rather meager, and for lack of sufficient documentation, Sâr Dubnotal was unable to administer the *coup de grâce* to the remnants of the Chessmen—remnants that were still redoubtable and which, like the necks of the Hydra, retained sufficient life to reconstitute it someday. Who could tell whether that might already have been done?—whether Tserpchikopf might have recruited new acolytes, created new Castles and, almost certain of impunity, resumed the course of his bloody exploits? As long as the utter rogue enjoyed his liberty, the worst eventualities had to be envisaged by Sâr Dubnotal, whose investigators, since their return to Paris, had search the capital in vain for traces of the Russian and his accomplices.

Did the Great Psychagogue think that he might be able to take advantage of the hatred that the ex-Queen of the Chessmen must have sworn against Tserpchikopf, who was guilty of having forced her out in favor of Azilis? At any rate, in the wake of the conversation that he had with Panloude, he summoned his three secret agents and instructed them to resume their investigations.

"Try to find the Queen, at least," he said, "and I'll call it quits with respect to everything else."

"Yes, Master," said Otto, Frank and Fréjus, in chorus.

Let us leave Sâr Dubnotal plunged in his meditations and accompany the three investigators.

As they left the house, Fréjus and Otto had the sullen expressions of people who do not quite know what they are doing, while the Englishman Frank, by contrast, seemed rather self-satisfied. "Well, comrades," he said, gaily, "one might think that you were going to attend your own funerals. What long faces you have!"

"Damn it!" said Fréjus. "It's not very amusing, this perpetual campaign against adversaries who make a game out of slipping between one's fingers."

"You'd prefer to put your hand on their collars right away, eh? But what merit would there be in that? We'd be no better than *sergents de ville* if we only had to apprehend malefactors. Personally, I like to have a strong opponent to deal with. It's more stylish, that's my opinion."

"I know you, Frank, old chap," said Otto. "You've got an idea."

"Well, yes," the Englishman admitted, squarely. "Do you know, comrades, that I made a rather curious observation yesterday."

"What?" the German and the Frenchman asked, swiftly.

"Wait! I was in Asnières, searching conscientiously without any great hope of finding Tserpchikopf there, or any of his worthy colleagues in the Chessmen, when I noticed a villa called the Tour Jaune on the Avenue de Courbevoie."

"What!" exclaimed Otto and Fréjus. "Why didn't you tell the Master that?"

"Because I don't know yet whether it's only a mere coincidence, or whether a stroke of good luck has led me to one of the gang's hideouts."

"You weren't able to find out?"

"No, because I was already late and I had to get back to Paris. All that I know is that the villa appeared to be inhabited. The shutters and the gate were closed."

"Off to Asnières, then!" said Fréjus. "We mustn't lose another minute."

The three investigators took a cab to the Gare Saint-Lazare, where they took the first train to Asnières.

Frank had been careful to make a note of the villa's address. He went along the interminable Avenue de Courbevoie, which was planted with trees whose branches as been laid bare by winter. His comrades followed him confidently, and the three of them soon arrived in front of the villa, which stood at the rear of grounds enclosed by a wall and railings.

The gate and the shutters were closed, as Frank had said, but there was no placard to indicate that the house was for sale or to let. Otto and Fréjus observed that their friend had not been mistaken; a marble plaque fixed to the bars of the gate bore three words in gilded letters: *LA TOUR JAUNE.*

Although the avenue was not very busy, Sâr Dubnotal's sleuths, fearing that their behavior might attract the attention of the neighbors, did not linger long in front of the gate.

"Let me do this," said Fréjus—and a few steps further on, leaving his companions to wait for him outside, he went into a wine merchant's shop on his own.

"A large glass of wine, Patron," he said—and while the owner was pouring out the requested glass on the counter, Fréjus added, negligently: "By the way, Patron, do you know whether that villa called the Tour Jaune is to let?"

"To let?" said the man. "No, since it already has a tenant—but it wouldn't be, if people were more careful about where they take up residence."

"Why?"

"You aren't from Asnières?"

"No," said Fréjus. I work for a letting agency in Paris, and I'm looking for a number of houses in the suburb."

"Well, I wouldn't advise you to set your sights on the Tour Jaune, even if it were free."

"Why?" Fréjus repeated.

"Because extraordinary things happen there, Monsieur—things to make your hair stand on end, brave as you might be. To be frank, the Tour Jaune is haunted, and hereabouts we call it the Accursed Villa."

"I didn't think the people of Asnières were so superstitious," said the passing customer.

"It's not a matter of superstition, Monsieur; it's a matter of patent and undeniable fact."

"You think so?"

"I'm sure of it."

"Since the villa has tenants, though, they can't be afraid?"

"The Tour Jaune has but one tenant, Monsieur—a Swedish painter named Fritz Petersen, and the artist isn't there. I know that, for he's not proud, and he often comes in to sip a mominette[21] on the zinc with his models. He left Asnières two months ago, and if he had any inkling of what's been happening in his house since then, my opinion is that he'd never dare to set foot in its again."

"You intrigue me," said Fréjus. "What's been happening, then? Speak freely, Patron—I love ghost stories."

"Then you'll be served as you wish, Monsieur, for if the Tour Jaune isn't visited by a ghost every night, the Devil may carry me away!"

---

[21] In 1890 a "mominette" was a glass of absinthe—a tipple notoriously favored by Bohemian artists and writers.

"Every night? Since when?"

"Since last January 16, Monsieur."

Why, that's curious! thought Fréjus. *Wasn't it on the night of January 16 that Annie Stephenson's cadaver was stolen from the morgue?* Aloud, he said: "Ah! That's not long ago, I see."

"No," said the shopkeeper, "and that date is engraved in my memory, for that night, at about 3 a.m., after hearing terrible cries coming from the Tour Jaune, I got up in haste and ran to the gate of the villa, convinced that Fritz Petersen had come back the day before without my knowledge and that he was being murdered."

"But it wasn't that at all?"

"Of course not, Monsieur, since the painter hasn't yet returned—but what I saw was even more terrible than anything I could have imagined. In the grounds, lit by the moon, there was a phantom: the phantom of a young woman, so far as I was able to judge. It was that specter that was uttering heart-rending screams, screams that I shall never forget as long as I live, which had nothing human about them."

"It wasn't a hoax?"

"To be frank, I wondered that myself for a while, inasmuch as a light was filtering through the shutters of one of the villa's windows. But who would amuse themselves with a joke in such bad taste? Why? For what purpose?"

"Burglars, perhaps?"

"Get away! They would have drawn attention to themselves. As you can imagine, the whole neighborhood was disturbed and neighbors came running from all directions."

"And the phantom?"

"The phantom was seen by more than 100 people. As pale as a bed-sheet, and vaporous, if that's the right word, it was wandering along a pathway through the grounds."

"Didn't you try to get closer to it?"

"Yes, Monsieur—not me, but a policeman."

"And what happened?"

"The policeman, thinking that he was dealing with a malefactor, jumped over the wall and threw himself in pursuit of the specter—but the specter hurled a hail of stones at him. Wounded in the head, the poor man had to beat a retreat."

"Did the phantom stay in the grounds?"

"No, Monsieur—it disappeared."

"What about the light glimpsed at one of the windows?"

"It had gone out some time before."

Fréjus shook his head skeptically. "All that seems quite fantastic," he said. "What sort of man is this Fritz Petersen?"

"A man in his 40s, tall and solidly built."

"I didn't mean that—I meant morally."

"Oh, he's a nice fellow, simple and generous—I hold him in high esteem."

"Because he's a customer?"

"Of course!"

"Don't you consider him capable of having put on this show for his credulous neighbors? Artists are, for the most part, famous jokers, you know."

"No, no, a thousand times no! Monsieur Petersen isn't the sort of man to do that sort of thing. Besides, once again, he's not here. He's not even in France."

"Where is he, then?"

"In England, I think, or in America."

"He could have come back surreptitiously one evening."

"He would have been seen since."

"Isn't the villa—or, rather, its grounds—on the bank of the Seine?"

"Yes."

"Well, your painter could have come back that way."

"You don't know Monsieur Petersen—otherwise, you wouldn't suggest such a thing. It's only tenth-rate art students who play such jokes."

"You seem very sure of that."

"Certainly! Anyway, it wasn't just on the night of January 16 that the phenomenon was manifest—it's every night."

"At the same time?"

"Yes, about 3 a.m."

"Have the police been alerted?"

"Since the very first day."

"Have they investigated the affair?"

"Yes, very actively."

"Without result?"

"Without any other result than observing for themselves that our complaints are well-founded."

"Do you mean that other policemen have seen the phantom?"

"Exactly."

"Have they tried to catch it?"

"Yes, with the authorization of the owner of the property—to whom, in the absence of the tenant, the Commissaire addressed himself. One night, a dozen *sergents de ville* hid in the grounds. Convinced that a practical joker was making fun of them, I can assure you that they mounted a careful watch—which didn't prevent the rain of stones falling upon them at 3 a.m. and obliging them to flee."

"The phantom didn't appear on that occasion?"

"Yes, at one of the widows of the villa."

"At the back or in front?"

"At the back."

"Did anyone think to check whether there was anyone in the house?"

"I beg your pardon, Monsieur. The Commissaire ordered a search of the building before doing anything else."

"A scrupulous search?"

"Very scrupulous. He and his men scoured the villa from top to bottom."

"When was that?"

"Four or five days ago."

"The police haven't renewed their attempt since?"

"What good would it do?"

"So the phantom remains master of the terrain?"

"Very nearly."

"And the neighbors have still got the wind up?"

"Of course!"

"Has the Commissaire abandoned all surveillance?"

"No, but his agents are content to remain outside."

"They daren't go into the grounds?"

"They're careful not to do so, at any rate."

"Thank you," said Fréjus, finishing his drink. "It's quite bizarre, all the same!" He hastened to rejoin his comrades, and told them what he had just learned.

Otto and Frank did not bother to hide their amazement. "You're telling us old wives' tales, Sûreté!" they said. "What are we going to do? What if we were to renew the attempt made by the police on our own behalf?"

"Don't even think about it," said Fréjus. "The worst thing that might happen, if we want to get into the property by night, is that the police might mistake us for the authors of this farce, if that's what it is. On the other hand, if the phantom really exists, I'm not going to get mixed up in it myself. That's the Master's business, not ours."

"What do we do, then?"

"Let's return to Paris, of course, and warn Sâr Dubnot-al."

"You think it will interest him?"

"I'm absolutely sure of it."

The Frenchman's conviction was apparently infectious, for Otto and Frank ceased to resist and followed their friend as he drew away from the Accursed Villa.

VI *Sâr Dubnotal and the Phantom*

The three sleuths got back at 4 p.m. By 5 p.m., their Master had received their report, which seemed to interest him greatly.

"Rudolph," he said to his disciple, who was party to the conversation, "fetch your satchel and get ready to follow me.

We're going to Asnières. Check your photographic apparatus carefully. I might have occasion to take an astral photograph."

The young man did not bother to ask why Sâr Dubnotal wanted to go to the Accursed Villa to try to elucidate the mystery. He gave it no thought, and made his rapid preparations. He and Sâr Dubnotal put on ample cloaks, leapt into the Master's magnificent coupé, and set off for the station. Rudolph was carrying his heavily-laden leather satchel over his shoulder, as well as a small, photographic apparatus of a very special kind.

The two men disembarked at Asnières at 6 p.m. Sâr Dubnotal asked for directions to the police station and asked the officer on duty at the door to take him to his senior officer immediately.

The Commissaire received the two strangers politely, their majestic appearance having made a strong impression on him and predisposed them in his favor.

"Monsieur," said Sâr Dubnotal, offering him a visiting card bearing the pseudonym Severus el Tebib, as well as a pass signed by the Prefect of Police, "I am an amateur detective, to whose good offices the head of the Parisian Sûreté is sometimes not shamed to have recourse, and I take a special interest in such mysterious and troubling affairs as that of the Tour Jaune."

"Oh, you've heard about that!" the Commissaire said, interestedly.

"Yes, and I as I have some small acquaintance with the study of psychognosis—a science that, as you know, embraces all abstract knowledge—you will understand, Monsieur Commissaire, the desire that I have to elucidate the mystery of the accursed Villa."

The functionary bowed. "How can I be of service to you, Monsieur?"

"I would like your kind authorization to go into the grounds of the villa this evening."

At these words, the worthy functionary started with surprise and uttered an exclamation. "What? What are you saying?" he stammered. "You're going into the grounds of the Tour Jaune this evening? But Monsieur, don't you know what happened to me agents a few days ago? They were stoned like stray dogs, my dear Monsieur, and if you intend to go into the grounds on your own, I'm convinced that you won't get out alive."

"I shall go anyway, if you have no objection," Sâr Dubnotal said, simply. "In any case, the authorization I'm seeking from you is only designed to cover me in case your agents, catching sight of me in the park, should accuse me of being the author of the misdeeds of which they have been the victims."

The Commissaire reflected, and then asked: "What do you intend to do, then?"

Sâr Dubnotal smiled. "Permit me not to reveal my plan to you," he said. "All that I can tell you is that my intervention will produce the most fortunate results. I have an idea, and you can be certain that from tomorrow on the phenomena that are manifest every night in the gardens of the Tour Jaune and are frightening the inhabitants of Asnières will cease."

"I'd like nothing better than to believe you, Monsieur Severus," said the police chief. "I confess to you, however, that I'm afraid of…an accident."

"Danger doesn't frighten me."

"Permit me, at least, to let me agents lend you a hand?"

"No!" said Sâr Dubnotal, swiftly. He pointed to Rudolph. "This young man is the only one authorized to go with me. He is my disciple and he will profit from the lesson."

"Are you going to carry out an experiment?"

"Perhaps."

"And you're really not afraid for your life?"

"I'm not afraid of anything."

This response was so curt, and Sâr Dubnotal's expression so resolute, that the Commissaire ceased to persist. His acceptance was no longer in doubt. The Great Psychagogue took advantage of this benevolent disposition.

"It's agreed, then?" he queried. "I'm authorized to go into the grounds of the Accursed Villa tonight?"

"Since you're determined!"

"I am indeed determined, and this is what I propose. Tonight, you'll establish a double cordon of agents in the Avenue de Courbevoie, some distance away from the Tour Jaune. It's vital that I'm not disturbed, and those agents will take responsibility for preventing anyone without exception, from passing along that part of the avenue in which my...experiment will be carried out. That experiment will commence at exactly 3 a.m. At 4 a.m., I hope that you will know the result, and that henceforth, order will be restored in Asnières."

With that, Sâr Dubnotal and Rudolph bowed to the Commissaire and withdrew, delighted with the charming welcome that he had given them—which was doubtless explained by the fact that the two psychagogues had let him know about the close relationship they enjoyed with the top brass of the police force.

Having some time to kill, the Master and his disciple went to meditate on the bank of the frozen Seine. The excessive cold of the evening had no effect on their iron constitutions. They did not exchange a word in the course of their long nocturnal stroll. Rudolph rarely questioned Sâr Dubnotal, and the latter seemed to be so absorbed by his thoughts that the young man dared not even ask him what his plan was.

Eventually, at 2:30 a.m., Sâr Dubnotal abruptly shook off his reverie, took Rudolph by the arm and drew him in the direction of the Avenue de Courbevoie. The cordons established by the police stopped the psychagogues about 500 meters from the accursed Villa.

"I am Severus el Tebib," Sâr Dubnotal told the agents. Having received instructions from their chief, the latter allowed the two men to pass. The latter slid into the shadow of the walls of the deserted avenue, where the faltering light of widely-space street-lamps was insufficient to dissipate the opacity of the darkness.

Sâr Dubnotal moved forward prudently, his ears pricked and his eyes watchful. From his lips, which were agitated by a rapid tremor, a slight murmur sometimes emerged, the meaning of which Rudolph had difficulty perceiving.

"Above all, no noise!" instructed the Great Psychagogue. "Human being or shade, trickster or soul in torment, it's necessary to come upon the nocturnal guest of the Accursed Villa unexpectedly."

"Go on, Master," whispered Rudolph. "I'm right behind you!"

Muffling their steps, the two bold companions arrived at the corner of the high wall.

"Halt!" murmured Sâr Dubnotal. "No need to go as far as the gate. Let's hoist ourselves up on to the top of the wall, from which we can take a look around the grounds."

Rudolph gave his Master a leg up; with a singular agility, the latter scaled the wall. He joined him with a nimble cat-like bound and lay prone next to him on the coping-stones, placing his head next to that of the Great Psychagogue. Momentarily the two men became immobile.

Rudolph had his photographic apparatus in one hand, and a powerful electric torch in the other, which he had just take from his satchel.

"Watch out!" Sâr Dubnotal murmured, suddenly. "There's something in the air."

He and Rudolph redoubled their attention. Their eyes fixed upon the mysterious villa, and they remained motionless for a further interval. All of their life seemed to be concentrated in their eyes,

Suddenly, Sâr Dubnotal jogged Rudolph's elbow.

In the deserted grounds, where the glacial winter wind stirred the branches of the fir trees and where an intense obscurity reigned, a pale silhouette had just appeared and disappeared again behind a tree. It reappeared almost immediately, and its nebulous contours stood out with slightly more precision in the mist of the moonless and starless night.

It was the pale and vaporous figure of a woman draped in a shroud.

The silhouette, which was extremely diaphanous, differed from a material body in that one could see right through it, and instead of walking like a human being, she moved forward lightly without touching the ground. The sand of the pathways squeaked beneath her, however, as if it were being trodden by footsteps, and it uttered little moans, which reached the ears of the two men lying on the walls distinctly.

Thus far, she did not seem to suspect their presence.

They allowed her to draw nearer without saying a word or making a movement.

Her head was lowered and its hands were joined upon her breast. They could see her well enough to perceive that her beauty was remarkable, in spite of the expression of despair that contracted her immaterial features.

One might have thought it the personification, slightly blurred but of an incomparable symbolic verity, or Remorse or Dolor.

"It's definitely a soul in torment. Quickly, Rudolph! Take the picture!"

Softly as these words had been pronounced, the soul must have heard the murmur, for it pivoted abruptly and fled—but Rudolph had already activated the two switches of his searchlight and his photographic apparatus, and he exclaimed: "I've got it, Master! The plate might not be very vividly impressed, but it will be relatively easy for us to rectify the print."

"Be quiet!" said Sâr Dubnotal, almost rudely, placing his hand over the reflector of the electric torch, which had just projected a blinding beam of light upon the fugitive spirit. "Listen to the noise of pebbles striking the walls! We'll be well and truly stoned if you don't let me recite the magic formula." And in a voice of thunder, which rose above the suddenly-furious howling of the wind and the racket made by the fall of a deluge of rubble, Sâr Dubnotal pronounced an incantation with whose power he was familiar:

212

"Begone, guilty Soul, who art so cruelly expiating sins committed on the planet! Cease haunting this place and frightening humans! We pray to God to pardon your crimes, but do not trouble our quietude henceforth!"

Immediately, the stones ceased raining down, and nothing more was heard but the hoarse whistling of the wind in the foliage of the firs.

VII. The Astral Photograph

The anxiety with which the Commissaire of Asnières awaited the return of the two intrepid psychagogues is easily imaginable, as is the joy with which he saw them come back safe and sound.

"Well, Monsieur Severus?" he inquired, excitedly.

"Well, Monsieur le Commissaire?"

"Have you seen it?"

"What?"

"The phantom?"

"No," said Sâr Dubnotal, smiling. "It was a false alarm, I think."

"That's not possible. More than 100 people have seen it with their own eyes."

"Those people must have been mistaken," said Sâr Dubnotal, placidly. "In any case, I give you my word that the phenomena that have frightened the population of Asnières will not be repeated."

The Commissaire could not believe his ears. In order to convince him, Sâr Dubnotal was obliged to conduct him personally, and immediately, to the Accursed Villa, the grinds of which he was able to explore with impunity.

Leaving the worthy man simultaneously amazed and delighted by such an outcome, Sâr Dubnotal and Rudolph returned to the railway station to take the first morning train to Paris. The Great Psychagogue seemed to be very happy, and when he reached his domicile it was in a strangely jovial tone that he told his disciple to take a few minutes' rest.

It had not been daylight for long when Sâr Dubnotal summoned his investigators and said to them: "My friends, there's no need to search any longer for the trail of the ungraspable Tserpchikopf. Content yourself with going to Asnières, and remain there until you receive further instructions. Your mission is to maintain a discreet surveillance of the Tour Jaune, and not to let anyone—especially Fritz Petersen—enter it without my being immediately alerted.

"I shall be departing shortly with Rudolph and Annunciata for my residence in Trez-Hir, from which I expect to return tomorrow evening—or, at the latest, the following morning. If Fritz Petersen or anyone else turns up at the Tour Jaune before then, you will have to contact me by telegraph at Trez-Hir. In the contrary case, you have only to fold your arms. One of you, however, must station himself permanently at the Asnières Post Office, in case I have some urgent communication to address to you. As soon as I return, I'll come to join you there with Rudolph, and we'll review the situation."

"Understood, Master!" said the three sleuths, with one voice.

Shortly afterwards, Sâr Dubnotal, his disciple and his medium left the Champs-Elysées. That same evening, they arrived at Trez-Hir without having encountered any difficulty.

The bungalow's caretaker, alerted telegraphically, had brought a carriage to meet them in Morlaix.

A good fire was burning in the hearth of the laboratory, to which Sâr Dubnotal, Rudolph and la Gianetti retired without even taking the time to shake their snow-covered garments or absorb anything but a few white tablets taken from the silver casket that the Master always carried about his person. It had been pitch dark outside for several hours, but a chandelier hanging from the ceiling inundated the room with light.

"You can't imagine how anxious I am to develop the astral photograph that you obtained in the grounds of the Tour Jaune," Sâr Dubnotal said to Rudolph, who helped him take off his steaming overcoat, "so hurry up and make the necessary preparations. Annunciata will give you a hand."

While the disciple and the medium got busy, the Master let himself collapse into a chair, where he set about reflecting profoundly.

Rudolph had put his satchel and his photographic apparatus on the floor. Kneeling down, he seemed to be setting up the workings of a delicate and complicated machine, somewhat reminiscent of the powerful projectors nowadays employed in cinematic projection.

As for the young Italian woman, she was busy setting up a large white canvas screen at the back of the laboratory.

"Are you ready, Rudolph?" Sâr Dubnotal asked, eventually.

"There you are, Master," said the young man, standing up.

The Great Psychagogue immediately got up from his chair. His eyes shining and his forehead aureoled with a gleam of genius, he took possession of the as-yet-unilluminated projector and called to the Italian woman, who came to stand by his side. Then he instructed the young man to extinguish the chandelier. Rudolph pressed a switch, and the laboratory was plunged into complete darkness.

"Is the plate in the apparatus?" the Master asked.

"I've slipped it between the focal point of the lamp and the lens," the disciple replied. "There's nothing more to do but light the acetylene, and I hope that the proof obtained will be fixed, faithfully reproduced, albeit greatly magnified, on the sensitive canvas screen."

There were a few seconds of silence; then the click of a switch was heard, which Sâr Dubnotal had just activated.

Immediately, a luminous beam sprang from the lens of the reflector that the Great Psychagogue was holding, and a human skeleton appeared, outlined in black on the pale background of the canvas screen. That life-sized skeleton did not take long to fade away into a sort of gilded pink and white cloud, which, extraordinarily, gradually took on the appearance of a beautiful young woman with blonde hair and blue eyes, dressed in nothing but a night-dress.

"The phantom of the Tour Jaune!" murmured Rudolph.

"The quartered woman of Montmartre!" added Sâr Dubnotal.

VIII. The Revelatory Sign

At this declaration from the Great Psychagogue, his disciple could not suppress an exclamation of surprise.

"The quartered woman of Montmartre?"

"Yes."

"What! The spirit haunting the Accursed Villa was that of Annie Stephenson!"

"Of the so-called Annie Stephenson, yes, Rudolph," Sâr Dubnotal corrected. "I presume that you never really thought that Annie Stephenson was the unfortunate woman's real name?"

"But how do you know that?" exclaimed Rudolph, avoiding the question.

"I'll tell you in due course," replied Sâr Dubnotal. "For the moment, move closer to that astral photograph and tell me what the mark is that the young woman bears on her right arm."

"On the right arm?"

"Yes."

Rudolph ran to the screen, guided by the light of the projector, and uttered another exclamation: "Oh!"

"What do you see?" asked Sâr Dubnotal, coolly.

"A tattoo."

"Which represents?"

"A chess piece."

"The Queen, isn't it?"

"How did you deduce that, Master?"

Sâr Dubnotal, admirably self-composed, switched the chandelier on and extinguished the projector before replying. "I've deduced many other things too, Rudolph. So, do you want me to tell you why the so-called Annie Stephenson had that tattoo placed on her arm, who killed her, and what became of hr corpse, for which everyone is searching in vain?"

Visibly bewildered, in spite of his natural and acquired phlegmaticism, the young man stammered: "Certainly, Master!"

"Annie Stephenson had that tattoo done because she was then the Queen of the Chessmen."

"Her?" cried Rudolph.

"Her," said the Great Psychagogue, simply. "And now you know who murdered her."

"Tserpchikopf?"

"Tserpchikopf, indeed—the bloody hypnotist. It can only have been him, just as it can only have been him who subsequently went to steal the cadaver from the morgue. The man we have found to be mixed up in almost all the crimes we have investigated in the last six months! Tserpchikopf, who caused the ruination of Azilis de Tréguilly; Tserpchikopf, the forger, the burglar, the master crook, the sinister hero of so many known and unknown tragedies; the man of false passports and multiple pseudonyms, the Prince of Crime, the King of the Chessmen!"

Sâr Dubnotal put the inert projector down on the table, sat down and, with a strange calmness—the absolute calmness that reigns after a storm—he said: "Paris, France, Europe and the entire world shuddered at the news of the monstrous tragedy of the Avenue de Clichy, the author of which the theft from the morgue has prevented the police from discovering. But I, Rudolph, am not content to shudder. I have reflected, and I foresaw the discovery of that tattoo, which has allowed us to identify the pseudo-Annine Stephenson with the Queen of the Chessmen.

"That identification explains many points that the Parisian police have been unable to clarify and doubtless never will clarify: why no one knew the victim; why she passed herself off as a rich orphan; how the assassin obtained access to her home so easily; and why her cadaver was stolen from the morgue and transported to the villa of the Tour Jaune, where we shall certainly find it buried in the grounds."

"The Tour Jaune!" exclaimed Rudolph. "Oh, why didn't I realize the significance of the villa's name sooner?"

"That's true," said Sâr Dubnotal. "It should have intrigued you immediately, as it intrigued our investigators—for, after all, it's thanks to Frank's flair that I was able to bring my inquiry to a conclusion.

"To be sure, I had long suspected that the pseudo-Annie Stephenson must have particular reasons to hide her origins, her past and her real name. As soon as the day after the crime, I had built an entire edifice of well-connected conjectures. For instance, the table set in the victim's dining-room was a very clear indication that Miss Stephenson was expecting someone that she particularly wanted to impress. The bouquet of white roses could only have been given to her by that person, and I immediately assumed that the murderer had sought to lull the unfortunate woman's suspicions by means of that gesture.

"Annie, not wanting to receive the individual in her home overtly, had let him in surreptitiously by the window that opens on to the street. That precaution on the victim's part was to doom her and, by contrast, save the guilty party, who was able to carry out his hideous crime in perfect tranquility.

"Up to that point, I was able to explain the march of events well enough—but I didn't yet know the murderer's name or the motive that impelled him, and even I was disconcerted by the horrific details. Père Berton's adventure finally made me think of Tserpchikopf, the bloody hypnotist. That's why I instructed my investigators to pick up his trail—but, to tell the truth, it wasn't until I received Frank's report that I realized the whole truth.

"By comparing the dates, Frank had remarked that he macabre theft from the morgue had been immediately followed by the first appearance of the phantom in the grounds of the Accursed Villa. That observation was, for me, a decisive stroke of enlightenment."

"Your sagacity is prodigious, Master!"

Sâr Dubnotal wore a furtive smile. "Prodigious, no—for I required long reflection before I acquired the beginnings of certainty. I still did not trust myself entirely, since, before making you party to my suspicious, I had to obtain the astral photograph of the spirit of the Tour Jaune."

"Did that precaution serve any other purpose that to remove your last doubts concerning the identity of Tserpchikopf's victim?" asked the disciple.

"Certainly, Rudolph. Soon you shall reproduce, by means of magnesium light, a portrait of the Queen of the Chessmen on an ordinary photographic plate. Then you'll take a few proofs of that photograph—which will, I hope, allow us to locate Annie Stephenson's family. By that means, we might perhaps discover how the unfortunate woman made the acquaintance of Tserpchikopf and penetrate the veil of mystery that hangs over the criminal's past."

"But why did Tserpchikopf murder her?" asked Rudolph.

"I don't know anything for sure," the Great Psychagogue admitted, frankly. "In that regard I'm reduced to mere hypotheses, and I don't like giving my imagination free rein. I don't think I'm mistaken, though in attributing the whole affair to vengeance—not a crime of passion, for Pawn One affirmed that Tserpchikopf did not love the Queen, but one designed to prevent the pseudo-Annie from putting her own threats into effect. Indeed, it's probable that the Queen of the Chessmen, dispossessed of her title, was a threat to Tserpchikopf. Suppose that she had threatened to denounce him to the police, and also that she possessed some terrible weapon to use against the Slav—that she knew about his past, for instance. Would not Tserpchikopf have been afraid of her, and would he not have desired to get rid of an accomplice who had become a mortal enemy?"

"That would indeed, explain everything, Master!" Rudolph murmured.

"Everything," repeated Sâr Dubnotal. "Tserpchikopf would then have been a cornered wild beast, with only one means of escaping his fate—murder. Resolved to perpetrate the crime, he feigned a reconciliation with the poor girl. The latter, deceived by the monster's prodigious cunning, welcomed him with open arms and paid with her blind confidence with her life."

"That must be what happened, Master!" the disciple exclaimed, with conviction.

"We shall verify it," Sâr Dubnotal said, placidly. "And if I'm not mistaken, we shall have a further motive for dedicating all our efforts to Tserpchikopf's pursuit! The scoundrel has avenged himself atrociously, Rudolph! He must have hypnotized Annie before attaching her to the cage of the elevator, and it was probably only when she was bound and gagged that he brought her out of the 'second state,' so that she would know all about the frightful torture that he wanted to inflict on her.

"Ah, that death, Rudolph! The unfortunate woman's slow and terrible agony as the elevator, meekly set to work, gradually stretched her arms and legs, broke the blood-vessels, distended the muscles and tendons, ripped apart the flesh! Whatever sins the Queen of the Chessmen might have committed, God will treat her with indulgence, for she has expiated them by crucifixion!"

The Great Psychagogue pronounced these last words with an emotion so vibrant that tear came to Rudolph's eyes. "Poor girl! We shall avenge her, Master!"

"Yes, we shall avenge her terribly, Rudolph. No pity or forgiveness can enter our heats when dealing with a monster like Tserpchikopf. He knows very well, moreover, that he can expect no clemency from human beings, if he should fall into their hands. If the bread-porter had not disturbed him, he would certainly have disfigured his victim before fleeing, in order to make certain of preventing the police from discovering the unfortunate woman's antecedents, and his own. Obliged to flee precipitately, he believed that he would be lost if

Annie's cadaver were examined by the official physicians, who would have discovered the tattoo she bore on her arm: a tattoo that she had partly effaced herself—which is why it escaped the superficial examination made by the police—but which the doctors would have been able to reconstitute, just as we have, albeit in a different manner. Thus, he did not hesitate to take the risk of going to the morgue that same night to steal the corpse."

"Astral photography is a sublime invention, Master!" said Rudolph.

"An invention that I shall not divulge, however. In order to be happy, people need to refrain from disturbing the rest of souls. It would be dangerous to furnish them with the means."

With a nod of the head the disciple signified that he approved of his Master's opinion, and then he set about carrying out Sâr Dubnotal's instructions with respect to the portrait of Annie Stephenson, the Queen of the Chessmen.

When that was done, Sâr Dubnotal and he retired to their respective bedrooms, as did Annunciata Gianetti, who had not emerged from her habitual apathy throughout the scene, the Great Psychagogue having had no need to take advantage of her services.

The overman's two aides had received orders to get up very early the following day. Having nothing more to do in Trez-Hir, the indefatigable Sâr Dubnotal intended to take the fist morning train to Paris.

Like the symbolic figures in the celebrated painting by Prud'hon, *Justice and Vengeance in pursuit of the Crime*, the Great Psychagogue never gave any respite to malefactors when he had given himself the mission of tracing them down and punishing them.[22]

---

[22] The cited painting by Pierre-Paul Prud'hon (1758-1832) dates from 1808 and hangs in the Louvre.

IX. Check and Mate

"Well, Otto?"

"What is it, Frank?"

"The famous Fritz Petersen is in no hurry to appear. What do you think, my old Berliner? My opinion is that we'll take root in this damned Avenue de Courbevoie, where it's bitterly cold."

"What do you expect, Scotland Yard?" replied the placid Teuton. "War is war."

"And orders are orders, aren't they?" mocked the Englishman, who could find no better way of killing time than teasing his friend. "That doesn't prevent our pal Fréjus from laughing at us. Oh, that rascally little Frenchman knows how to look after himself! While we get frozen feet outside, in Siberian temperatures, Monsieur is lounging on a bench in the Post Office and smoking a cigarette, with his feet up on a nice heater."

"What do you expect?" Otto repeated.

"Yes, war is war!" said Frank, laughing. "I know the chorus." And his heavy Anglo-Saxon paw came down on the brave Otto's powerful shoulder.

This conversation, which took place the morning after Sâr Dubnotal's departure, was abruptly interrupted by Fréjus, who came running at the gallop.

"Speaks of the Devil..." murmured the German.

"And one sees the tip of his nose," Frank finished.

"The nose and the rest!" said the former Sûreté inspector, wiping the sweat from his brow. "Joking apart, though, friends, there's news!" So saying, Fréjus waved a telegram, which he had just taken out of his pocket.

"Is it from the Master?" asked Otto and Frank, excitedly, becoming serious again.

"Yes," said Fréjus, in a low voice. "Read it and hold your tongues, chatterboxes, for sidewalks have ears as well as walls."

The German and the Englishman leaned forward eagerly over the blue sheet unfolded by Fréjus and read:

Sutorf, Poste Restante, Asnières.

One of you start painting immediately; install yourself you know where in order to do you know what. The others will serve as models. If tenant should paint before my arrival, attend to him. Will certainly buy canvases this evening.

Severus.

The three investigators remained silent momentarily. It was Fréjus who broke the silence. "The Master sometimes put us to a rude proof with his codes, eh? Do you understand what it means?"

"Not yet," said Otto, "but we'll soon succeeded in deciphering it, if we take the trouble."

"Sutorf means the three of us," Frank observed. "The word can be broken up as Su…To…Rf—which is to say, after inverting the letters, Us...Ot...Fr. 'Us' is the last two letters of the name Fréjus; 'Fr' the first two letters of my name, and 'Ot'…."

"The first two letters of Otto," the Frenchman put in., "Yes, we know that perfectly well—but it's the rest that it's important for us to deduce, and which we aren't deducing."

"Just a minute," murmured Otto. "I think I have it."

"Me too," Frank hastened to say.

" 'One of you start painting' signifies that one of us has to disguise ourselves as a painter."

"And play the role of Fritz Pertersen," the Englishman added.

"You're right, of course!" said Fréjus. "That gives me the key to the puzzle, and, if there's no mistake, this is how the telegram translates: 'Frank, Otto, Fréjus, Post Restante, Asnières. One of you disguise himself as Fritz Petersen and install himself in the Tour Jaune in his stead to mount guard. The others, whom he will pass off as his models, will lend him a hand if need be. If the villa's tenant should arrive before I do, arrest him. I'll certainly rejoin you this evening. Sâr Dubnotal.' "

223

"Bravo, Sûreté," said Frank, ironically. "Your translation, belated as it may be, deserves an ovation."

"You're too clever by half, Scotland Yard!" said Fréjus.

"As clever as you, my lad—don't get upset about it!"

"That's not proven."

"Come on, come on!" said the wise Otto, seeing that the discussion was threatening to turn hostile. "Let's stay calm. You're as subtle as one another, and I make no concessions to you in that regard. There, are you happy! Now let's talk less, and more to the point. The Master has sketched out what we have to do. It's up to us to figure out how. First, which of us is going to play the role of Fritz?"

"Not me," said Fréjus. "I'm too thin."

"Nor me," said Frank. "I'm too tall."

"It'll be me then," Otto decided. "One of you will be my valet, the other my model. But it's necessary that I get an exact description of the man whose skin I have to get into. We know already that he's a sturdy fellow. By interrogating the suppliers in the neighborhood, especially his friend in the bistro, we'll soon find out. On the other hand, I wonder if I should just go straight into the Tour Jaune as if I were returning from a trip, or whether I should slip in surreptitiously after nightfall."

"In my opinion, you shouldn't do either," said Frank.

"Why?"

"You shouldn't draw needless attention to yourself, but it shouldn't appear that we're hiding. In a word, we wait for nightfall, when there won't be many passers-by, and if one of them sees us, they'll assume that they're seeing Fritz Petersen and his companions."

"What do we do once we're inside the villa?" asked Fréjus.

"It won't be long before the master rejoins us. We can lie low while we're waiting for him."

"And if the real Fritz Petersen turns up before him?"

"That will be the time to put our hands on his collar. The Master's counter-passes[23] will render us invulnerable, and even if it's Tserpchikopf in person, we'll get the better of him easily enough."

On this reassuring reflection by Frank, the three investigators separated, after having arranged a rendezvous at the Post Office three hours later. Each of them went to collect information on the subject of Fritz Petersen, his valet and some of his usual models.

The friends met up again at the agreed time; all three of them were sufficiently well-furnished with information. Leaving the Post Office, they went to a local shop to buy clothes almost identical to those of the artist and his employees. With that done, they looked for a discreet corner in which to disguise themselves, and found it under a bridge over the Seine. They underwent a rapid and radical transformation of their appearances, then hailed a cab and climbed into it, initially giving the coachman instructions to take them to a department store, where they purchased trunks, canvases and easels.

Otto was made up with particular perfection. A handsome false beard flecked with grey and a false nose made him look exactly like Fritz Petersen, who had been described to him as a rather stout man in his forties, good-looking but already going grey and afflicted with a large nose.

As they came out of the department store, the investigators, seeing that it was already after 5 p.m., gave their Automédon the painter's address.[24]

The carriage stopped outside the gate of the Tour Jaune as dusk was falling. They got down before the astonished eyes of one of the local tradesmen, who was passing by.

"Ah! Is that you, Monsieur Petersen?" the man said.

---

[23] A *contre-passe* [counter-pass] is usually some sort of endorsement, but in this instance it presumably refers to some sort of precautionary shield against a hynpotist's "passes."

[24] Automédon was the name of Achilles' charioteer, which was borrowed for application to all skillful drivers.

Otto, feigning a violent coughing fit, replied in a hoarse voice; "Damn! It's not warm, is it?"

"No, it's not like last week," said the merchant, with a wink.

Otto thought he had been found out and shivered. "What do you mean?" he asked.

"You don't know what I'm talking about, then?"

"No."

"Well then, I ought to tell you…"

And whether they liked it or not, Otto, Frank and Fréjus were obliged to hear the story of the events of which the Accursed Villa had been the theater. The tradesman put particular emphasis on the descent of the police and the intervention of a certain Severus el Tebib, who had put the phantom to flight.

"Now you can sleep soundly, Monsieur Petersen," the gossip concluded. "If you'd come back a little sooner, though, I don't know how you'd have been able to get back in."

Finally rid of the unwelcome individual, Otto, Frank and Fréjus hastened to dismiss the coachman, opened the gate with a skeleton key and carried their improvised luggage into the house, which they entered by the same means. There they burst into laughter.

"The tradesman didn't suspect a thing!" said Fréjus.

"Which didn't prevent him from giving us quite a fright!" said Frank.

"A fright?" said Otto. "Us? Get away!"

Closing the door to the villa behind them, the three investigators went to lie in wait in a room whose windows, equipped with Venetian blinds, had a view of the grounds and the gate.

"If anyone turns up, comrades, it's understood that we take them prisoner!" said the Frenchman.

"As long as he's not one of ours," remarked Frank.

"That goes without saying, you fool!"

"Silence!" Otto ordered.

The gate had just opened and closed again. A man was striding along the principal pathway toward the Tour Jaune.

The darkness, which was already profound, prevented Sâr Dubnotal's aides from making out his features. Even so, they noticed that the visitor was poorly dressed.

The man came up the front steps and knocked on the door.

"Go see what he wants!" Otto whispered to Frank, who was playing the role of valet. "We'll follow you along the corridor, ready to help you if need be."

"No need!" said the Englishman, showing his pugilist's fists. "If he puts a foot wrong, I'll knock him down."

Otto and Fréjus followed their comrade on tiptoe, though.

"Who's there?" interrogated the fake valet, disguising his voice.

"It's me," the man replied, swiftly. "Open up, quickly."

"Who's *me*?"

"Don't you recognize me, Octave?"

It seems that my name is Octave, Frank thought, as he grumbled: "No, I don't recognize you, friend. Who are you?"

"The Knight, damn it!"

"Oh, the Knight!" said Frank, as naturally as possible— and he withdrew the bolts on the door, into the opening of which the man immediately dived...to find himself face-to-face with three individuals who certainly resembled those he had expected to find there, but who leapt upon him and manhandled him, reducing him to helplessness in spite of his indignant protestations.

"Let's take him into one of the rooms at the back, where Fréjus can keep watch on him while we resume our interrupted sentry duty," said Otto. "Fréjus, you might take advantage of the situation to worm something out of him. The affair's getting complicated. Is Fritz Pertersen one of the Chessmen, perhaps, and the Knight we've captured one of Tserpchikopf's emissaries?"

"I'll try to find out," said Fréjus.

While the Frenchman pressed his prisoner with questions, Otto and Frank returned to the embrasure of one of the

227

windows overlooking the grounds and continued watching the gate.

It was 9 p.m.

The watchers suddenly shivered; three people had just crept into the grounds: two men and a woman.

"The Master!" Otto murmured.

"With Rudolph and la Gianetti," said Frank.

They threw themselves into the corridor to open the entrance door. Five seconds later, it gave passage to Sâr Dubnotal and his companions.

"We've carried out your orders, Master," Otto said, "And that has permitted us to capture an individual who presented himself here under the name of the Knight."

"Where is he?" asked Sâr Dubnotal.

"With Fréjus, in that room over there."

"Good. Return to your post, my friends. Rudolph and Gianetti, come with me."

Fréjus bowed respectfully to the Great Psychagogue as he came into the room, and then shone the light of a torch he had just illuminated on to the captive's face. Rapidly, he explained: "This individual belongs to the Chessmen, Master. He's just confessed to me that Fritz Petersen is none other than Tserpchikopf. He's one of the Knights, or emissaries, or the famous gang, which has been recently reconstituted by our enemy. A tradesman that we met on arriving here, who mistook Otto for the painter, has spread the news of the latter's return around Asnières. The Knight, thus informed, came right away to put himself at his King's disposal, and was stupidly captured by us."

"So he wasn't astonished by this abrupt return?" asked Sâr Dubnotal.

"No, for it seems that, by a strange coincidence, Tserpchikopf is due to come back tonight."

"In that case," said Rudolph, "we have the upper hand."

The Great Psychagogue, whose brows were furrowed, did not share his disciple's optimism. "I only wish that were true," he said. "We shall see, though. Continue watching this man, Fréjus. Has he told you what time the King is supposed to be coming back?"

"Yes, Master—but the 12:30 train. Having heard that he had arrived at Courbevoie at 6 p.m., the Knight simply thought that he had taken an earlier train."

"Does he know where Tserpchikopf has been?"

"No. All that he can say is that the false painter isn't supposed to arrive at the villa before 1 a.m."

"Good. We'll wait for him here. It's not yet 10 p.m. Annunciata and I have all the time we need to do what has to be done."

The medium immediately armed herself with a small black wand and followed her Master, who also summoned Rudolph

"Isn't there a possibility that we'll be seen from the street?" asked the young man.

"We'll take precautions," Sâr Dubnotal replied. "As it's necessary to avoid being seen at all costs, our investigations will only be undertaken in the sector of the grounds masked by the villa. That's probably where Annie Stephenson's corpse lies."

"What if Tserpchikopf buried her in front of the house?"

"I don't believe he would have been so imprudent. Let's make haste, in any case. We have to be back in the Tour Jaune before he arrives."

Sâr Dubnotal, Rudolph and Annunciata glided like shadows through the dark pathways in the grounds, taking care to remain in the sector protected by the building. Suddenly, the Italian woman stopped, her eyes on the ground; the wand was trembling in her hand.

"I wasn't mistaken," the Great Psychagogue murmured. "The murderer passed this way with his victim. My medium's disturbance tells me as much."

In fact, the two men were not long delayed in finding a slight bulge in the ground.

"Annunciata!" Sâr Dubnotal called, softly. "Isn't there a grave here?"

"Yes, Master."

"To work, then!"

The medium was about to place her magic wand over the mound, within whose interior the Great Psychagogue was convinced that mortal remain lay, when his trained ear caught a faint whistle coming from one of the rear windows of the villa. "Stop, Annunciata!" the murmured, immediately. "You can proceed with the incantation later. Our investigators are calling us back."

The Great Psychagogue ran soundlessly from tree to tree toward the door of the Tour Jaune, followed by Rudolph and the Italian, who imitated his maneuvers. They went into the house and along the dark corridor that ended at the front door.

Frank, Otto and Fréjus were crouching behind that door, and people could be heard moving about on the far side of it.

"Open up, then, Octave!" said one of them.

"I can't find the key!" replied another.

"Look out!" murmured Sâr Dubnotal. "This time, it's them. They've arrived sooner than we expected."

Suddenly, a key was introduced into the lock and the door opened, to reveal three individuals standing on the threshold with bags and cases in their hands. One of them looked exactly like Fritz Petersen!

"Finally!" roared Sâr Dubnotal, pouncing on him, while his aides grabbed the other two, who seemed more dead than alive. "So I've got you at last, Tserpchikopf! Ah, you didn't expect this, did you? Check and mate!"

Suddenly, though, Sâr Dubnotal relaxed his grip. Outside, near the gate, a sarcastic voice replied to him thus: "Check and mate? Not yet, Severus el Tebib! You've taken a Knight, a Castle and a few Pawns, but you haven't captured the King!"

What had happened?

Sâr Dubnotal understood immediately. The man he had arrested was only a subordinate of the King of the Chessmen—a Pawn, like Gustave Panloude. Tserpchikopf had taken

230

the precaution of having his role played by the man, who was almost the same height and to whom he had given his clothes.

While the three Pawns obediently went to open the door of the villa, their leader had prudently held back, having scented a trap and not wanting to enter the house before his aides had made certain that he was no running any danger by doing so.

When he understood that—which is to say, after a split second—Sâr Dubnotal stopped his investigators, who had already launched themselves outside in the direction from which the enemy's voice had come, with a gesture.

"Too late!" he told them. "Tserpchikopf is right—we still don't have the King of the Chessmen. There's no point in launching yourselves in pursuit—he's already far away. We've compromised the results of our laborious campaign by being in too much of a hurry, and lost the game at the very moment when we should have won it. If we'd let these men enter the villa, their leader might perhaps have risked following them, and we would have captured him. What am I saying? A moment's reflection should have put us on our guard against that redoubtable adversary's trickery—and then again, I should have been able to take possession of him with a single word. Would it not have been sufficient for me to order my medium to lift her wand in order for Tserpchikopf to be nailed to the spot?"

The Great Psychagogue paused, then murmured: "But one can't think of everything. God alone is infallible, and I'm merely his servant. I can't complain about being worth no more, in certain cases, than other men. What merit would I have, in fact, if I only had to express my desire in order for it to be realized?"

Pointing to the three bandits held by his aides, the Great Psychagogue went on, in a firm tone: "After all, our expedition has not been fruitless. These Pawns will join Gustave Panloude and Azilis de Tréguilly. As for the King of the Chessmen, he's been able to slip through my fingers, but I shan't allow myself to be stopped by any obstacle, and the war

I've declared against him will only end with his capture or his death. Let's all go back into the Tour Jaune. While Fréjus and Frank watch the four prisoners, Otto can go in search of cabs, and Rudolph and Annunciata can help me disinter the mutilated body of the sinister King of the Chessmen's last victim."

Otto carried out his task quickly, and at daybreak, the Great Psychagogue, his followers and the four captives drew away from the Accursed Villa in carriages to return to Paris. But the search that the Master, his disciple and his medium had undertaken had had an unexpected result. Sâr Dubnotal found, in fact, that Annie's cadaver, buried in the grounds of the Tour Jaune on January 16, had been exhumed since then and taken elsewhere.[25]

---

[25] Although this is by no means the only lacuna in the unfolding plot, it is a particularly significant one. Presumably, "Annie Stephenson" was only haunting the grounds of the Tour Jaune because her body had been buried there, and it must still have been there when the astral photograph was taken. But when in the interim between then and now, was the body removed, and by whom? More importantly, *why* was it removed? If Tserpchikopf had buried it there in order to hide it, why move it again? And if, as seems likely, Tserpchikopf had taken advantage of Sâr Dubnotal's exorcism to recover the body—for whatever purpose—before the investigators returned to watch the house, then why did he return to the house later as Fritz Petersen? Is it possible, perhaps, that he only dug up the body in order to move it to another part of the grounds, and only sent his lackeys to the house to distract Sâr Dubnotal long enough for him to receive it again? If so, he must have some powerful reason to move the body—some motive much more powerful than merely concealing the tattoo, the discovery of which by his adversaries he must now assume and accept. The desire to conceal that tattoo might, however, have been one reason for the peculiar means of execution he chose—had the quartering been properly completed, he would

Where, then, had Tserpchikopf hidden her?

The place remains unknown to us at present, but our next chapter will contain all the relevant details necessary to satisfy our readers, who will tremble at the narration of further tragic vicissitudes through which Sâr Dubnotal, the Grandmaster of Psychognosis, was to pass before bringing the bloody career of the King of the Chessmen to a definitive close.

---

have been able to take the severed arm away with him from the crime scene.

Et Jack l'Éventreur fut projeté en plein air où il demeure suspendu, la tête en bas.

JACK THE RIPPER

I. The Mysterious Hut

One evening, Frank, one of the Great Psychagogue Sâr Dubnotal's three investigators, was in the process of conscientiously searching the sordid and unsafe streets of the wretched district of Whitechapel. His colleagues, the Frenchman Fréjus and the German Otto, were undertaking their investigations in other parts of the great English metropolis, so he was alone.

A pure Anglo-Saxon and a native of that very city, formerly attached to the central office of the Metropolitan Police at Scotland Yard as a detective, Frank knew Whitechapel like the back of his hand and could, so to speak, find his way with his eyes closed through the inextricable labyrinth of streets that lay between the High Street, the long principal thoroughfare of Whitechapel, St. Catherine's Docks and the London Docks. He was not about to close his eyes, though, and never ceased to be watchful. Rain was falling and he advanced prudently along tortuous and muddy back-streets, floundering in the ruts of the insufficiently-macadamized roadways, transformed into sewers, and even more badly lit.

He had put on velvet trousers tightly cinched at the knees by leather thongs for the occasion, along with a mud-spattered mackintosh that was three-quarters threadbare, a pair of old boots and a filthy cap. It was a wise precaution, for, at that time, a decently-clad gentleman would not have ventured alone in the twilight into that district infested with malefactors, who mounted continual attacks against inoffensive passers-by under the very noses of the police.

Frank hugged the walls of the centenarian hovels. Although he pretended to be shivering under the glacial deluge of the April evening, he scarcely paid any heed to the cold and damp, which had gained no purchase on his iron constitution. He had lifted up the collar of his mackintosh and pulled his cap down over his eyes. He was walking bent over, with his head lowered and his hands in his pockets. Nothing of what was happening around him escaped his notice, however, and the furtive glances he darted in all directions, at the passers-by and into dark alley-ways or bars, testified to an ever-alert attention.

What trail was he following thus?

A few months earlier, Sâr Dubnotal had been suffered a defeat of sorts in the war in which he had engaged against a redoubtable hypnotist named Tserpchikopf. This Tserpchikopf, a sort of Proteus of Crime, who lived like a king on the fruits of his plunder, was ungraspable by virtue of his continual changes of identity. Possessed of false papers in the names of twenty different individuals, he could as easily pass for a Russian boyar as a Belgian courtier, and English lord, a Swedish artist or a French rentier, for he spoke seven or eight languages fluently and could disguise himself to perfection.

Tserpchikopf really was the Prince of Crime, and he had certainly not usurped the title of King that had been conferred upon him by a band of cut-throats known as the Chessmen. Sâr Dubnotal had administered the *coup de grâce* to that tenebrous association, enveloping with the same thrust of the net one of its Knights, or emissaries, and three of its Pawns, or subalterns—but Tserpchikopf had not fallen into the trap that had been set by the Great Psychagogue, for his mistrust was extreme and he was always on his guard. Tserpchikopf knew far too well what fate was reserved for him if he fell into the hands of the law not to take the most minute precautions. He only knew the Great Psychagogue under the pseudonym of Severus el Tebib and undoubtedly did not suspect the true nature of the overman, although he was wise enough to fear him, for Sâr Dubnotal had almost captured him several times already.

The Grandmaster of Psychognosis was all the more eager to get his hands on Tserpchikopf because the latter was the author of the most atrocious crime that had bloodied Paris for a long time. Threatened by being betrayed to the police by the former Queen of the Chessmen, from whom he had separated and who was living in the Avenue de Clichy under the pseudonym of Annie Stephenson, Tserpchikopf had tied her to the cage of an elevator and quartered her alive, after having cut the throat of the house's concierge. Disturbed just as he was about to disfigure Annie, however, and fearing that he might be discovered if the latter's identity became known, he had stolen his victim's cadaver from the morgue the following night. Under the false name of Fritz Petersen, a Swedish painter, he had rented a villa named La Tour Jaune, in the Avenue de Courbevoie in Asnières. As Sâr Dubnotal succeeded in establishing, it was in that villa's grounds that he had buried the remains of the fake Annie, but he had disinterred them shortly afterwards and transferred them to a mysterious destination. Thus, once more, the author and victim of that extraordinary drama had disappeared without a trace, without the least clue permitting the recovery of the trail.

It was then that Frank, Otto and Fréjus had set out on campaign.

At Asnières, their master had arrested three Pawns of the Chess Gang, who had gone to join Gustave Panloude, one of their colleagues who had been captured previously. The revelations of these rogues had informed the Master Psychagogue, who suspected it already, that Tserpchikopf had crossed the Channel. The three sleuths had, therefore, received orders to go to England, where a skillfully-undertaken inquiry has permitted them to infer that the audacious Slav had succeeded in deceiving the English customs regarding the contents of a certain large-sized and heavy trunk—which, he affirmed, was full of second-hand clothes, but which, in reality, must have enclosed the cadaver of his former accomplice, presumably embalmed.

Unfortunately, the criminal's trail, picked up and successfully followed as far as Charing Cross Station, had not been able to take the three investigators any further. They knew that the Slav had loaded the trunk into a hired carriage, but they did not know number of the cab. They did not know the identity of the driver and, in consequence, had no clue as to the place to which he had taken the trunk.

Since then, Frank and his friends had been reduced to trusting in luck to recover the fugitive's trail. They had every reason to suppose, however, that Tserpchikopf was still hiding in London, and probably in Whitechapel, where Panloude, alias Pawn One, had told them that he had a special relationship with a particular society.

Slavs were swarming all over Whitechapel, and the investigators, who spoke Russian fluently, hoped to gather precious information with regard to their slippery enemy, of whom they possessed an exact description—exact enough that his multiple and accomplished disguises would not be sufficient to deceive them. In any case, they had time in hand, for Sâr Dubnotal had moved to London himself and had bought a sumptuous property in the tranquil quarter of Chelsea, on the delightful promenade of Cheyne Walk on the bank of the Thames.

That was why Frank found himself in Whitechapel on that foggy and rainy April day. His mission, and that of his comrades, was rather complicated. They had orders not only to search for the cadaver of Annie Stephenson but also to try to establish her true identity. Sâr Dubnotal did not in fact, imagine that he would be able to put his hands on the cunning Tserpchikopf directly, but he hoped that his investigators might be fortunate enough to discover one of his new criminal accomplices and the real name, relatives or former acquaintances of Annie Stephenson, who was said by the captured Pawns to be a native of London. If he could discover the true identity of the ex-Queen of the Chessmen, the Great Psychagogue would have a new trump card in his hand. Tserpchikopf might even be hiding in the milieu in which he had made the woman's acquaintance.

Frank had been wandering around Whitechapel for several hours when he came to an abrupt halt as he was moving alongside the fence of some waste ground near to an old abandoned factory. Fifty meters in front of him, a man was crossing a somber and deserted street and heading at a rapid pace toward the entrance to the waste ground. The darkness prevented him from being seen distinctly. The man had not seen Frank, for the latter had swiftly hidden in the dense shadow of the fence.

The individual was bent over by a heavy burden, and it appeared—so far as the obscurity permitted Frank to judge—that the burden was wrapped in a large canvas sack. Before venturing into the roadway, the mysterious porter, who had come out of a house nearby, had taken care to look both ways along the street.

Intrigued by this conduct, which seemed suspicious, Frank took care not to emerge from hiding. He let the other reach the gate of the waste ground without losing sight of him.

Supporting his sack with his left hand, the man stuck the other hand into his pocket, from which he took a shiny object that might have been a key. Indeed, Frank's ears perceived a significant grating sound, and the gate opened in front of the individual, who went through it hastily, then closed it behind him, without letting go of his burden.

The Great Psychagogue's investigator did not know what to think. He took the opportunity to note the name of the street—Lambeth Street—and then slid a prudent gaze through the planks of the fence.

In the middle of the waste ground there was a wooden hut that was one of the outbuildings of the old factory. The man with the sack lost no time in reaching its threshold. Frank saw him open the door and go in.

Although the street was completely deserted, the investigator, increasingly intrigued, hesitated to climb over the fence

239

into the waste ground—but curiosity soon overcame his scruples and he groped his way along the fence, searching for a handhold that would allow him to climb over or a gap through which he could slip.

The worm-eaten planks were hardly held together. Becoming impatient, Frank ended up applying a thrust of his shoulder to two or three of them, which gave way and produced a passage through which he could insinuate himself. After replacing the planks as best he could and darted a final glance along Lambeth Street to make sure that no one had seen him, he moved forward quietly, crouching down, in the direction of the hut.

He was careful to follow the arc of a circle in order to stay out of the individual's line of sight in case the other suddenly opened the door again. When he reached the back of the small building without incident, Frank took a deep breath. He was now more anxious than ever that he might be taken by surprise. In spite of the rain-soaked ground, he crept up to the wall of planks on his hands and knees, stuck his ear to it and listened hard. Strangely enough, he could not hear any sound at all—and when he put his eye to a crack in the wall he could not see anyone inside.

Had the individual taken cover? Had he detected Frank's presence? That seemed improbable, in view of the precautions that latter had taken as he approached.

For eight or ten minutes, the investigator remained in a state of prudent expectation. Nothing moved inside the hut, and the silence was beginning to seem disconcerting. He had not been imagining things, though. He was certain—as certain as one can be—that the man with the sack had gone into that hut and had not come out again.

By Jove! he said to himself. *What can the lascar be doing in there? Has he suddenly dropped dead or fallen into a catalepsy?*

Frank waited for a few seconds more and then, wanting to solve the mystery, slowly and soundlessly approached the door. Before taking the risk of turning the handle, he checked that he had his revolver and his electric torch handy. Reassured on both points, the bold fellow turned the door-handle. The door opened without difficulty, letting him through.

"Hey there, fellow!" he shouted, as he went in. "Where are you and what are you doing?"

To his great surprise, there was no reply. When he pushed the door to behind him, he found himself in pitch darkness. Before repeating his question he pressed the switch of his torch, which darted a luminous beam into the darkness—but Frank did not see a living soul. He shone the beam of the torch into every corner in vain; he saw nothing but a heap of old scrap iron. The man with the sack had vanished into thin air.

"That's odd!" the investigator murmured, continuing to search ever last corner of the hut with his gaze. What is this phantasmagoria?"

To salve his conscience, he moved a few iron bars that were piled up in a corner of the hut, mingled with old locks and rusty tools. No one would have been able to hide underneath them, and Frank was just about to abandon his investigation when he made a discovery that encouraged him to persevere in his efforts. At one point in the floor that he had just cleared there was a sort of button made of wood and bone, reminiscent of an electrical commutator-switch.

The investigator observed that the button was solidly embedded in one of the floorboards, positioned in such a way that by stretching out an arm one could reach it through the heap of scrap iron that had covered it over a little while ago.

Right! he said to himself. *Is the floor false, and is there a subterranean passage underneath it into which the man with the sack went after activating the switch? I have to clarify the enigma!*

He made a tour of the room, holding his torch close to the floor, and noticed that there was a crack extending along the entire length of the four walls. Convinced that he had the key to the puzzle and that the floor of the hut was some sort of platform—a platform capable of descending into the ground and then resuming its original position by virtue of some simple mechanism—Frank went back to the button. As he examined it more carefully and attentively his last doubts dissipated.

I'm not mistaken, he thought. *The subterranean space definitely exists, and that's how my man disappeared so easily. I wish I hadn't disturbed the heap of iron. If I'd been cleverer, I'd have been able to discover the button without touching anything. Let's put everything back in place—although I fear that my man might perceive that an intruder has discovered his secret anyway.*

The investigator set to work. He was trying to erase every trace of his presence when he touched the button by mistake. An exclamation of surprise escaped his lips. The floor abruptly started to move, and he had the impression that all solid support was disappearing under him. At the same time, a stale, damp and nauseating odor caught in his throat and made him sneeze.

"By Jove!" he exclaimed. And he knelt down on that sort of trapdoor, which continued to descend into empty space like a cage of an elevator.

II. The Telepsychic Warning

At about 10 p.m., Fréjus and Otto returned to the Cheyne Walk residence to make their reports to Sâr Dubnotal. The Frenchman and the German had nothing interesting to tell him. They offered their apologies and expressed the hope that Rank—who had not yet returned—might have been more fortunate.

The Great Psychagogue had new instructions to give his three sleuths. He therefore invited Otto and Fréjus to await the arrival of their colleague in his study. Rudolph, the Master's favorite disciple, was also there. To pass the time, the four men engaged in a conversation that soon took a particular turn.

It was then the sinister era when the monstrous exploits of Jack the Ripper were bloodying Whitechapel and shaking the entire world with a great spasm of fear and horror.[26] The crimes of that mysterious murderer had been succeeding one another with a disconcerting regularity for some time. Scarcely a week went by without one of his victims being found, mutilated in the most barbaric fashion.

Jack the Ripper, as his name indicates well enough, was not content to take the lives of the poor women he was accustomed to attack; he took pleasure in literally disemboweling them. With a thrust of his knife he opened the abdomen, drew out the entrails from the quivering body and, by an inexplicable caprice of monomania, plunged the dead woman's shoes into the frightful wound. That was the seal with which he marked his victims, his bloody signature—an atrocious challenge issued to the London police, whose powerlessness to do

---

[26] The first two episodes of the saga were explicitly set in August 1889 and *The Quartered Woman of Montmartre* in January 1890, with *The Astral Trail* presumably occurring sometime between August and December 1889. Therefore, the implication of "a few months later" is that the April in which this story begins is that of 1890. Although the five "canonical" murders nowadays attributed to "Jack the Ripper" were all committed in a period of a few weeks in 1888, the contemporary scandal lasted long after that; the police and newspapers of the day continued to make possible connections between subsequent murders and the unapprehended Ripper until the early months of 1891, and anxiety was certainly still very widespread in April 1890, when it was anyone's guess how many of the murders already investigated might have been committed by a single individual and how long the relevant killings might go on. Very few bodies except for the canonical five suffered any extensive mutilation, let alone mutilations as specific as those cited here, but rumor routinely overshadowed mere facts at the time. It is also worth noting that Tserpchikops was in London in the fall of 1889.

anything was terrifying for the honest people of Whitechapel. When would the bloody sequence stop?

A dozen women, young and old, had fallen to the monster's dagger in succession. For preference, he attacked beggar-women, who were doubtless less reluctant than others to follow him when he lured them into the inhabited house, cellar or stable in which he had chosen to perpetrate his crime at his ease. When beggars were in short supply, the working class also furnished easy prey. The working girls of Whitechapel no longer wanted to go home after nightfall, for fear of running into him at the corner of a deserted street and being subjected to the same fate as two or three of their comrades, whose sudden disappearance had been initially attributed to their having run away, but whose odiously mutilated cadavers had been discovered at a later date.

The monster's audacity equaled his ferocity. His diabolical skill in evading the sleuths launched against him was almost prodigious. People had even begun to wonder whether Jack the Ripper might not be a myth, and whether the crimes so long attributed to a single malefactor might not be the work of several monomaniacs who, attracted by exemplary contagion, were mechanically repeating the method of the initial murderer. The latter hypothesis appeared increasingly plausible, for the arrest of any individual caught *in flagrante delicto* in the murder of a woman and accused of being Jack the Ripper was immediately followed by the discovery of a new crime. Sâr Dubnotal did not, however, seem to find that fact conclusive, and his aides had often heard him say that once Tserpchikopf had been arrested, he would take it upon himself to prove that Jack was no myth by arresting him too.

At any rate, seeing that Frank was so late in coming back that evening, and knowing that he had carried his investigations into the very theater of Jack the Ripper's sinister exploits, the Master Psychagogue and his aides wondered whether chance might not have put him in the presence of the redoubtable criminal and whether something bad might have happened to him.

"I know that Frank is a stout fellow who isn't afraid of anything and prides himself on being able to knock any man down with a single punch," Sâr Dubnotal said, "but his very intrepidity might have caused him to fall into a trap, and I won't be tranquil until I see him again."

"It's after midnight," said Rudolph. "I fear that waiting up might be pointless."

"Go to bed, if you wish, my children," said Sâr Dubnotal. "I'll wait up on my own."

"We shan't leave you, Master," the disciple replied, respectfully. "We're too worried ourselves to get a wink of sleep—but, if our presentiment isn't mistaken, and Frank is in real danger, how can we relieve the uncertainty? What can we do?"

The Great Psychagogue reflected momentarily, and eventually said: "Fetch Annunciata, Rudolph."

The disciple hastened to defer to his Master's desire and soon returned with the young Italian woman, Annunciata Gianetti—one of the most famous mediums in the entire world.

Rudolph and the two investigators wondered what Sâr Dubnotal intended to do. Was he going to interrogate the Beyond via the intermediary of the Italian, in order to find out what had become of Frank? Their curiosity did not last long.

"Annunciata," said the Great Psychagogue, fixing the powerful gaze of his green eyes upon his medium, "I'm going to put you into a hypnosomnambulistic trance."

"Why, Master?" asked the Italian woman, who was already quivering in a magnetic spasm, in an anxious tone.

"Because Frank, of whom we have no news, might have need of us and might send us a telepsychic call for help."

The explanation satisfied and visibly reassured the Master's aides. They knew that telepsychy, or human telephony, sometimes rendered the Great Psychagogue signal services. Annunciata, or some other medium, served him as a transmitting and receiving apparatus, and he could communicate his thoughts by that means, or register those of a third party, no matter how far apart they might be.

In order to do that, it was sufficient for him to put his medium in what is called the "second state"—which is to say, into a sort of attenuated hypnotic trance—which rendered her capable of producing, in the purely psychic order of things, phenomena analogous to those of wireless telegraphy. This was what he did once again, and the magnetized Annunciata let herself collapse on to a sofa as if she were dead.

"Are you asleep?" asked Sâr Dubnotal.

"Yes, Master," she replied, without opening her eyes or moving.

"Good! Concentrate your thoughts on Frank, and if he gives any sign of life, don't hesitate to inform us."

The Italian woman released a resigned sigh and remained motionless. An hour went by without her prostrate body being shaken by the faintest quiver. Even her respiration seemed to be suspended, and her face was as white as a sheet,

Sâr Dubnotal, Rudolph, Otto and Fréjus contemplated her silently, their expectation full of anxiety. Might it already be too late to enter into communication with Frank? Might the Englishman have succumbed to the blows of a mysterious enemy, without having time to utter a mental cry for his Master's help? It seemed only too possible.

All of a sudden, however, the four men's hope was renewed. With a single bound, Annunciata had just left her improvised couch. Haggard and pale, she stood up to the full extent of her height and her extended arms pointed to something invisible, while her lips moved feverishly.

"There...there!" she stammered. "Look!"

"At what?" asked Sâr Dubnotal.

"Look...Frank."

"Did he call you?"

"Yes."

"Where is he?"

"There...there!" Suddenly, she collapsed in a heap on the study carpet, stammering these seemingly incoherent words: "Lambeth Street... Whitechapel... waste ground... hut... subterranean space... chloroform... evildoer!"

III. A Savage Duel

We left Frank at the moment when the false floor of the mysterious hut in Lambeth Street fell away beneath him, drawing him into the bosom of the Earth.

The descending movement accelerated. Then, after several seconds, there was a shock and an abrupt stop.

Frank had not let go of his revolver or his electric torch. When the platform was no longer moving, his first concern was to aim the beam of his torch into the thick darkness surrounding him. At the same time, he raised his revolver, ready to fire if anyone threatened him—for he expected to find himself face to face with the man with the sack, who, furious at the realization that he had been tracked into his most secret refuge, would probably greet him with a weapon in his hand.

The investigator could not see anyone, though. The light of his torch only illuminated a narrow space in front of him. He found himself at the entrance of a subterranean passage that must be fairly long, whose far end he could not see.

Prudently, Frank stepped off the platform. Scarcely had he set foot on the muddy and fetid soil of the passage than the floor, relieved of his weight, rose up again automatically into the well into which it had descended. The roof of the tunnel seemed to close in over Frank's head; he was momentarily dumbstruck, wondering how he was going to get out of that tomb.

He soon made a discovery that reassured him. Set in the wall—which must have been several centuries old, so many of its stones were crumbling—there was a button identical to the one that Frank had found in the mobile floor of the hut. When he pressed the button, he saw the platform coming down again. Certain now that he would be able to leave the subterranean workings at will, he stopped pressing and allowed the apparatus to go back up.

"That's a stroke of luck," he murmured. "The man must have gone along this dark corridor; he probably doesn't suspect that I'm here." He carefully altered the controls of his torch in such a way as to mask almost all of the lens, so that only a trickle of light would filter through, permitting him to guide himself without betraying his presence. Then he took his shoes off, in order to move forward more quietly through the sticky mud, whose putrid emanations continued to sting his nostrils unpleasantly. Tying his shoes together and slinging them over his shoulder, he set off on the perilous exploration of the tunnel that chance had allowed him to discover.

From Sâr Dubnotal's schooling, Frank had learned that prudence is the mother of safety. As brave and strong as a lion, the investigator only felt an easily-comprehensible sentiment of suspicion, not of fear; but he did not want to take any unnecessary risks. Hugging the wall and inching forward, he took 20 minutes to travel the 30 or 40 meters that the tunnel extended, in a straight line, before arriving at a sort of broad fork, where it bifurcated at an obtuse angle, dividing into two from then on.

When he reached the fork, Frank was only slightly hesitant as to which way to go. In fact, footprints deeply encrusted in the mud indicated to him which route the man with the sack had taken. That exceedingly fresh trail extended into the tunnel on the right, and it was that direction that the investigator took, after having crossed the fork carefully.

This tunnel was much narrower and more tortuous than the first. Two men could not have passed through it abreast, although its ceiling—which was threatening to collapse in places—was high enough for a man of Frank's stature not to have to lower his head.

After many turnings, the Englishman remarked that the tunnel ended in a sort of excavation that seemed to be the work of nature, and he hesitated before going any further. He dared not unmask his torch completely, so he could not measure the dimensions of the hole. In front of him, the ground slanted away in a steep and slippery slope. He had to hold on to a projection of the side-wall in order not to slide down to the bottom of a sort of basin whose depth he did not know and which infiltrations might have filled with water.

He listened; there was no sound.

Convinced that, if he had come this far, the man must have gone on through a corridor whose entrance was hidden from him by the darkness, Frank decided to project the full beam of his torch into the hole and around its walls.

A dull exclamation of horror escaped him. The excavation was not full of water, as he had imagined, but full of bones.

Hundreds of fleshless whitened skeletons were heaped up in the hollow. Skulls tibias, ribs and spines were inextricably entangled there—but what made the deepest impression on Frank, what congealed the blood in his veins, was seeing a living human being—the man with the sack—crouching on the macabre heap of bones!

The sack, now empty, lay at his feet. The cadaver of a woman had rolled out upon the skeletons, and the man was looking at Frank with an expression so ferocious that in spite of his bravery, the Englishman felt a chill in the marrow of his bones.

That weakness was, however, temporary. In the blink of an eye, Frank recovered his self-possession. Immediately, he extinguished his torch, so that it would not offer a target to the other, who had made as if to take a weapon out of his pocket.

Protected by the darkness, Frank changed his position and then called out: "Hey, fellow, what are you doing here?"

"What are you?" replied a rude voice.

"Me?"

"Yes."

"I'm tracking a fine gallows-bird, if I'm not mistaken."

"Really?"

"Chances are that that's the case, at any rate."

"And what makes you think so?"

"Everything, by Jove! Would an honest Englishman find himself where you are, in the company of these skeletons and that corpse?"

"I don't have to account to anyone."

"That remains to be seen."

"It's definite."

"What if I don't share your opinion?"

"The difference is easy to put right," the man said. "Are you a policeman?"

"No," said Frank.

"You're lying!"

"That's an insult that is never addressed to me without it costing the speaker dear," Frank roared. "Believe me or don't, it doesn't matter to me. You won't be long delayed in regretting your insolence either way."

"Who are you, if you don't belong to the police?"

"I'm a curiosity-seeker who happened to stray into these catacombs," the Englishman said, laughing sardonically.

"You're lying!" the voice repeated.

This dialogue was exchanged in the most absolute darkness. Frank, who knew that the other was as wary as he was himself, sought in vain to pierce the darkness. "Enough discussion," he said, dryly. "I've got you—give up."

It was the turn of the other to laugh sardonically. "You've got me? Come and take me, then!"

"That's what I'll do, be assured."

"How, and why?"

"How? I don't know yet, but one way or another, which I promise you won't be long delayed. Why? You know very well."

"No,"

"You've nothing for which to reproach yourself?"

"Nothing!"

"What about the cadaver that I saw at your feet? You can't tell me that it was one of the skeletons of this ancient ossuary."

"You're too curious, friend."

"Possibly—but answer me."

"I don't have to answer. Since you aren't with the police, what right do you have to question me?"

"The right that every honest man has to ask a scoundrel the reason for his conduct."

"Are you quite sure that I'm a scoundrel?"

"If you weren't one, you wouldn't have taken so many precautions in bringing the sack containing that woman's body here."

The man uttered a terrible stream of oaths. "Curse you! Curse you! So you've spied on me, followed me and lied to me impudently by saying that chance alone led you here?"

"I didn't lie. It was chance that put me on your track, and it was involuntarily that I descended into these subterranean workings—but now that I'm here, I'm staying here, and I'm not leaving until I've put my hand on your collar."

"Oho! You'll have to put a bullet in my flesh beforehand."

"I'll do that, if necessary."

"You talk as if I counted for nothing. Tell me, friend—are you a man of honor?"

"That's not for you to doubt."

"All right! Well, I have a proposition to make to you."

"Go on," said Frank, calmly, "but be quick, for my time is limited."

The same sinister laugh echoed within the hole. "You couldn't have put it better. Your time is indeed, limited, and you shall know what it costs to meddle in my affairs. But since you're a gentleman, I'll show myself to be a good prince and give you a chance to get out of this hornet's-nest alive. Are you armed?"

"Yes," said Frank.

"Good. Do you want to fight?"

"A duel?"

"A duel."

"You're armed too?"

"To the teeth."

"I'd like that," said the investigator, "but I warn you that you'd do better to surrender. I have some skill as a marksman."

"I shan't surrender, though," cried the man—who must have changed his position just then, for Frank heard the bones of the charnel-house creaking.

"You'd prefer to run away?"

"Run away? This is how I run away! Take that!"

At the same instant, a sharp detonation echoed noisily in the cavities of the subterranean space, and a bullet whistled past the investigator's ear.

Before returning fire, Frank lay down on the ground and darted a rapid beam from his torch in the approximate direction of his adversary—but the latter must have found a safe hiding-place, for he remained invisible, and it was at hazard that Frank discharged his weapon. Another detonation was confused with that of his gun, and his torch slipped out of his hand, shattered by a bullet.

"Aha!" exclaimed the man, mockingly. "You're a good shot, it seems. What do you think of that one?"

Frank, profoundly annoyed at having been placed at a disadvantage at the very commencement of the duel, uttered a groan of irritation. The loss of his torch put him in an awkward situation, inasmuch as his antagonist had a torch of his own, which he put to use with diabolical skill. Immediately, a beam of light cut through the darkness and struck the place where Frank was lying prone.

The latter tried to do the same to his opponent and shatter his torch, but the individual maneuvered it so cleverly that several attempts failed. The bullets struck the walls around the brilliant dot without extinguishing it.

Fortunately, Frank had been able to lie down behind an outcrop of rock, and he was shielded from the hail of projectiles that the man rained upon him.

When his revolver's magazine was empty, the investigator, who still had a dozen cartridges in his pocket, hastened to reload it. Then he started firing again, but less hurriedly. Even so, it was not until the final shot that he succeeded in emulating his antagonist's feat; the other's torch finally burst into shards.

"Curse you! I don't have any more bullets!" howled the man.

"Me neither," Frank replied. "But I have a knife."

And he crept toward his adversary, groping his way forward.

The man had made use of a stratagem that was nearly fatal for Sâr Dubnotal's intrepid agent. More shots suddenly resounded, and Frank often wondered how he escaped that hellish fire. "Ah! Cheat!" he roared, leaping to his feet and diving straight ahead, armed only with his knife.

This time, the man was really out of bullets, for no gunshot stopped the investigator's progress—but the latter was almost immediately paralyzed in another manner.

The characteristic odor of chloroform had just spread through the cave, and Frank was seized by a sudden dizziness. His head was buzzing, and his legs gave way beneath him as sparks danced before his eyes. A large jar or demijohn full of chloroform must have been placed there among the bones to serve in case of need, and the bandit had broken it as he drew back.

The stupefying vapors of the liberated liquid rose up so densely that Frank as unable to resist them. He tried to beat a retreat, but his strength let him down. Like an inert mass he fell into the ossuary.

Feeling life abandoning him, he had but one thought: to concentrate the last remnants of energy that still remained to him to send a telepsychic cry for help to the Master and give him the means if not to help him, at least to avenge his death.

IV. To the Rescue

Annunciata Gianetti's unconsciousness did not last long. Scarcely had she finished speaking than Sâr Dubnotal ran to her aid.

"I understand everything," he murmured, as he leaned over the young woman's inert body and lavished cares upon her that soon brought her round.

With that first duty fulfilled, the Great Psychagogue was no longer thinking of anything but flying to Frank's rescue. "Get your satchel, Rudolph," he said to his disciple, swiftly. "We might need it. You, Otto, run and tell the coachman to hitch up the coupé right away."

While Rudolph and the German investigator ran to carry out the Master's orders, Fréjus lifted Annunciata up, and then helped Sâr Dubnotal to wrap her in a warm fur cloak. "Where are we going?" he asked.

"You? Nowhere. You'll stay here, awaiting further orders. Only Otto and Annunciata will go with me."

"Very well, Master," said Fréjus, slightly annoyed not to be a member of the party.

"Above all," Sâr Dubnotal instructed, "Don't leave for a moment. I might have to send you a message tonight, summoning you urgently."

"A telepsychic message?"

"Yes."

"Very well, Master," Fréjus repeated, is a more satisfied tone.

Five minutes later, Sâr Dubnotal, Rudolph, Otto and Annunciata took their places in the coupé. "We're going to Lambeth Street, Whitechapel," said the Great Psychagogue to his coachman, Joseph. "Go at top speed. Stop some distance away from Lambeth Street."

The speedy rig flew through the night along the right bank of the Thames as far as Blackfriars Bridge, and then plunged into an interminable labyrinth of side-streets. A little less than two hours sufficed, however, to complete the long journey. The carriage stopped at about 3 a.m. at the junction of Whitechapel High Street and Commercial Road, which was a few minutes away from Lambeth Street.

"Wait for us here until 5 a.m., Joseph," Sâr Dubnotal said. "If we haven't returned by then, go back to Chelsea on your own, and we'll come back by cab, or by the District Line."

"What are we going to do, Master?" Rudolph asked, respectfully.

"You understood that Frank was in danger?"

"Yes, but are you sure that he'll be in Lambeth Street?"

"He was there when Annunciata registered his telepsychic call for help, at any rate. Unless there's some mistake, there must be a waste ground bordering the street and a hut on the waste ground. If I understand the broken message that my medium transmitted to us correctly, it's in that hut that we'll pick up Frank's trail."

"Didn't Annunciata pronounce the word *chloroform*?"

"Yes—I fear that Frank might have fallen into a trap." Sâr Dubnotal paused for reflection. "But let's hurry. We have no more than two hours of darkness before us, and that might not be enough. We'll go two by two—Annunciata with me and you, Otto, with Rudolph. Try to be as inconspicuous as possible."

The Master Psychagogue took the lead, with his medium, and his little troop followed his instructions. It was still raining, favoring Sâr Dubnotal's plans. They did not encounter any policeman on the way—or at least, none that they could recognize.

Having arrived at the fence, the Great Psychagogue observed, to his satisfaction, that there was a hut standing in the middle of the waste ground. He made a sign to Otto and Rudolph, who were walking behind him on the opposite sidewalk. Then he moved aside two or three planks, as easily as if they were wisps of straw, and held Annunciata to pass through the opening—which he blocked up again as soon as he and his aides had gone through in their turn.

"Surround the hut," he whispered to his two men.

In the blink of an eye, Rudolph and the German were in position.

Certain that no one could escape from the hut, Sâr Dubnotal headed directly for the entrance and knocked on the door. Having obtained no reply, he summoned his companions an opened it. The hut was, of course, empty. It did not take them long to make sure of that and to recommence the search that Frank had carried out before them. It was equally brief.

Rudolph had lit a lamp taken from his satchel. On bending over, Sâr Dubnotal perceived the elevator-button next to the heap of scrap iron and guessed the truth. He put out his hand, saying: "Look out! There must be a cellar into which we shall probably descend. Lean on one another, and don't move."

He pressed the button, and the apparatus started moving, without the aides getting overly excited, having been forewarned. Even so, when the platform rose up again automatically, Otto and Rudolph could not help shivering. The subterranean space was reminiscent of a tomb, and they thought that if the elevator mechanism were to go wrong they would have a great deal of trouble getting out of it.

We shall soon see that their presentiment was not deceiving them.

Sâr Dubnotal's calm attitude reassured them, however. The Master, armed with the electric lamp, inspected the ground carefully. "Look!" he said to his companions. "Frank came this way—I recognize his footprints."

"Let's go!" said Rudolph, with the impetuosity of youth.

"Gently!" said Sâr Dubnotal. "Stay behind me and we'll go forward in Indian file."

Having formed up, the little troop did not take long to pass the fork and go along the narrow tunnel, in which Frank's tracks continued to be distinctly marked in the mud.

Suddenly, the Great Psychagogue was confronted by the ossuary. "Great God!" he said.

Two bodies were lying on the bones: Frank's and that of a young woman. They could not tell whether the investigator was dead or simply unconscious, but with respect to the woman there was no possible doubt. When Rudolph, Otto and Annunciata rejoined their Master, a triple exclamation of horror awoke echoes in the cave.

At first glance, the Master's three aides had recognized the two victims—not just Frank, but also the young woman whose cadaver lay beside him. The second cadaver was that of Annie Stephenson, the quartered woman of Montmartre. Her body, evidently embalmed, was in a state of perfect conservation, although it was frightful to behold with its waxen face, its bulging eyes, its disheveled hair and the hideous wounds in its limbs, half-detached from the trunk.

The unfortunate woman was still in her night-dress, and the canvas sack that lay beside her explained how the murderer had brought her here.

"Tserpchikopf!" said Sâr Dubnotal dully. "It's Tserpchikopf who has also passed this way. Frank has discovered his lair, but the wretch has done for him."

"Is he dead?" asked Rudolph, breathless with emotion.

Without replying, Sâr Dubnotal advanced toward the inert form of his follower, but as he descended into the hollow of the ossuary suffocating emanations of chloroform forced him to renounce the project for the time being. Stopping his nostrils with his handkerchief, he returned to his companions. "Tserpchikopf has chloroformed him," he said.

"Oh!" said Otto, at that moment. "A revolver, Master!" Crouching down, he picked up a weapon whose barrel and magazine were black with powder.

"It's his," said Sâr Dubnotal. "If he's succumbed to the force of a treacherous enemy, at least he put up a desperate resistance."

"What a pity we weren't able to get here sooner," sighed the German.

"The Slav might not have left the subterranean workings," Rudolph remarked. "There's another tunnel, which we'd do well to explore."

Sâr Dubnotal shook his head. "I fear that he has indeed escaped by that route," he murmured. "We'll explore the tunnel, of course, but let's take care of more urgent matters first."

Under the Master's orders, Rudolph a strip of antiseptic cloth from his satchel, which the former knotted behind his head, being careful to cover the mouth and the nasal passages completely. This protected against the action of the chloroform vapor that was still emerging from the ossuary, the Great Psychagogue was able to approach the dangerous spot with impunity. Rudolph provided him with torchlight from a distance.

First, Sâr Dubnotal lifted Frank's body, loaded it on to his shoulders as he might have done with the body of a child, and deposited it at the feet of Rudolph and Otto, who hastened to sound his chest. Then he returned to Annie's body, put it back into its sack, and carried it away in the same fashion.

Then the Master took off the antiseptic strip, which was making it awkward for him to breathe and speak, and asked anxiously: "Is he still breathing?"

"Yes," said Rudolph, "but very feebly."

"God be praised!" said Sâr Dubnotal, fervently. "If he's breathing, I can save him."

For several minutes, there was a tragic pause, which put an atrocious pressure on Rudolph's and Otto's nerves and even tormented those of the impassive Annunciata. Might Sâr Dubnotal be taking his science a little too much for granted? Could he really bring that human wreck back to life?

By means of a spatula, he separated Frank's clenched jaws, and trickled a thin stream of brown liquid from a bottle taken from his disciple's sack between the poor fellow's lips...

"He's coming round!"

At these words from the Master, his companions leaned over the quasi-cadaver eagerly, and observed with great joy that he was indeed coming out of his lethargy. His eyelashes were fluttering and his lips were moving. Respiration, hesitant at first but becoming increasingly powerful, lifted his breast. Finally, a feeble murmur reached Sâr Dubnotal's ears and those of his aides.

"Where am I? My God, what happened?"

"Rub his limbs," the Master said to Otto and his disciple, simply. "His memory will come back along with the feeling."

V. Between Scylla and Charybdis

Ten minutes later, Frank was back on his feet, offering warm thanks to his Master, who had just snatched him from the jaws of certain death.

Pressed with questions, he told the story of his duel with the man with the sack, and was only half-surprised to learn that his adversary must have been Tserpchikopf. By contrast, he nearly fell over when Sâr Dubnotal told him who the dead woman was.

"What? That's Annie Stephenson?"

"There's no doubt about it," said Sâr Dubnotal. "I have a photograph of the unfortunate woman, and the resemblance is striking."

"But the murder took place several months ago," Frank remarked.

"Tserpchikopf has embalmed the corpse. Since he was carrying it with him, the odor would have betrayed him if he had not taken that precaution."

"Oh, the blackguard! The infamous scoundrel!"

"Yes," said Sâr Dubnotal. "But he'll be punished for his crimes, and if you can, we'll set about searching for him immediately."

The ossuary had no other exit than the tunnel through which they had come, so the five companions had to retrace their steps and continue their investigation of the other passage leading from the fork. That tunnel, much broader and longer than the first, was explored from end to end by Sâr Dubnotal and his aides, but, like the other, it appeared to end in a cul-de-sac. If there was a concealed entrance therein, they could not find it.

Whether it was by that route or by means of the elevator to the hut, Tserpchikopf had, at any rate, escaped. Given the obvious futility of his search, Sâr Dubnotal appeared to give up. He consulted his watch and said: "4:15 p.m. Quickly, my children! We'll go back up with Annie Stephenson's corpse, and one of you can run to the coupé, which should still be at the junction of the Commercial Road."

In all haste, the little troop returned to the ossuary. The robust Otto put the funeral parcel over his shoulder and, following the Great Psychagogue, everyone headed for the elevator.

"How were you able to get down here?" Frank asked his Master.

"Your telepsychic cry for help put us on the right track," said Sâr Dubnotal. "Once we were in the hut, it wasn't difficult to find the button that activated the elevator."

"Another button set in the wall will allow us to go back up," said the Englishman.

"I know," said Sâr Dubnotal. "I too saw that button, which must operate the hidden mechanism of the elevator."

"Where do you think the mechanism is, Master?"

"Within the thickness if the wall, undoubtedly. It seems to me to be built on the model of a dumb-waiter mechanism."

"That's extraordinary," said Rudolph. "How was Tserpchikopf able to obtain a refuge so discreet and so safe?"

"Nothing simpler," replied Sâr Dubnotal. "Beneath the surface of London, as of almost all the old European cities, there is a vast labyrinth. Our ancestors liked nothing better than hollowing out mysterious subterranean workings in which, in case of necessity, they could take refuge with their wealth and their families. Sometimes they're transformed into ossuaries, like the famous catacombs of Paris."

"So the skeletons in the cave will have been there for a long time?"

"For centuries, my friend. Chance, or the study of an old map of London, revealed the existence of that subterranean den to Tserpchikopf, of which he immediately thought of making use. The installation of the dumb-waiter was child's play for that accomplished evil-doer, and it might be that we now hold the key to a certain enigma."

"What enigma, Master?"

"That pertaining to the identity of Jack the Ripper. You know as well as I do that the sinister villain of Whitechapel has always avoided the most active researches of the police. Why? How? That's what I think we've discovered."

"What?" cried Rudolph, Frank and Otto in unison. "Tserpchikopf and Jack the Ripper are one and the same?"

"That's my thinking, at least," Sâr Dubnotal replied, coolly. "By meditating on the subject of the King of the Chessmen, I've ended up thinking him capable of anything."

"But why would Tserpchikopf amuse himself with the cowardly massacre of so many unfortunate women?"

"I can't explain that yet," said the Master Psychagogue. "That's something that disconcerts me, something that would almost plunge me into doubt, if…"

"If?"

Sâr Dubnotal put on a somber smile. "Time is too pressing, my children, for me to satisfy your legitimate curiosity now. We'll resume this conversation later. Let's hurry up and get out o this vestibule of Hell—otherwise Joseph will leave and we'll have a great deal of difficulty getting back to Chelsea with Miss Stephenson's body."

The group had arrived at the end of the large tunnel, beneath the trapdoor in the hut. Swiftly, Frank pressed the button—but, to the amazement and extreme disquiet of his companions, the mobile floor of the hut did not budge. It appeared that the mechanism of the elevator was no longer working.

Very pale, Rudolph, Otto and Frank looked at their Master—who, along with Annunciata, seemed to have preserved his tranquility.

"We're immured in this pit, Master," the Englishman stammered. "The mechanism won't work."

Sâr Dubnotal was about to answer when a distant voice, muffled as if by the thickness of the vault behind which it seemed to resound, cut him off.

"Immured—yes you are, you vile rogues! Oh, you wanted to ruin me, Severus el Tebib. You and your clique have sworn to track me down without truce or respite, but you don't know who you're dealing with! You might as well put ropes round your necks right away! I've got you now. No human power can extract you from my claws, and you shall know the cost of declaring war on me."

"Tserpchikopf!" exclaimed Rudolph and the two investigators.

"Tserpchikopf indeed!" the voice repeated, sarcastically. "Tserpchikopf, who is finally taking his revenge—a complete and definitive revenge! Ah, you didn't expect this, eh, Gentlemen? You'll be able to reflect with rested heads on the inconveniences that can result from getting mixed up in other people's business. One of your friends is already waiting for you in the depths of this hole—rejoin him. As for me, I'll go to see the parish priest so that he can say the prayer for the dead on your behalf. You can get into my subterranean vault but you can't get out as easily."

"I shall, however, get out!" shouted Sâr Dubnotal, who was not in the least intimidated by his enemy's ignoble threats.

"I'm curious to know how you'll do it. I've destroyed the elevator mechanism, and I defy you to get through the walls of the tomb into which foolish recklessness has caused you to descend while alive."

Sâr Dubnotal made a sign bidding his companions to be silent. Then, turning to the Italian woman, he murmured in a voice fainter than a breath: "Annunciata, my girl, you have to get us out of this mess. As Tserpchikopf said, no human power can deliver us—but no obstacle can resist the magnetic fluid and it's a matter of proving to this fool that we're able to scorn his threats and recover our liberty."

At these words, Rudolph, Frank and Otto recovered all their serenity, for they had already guessed their Master's plan.

By virtue of her aptitude in provoking the phenomenon of levitation, there was scarcely a prodigy that Sâr Dubnotal's remarkable medium could not accomplish.

Extremely nervous and impressionable, it was as if Annunciata Gianetti were saturated with the mysterious fluid whose existence the most skeptical of scientists have ended up admitting. Sâr Dubnotal is still alone, however, even today, in knowing its exact nature, just as he alone has established the laws of the automatic attraction and repulsion of bodies. By condensing the subtle and powerful effluvia emitted by her nervous system, la Gianetti could work veritable miracles. Thus, without the slightest effort, she could lift or displace weights that ten strong men would not have been able to disturb.

Extending his hands toward his marvelous medium, Sâr Dubnotal directed a few rapid passes at her, while Rudolph armed her with a little black wand that he had just taken out of his satchel.

"Annunciata," the Great Psychagogue said then, in a low voice. "I want you to piece the wall of this cellar and unmask the mechanism of the elevator.

"Yes, Master," the Italian woman murmured. In response to Sâr Dubnotal's instruction, his aides stepped back, leaving the medium at the foot of the wall in front of the lift-button.

"Go!" said the Great Psychagogue.

Annunciata pointed the wand at the button and sketched a large circle on the stones.

What happened then defied all description. One by one, the blocks of stone peeled away and fell to the ground, opening a breach in the wall that became increasingly broad and deep. The noise made by the falling stones must have reached the ears of Tserpchikopf, who had not left the hut.

"Hell and thunder!" the wretch swore. "Ah! You're going to escape anyway, Severus el Tebib. Very well! It won't change anything."

"Possibly," Sâr Dubnotal replied, coldly. "But one thing that's certain is that you're doomed!"

This time, the Slav made no reply, and the silence was no longer troubled by anything except the dismantling of the wall, cut up as if by a jigsaw by the action of the magnetic fluid.

When the opening was large enough, Sâr Dubnotal shone the beam of the torch into it. All of the delicate and complicated machinery, which Tserpchikopf had put temporarily out of commission by cutting of the electric current that alimented it, was exposed. Rapidly, the Master Psychagogue located a switch inked to a metal wire, whose extremity had to extend into the hut, probably between two planks of one of the side walls. By tugging that steel thread, Tserpchikopf had closed the switch and cut off the current, but Sâr Dubnotal had no difficulty in putting the former in place and restoring the latter. To prevent the Slav from repeating his maneuver, he cut the metal wire, then pressed the elevator button and observed with pleasure that the apparatus was functioning again.

Indeed, the platform began to descend, and if Tserpchikopf had still been in the hut he would have been drawn down by the movement—but the cunning scoundrel had evidently scented danger. Sâr Dubnotal, who had not expected to capture him in that fashion, was only slightly disappointed. At any rate, the overman did not waste any time deploring the failure of his trick. With a gesture he invited his aides to take their places on the platform, and when they had joined him he pressed the button again.

In spite of the weight of the five people and one cadaver that it was supporting, the platform rose up immediately. Once again, the Great Psychagogue and his medium had triumphed over all obstacles.

The Great Psychagogue's tribulations were not at an end, however. He had fallen, as they say, between Scylla and Charybdis. He was just about to leave the hut with his friends when the blast of whistle sounded outside. At the same instant, Frank, who had been charged with fetching Joseph, came precipitately back into the hut, whose door he had just opened by a crack. "Master!" he stammered.

"What?"

"Police constables!"

The Great Psychagogue realized that a police patrol had discovered his presence and that a very regrettable misunderstanding might perhaps ensue, because of the cadaver that one of his aides was carrying on his shoulders. Even so, he did not take long to recover his self-composure.

"Very good!" he said, to the surprise of his companions. "I didn't want to involve the police, but since they're here, doubtless summoned by Tserpchikopf, I won't seek to avoid them."

"Couldn't we go back down into the tunnel?" Rudolph suggested.

"Yes, but there's no need."

"Are you going to denounce the Russian?"

"No."

"What, then?"

"My children," the Great Psychagogue said, gravely, "let me act as I wish, I beg you. I have an idea. Whatever happens, conform to my instructions, which are not calculated to exculpate us in the eyes of the constables.

"Otto, open the sack and take out the cadaver. Rudolph, aim your torch in such a way that the light can be seen from the waste ground. You, Frank and Annunciata, lean over the mortal remains of Annie Stephenson."

Sâr Dubnotal fell silent. The door was pushed open violently from outside, and a dozen policemen hurled themselves upon the group assembled around the cadaver.

"Hurrah!" the cried. "We've got Jack the Ripper and his gang!"

VI. In Which Fréjus Thinks He Is Dreaming

We left Fréjus in Chelsea, awaiting a possible message from Sâr Dubnotal. The brave lad spent a sleepless night without receiving the slightest magneto-aerial communication.

At 7 a.m., the coachman Joseph came back with the coupé empty, and was unable to tell the French investigator anything. All that he knew was that he had waited for Sâr Dubnotal in vain at the junction of Commercial Road.

Fréjus was beginning to get anxious. He went back to his Master's study cursing his assignment, which left him kicking his heels at the house while his comrades might be in great danger.

More time went by, which left him profoundly anxious. No longer able to bear it, he was just about to set forth on campaign on his own initiative when, at about 9 a.m., the expected message reached him, in the formed of a few sentences that plunged him into the greatest astonishment.

"Fréjus," pronounced Annunciata Gianetti's voice, "The Master instructs me to tell you that we have all been arrested on suspicion of murder and we shall appear at 3 p.m. before the Worship Street Magistrates' Court. Come to the session, but don't attempt to make contact with us in public. Content yourself with addressing a small sign of intelligence from your place. If necessary, I'll transmit further instructions telepsychically."

"Now then!" said the investigator, looking round. "Am I really awake, or am I going mad? Arrested? Them! What can it mean?"

For a moment, Fréjus did not know what to think. There was no one beside him, but he was sure that he had heard Annunciata's voice. What he had just been told, however, was so strange, unexpected and disturbing that he was almost inclined to think that he was the victim of a hallucination.

"I shall certainly see!" he ended up deciding. "I'll go to Worship Street and I'll take up a position there. But if the London police have arrested the Master, what a gaffe, milords! What a colossal gaffe!"

Entrusting the care of the house to Naïni, Sâr Dubnotal's gigantic Hindu servant, Fréjus left immediately, seething with impatience. He leapt into a cab and gave the court's address to the driver.

I have time in hand, he thought, *but I'd better arrive early. I might gather some information from the curiosity-seekers who want to watch the session.*

The rapid carriage only took an hour and a half to get him to his destination. Fréjus got out at the intersection of Worship Street and Curtain Street and mingled with the numerous idlers who were assembled there.

A lively curiosity seemed to have taken possession of all of them, as they pressed around a man who was ranting at them in poor English. Dressed, like an art student of the lowest class, in a threadbare velvet suit, the man was carrying a soft and pointed felt hat in his hand and had a large cloak over his arm. With his big black mustache, his unhealthy complexion and his jet back pupils, he looked like one of those Italian sketch-artists who earn their living in the street by drawing caricatures of passers-by for the modest price of sixpence a portrait.

The investigator drew nearer and pricked up his ears.

"I tell you that Jack the Ripper is under lock and key," jabbered the artist. "He's been arrested with fur accomplices in Lambeth Street, where the wretches had gone to hide the body of a woman they'd just murdered in an abandoned hut. The proof is that they're due to appear this very day, at 3 p.m., before the Magistrate at Worship Street Court."

"You say they're under lock and key?" asked Fréjus.

"Yes. They were taken to the police station initially, then to Pentonville Prison."

"Hurrah for the police!" cried the cunning investigator.

"Hurrah!" repeated the idlers.

Fréjus was now liberated from his uncertainty regarding the telepsychic message he had received shortly before, but his astonishment was only redoubled.

What a gaffe! he repeated. *What an almighty gaffe! The Master taken for Jack the Ripper? No, that's side-splittingly funny!*

On this reflection, more outraged than joyful, the investigator joined the crowd that was beginning to form a queue at the door of the court.

The courtroom itself was overcrowded; everyone was waiting feverishly for the appearance of the five prisoners.

In spite of professional custom and his phlegmatic temperament, the Magistrate was very excited. The public was breathless with impatience, closely watched and frequently called to order by the ushers and the guards.

Outside, the compact crowd of those who had been unable to get into the courtroom, held back with great difficulty by a double cordon of constables on foot and on horseback, stirred anxiously like a human tide and uttered deafening shouts:

"Hurrah for the police!"

"Death to Jack the Ripper!"

"To the gallows with the monster!"

"No, into the Thames!"

Finally, at 3 p.m., a profound silence fell in the hall, one of whose lateral doors had just opened, giving passage to an entire squad of warders from Pentonville Prison, framing four men and a woman.

At that moment, Fréjus, who had retained a slight doubt regarding the identity of the prisoners, had difficulty suppressing an exclamation of anger, for the four men and the woman were Sâr Dubnotal, Rudolph, Frank, Otto and Annunciata Gianetti!

VII. An Animated Hearing

We shall proceed to an explanation of the strange ordeal to which the Psychagogue and his followers had just been subjected without further delay.

On seeing the policemen enter the hut into which the elevator from the subterranean passage, repaired by Sâr Dubnotal, had permitted them to rise up, Rudolph, Otto and Frank—in spite of the orders received from their Master—had initially thought of resisting their aggressors. A few words spoke in Hindi by Sâr Dubnotal had soothed that impulse.

"Be calm, I said, my children! These constables are already convinced that they've captured the Whitechapel murderers, and the whole of London will soon share in their error. Only the real guilty party, Tserpchikopf, will not be deceived by appearances, and with good reason! But believe me, my children, the wretch will be all the more anxious to enjoy his triumph, and I'll bet my fortune to a penny that when we appear in court, charged with homicide, he'll be in the front row of the spectators."

An abrupt intervention by the sergeant in command of the patrol prevented Sâr Dubnotal from saying any more. "What are you jabbering about there?" said the officer, rudely, putting his hand on his shoulder.

"Nothing."

"Shut up, then."

The Master Psychagogue obeyed. The other constables took possession of his aides and handcuffed their wrists.

Soon, the entire company set off for the police station, where the prisoners learned that they had been arrested after being denounced by an unknown individual, and where, after having been conscientiously searched, they were subjected to a preliminary interrogation, to which they obstinately refused to respond. From there they were taken in a "Black Maria" to Pentonville Prison. Along the way, Sâr Dubnotal was able to slip a few more words in Hindi into the ears of his companions.

"Let matters take their course! He who laughs last laughs longest. I repeat that I'm convinced that Tserpchikopf will be at the hearing. He'll take the precaution of disguising himself, of course, but his make-up skill won't deceive me. I'm sure I'll recognize him at first glance. Besides, his attitude is bound to betray him. You'll observe that, among the innumerable curiosity-seekers who are staring at us, there will be one more indiscreet than all the rest. That will be our man."

"And what are you going to do then, Master?" murmured Rudolph.

"I'll exonerate myself of course! The unknown individual who denounced us is not unknown to me! It's Tserpchikopf. It will be easy for me to establish the proof of our honorability, inasmuch as the senior police officer who has taken possession of our papers won't take long to realize that there has been a mistake."

"You think so?"

"I'm sure of it. Doesn't my wallet enclose, among other documents, an accreditation card signed by the Prefect of the Parisian Police?"

"Why didn't they release us right away, in that case?"

"Because we haven't protested our innocence. The senior officer was able to believe that I've stolen the documents, but the detectives that he must have sent to make enquiries will have established my identity firmly after a visit to Cheyne Walk."

"Fréjus will receive them there?"

"No—I've summoned him to the hearing."

"How?"

"You know that very well."

"By telepsychic message?"

"Of course."

"But Master, even admitting that everything happens as you say it will and that the judge releases us, won't Tserpchikopf, forewarned, have the time to make himself scarce?"

"Undoubtedly—but Fréjus, forewarned telepsychically, will be able to follow him."

"I see," said Rudolph.

For the moment, the conversation stopped at that. The accused were locked up shortly afterwards in the cells of Pentonville Prison, and it was then that Annunciata, magnetized in advance, succeeded in sending the message that so intrigued Fréjus.

The defendants' sojourn in prison did not exceed two hours. After a meal, of which they refused to partake, the prison van transported them to Worship Street court. The police were so fearful of an escape that the constable charged with escorting the captives had received orders to chain himself to them.

By reason of the evident authority that he exercised over his companions, Sâr Dubnotal was considered to be the most guilty of the five, and only he was designated by the infamous soubriquet as Jack the Ripper. Nevertheless, on seeing the defendants enter, the Magistrate, Mr. Bringham, could not retain a slight exclamation of surprise. The imposing appearance of Sâr Dubnotal, his imperturbable self-possession and the simultaneously arrogant and piercing gaze that he paraded over the assembly—in brief, everything about the principal defendant—disconcerted the Judge.

The interrogation commenced as soon as the five accused were lined up with their warders at the bar. Mr. Bringham began by asking them whether they pleaded guilty or not guilty.

"Not guilty," replied the Great Psychagogue, in excellent English.

"Well," said the Magistrate, "that's up to you, but I feel obliged to tell you that your denials have little chance of convincing me and that, if you plead not guilty, you will have to establish the proof of your innocence."

"That is exactly what I intend to do, Your Honor."

"Soon?"

Sâr Dubnotal smiled.

"The police caught you in the act," the Magistrate continued, "and you have refused to respond to the interrogation of the inspector at the police station. I therefore have the right to consider you as guilty and I call upon you to state your names and occupations."

Instead of complying immediately with the Magistrate's order, Sâr Dubnotal exchanged a few words with his companions in Hindi, which attracted a stern admonition on the part of Mr. Bringham. As this reprimand left him unmoved, the public became indignant. Threats addressed to the defendants came from all directions, and to restore order in the courtroom Mr. Bringham had to declare that he would have it cleared.

When silence was re-established, Sâr Dubnotal finally explained. He did so calmly, with no hint of anxiety or conceit.

"What is your name?" Mr. Bringham repeated.

"Severus el Tebib," he replied.

"Your nationality?"

"My original ancestry is European, Your Honor. Personally, I was born in Bombay, where my family had been resident for centuries."

"What is your age?"

"I have no age."

"Your profession?"

"I do not follow any, Your Honor."

"You have means of existence?"

"More than sufficient," the Great Psychagogue replied, modestly, "and that permits me to dedicate my abundant leisure to science."

"You study, then?"

"Day and night."

"Surgery, perhaps?" mocked the Magistrate.

"And anatomy," added Sâr Dubnotal, placidly.

"When did you arrive in London?"

"A month ago."

"Where is your domicile?"

Sâr Dubnotal, faithful to his pretence, made no reply.

"Who are the men who are accompanying you?"

"My friends."

"What was your purpose in coming to London?"

"Permit me to maintain silence on that point."

"You refuse to answer?"

"Provisionally, yes."

"What was your reason for being in Lambeth Street?"

"I might perhaps tell you that shortly."

"Why not right away?"

"Your Honor," said Sâr Dubnotal, "I have my reasons for keeping silent, believe me. Are the detectives charged with the inquiry present?"

"No, but they will arrive at any moment."

"Good. I shall await their arrival before explaining myself."

The Magistrate suppressed a movement of impatience. "Who was the woman whose body was found with you by the police?"

"There is no point in persisting, Your Honor; I shall not reply."

"Do you persist in denying that you are the author of the crime?"

"Absolutely."

"According to you, the police have made a mistake?"

"A serious mistake."

"They should not have arrested you?"

"No."

"You don't possess any papers establishing your honorability?"

"Yes, but they were taken from me at the police station."

"Well," murmured Mr. Bringham, "let us pass on to the other accused individuals."

While the clerk recorded the declarations of Sâr Dubnotal and those of Rudolph, Otto, Frank and Annunciata, who limited themselves to protesting against the arbitrary arrest to which they had been subjected, Sâr Dubnotal never ceased searching the compact ranks of curiosity-seekers with his

273

gaze. Observing, to his satisfaction, that Fréjus was among them, he concentrated his attention on a man that he had just spotted in the auditorium.

Seated on one of the benches closest to the bar, this man—who was none other than the artist already noticed by Fréjus—appeared to be very interested in the interrogation of the accused; he was particularly noticeable by virtue of the ardor that he put into calling for their deaths. Threatened with expulsion by the Magistrate, he calmed down somewhat, and contented himself with muttered vague imprecations as he listened to Rudolph, Otto and Frank make their evasive replies.

After a momentary examination, Sâr Dubnotal ceased to occupy himself with the artist and stared at Fréjus, strangely and at length. The latter, breathless with emotion, guessed that his master was trying to communicate thoughts to him automatically; concentrating all his psychic energy, he prepared himself to receive them.

He was quickly informed. What Sâr Dubnotal wanted him to do was not to lose sight of the artist who was present in the hall, and to follow him if the latter left before the end of the hearing.

The investigator replied to his Master's mute order in the same fashion, saying that he would carry out his mission punctiliously.

An incident caused a diversion.

Three or four men had just come into the hall and taken their places on the witnesses' bench. At the sight of them, the artist seemed singularly displeased. When the Judge asked them whether they were the detectives charged with the inquiry and they relied in the affirmative, that mysterious individual hurriedly got to his feet. Elbowing his way through the crowd of spectators, he was outside in the blink of an eye, but Fréjus was on the alert and Sâr Dubnotal saw, with satisfaction, that his sleuth had left the courtroom hot on the artist's heels.

Meanwhile, the detectives commenced their testimony. It was entirely favorable to the accused and provoked an unexpected change of direction in the opinion of the Magistrate and the public.

"Your Honor," said the senior detective, "the few indications furnished by the accused have proved to be accurate. Their role in this affair remains rather shady, but they are obviously innocent of the murder of this woman, whose death—according to the medical examiners—took place several months ago."

"That is true," said Sâr Dubnotal, in a voice that caused a stir throughout the audience, so redolent was it with frankness and gravity. "And now, Your Honor, there is nothing to prevent me from exonerating myself completely. As God is my witness, I swear that the death of that woman is not attributable to me. I swear that, far from being a murderer, I am myself an agent of justice, a man who spends his life tracking down evildoers. That is why my companions and I were in that hut in Lambeth Street in the company of the cadaver."

Rapidly, but with convincing details and a luminous clarity of exposition, the Great Psychagogue told the story of his dealings with Tserpchikopf, and explained how he had learned that Annie Stephenson's murderer had taken refuge in London with the cadaver of his victim, and how Frank had almost capture the villain.

"But why didn't you tell me all this sooner?" exclaimed the Judge.

"Because, having allowing myself to be arrested, I hoped that the real guilty party, impelled by curiosity, would present himself at the hearing," said Sâr Dubnotal, simply.

"You were mistaken?"

"No, Your Honor."

"What? You're saying that the murderer is here now?"

"He was here a little while ago."

"You recognized him?"

"Yes."

"And you allowed him to leave?"

"I allowed him to leave."

"Great God, why? Why?"

"Could I have done otherwise, Your Honor? If I had denounced him squarely, would you have believed me?"

"No, of course not," murmured the Magistrate, "but I would have ordered the ushers to keep him in custody until further instructions."

"Pardon me, Your Honor," Sâr Dubnotal said, respectfully, "but you don't know Tserpchikopf. He is the most arrant scoundrel that the Earth has ever seen, and his perversity is only equaled by his extreme cleverness. At the first word, he would have been put on this guard. He would have escaped, and we would never have seen him again."

"Do you expect to see him again, then?"

"Yes, Your Honor, and even to capture him. One of my friends, who was waiting in the courtroom, has undertaken to follow him, and a few hours from now I hope to be able to proceed to his arrest, if you don't refuse to set us at liberty."

"You are free to go, Severus el Tebib," said the Magistrate, a trifle embarrassed by his discomfiture. "But who was the man of whom you spoke? I only saw one individual leave the courtroom, and that was an excitable Italian who was one of those most hostile to you."

"That's correct," said Sâr Dubnotal, with a tranquil smile. "That Italian, Your Honor, was none other than Tserpchikopf."

VIII. The Sûreté At Work

On leaving Worship Street Magistrates' Court, Fréjus—whom his comrades ordinarily designated by the soubriquet "the Sûreté"—had thrown himself upon the heels of the man that Sâr Dubnotal had ordered him to follow. Such a mission held no difficulty for such a fine and clever sleuth. Certain that the pretended Italian artist had paid no heed to him, he allowed the latter to move a few paces ahead, in order to follow him at his leisure.

On leaving the hearing, the artist had wrapped himself up in his cloak, the hood of which he put up over his head even though it was not raining. He ploughed through the ranks of the massive crowd in front of the building and left Worship Street by turning into Curtain Street, and then into Hearn Street.

Where is he going and who is he? Fréjus wondered, taking care to stay on the opposite sidewalk and pretending to read his newspaper, while never taking his eyes off the suspect individual. *Who is he?* he repeated, after several seconds of reflection and scrupulous attention. *But it's our friend Tserp-chikopf, of course! The scoundrel, who has more than one avatar, is disguised as an artist. That black moustache and those hairless cheeks give him a new physiognomy, and I was deceived at first, but now I recognize his Kalmuk profile, his flat nose and his phosphorescent eyes. I'd swear on the Bible that he really is the pseudo-boyar, the ex-King of the Chess-men, the murderer of Annie Stephenson, the bloody hypnotist!*

Right! So the Master...yes, of course! I get it! The Master recognized him at the first glance, and that's why he ordered me telepsychically to follow him. Oho! Pay attention, the Sûreté. You must distinguish yourself, old chap! If you have a chance to get your hands on Tserpchikopf, Otto and Frank will be insane with jealousy. But where is the damned black-guard going? Where?

The artist had not lingered long in the short and winding Hearn Street. Still tracked by Fréjus, he crossed Shoreditch High Street at an angle, and then went along Church Street, a rather busy street in the Bethnal Green district. At the end of that street he seemed to hesitate. He even turned round to dart a suspicious glace behind him, and the investigator only just had time to step inside a newsagent's shop, from which he emerged as soon as his quarry had gone into Mount Street.

Shortly afterwards, Fréjus saw him slip into the corridor of a house at the corner of Mount Street and Virginia Road.

He went to take up a position two or three doors further on. Not knowing whether the artist really lived in the house into which he had just gone, the intelligent fellow did not want to abandon his pursuit yet. Time was not pressing, and he did not want to leave anything to chance.

Two hours passed. Night fell. Not having seen the painter come out again, Fréjus was beginning to believe that it really was his domicile, and he was about to leave to send a telegram to the Hindu Naïni—who would give it to the Great Psychagogue as soon as he returned—when the man reappeared at the entrance to the corridor. Briefly, he scanned the vicinity of the house on whose threshold he was standing. Fréjus had hastily ducked around the corner of Mount Street.

Presumably reassured by seeing no one in the street but a few placid passers-by, the painter, still cloaked and hooded, went back the way he had come as far as Rock Street, a little side-street leading to Arnold Circus. When he went into the alleyway, the Frenchman had not dared to get too close to him, and when the latter arrived in his turn at the corner of Mount Street and Rock Street he uttered a dull exclamation of disappointment. The painter was no longer in sight! The man in whom the sleuth and his Master had recognized Tserpchikopf had vanished into thin air!

The first thought that came to Fréjus' mind was that the Slav had gone into another house, for he certainly had not had time to get to the end of Rock Street, and the only man now visible in hat street did not resemble him at all—he was a respectable old man in a frock coat and a top-hat; he had a long white beard and spectacles, and he walked painfully, bent over a stout cane, with a overcoat draped over his left arm.

Should I accost him? Fréjus thought, horribly vexed. *Perhaps he noticed the artist and will be able to tell me which way the rascal went.*

The investigator increased his pace in order to catch up with the old man, who was limping along in front of him; half way, however, he stopped indecisively.

"No, no!" he murmured. "I won't speak to him. So much the worse if I'm mistaken, but I've got an idea."

The old man went around Arnold Circus without Fréjus appearing to pay any further attention to him, but as soon as he had disappeared, the investigator ran across Rock Street, also went around the square and arrived in time to see the old man go into a house in Camlet Street, another street that ended at Arnold Circus. The seemingly-shabby house bore the number 63A. Possessed of two upper stories, its ground floor was occupied by a low-class public house. A corridor opened to the side of the pub, which permitted the tenants to reach their homes without passing through the establishment.

There's a worthy old fellow who resides in an exceedingly wretched place! Fréjus remarked to himself, having darted a rapid glance over the house's façade. Prudently, he made sure that no one was spying on him, and watched the windows of number 63A. A few seconds later, a light came on in one of those windows.

"The old man has just gone in," Fréjus murmured. "His lodgings, it appears, are on the second floor. Now I know. The barmaid or the drunks in the pub will give me more details, I hope."

The investigator went into the establishment's "glass section," ordered a glass of beer that would not have been served to him in the neighboring "pot section," and, setting his sights on an old woman who was standing at the counter sipping a glass of whisky, engaged her in conversation.

At first, he only talked about the rain and fine weather, but he gradually led her to reveal that she lived locally and knew Camlet Street perfectly.

"In that case, Mrs…"

"Mrs. Clarke," said the woman, sketching a bow.

"In that case, Mrs. Clarke, I'd be most obliged if you'd tell me whether you also know an old gentleman whose description I'll give you. Can you imagine, my dear lady, that in passing through Rock Street just now, I thought I saw a pickpocket slip his hand into the pocket of an old man dressed in a

279

frock-coat and a top-hat. I ran after the thief, but I lost track of him, and when I got back to Rock Street the old gentleman was no longer there. I'd like to find him, though, in order that he can tell me whether he really has been a victim of theft—in which case I'll willingly serve as a witness."

"The old man was wearing a frock-coat, you say?" asked Mrs. Clarke, very interested by the cunning investigator's fanciful story.

"Yes, and had a fine white beard, as well as a cane and a pair of spectacles."

"Oh, then I do, indeed, know him," said the woman, excitedly. "It can only be that nice Mr. Graham, who lives in this very house, on the second floor."

"Do you think so?" said Fréjus, naively.

"I'm sure of it! There aren't two men like Mr. Graham in the neighborhood."

"I don't like to disturb him at this late hour," the investigator murmured, as if regretfully, "but it would be better to alert him right away."

"Oh, you won't disturb him much," Mrs. Clarke affirmed. "He's used to these little annoyances, you know."

"Used to being robbed?"

"No, sir!" said the woman, laughing. "Not that—used to being disturbed is what I meant."

"Oh, good!" said the investigator, quite naturally. "What does he do for a living, then?"

"He's a doctor."

"Thank you, Mrs. Clarke," Fréjus said, immediately, paying for her next glass of whisky. "On due reflection, I shan't call on him this evening, but I'll be do so without fail tomorrow morning. Does he ever go out at night?"

"Too often for a man of his age. He has a lot of clients, and cares for them with admirable devotion. Oh, he hardly gets any sleep, for sure!"

"Has he lived here long?"

"I think so. All the poor people know and love him. He works more often for honor than money, that's all I can tell you. Personally, I only made his acquaintance three or four months ago, but I think he's been here much longer than that."

"Thank you, Mrs. Clarke," the investigator repeated, making his exit without further delay.

On returning to the street, Fréjus began to stride back and forth along its length. He seemed singularly perplexed, and murmured: "After all that, they'll surely say that I lost the right trail. This worthy doctor can't have anything in common with Tserpchikopf—and yet, I was quite proud to have found a plausible explanation for the artist's disappearance. Since the old man was alone in the street, if Tserpchikopf hadn't gone into a house in Rock Street, it followed logically that Tserpchikopf and the old man were one and the same. But how did he contrive such a rapid metamorphosis? Bah! It's quite simple. Let's suppose in fact, that the Slav, the Italian artist and the English physician are the same person.

"On coming out of the hearing, Tserpchikopf, then dressed as a painter, first went to Mount Street, where he has a pied-à-terre. There, he could have quickly changed clothes, replacing his velvet suit with a more decent frock-coat, sticking a false beard and wig, spectacles and a collapsible hat in his pockets, and anything else he needed to disguise himself with a flick of the wrist. Hiding his change of clothing beneath his cloak, he presented the same appearance to me that he had two hours earlier—but in Rock Street, no one being there to inconvenience him, he would have been able to cast off his cloak with a single gesture without stopping, throw it over his arm, after folding it like an overcoat, put on his false hairpieces and spectacles, replace his fur cap with the collapsible topper and thus be reclad almost instantaneously with the appearance of old Mr. Graham.

"Yes, there's nothing impossible about any of that, and the master, my comrades and I have seen Tserpchikopf play many tricks even more disconcerting. But what prevents me from being satisfied with my hypothesis, and makes me dread that Mr. Graham might be a real doctor while I've stupidly let the real Tserpchikopf escape, is the conversation I've just had with the worthy Mrs. Clarke. Beneath their unprepossessing appearances, lower class people often conceal more perspicacity, common sense and, especially, mistrust than upper class folk. Where a lady from the West End would allow herself to be deceived by appearances, there's every chance that Mrs. Clarke would have seen clearly. In brief, I don't know what to think any longer—and if Tserpchikopf has given me the slip, I don't know how I'm ever going to dare to tell the Master."

While indulging in this monologue, Fréjus continued mechanically walking back and forth along the sidewalk opposite number 63A. He stuck close to the wall in order to remain in the shadow of the houses, and never ceased watching Mr. Graham's illuminated window.

Suddenly, he stopped dead, as if turned to stone by an extraordinary spectacle.

The doctor had lowered the white fabric blind that shielded his window, but his shadow was outlined in black there as if on a screen, and Frank was able to follow the gestures of the dark silhouette with his eyes. Now, it certainly seemed to the investigator that the pretended Mr. Graham was in the process of removing the fine white beard that had given him such a worthy and venerable appearance!

"My God, yes!" said Fréjus. "He's taking it off! Unless I'm seeing things, he's taking it off! The beard is fake. The profile of the face is no longer the same! Oh, how happy I am!"

Holding himself firm in order not to execute an entrechat, Fréjus ran to the nearest Post Office, wrote out a brief telegram, had it sent right away, and then returned to his sentry duty in Camlet Street.

IX. The Mouse-Trap

Sâr Dubnotal, Rudolph, Otto, Frank and la Gianetti, set at liberty with profuse apologies by the Magistrate at Worship

Street, returned immediately to the house in Cheyne Walk, where they arrived at about 7 p.m. There, the four men held a Council, for the expected telegram from Fréjus had not yet arrived and the Great Psychagogue was beginning to fear that the French investigator might have experienced great difficulty in fulfilling his mission.

"My children," said Sâr Dubnotal, "if the telegram hasn't arrived in another hour, we'll have to go in search of Fréjus without further delay. As I've told you, I'm convinced that the artist whose equivocal attitude and sudden departure I pointed out to you as none other than Tserpchikopf. Nine times out of ten, an unhealthy curiosity drives the worst malefactors to their doom, and that's what should have happened this time.

"Unfortunately for us, and fortunately for him, we couldn't think of arresting the wretch in the middle of the court hearing. I want him to expiate his crimes in an exemplary fashion, and that would not be the case if we had deliver him into the hands of English law; I'm convinced that he would have found the means to escape his guards yet again.

"It remains to be seen whether your comrade, charged with following him, was dealing with too strong an opponent. Tserpchikopf has more than one trick up his sleeve, and we have to be ready for anything, on his part. If Fréjus has put him on the alert, we might perhaps have a new misfortune to regret."

"Can't you get us out of this frightful uncertainty, Master?" asked Rudolph.

"Yes," said the Great Psychagogue, "and I think I shall—what is it Naïni?" The Hindu had just come into the room.

"A telegram, Sahib," the gigantic servant replied.

"Ah!" sighed Rudolph, Otto and Frank, while their Master took the folded dispatch and tore it pen. "It's from him!"

"Yes," said Sâr Dubnotal. And he read, aloud: "All right! After nearly giving me the slip by means of a rapid and adroit change of clothes, the man that you ordered me to follow has gone into number 63A Camlet Street, Bethnal Green, where he resides under the name of Dr. Graham. If you want to catch him at home, come quickly, for it appears that the respectable doctor—who is unfortunate enough, when he removes his beard, to bear a strong resemblance to Tserpchikopf—dedicates himself body and soul to the salvation of his patients, and spends entire nights at their bedsides. If he goes out before you arrive—which is hardly probable, since he has just taken off his false beard and wig—I shall continue to follow him discreetly. In the contrary case, you will find me in Arnold Circus, on the corner of Camlet Street, from which I can see number 63A. See you soon, I hope. Fréjus."

Sâr Dubnotal recovered his breath and said; "Fréjus too has recognized Tserpchikopf. It's a good sign, and you shall see that the Slav and the mysterious Jack the Ripper are identical. Let's go to Camlet Street right away. If we capture the scoundrel, we can force him to tell us the whole truth, including who the mysterious Annie Stephenson was, before he made her the Queen of the Chessmen."

Annunciata, Rudolph and the two investigators followed their Master and took their places with him in his coupé.

On Sâr Dubnotal's orders, Joseph whipped his horses, which literally galloped all the way from Cheyne Walk to Church Street, where Sâr Dubnotal called a halt for reasons of prudence. The Great Psychagogue and his aides jumped down from the carriage and dispersed in such a fashion as not to attract attention from the inhabitants of the neighborhood. They had agreed to meet up in the pub at number 63 Camlet Street, with the exception of Otto and Frank, who were to mount guard at either end of the street in question.

Sâr Dubnotal took a route via Rock Street and Arnold Circus, where he had the pleasure of meeting up with Fréjus, who had not had to move from his sentry-post.

"Your quarry is still in his den, then?" asked the Great Psychagogue.

"Still, Master. Look at the lighted window on the second floor of number 63A. That's his room."

"There's no doubt of it?"

"None."

"You're sure?"

"Absolutely sure."

"Good—continue your watch, old man. Otto will join you without delay. Frank will take up position at the far end of Camlet Street. As for Rudolph and Annunciata…."

"They're already in the pub, Master. I've just seen them go in, one after the other."

"Perfect. In that case, I only have to join them. Do I need to tell you what to do?"

"Leap at Dr. Graham's throat if he tries to flee, and call you, Master. That's it?"

"That's exactly it. But if the doctor goes into the pub, into which I'll try to draw him, it's vital that you let him be!"

"Have no fear."

"I've also warned your comrades, and they'll only intervene if the pretended physician tries to run away."

After shaking the hand of his zealous sleuth, Sâr Dubnotal strode forthrightly toward the pub and went into the establishment's "Private Saloon." That title, inscribed in enamel letters on the glass door, only lent a meager pretension in the circumstances, for the room into which the Great Psychagogue did not hesitate to venture was more like a low dive than an honest tavern.

It was a high-ceilinged room whose dimensions were considerable, but still insufficient for the large number of drinkers who were assembled there. Pipe-smoke blurred the light of the gas-lamps and rendered the air—which was already saturated with alcohol vapor and the stench of beer—unbreathable.

At first, Sâr Dubnotal could only make out the indecisive forms of a dozen individuals standing at the zinc counter. Then, becoming accustomed to the semi-darkness that reigned in the room, he was able to see the décor more clearly.

Behind the counter laden with bottles of gin, brandy, whisky and various wines stood a barmaid, her hand on the lever of an apparatus for pumping beer. The blonde young woman, whose face and figure were pleasant but had a rather

285

profligate air about her, was pulling stout, ale and half-and-half—which is a mixture of the two—into pint glasses, which she passed to her numerous customers, without any respite. The customers turned to look at the stranger who had just come into the saloon, but without any suspicion.

Rudolph and Annunciata had joined the drinkers, and stared at their Master as if they were seeing him for the first time. They had been careful to go in separately, and were pretending not to know one another. There was nothing about the anonymously-dressed young disciple to attract attention, and his arrival in the pub had therefore passed unnoticed. As for the pretty Italian woman, she had doubtless been mistaken for one of the good-time girls who are ten-a-penny in London, and no one had take the trouble to address a word to her.

With his black frock-coat and white trousers, however, his cravat pinned with an enormous sapphire, and his turban most of all, Sâr Dubnotal made a certain impression on the pub's clients, who were not used to seeing such an imposing individual in such an exotic costume in their sad environment.

Taken by surprise, the barmaid stopped plying the beer pump, and the drinkers were no longer thinking about emptying the glasses they held in their hands. The Great Psychagogue did not appear to take offence at the curious stares that he provoked in the "private saloon." He went up to the counter.

"A glass of Pale Ale, if you please," he said to the barmaid, politely. The latter filled the order awkwardly, intimidated by the new customer's grand manner, his black beard, his admirable eyes, his superb bearing, his deep and harmonious voice and his oriental headgear.

Sâr Dubnotal raised the glass to his lips and, pretending to have just caught sight of la Gianetti, said as if to himself: "An Italian! Ah, what luck to be able to converse for a while with someone who speaks the sweet language of Dante and Petrarch!" Addressing his medium, he continued in Italian: "These people can't understand us, Annunciata. Pretend to smile, as if I were speaking of your homeland and addressing gallantries to you, but pay attention. My investigators have

286

just set a mouse-trap in which it's necessary that Tserpchikopf be taken. Everything leads us to believe that the Slav is living in this house in the guise of an honest doctor of medicine. My intention is to attract him into the pub, but I can't do that without your help. In a few moments, I'll give you a sign and you must immediately pretend to have suffered a stroke. I'll ask these people if they know of a doctor, and they can't fail to point me in the direction of the one who lives upstairs. I'll have the barmaid summon him, and then Rudolph and I will arrest him. If these people try to help him, you'll reduce them to impotence—so concentrate all your reserves of fluid and prepare to intervene."

"Yes, Master!" said the Italian woman, bursting into laughter to deceive the customers.

Rudolph had listened to the rapid speech and, as he understood Italian, the Great Psychagogue's plan was as clear to him as to la Gianetti. *The mouse-trap is well-laid*, he thought. *If Tserpchikopf escapes us again, I think we'll have to abandon all hope of ever catching him!*

With that judicious reflection, the young man swallowed a draught of the foul beverage contained in his glass and drew closer to his Master, holding himself ready for any eventuality.

X. The Tragic End of a Monstrous Criminal

Rudolph did not have to wait long.

Seeing that several of the people assembled in the bar were moving around him, as if torn between the desire to pick a fight with him and the fear of being made to look like fools, Sâr Dubnotal judged that it was necessary, at all costs, to avoid a quarrel. His superhuman power would have no difficulty in disposing of any attackers, of course, but it might put the so-called doctor on his guard and further complicate a situation that that was already very delicate. Holding the churls in thrall with his cool and resolute gaze, he made a sign to la

287

Gianetti, who immediately dropped the glass that she was holding in her hand and collapsed in a heap on the floor.

The incident caused considerable excitement among the customers. The men who might perhaps have been inclined to rough up a rich stranger had no other thought than to offer help to an unconscious woman. Sâr Dubnotal and Rudolph got in ahead of them. They knelt down beside the Italian woman's seemingly-inanimate body.

Rising to his feet again almost immediately, Sâr Dubnotal exclaimed: "It's a stroke! Is there a doctor in the vicinity?"

"Yes," replied the barmaid, greatly distressed. "There's Dr. Graham, who lives directly above us."

"Is he at home?"

"I don't know," the girl said. "I'll go see."

"Don't bother," said one of the customers. "Don't worry about it, Betsy—I'll go!"

The man ran out like a gust of wind and was heard calling to the doctor from the street.

Eight or ten minutes went by. The man came back in and, annoyed at not seeing the doctor already there—the latter having replied to him immediately and told him that he would be down right away—went back out into the street, where he shouted more loudly.

Meanwhile, Sâr Dubnotal appeared to be hurriedly giving the Italian woman first aid. He moistened her temples and rubbed her hands. His back was turned to the door; he left it to Rudolph to watch the street.

Finally, the obliging customer came back into the room, declaring that Mr. Graham was on his way. "The doctor was already in bed," he explained, "and had to get dressed."

Knowing that the critical moment was near, Sâr Dubnotal signaled to Rudolph, instructing him to take up a position close to the door and to close it again as soon as the doctor was inside.

They waited a few more seconds, and then a sigh of relief escaped the clients' lips. "Here he is!"

"Over here, Dr. Graham!" called the barmaid. "Quickly—this woman's dying!"

An old man with a white beard had just hurried into the establishment. If Frank had been there, he would immediately have recognized the man he had earlier followed from Rock Street to number 63A Camlet Street. As soon as he was inside, Rudolph shut the door of the room. Under the pretext of preventing the drinkers from the others rooms and the idlers who were beginning to gather in the street from forcing an entry, he put his back to the door, while Sâr Dubnotal stepped back quickly into the darkest corner of the room.

The pretended Dr. Graham was carrying a doctor's bag in his hand. He knelt down beside the Italian woman lying full-length on the floor, adjusted his spectacles, took hold of the stricken woman's wrist and felt her pulse.

By the simple means of a single magnetic pass, the Great Psychagogue had just interrupted his medium's vital functions.

"But this woman is dead!" exclaimed Dr. Graham. "Her pulse isn't beating and she isn't breathing." He sounded Annunciata's chest then, perceiving no heartbeat, and declared: "Nothing to be done! It only remains to inform the police, gentlemen!"

"Pardon me!" said Sâr Dubnotal, abruptly emerging from his corner. "Are you quite sure that this woman is really dead, Dr. Graham?"

At these words, pronounced in a sarcastic tone, the doctor raised his head, and his gaze, veiled by his spectacles, met that of the overman.

"Curse you!" he cried. "Severus el Tebib!"

"Severus el Tebib indeed," said Sâr Dubnotal, coldly. And, pouncing on the kneeling doctor, who seemed petrified, he grabbed him by the hair and beard,

To the amazement of the witnesses, the old man's fine white beard and snowy hair were detached from his chin and his skull, and the suddenly-rejuvenated Dr. Graham appeared to them as a man in the prime of life.

"Ah, you won't escape me this time, Tserpchikopf!" thundered Sâr Dubnotal. "Stand up, Annunciata!"

The Italian woman came to her feet in a single motion—which had the effect of bringing the astonishment and fear of the pub's customers to a peak.

The false Dr. Graham also got to his feet and stared at Sâr Dubnotal, with his teeth chattering, shaken by a thrill of fear.

"Gentlemen," the Great Psychagogue went on, addressing the customers and pointing at the doctor, "may I introduce you to the monomaniac of Whitechapel, the sinister Jack the Ripper!"

Looking around wildly, Tserpchikopf howled: "It's not true, gentlemen! The man is a brazen liar!"

"Do you really dare to make that claim, wretch?" said Sâr Dubnotal, in a wrathful voice. "Ah, I shall soon reckon with you now, murderer!"

There was a second or two of fragile silence. Tserpchikopf continued to dart bewildered glances in every direction, seemingly imploring the protection of the customers in the pub—but they did not move or speak. Seeing that the pub door was barred by Rudolph, while Severus el Tebib was standing between him and the counter, the bloody hypnotist recoiled as far as the wall of the saloon. Uttering another howl of range, he plunged his hand into his pocket and withdrew it holding a dagger.

"You admit it, then?" said Sâr Dubnotal. "Finally unmasked, you have no other recourse but to attempt to reconquer your liberty at the price of a new crime?"

"You're attacking me—I'm defending myself!" howled the Slav. "So much the worse for you!" He tensed himself on his muscular legs and, brandishing his weapon, made a mighty leap toward Sâr Dubnotal. Without taking a step back or unfolding the arms he had crossed over his broad chest, the Great Psychagogue waited for the impact—but Tserpchikopf had counted without Annunciata. The medium was on the lookout for a propitious moment to intervene. Seeing the wretch hurl himself against her Master, she seized her wand and swiftly extended it toward Sâr Dubnotal and Tserpchikopf.

Stopped dead by the fluidic current, the latter tried to turn his rage against the Italian, but she made an abrupt rotary movement with her wand and, turning upside-town, Jack the Ripper was lifted from the ground and thrown against the ceiling, where he remained suspended by his feet, head down.

The wretch did not let go of his dagger, though. Maddened by panic, not understanding any of what had just happened to him, and perhaps thinking himself the victim of an atrocious nightmare, he begged: "Help me gentlemen! For pity's sake, help me!"

"You had no pity on your victims, monstrous criminal!"

"Mercy, Severus el Tebib!"

"Do you confess?"

"Yes! Forgive me! In the name of God, forgive me!"

"God, whose indulgence is infinite, might perhaps forgive you, but first you shall expiate your crimes in this world. Stop struggling, since your efforts cannot detach you from the ceiling to which you are pinned by magnetic waves of irresistible force. You shall not set foot on the ground again until you have made a full confession."

The Great Psychagogue turned to the spectators, who were still mute and petrified, and said: "Listen carefully, gentlemen! Hear with me the confession of Tserpchikopf, the ex-King of the Chesssmen of Paris, who is also Jack the Ripper. Will you speak, Tserpchikopf?"

"Yes," murmured the murderer, feebly. Under the influx of blood, his head was buzzing and the veins in his temples beating as if to burst.

"Why did you quarter Annie Stephenson?"

"Because she intended to give me up to French justice."

"I know that," murmured Sâr Dubnotal, who added, more loudly: "Where did you meet that unfortunate woman."

"In London."

"What was her real name?"

"Lily Harrods."

291

"What did she do at that time?"

"She was an orphan selling flowers in the streets of Whitechapel."[27]

"It was you who corrupted her, wretch!"

"Forgive me!" groaned Tserpchikopf.

"And why, after many other known crimes, did you come to sow horror in Whitechapel?"

"I knew that you were tracking me down pitilessly, Severus el Tebib. I've seen the terrible instrument of justice that you really are, and I hoped by that means to turn your attention away from me. If you had been deceived, if you had occupied yourself with the Whitechapel murders, I would have escaped you—all my precautions were taken."[28]

---

[27] The reader will recall that the allegation was made in the previous episode that the Chessmen's Queen was very well-educated and spoke numerous languages. Evidently therefore, Tserpchikopf must have taken the orphan in hand and shaped her, much as the sinister hypnotist Svengali shaped Trilby Mackenzie in George du Maurier's novel *Trilby* (1894). That does not explain, in itself, why he stole her body, but might offer a clue. Since he moved her body after her phantom appeared in the grounds of the Tour Jaune, presumably following the exorcism carried out by the man he knew as Severus el Tebib, he must have suspected then, if not before, that Severus had occult powers, and might be able to recruit the posthumous assistance of his Queen—who would inevitably, be very keen to take revenge for being murdered so horribly. That suspicion, reinforced when Severus tried to recover the body, must surely have been why he became so determined to keep the body out of Severus' reach and hide it in a place where (saving some outrageously unlikely coincidence like the one that actually occurred) it would never be found.

[28] This makes no sense whatsoever, as Sâr Dubnotal must surely have realized, although he obviously refrained from pointing it out to his ghost-writer. It would be patently ridiculous for a perpetrator to deflect the attention of a pursuer by

"Did your victims put their trust in you, then?"

"Wasn't I their doctor?"

"And you hoped that I would never discover the identity of Jack the Ripper?"

"I hoped so, Severus el Tebib, for I had intended to leave London this morning, and I only stayed a few hours longer in order to attend the hearing at Worship Street Magistrates' Court."

"I see that all my expectations have been realized, point by point," the overman said to his disciple." He asked Tserpchikopf: "Was it you who denounced us to the police?"

"Yes," the scoundrel confessed, dully.

And when you left the hearing, you didn't suspect that one of my aides was following you?"

"No! Even so, I disguised myself en route, as usual, for I have a room in Mount Street where I pass for a painter, while I'm always Dr Graham here."

"Everything is explained!" said Sâr Dubnotal.

"Yes," said Rudolph. "We finally hold the key to the enigma, and now it only remains to punish this monster."

---

committing more crimes whose successful investigation would lead to him just as surely as successful investigation of his previous crimes would have done. In any case, Jack the Ripper's crimes began long before Sâr Dubnotal had ever heard of Tserpchikopf or suspected his existence. Evidently, the fake Dr. Graham had some other motive for butchering his patients so horribly, of which he is so desperately ashamed that he will not reveal it even *in extremis*—or which is too shocking to be revealed in a work of popular fiction, whose author would be forbidden by prevailing standards of decency to spell out the full details of Tserpchikopf's compulsive sadism, necrophilia and worse. Obviously, I am constrained by the same standards, and can do no more that point out the sinister logic of the diplomatic omission—which will, however, assist the reader to figure out the true logic of what happens next.

"The punishment will be proportionate to the crime," said Sâr Dubnotal.

The overman was turning to Annunciata in order to ask her to release Tserpchikopf when a catastrophe occurred. Misunderstanding her Master's intention, or prey to a sudden fainting fit, the medium let go of her wand.

Abruptly interrupted, the magnetic current ceased to sustain Tserpchikopf. Falling head first to the floor, the sinister bandit fractured his skull, while the dagger that he held in his hand perforated his abdomen.

Before the customers in the pub were able to shake off the terrible emotion that the criminal's revelations and his tragic end had caused them, Sâr Dubnotal, Rudolph and Annunciata left the establishment, leaving Tserpchikopf's corpse behind.

Outside, they met up with Otto, Frank and Fréjus, to whom they announced the death of their enemy.

Having arrived in Church Street, where Joseph was waiting for them, all six of them took their places in the Master's coupe, Frank and Fréjus squeezing into the seat beside the coachman—who conveyed them rapidly to Chelsea.

The Great Psychagogue was taciturn. A cloud passed over his noble face and obscured the magnetic gleam of his black eyes. Rudolph asked him what was wrong.

"I'm thinking about the unexpected and terrible end of that wretch Tserpchikopf," he replied. "Jack the Ripper did not have time to repent his crimes. Having died in a state of sin, it's in the afterlife that he'll expiate the atrocities of which he was guilty on Earth. He's dead—may the *larva* that his soul becomes never oblige us to occupy ourselves with him!"

Unfortunately, the Great Psychagogue's wish was not to be granted. Instead of accepting the dictates of Destiny, the bandit's *larva* was to attempt an insurgency against his fate and to harass the humans who had sent him to expiate his crimes in the infernal spheres. That posthumous hatred was to cause Sâr Dubnotal and his aides a great deal of trouble; we shall soon see how it was manifest and how it reached its conclusion.

At any rate, since Tserpchikopf's execution, London has heard no further mention of Jack the Ripper, whose disappearance would have remained as mysterious as his crimes if the Great Psychagogue had not consented to the publication of his memoirs. Indeed, when the police, summoned by the landlord of the pub to take away the body, interrogated the barmaid and her clients, all of them, fearful of being implicated in the affair, were united in declaring that the victim—whose false hair and beard someone had taken the opportunity to remove—was unknown to them. According to them, the man, suddenly seized by an attack of *delirium tremens*, had struck his head against the wall and pierced his belly with a knife-thrust.

Accepting these witness statements without digging any deeper or attempting to verify them, the coroner, who had found no identity papers on the cadaver, instructed his jury to return the verdict of "Person unknown, died of suicide"—and Tserpchikopf's fate generated no more echoes in London than that of a rat in a gutter.

SÂR DUBNOTAL

Chaque fascicule contient un récit complet.

Cette buée blanchâtre prenait peu à peu l'apparence d'un fantôme humain.

POSTHUMOUS HATRED

I. Eyes of Fire

"Comtesse, I have some good news for you. Sâr Dubnot-al, whom you knew by the name of Severus el Tebib, has just sent me a telegraphic message to tell me that, touched by your sincere repentance and judging your penitence sufficient, he consents to your return to France, where you left your daughters. I've just given orders for you to be taken directly to Yo-kohama, where you will take the first steamship departing for Europe."

"My children! I'll be able to see my children again? You're not deceiving me, Governor?"

"No, Comtesse, and I'm not even surprised to have received the telegraphic message, for I'm the one who prompted Sâr Dubnotal's decision by giving him a most eulogistic account of your progress.

"Oh, how grateful I am to you!" the unfortunate woman sobbed. "Andrée, Jeanne, my dear little ones! Oh, my God—it's too much happiness!"

This dialogue took place between Azilis de Tréguilly and Lieutenant-Colonel Tedworth, a former officer-instructor in the Chinese army.

American by nationality, Tedworth had been obliged to leave Canton after a rebellion by troops placed under his orders. Having been befriended by the Great Psychagogue, he had undertaken a long voyage around the world aboard a yacht belonging to that individual. That voyage having resulted in the discovery of a recently-formed atoll in the Pacific Ocean,

297

entirely unknown to cartographer and navigators, Tedworth had manifested a desire to found a little colony on the new coral island. Accompanied by a few old soldiers he had disembarked there with water, weapons, food supplies, tools and seeds—in brief, everything necessary to provide the primary necessities.

The colony's beginnings had been difficult, but after Sâr Dubnotal had re-supplied it several times they were not long delayed in seeing their conditions ameliorated. After several years, the atoll, now covered in vegetation, seemed like an Eden to those who had known it before. Tedworth was so delighted by it that he no longer wanted to leave, and is companions shared his enthusiasm.

The Colonel had baptized his islet Redemption Island, because the Great Psychagogue had had the idea of sending a few repentant malefactors there. Instead of delivering them to human justice, Sâr Dubnotal sent unfortunates who were more to be pitied than blamed to the Pacific atoll, and confided them to Tedworth's care. There, they were gradually regenerated by work and prayer, and when the Colonel considered them to be morally healed, he advised Sâr Dubnotal of his opinion. The Master Psychagogue immediately gave orders for them to be set free.

It was for this reason that Azilis de Tréguilly found herself on the island, in conversation with the brave Colonel Tedworth, Governor of Redemption Island. More emotional than he wanted to appear, Tedworth silently strode back and forth on the floor of the cell in which the Comtesse had been detained for several years. His prisoner had certainly accumulated a great guilt.

Azilis was the daughter of a poor Breton clockmaker resident in Kerambellec, not far from Morlaix, Père Le Floch. Young and pretty, her charms had seduced Come Jean de Tréguilly, whose manor was built on a nearby promontory, overlooking the lovely seaside resort of Trez-Hir. Instead of cherishing her husband, who had taken her out of poverty and to whom she had given two daughters, Azilis had rid herself of him by a crime! Horrible as it was, though, that crime was one of those with respect to which extenuating circumstances could be invoked.

Softened by the abundance of tears that the captive shed, the Colonel went on: "Comtesse, I can see that you find Sâr Dubnotal's clemency particularly touching, even though you have had occasion to appreciate his generosity many times before. Incarcerated here, far from all human aid, you have scarcely conserved the hope of ever recovering your liberty. On the other hand, you have been able to measure the full extent of your sins—sins that you would perhaps not have committed, admittedly, if you had not fallen victim to the criminal suggestions of the infamous Tserpchikopf."

"Oh, Governor, that is only too true: it was that wretch who caused my ruination!"

"I know that," said the Colonel, gently, "And Sâr Dubnotal knows it too. Did Tserpchikopf love you? It's hardly probable—but your marriage had made you rich, and the scoundrel, who coveted your fortune, intended to marry you after your husband's death Thanks to the Great Psychagogue, my friend and benefactor, that plan was not entirely realized. Guilty of the most frightful crimes, Tserpchikopf—who, under the names of the King of the Chessmen and Jack the Ripper, had bloodied Paris and London in turn—has paid for his crimes with his life. And you, Comtesse…"

"I, Governor, have benefited from an excessive indulgence, for I should have shared the fate of my accomplice."

Increasingly emotional, Colonel Tedworth shook his head. "No, no, Comtesse! Sâr Dubnotal, always merciful, did not judge that necessary, and he has done well, since you have been touched by repentance and grace. Redemption Island is not a labor camp in which malefactors die in pain after a long incarceration; as its name indicates, it is a place where repentant sinners can gradually attenuate the violence of their remorse. It is, in effect, a sort of terrestrial Purgatory, which Sâr Dubnotal wished to create."

299

The Colonel took Azilis by the hand and continued: "While you have been here, I have had time to convince myself of the sincerity of your conversion. Since the day when you escaped Tserpchikopf's influence—his hypnotic passes, and his occult and perfidious injunctions—you have led an edifying life. Like Mary Magdalene before you, your tears have washed away your sins. I have never had to complain about you. It is with the most perfect submission that you have yielded to the regime of severe but equitable regulations to which my prisoners are subject. Your hair has gone white, your complexion has faded and your eyes have become almost blind, by force of weeping. The punishment is sufficient."

"Dare I present myself to my daughters, though?" the unfortunate woman sobbed.

"Your daughters have never known the truth," the Governor hastened to reply. "The poor children have thought themselves orphaned of their mother as well as their father for a long time. After your arrest, Sâr Dubnotal saw to it that their interests were safeguarded, and had them fostered by worthy farmers before being sent to a boarding school, where they still are. It's only for a year that they've suspected that their mother is still alive."

"What must they think of me?" Azilis murmured, sadly. "To what can they attribute the inconceivable abandonment of which they have been the victims?"

"Sâr Dubnotal, who has served them as a sort of tutor under the pseudonym of Severus el Tebib, has made all the necessary provisions to prepare them to see you again. He has old them—and God will pardon him, I feel sure, for the small lie—that you lost your reason as a result of the death of Comte Jean, their father."

"He has taken his generosity that far?" exclaimed Azilis, in a great outburst of joy.

"Yes, Comtesse. Mademoiselles Andrée and Jeanne de Tréguilly imagine that you are interned in a sanatorium, and that he has forbidden them to see you for fear that the emotion of such a meeting might prove fatal for you. But Sâr Dubnotal has taken care to add that you were making good progress toward a cure, and that he hopes that you will be able to render your affection to them before long…"

While the conversation continued, Azilis was prey to the most contradictory sentiments and impressions.

Finally, she would be able to take the poor little things in her arms, hug them, caress their young heads and piously kiss their pure lips! That hope would have sufficed to make her forget all the mental and physical suffering that she had endured on Redemption Island, if she had been able to efface the memory of her crime from her memory.

Alas, she could not forget the death of Comte Jean, nor her guilty liaison with Tserpchikopf, and she wondered anxiously whether, in spite of what the Colonel had just told her, she would ever dare appear before Jeanne and Andrée. Had she not steeped her hands in their father's blood? It seemed to her that the girls would read the truth in her eyes and disown her, turning away from her in horror and disgust.

In any case, today was not the first time she had envisaged the eventuality of her return to France, for Colonel Tedworth had already told her that it would not be long before the door of her prison would be flung open for her. Strangely enough, though, she had never felt unhappier than since he had begun to nurture the hope of recovering her liberty.

She had frightful nightmares, terrifying hallucinations, and visions of murder and carnage. The obsession haunted her day and night. Her overheated neuropathic imagination gave birth to atrocious scenes, in which she imagined Comte Jean lying on his deathbed, as pale as the wax of the candles that burned at his bedside.

Usually, the image of the dead man disappeared, leaving nothing in its place but two large eyes, soft and sad at the same time, which Azilis could not contemplate without dissolving in tears. In her breast, elevated by convulsive sobs, her heart would contract to breaking point and, falling to her knees on the floor of her cell and putting her hands together, she would beg: "Forgive me, Jean! Forgive me, my poor husband!"

Then the immaterial eyes—the huge eyes suspended in mid-air—would weep inexhaustibly themselves, and Azilis' desolation would be redoubled.

Even that was not all.

In the shadow of her narrow retreat, another pair of eyes would light up flamboyantly, hypnotizing the unfortunate woman as soon as she turned her eyes in that direction. Those eyes were green—a luminous phosphorescent green—and possessed a magnetic gleam.

To whom did they belong?

From Azilis' trembling lips, a word would spring forth irresistibly—a word that chilled her through and through: "Tserpchikopf!"

Yes, those fiery emeralds, those diabolical pupils, could only be those of the powerful hypnotist.

When Cain, after the murder of his brother, fled in desperation, he could not see anything but Abel's eyes shining in front of him. The unfortunate Comtesse saw both the eyes of her victim and those of her accomplice! That double apparition recurred so frequently and with such intensity that the captive had lost sleep and her health declined. Prematurely aged and withered, she was dying by degrees, like a plant etiolated for lack of air and light.

Remorse, that ulcer of guilty souls, ate into Azilis de Tréguilly.

The worst thing was that she dared not complain to the Governor—although, if he knew that she was ill, he would not treat her harshly. And the most curious thing was that he frequency of these phenomena increased as Azilis saw her chances of being granted mercy increase. One might have imagined that, at the thought of that imminent release, the spirit of Comte Jean experienced more chagrin, and the *larva* of Tserpchikopf more wrath.

Although he was far from guessing the truth, Colonel Tedworth could not have witnessed the slow agony of his prisoner without feeling compassion for her. Observing that Azilis de Tréguilly was wasting away day by day, and no longer doubting the sincerity of her repentance, the honest Governor had hastened to inform Sâr Dubnotal, then resident in France with his following of disciples, mediums and investigators.

The Great Psychagogue's response has not been long in coming. By wireless telegraph, he had sent orders to Colonel Tedworth to repatriate Azilis immediately, and Tedworth had made all the necessary arrangements immediately.

"Come, Comtesse," he said. "The yacht that will take you to Japan is already under steam. In his telegraphic message, Sâr Dubnotal informs me that Naïni, his Hindu servant, is in Yokohama at present, and that he has sent him a telegram asking him to wait for you. You'll return to France with him, and he will look after you during the voyage. Come on! Don't cry anymore!"

Azilis shook her head and abruptly snatched away the hand that the worthy Colonel had been squeezing in his own. "No, Governor!" she said. "No, no, no!"

"What?" exclaimed Tedworth. "You don't want to leave?"

"No, no, no!" the prisoner repeated, obstinately. She laughed hysterically. "Leave? Why leave?"

"To see your daughters again."

"Do I still have daughters? Have I the right to have any? No, no, Governor. Leave me in my prison. I no longer have children!"

Not understanding this singular resistance, the Colonel studied Azilis more attentively. She seemed to have changed completely. The tears were no longer streaming down her hollow cheeks, but an expression of terror and distress was contracting her fleshless features. Turning toward the back of her cell, she stared fixedly at the whitewashed wall, and the Colonel wondered vainly why she had adopted that bizarre attitude.

Suddenly, Azilis' entire body stiffened; her right arm stretched out toward the wall and, in a voice punctuated by terror she stammered: "There! There!"

"What? What is it?" asked Tedworth, who could not see anything.

"There, I tell you," groaned Azilis. "There, on the wall—can't you see it?"

"The fact is…"

"You can't see those two eyes of fire?"

"I don't…"

"You can't see them? You can't see them?"

"Er…no, Comtesse!"

"Ah, he's blind!" said Azilis. "Would that I were, too! Oh, those eyes, those eyes of fire! My God! My God!"

"What's the matter, Comtesse?" said the Governor, moving forward to support the unfortunate woman as she became unsteady. "Calm down, for mercy's sake! I assure you that I can't see anything."

"I can see for myself! I can see those two diabolical eyes looking at me…look! There, Governor, very close, in front of us. I'd only have to reach out my hand to touch them—but I don't want to! I don't want to. They're burning me, those eyes of sulfur and phosphorus!"

Abruptly, she pushed the Colonel away and went to thrown herself on the bed—which, along with a table and a chair, comprised the entire furniture of the room—and buried her face in the bolster.

Tedworth, momentarily disconcerted, did not take long to pull himself together. "I understand," he murmured. "Joy has disturbed the unfortunate woman's mind, and that has brought back these strange hallucinations, the disquieting recrudescence of which was recorded in my warders' reports. I'll try to get her away from here. The open air will do her good—and besides, it's time for her embarkation. The Master had asked me to start her journey at 5 p.m. precisely—although I can't imagine why! It's 4 p.m. now, and orders are orders. Sâr Dubnotal is not a man from whom one can conceal anything, or whose orders it is permissible to disobey."

With that, Tedworth drew nearer to Azilis and said to her: "Come on, Comtesse—a little courage! Please stand up and follow me."

Azilis made no reply.

Slightly impatient, the Governor was about to take her by the hand when she suddenly sat up on the bed.

"Oh, those eyes!" she cried. "Those eyes of flame! Am I condemned to see them for as long as I live? Jean, my Jean, if they were still yours-but you have taken pity on me and only look at me once or twice a day, while that monster never ceases to feed on the spectacle of my pain…

"He's there, look, Colonel Tedworth! You can't see his head or his body, nor anything other than his phosphorescent eyes. Ah, they're burning! They're burning! Flee, Governor! The fire will take hold of you in the cell. The flames darted forth by those infernal eyes are getting closer; they're all around me! I want to die! Let me die!"

"Comtesse, I beg you! Pull yourself together, Comtesse, wake up!"

"Flee, I tell you!" Azilis groaned, pushing him away.

Tedworth was a colossus. His torso, shoulders, arms and everything else about him were Herculean. He could have felled an ox with a single blow of his fist, and had given proof of his prodigious strength—which equaled, if it did not surpass, that of the gigantic Naïni—on many occasions. He thought, therefore, that he could easily overcome the resistance that the poor woman was offering to him; seizing her by the wrists, he set about pulling her away from the bed on which she was sitting.

To his extreme surprise, he could not do it. He braced himself against the bed and pulled Azilis' arms with all his strength, but in vain; he could not budge her, any more than if she had been made of stone. She remained upright, seemingly riveted to her bed, as stiff as a cataleptic, and continued uttering increasingly fearful screams.

Exhausted, Tedworth had to let go. "By all the devils!" he exclaimed, sponging his sweat-bathed brow, "that's the most amazing thing I've ever seen. If a strong man like me can't budge a small woman, the suffragettes who are proclaiming the equality of the sexes are 100% right."

The brave Colonel seemed quite perplexed. "All the same," he murmured, "something has to be done. I regret that the Master's not here, for all this is extremely mysterious. I don't understand it at all…not at all!"

He went out of the cell in order to call the warders. Half a dozen men came running in response to his summons.

Azilis was still shouting. "What do you want with me? Why are you staring at me like that, accursed eyes? You've scorched my body; are you going to set fire to my soul?"

"She thinks she can see two gleaming human eyes on the wall," Colonel Tedworth explained to the astonished warders. "The news of her repatriation must have sent her completely out of her mind, for she's never been in such distress before today. You, who are in your right minds, search the cell with your eyes. Are there two bright dots there that the Comtesse might have mistaken for eyes?"

"No," said the warders, after looking everywhere. "There's nothing there."

"It might be nothing more than a hallucination. The woman has been struck by dementia, that's all. In telling her daughters that she's a madwoman, Sâr Dubnotal never said a truer word—but that's all the more reason for her to return to France. Come on, my friends! Get hold of her, as gently as possibly, and take her to the harbor, where we'll immediately confide her to the Captain of the yacht."

The warders advanced. As we have said, they had formerly been seamen in the employ of Sâr Dubnotal. Recruited with care by the Great Psychagogue, the torrid climate of Redemption Island—which was situated on the Tropic of Cancer—had not debilitated them. Each of them could easily have carried two women like Azilis on his titanic shoulders. Lifting her off the floor should have been as easy for them as picking

306

up a rifle that had fallen to the ground. Nevertheless, although they exerted their muscles of steel to the full, they had no more success than Colonel Tedworth. They moved the bed without being able to remove Azilis from it.

"Let me be!" she howled, persistently "Can't you see, you fools, that I don't have the right to leave? They don't want me to go! No, no, they don't want it!"

"Who are *they*?" Tedworth asked, nervously.

"The eyes!" Azilis said, through chattering teeth. "I can see them, even if you can't, and I can read their thought. They're forbidding me to leave."

"It's extraordinary," said the Governor, turning to his warders. "The Comtesse is evidently the victim of a hallucination—I'm increasingly convinced of it. On the other hand, I can't explain how that frail woman, whose illness seemed to have worn away all her strength, can offer us so much resistance."

"It's not me that's resisting," said Azilis, in a blank voice. "It's them!"

"The eyes?" Tedworth asked.

"Yes."

"They're ordering you to remain here?"

"Yes, Governor."

"Damn it!" the Colonel cursed. "What can I do? I can't do any more, but time's pressing—what will Sâr Dubnotal think if I don't carry out his instructions?"

Scarcely had Tedworth finished formulating this reflection when Azilis fell backwards on the bed.

"God be praised!" stammered the Colonel. "I hope that's the end of the crisis!"

It was indeed the end—but it was a very different conclusion from the one anticipated by Tedworth. Emerging from her abrupt torpor at the very moment when the warders were about to take hold of her, Azilis leapt from the bed, opened her arms wide in the form of a cross and pronounced, as if in ecstasy:

"Thank you, Severus el Tebib! You've saved me. Thanks to you, the accursed eyes have ceased to frighten me. Yes, yes…I can see you, now Severus el Tebib! You're at Trez-Hir, in your laboratory, and I can hear your grave voice, which reassures me. Yes, I'm healed, Master. I'm no longer suffering. I can no longer see them—they've gone! It's over, I assure you."

She turned back to the astounded Colonel. "Haven't I become reasonable, Governor?" she asked, with a fugitive smile. "Tell the Master that, in order that he'll believe me. Tell him that I'll embark, that nothing retains me here any longer, that the eyes of fire have disappeared from my cell."

"I will indeed tell him all that," Tedworth replied, mechanically, passing from one surprise to another. "But let's hurry, Comtesse. Since you've just promised Sâr Dubnotal to leave prison immediately, it's necessary to keep your word."

At that moment, Azilis de Tréguilly passed her hand over her forehead and looked around fearfully. She seemed only to perceive the presence of the governor and the warders. Inadvertently catching sight of herself in a mirror hung over the table, she uttered a faint cry of alarm. "What's become of me? Why am I livid and disheveled? What happened, Governor?"

"Nothing," said the Colonel, with difficulty, having understood that Azilis could not remember her crisis and not wishing to refresh her memory. "I've come with these men to take you to the yacht that will carry you away this very day, that's all."

"So it's true—I'm leaving?"

"You're leaving."

"Oh, what luck!" the prisoner cried, joyfully.

Meekly, she allowed herself to be taken to the yacht.

II. *The* Flying Dutchman

Sâr Dubnotal owned several ships, and one of them, specially appointed to carry supplies to Redemption Island, shuttle back and forth between the atoll and Yokohama, the nearest large port served by European shipping companies. The atoll only had a surface area of a few dozen hectares, but its northern coast, steeply inclined, formed a sheltered and secure harbor where the *Brahma*, as the ship in question was called—it was rigged out as a pleasure-yacht—found a refuge from all the shocks of typhoons.

As 5 p.m. chimed, Azilis de Tréguilly climbed aboard the *Brahma*, which immediately raised anchor.

Colonel Tedworth watched the ship draw away with a sigh of relief. Nothing in the world could have persuaded him to disobey the Master, even in the most minimal detail.

The most important thing is done, he said to himself, *since I've been able to conform to Sâr Dubnotal's instructions exactly. He insisted that the Comtesse should embark at 5 p.m.; his orders have been followed to the letter—but by Jove, what a singular adventure! I shall have to tell the Master all about it, and ask him to give me an explanation.*

What were those diabolical eyes that the Comtesse claimed to see in her prison, and which seemingly prevented her room leaving the cell? Were they, as I believed until now, merely a hallucination? If so, how was the poor woman able to resist the efforts of six athletes like my warders? And what is the significance of the vision she had afterwards? She really seemed to be seeing Sâr Dubnotal, talking to him and yielding to his orders.

I know very well that the Master' power is marvelous, but, all the same, I don't understand this prodigy at all. I've acted prudently, I think, in giving the Captain of the Brahma *a letter for Naïni. Apprised of the facts, the Hindu will be less fearful if the Comtesse suffers another crisis in the course of the voyage…*

Let us leave the brave Governor to talk to himself in peace and accompany Azilis de Tréguilly in her long and painful voyage of repatriation.

A speedy vessel, the *Brahma* covered the 1200 miles of the crossing in five days and reached Yokohama without the slightest incident.

Naïni was waiting for Azilis. He read the letter from the Governor of Redemption Island without raising an eyebrow, and immediately embarked with the Comtesse on a Lloyd's-registered Austrian steamer that was due to leave that same day for Trieste.

"Madame la Comtesse," he said, politely, "Sâr Dubnotal will not be at Trez-Hir when we arrive in Europe. He will be in Bordighera in Italy, where he has just acquired a property. You will meet him there before going to see your daughters."

Too emotional to reply, Azilis de Tréguilly wiped her moist eyes and installed herself in the comfortable cabin that Naïni had reserved for her.

Until they reached the vicinity of the Maldives in the Indian Ocean, the *Budapest*—that was the steamship's name—enjoyed a peaceful journey, whose monotony was only broken by brief stops in the ports that it served. In that region, however, something happened that the vessel's crew and numerous passengers were to remember eternally.

It was about 2 p.m. on a warm and sunny day in April. Thrashing the calm waters with its twin propellers, the *Budapest*—which had left Colombo on the previous evening and was out of sight of land—was racing forward at 18 knots. The line of the horizon seemed to be retreating into infinity. Not one cloud stained the gilded azure immensity of the sky, not a single wave was visible on the surface of the sea cleaved by the ship's powerful bow, and no sail was discernible there.

One the bridge, Captain Schlacht was strolling back and forth calmly smoking his pipe, while his first mate, Lieutenant Krieger, was monitoring the compass, and two sturdy seamen named Karl and Friedrich manned the tiller and the cathead respectively.

Suddenly, Captain Schlacht stopped in his tracks, his gaze focusing on a point of the horizon situated in front of the ship to port. "That's strange," he murmured. "The barometer hasn't gone down, though, so far as I know, and there's been no indication of any atmospheric disturbance." In a louder voice, he added: "Look at that grey cloud forming in the distance, Krieger."

The lieutenant looked in the direction indicated by his senior officer and exclaimed: "It looks like a squall!"

"Or a waterspout," muttered Karl.

"Yes, indeed!" the mate went on. "What can it be, Captain?"

"I was just asking myself the same question," Schlacht replied. "I thought of a cyclone myself, but we're not in the region of cyclones here and our instruments haven't budged." He pointed to the barometer. "Look! The needle's stuck firm!"

"Perhaps the instrument is out of order," suggested Friedrich.

"Get away!" said the Captain. "A precision barometer, formally guaranteed, doesn't break down like that without rhyme or reason." Schlacht took up his binoculars and continued: "Besides, that's neither a squall not a waterspout. It looks to me more like a bank of fog."

"Where can the fog have come from?" asked Krieger. "We're a long way from land, and the sky is clear."

"I don't know any more than you for the time being," Schacht grumbled, visibly perplexed and intrigued. It looks to me—as it will soon seem to you, since it's approaching rapidly—like a livid cloud floating very low above the surface of the sea."

"I can make it out quite well, in fact," said Krieger.

"Us too," said the seamen.

"Damnation!" said Schacht. "We'll have to reduce our speed, lads. That damned fog is about to descend upon us."

311

Indeed, the mysterious cloud was advancing toward the *Budapest* at a prodigious speed, and even before the Captain had raced to the telephone to give the chief engineer an order to slow down, thick wisps of a sort of grey smoke descended upon the steamer's deck. At the same time, a bitter odor of alkaline and sulfurous vapors took the crew and passengers by the throat as they lined the ship's side in order to contemplate the bizarre phenomenon.

"There's no volcano in the vicinity, though," said the first mate.

"No," said Schlacht. "No submarine crater would have been able to open five or six fathoms down up in these depths—although volcanic clouds can travel considerable distances from the erupting cone."

"Not on their own," Krieger said. "To do that, they have to be chased by the wind, and there's not a breath of air. Then again, Captain, note that the cloud isn't charged with scoria dust."

The Captain frowned. Leaning over the guard-rail of the bridge, he peered into the leaden mist—which, bizarrely, seemed to stick to the ship instead of continuing in its progress. The *Budapest* was still decelerating, in order to let the cloud pass, but it did not pass.

"One might think that we were attracting it and that it's taken it into its head to travel with us," Friedrich murmured, not without a certain alarm.

"There's witchcraft in this," Karl confirmed.

"Silence!" ordered Schlacht "Spare me your stupid remarks, will you? Stick to your posts—that's all I require of you."

The seamen shut up. Their commander, raising the binoculars to his eyes, seemed to be studying the composition of the cloud, which did indeed seem to be clinging to the *Budapest*.

"It's not smoke and it's not fog either," Schlacht continued, between two sneezes provoked by the inhalation of a draught of air. "Notice, Krieger, that the cloud is much more transparent than we thought at first."

"Yes," the mate replied. "I can even see the Sun through it. But what the Devil is it made of, then, Captain? I swear that it's making the air unbreathable!" And Krieger sneezed in his turn, while, from one end of the ship to the other, nothing could be heard but coughing fits and the sounds of handkerchiefs being energetically deployed.

"It's necessary to support that which can't be helped," Schlacht declared, eventually, his innate philosophical attitude getting the upper hand again. "We'll wait until the cloud consents to dissipate; then we'll resume our original speed and try to make up the time we've lost. I'll enter the incident in the ship's log; perhaps some scientist in Vienna or Berlin, or somewhere else, will eventually be able to give us a plausible explanation of the phenomenon that's confused us so completely."

Schlacht was about to put his binoculars back in their case when something else appeared to attract his attention. "Hell and damnation!" he blasphemed, turning toward the point at which he had seen the enigmatic cloud form. "There's a nasty complication!"

"What is it now?" Krieger inquired, anxiously.

Before answering, the Captain put his lips to the telephone transmitter and shouted: "Full steam ahead! Maximum power!"

"Sailing-ship for'ard to port!" roared Karl and Friedrich, simultaneously.

"Which is heading straight for us at an angle, as if to render a collision inevitable," said Schlacht. "Do you see, lieutenant?"

"Yes, I see her now," Krieger replied. "But, Captain…oh!"

"What?" asked Schlacht, nervously.

"Oh!" the first mate repeated, pointing at the sailing ship. "Look how rapidly she's traveling, Captain! She'll hit us amidships if we don't watch out!"

"Helm to starboard, full!" said Schlacht to Karl.

The seaman rapidly turned the tiller-wheel and, leaning over, the *Budapest* veered to starboard in order to avoid the sailing-ship. The latter was a two-master rigged as a brig.

The cloud, which the other ship had just entered in its turn, inevitably lent it a vaporous appearance. The blurred lines of her hull were confused with the grey background of the cloud, although the white sails covering her masts stood out clearly against the same backcloth.

The *Budapest*'s maneuver was successfully executed, and if the sailing-ship had not modified her direction just as the steamer modified its own, all danger of a collision would have been averted. Incredibly, though, scarcely had the steamship veered sharply to starboard than the brig did likewise.

"Hell and damnation!" Schlacht repeated. "Do you think that she's trying to chase us? Now, then—have we returned to the age of piracy, and does that rascally sailing-ship intend to ram us?"

What put the cap on the astonishment of the two officers was that, in spite of the flat calm, the two-master seemed to be moving as rapidly as the fast steamship. She was even gaining on her, and her slender form became ever-more-clearly visible in spite of the cloud that obstinately enveloped the two vessels.

In order for her to steer straight for a transoceanic steamship in that manner, of course, either her Captain was ignorant of the ABC of maritime regulations, or she was manned by a crew of pirates intent on capturing the *Budapest*. That did not explain, however, how she came to be endowed with such great speed, since her only means of propulsion seemed to be sail, and there was no wind.

"I think I have it," said Schlacht, suddenly. "Perhaps she's powered by electricity. In that case, it's probable that her intention really is to attack us."

"Well, we'll defend ourselves," said Krieger, resolutely. "We've got Gatling guns aboard—we'll have to use them."

314

"Undoubtedly," the Captain approved. "A 15,000-ton steamer with a solid crew can't give in to such an adversary without a fight. Mercantile mariners we may be, but we have to remember that, in case of war, Lloyd's-registered ships will serve as cruisers in the Austrian fleet! First, though, let's change heading one more time to see if that dog of a sailing-ship will dare to continue the pursuit."

Schlacht took the wheel himself and caused the vessel to describe a series of curves designed to put the singular two-master off the track. After a quarter of an hour of clever maneuvers, however, he was able to judge the sterility of his efforts; the sailing-ship was still traveling at top speed, and appeared to be maneuvering as if to cut his own vessel in two.

"Give the signal to clear the decks!" said Krieger. "Make ready to fire!"

"What good will it do, Lieutenant?" Karl stammered. "Shall I tell you the truth? Your bullets will go right through that ship without stopping it, for she's no more nor less than the *Flying Dutchman*."

At these words, Schlacht and Krieger looked at one another, and could not help going pale. To be sure, neither of them was superstitious—they were officers of the modern school, intelligent and educated men—but they had often heard mention of the Dutch sailing-vessel, the accursed brig condemned by the Divine Will to wander eternally from sea to sea. The mysterious speed of the two-master, and the inexplicable phenomena that had heralded her arrival—and were still persisting before their very wyes—obliged them to be less skeptical with regard to the legend. Returning their attention to the suspect sailing-ship, they examined her anxiously.

"There are people on board," stammered Schlacht.

"Yes," said Krieger. "An entire crew busy on the deck."

"They're not men of flesh and blood, and that ship isn't made of wood," said Karl, who was trembling like a leaf.

The fact is that the two-master, which must now be very close, since the crewmen manning her could be counted, still seemed distant and unobtrusive. She was more like a phantom of a ship than a ship. No noise could be heard from her direction. Her seamen, dressed like the filibusters of yore, slid silently over her decks; her maneuvers appeared to be carried out by a mute population. Next to the Captain, who was standing on her bridge and seemed to be a specter himself, a huge black Newfoundland dog was capering about and opening its mouth as if to bark, but its baying was inaudible.

Such terror emanated from that silence that those of the *Budapest*'s passengers who were still on deck fled in disarray to their cabins. Only Naïni and the Comtesse de Tréguilly remained in their places. The impassive Hindu's lips were sealed and Azilis did not appear to be at all afraid.

It was only much later that anyone learned, with amazement, the reason for their firm attitude, at that moment of indescribable panic—in which even the crew-members ran away to take refuge in the hold, and the Captain, mastering his own fear with great difficulty, was aggrieved to see Krieger, in the grip of a sudden fit of madness, hurl himself into the sea, while Friedrich fainted like a girl and Karl fell to his knees, calling loudly to Heaven: "Help us, Lord! Save us from the *Flying Dutchman*!"

The fact is that Naïni and Azilis, once the alarm was over, affirmed on oath that they had not seen either the leaden cloud or the two-master. Save for certain points of detail, of which we shall speak at the appropriate time and place, their testimony was in stark contradiction to that of the Captain, the crew and the majority of the *Budapest*'s passengers.

Meanwhile, on the bridge, Schlacht, white and shivering, was crouched over his wheel, still trying to escape the infernal brig that had set a course straight for the bowels of the steamer and was advancing at lightning speed.

"Curse you!" said the valiant officer, suddenly. The steamboat's engines had just come to an abrupt stop. The propellers ceased to thrash the sea and the rudder ceased to obey the Captain. Completely immobilized, the enormous leviathan offered its flank to the bow of the two-master that was racing toward her.

Glued to the wheel, the horrified Schlacht awaited the imminent collision.

The impassivity of the mariners on the sailing-ship, who were busy hailing in a sail as if nothing were happening, seemed to Schlacht to have a hint of madness about it.

Fortunately, the wait was brief. So closely had the *Flying Dutchman* kept company with him that it was only a short distance away. It came upon the *Budapest* with stupefying rapidity—and there was an impact.

A strange impact!

Was it, in fact, even an impact?

Did a collision actually occur, as Captain Schlacht was later to affirm? Did he really see the phantom brig cut completely through the Budapest with its immaterial bow and continue on her course without any longer seeking to harass the steamer?—which immediately departed herself at full steam and, finally emerging from the tenacious grey cloud, returned without transition to the vivid sunlight.

At any rate, at the moment when that extraordinary contact was made, according to Schlacht, the temperature became exceedingly cold. In the cabins and below decks alike, the passengers and the crew—who had been suffocating in the heat a moment before—felt a mortal chill freeze the blood in their veins, and that frisson was not the thrill of fear. Cold alone had caused it, the proof of which was given by the discovery of a thin layer of frost on the deck.

In that respect, at least, Naïni and Azilis were of the same opinion as the other passengers, and their good faith—which people were beginning to doubt—appeared obvious when they complained spontaneously of having experienced a sensation of Siberian cold themselves.

As soon as Schlacht had recovered from his emotion, he observed that the *Budapest* was alone within the circle of the horizon. So far as the eye could see, there was no longer any trace of the grey cloud, or of the phantom brig. The Sun was shining, the sky was gold and azure, the sea seemed to be a vast blue plain that no other ship, moved by sail or steam, was laboring with its keel.

The Captain had not been dreaming, though. There was no longer anyone beside him but Karl, still on his knees, and Friedrich, still fainted. The unfortunate Krieger had vanished, and when Schacht, calling everyone on deck, took a roll call of the crew, his last hope of seeing the first mate again vanished. Krieger did not respond to the call, and no one doubted that his suicide had been caused by an abrupt fit of dementia consequent on the violent emotion that he had experienced.

Schlacht had the second mate take over the watch, replaced the men at the tiller and the cathead and, observing that the ship was calmly following her course, mingled with the groups formed by the seamen and the passengers.

"I don't understand the terrifying adventure that has just overtaken us at all," he told them, in an unsteady voice. "It's necessary to believe that ghost stories are not as chimerical as people think, and as I thought myself until now. We have all seen the phantom brig, and how can we doubt that the accidents that occurred in parallel—the stopping of the *Budapest*, the death of my poor first mate and the abrupt decline in temperature—were caused by the action of a supernatural power?"

III. The Enigmatic Newfoundland

At these words from Captain Schacht, one of the passengers—an old man with an intelligent manner—shook his head skeptically.

"I beg your pardon," he said. "I saw nothing, myself."

"Were you on deck?" asked Schlacht.

"No," said the old man.

"Well, then?"

"But I've questioned my traveling companions, and my conviction is formed."

318

"What do you believe then?"

"Before answering you," said the old man, expressing himself correctly in German, "permit me to introduce myself to you, Captain Schlacht."

The officer looked down at the card that his interlocutor was holding out, and read: *LUDOVIC GRANGER, Doctor of Science, University of Paris*.

"I see that you're a French scientist, Monsieur," said Schlacht, coldly.

"My God, yes, Captain," said he old man. "That is to say, I am occupied in resolving certain scientific problems."

"And you claim to have an explanation of the phenomenon that we have just witnessed?"

"I believe so, at least," said Monsieur Granger, modestly. "In my opinion, Captain, you have all been victims of an optical illusion. You have, in fact, witnessed a phenomenon as curious as it is rare, similar to that which is sometimes produced in the Sahara, to the great disadvantage of caravans."

"You mean that the apparition of the *Flying Dutchman* was nothing but a mirage?"

"Precisely, Captain."

"What makes you think so?"

"If you would care to hear me out," said the scientist, "I think I can convince you. In 1900,[29] a German ship, the *Sachsen*, traveling from Japan to New York, had just crossed the equator when the officer of the watch perceived a sailing-ship above the line of the horizon, whose hull, masts and rigging stood out with such clarity from the zone of the sky in which it was sailing that all of its maneuvers could be tracked by eye, down to the slightest operation of the crew. A seaman hauling in a sail having lost his footing and fallen into the water, a launch was seen to set off from the ship and row toward the drowning man. The apparition lasted several minutes, then

---

[29] The text will subsequently assert that Azilis has been sequestered for "nearly 15 years," indicating that the present story is set in 1904.

faded away and vanished completely. It was witnessed by the majority of the *Sachsen*'s crew, who answered the summons of the officer on watch—and those men, like yours, Captain Schlacht, were allowing themselves to be overwhelmed by superstitious terror when, at about noon on the following day, the *Sachsen* encountered an English sailing-ship exactly similar to the apparition of the previous day but heading in the opposite direction and sailing on the surface of the water. After which the crew-members realized that it had been a simple matter of solar refraction, and their dread dissipated…"

Before Schlacht could say a word, a second passenger, who seemed to have been listening to the story told by the first with great attention, spoke in his turn. "The *Sachsen*'s adventure wasn't new," he said, "and it won't be the last. More recently, the American transatlantic liner *Philadelphia* had an exactly similar experience. Its crew and passengers saw a French steamer, the *Lorraine*, coming toward them through the clouds, although it was really 25 miles away, as they were able to establish by getting in touch with her via wireless telegraphy. It's rare, however for adventures of that sort to terminate as well as those of the *Sachsen* and the *Philadelphia*, as we have just seen, Monsieur. You would do well if you could get it out of the heads of sea-goers that what you call mirages are in fact what they themselves call omens or signs, and that their appearance is always followed, more or less distantly, by a catastrophe.

"I might mention phenomena more extraordinary still, like the one that was observed in the month of August 1888 in Hungary, near Wasarden, and accepted without further explanation by the scientists of the entire world. Above the vast plains that surround the town, an army of several thousand men was seen marching in mid-air. The surrounding populations, who came running in large numbers, witnesses the maneuvers of those phantom soldiers three days running, with a curiosity mingled with fear. That could not have been a mirage, though, since there was no army in the vicinity, or within a radius of many miles."

"Furthermore," said Schlacht, addressing Ludovic Granger, "how do you explain the drop in temperature that occurred at the moment of the collision?—a drop that was felt to your detriment as well as ours, to judge by your red nose."

"It's true," the scientist murmured, somewhat embarrassed, "that the latter phenomenon…"

"Is no more explicable than the others, if one entrenches oneself behind pure science," said the Captain, shaking his head. You weren't on deck, Monsieur, so you cannot affirm anything—but I can guarantee that it was no mirage, or any other such nonsense. That two-master wasn't sailing in the sky like the vessels perceived by the seamen of the *Sachsen* and the *Philadelphia*; its hull was gliding through the water and cut straight through us. I saw the phantom brig with my own eyes, with its crew of specters, and nothing you can say can make me say otherwise."

"The Captain's right," said several other passengers. "We didn't stay on deck until the end, but we had time to see the *Flying Dutchman* perfectly. The proof is that we clearly distinguished a large black Newfoundland dog standing on the bridge next to its Captain."

At that precise moment in the conversation loud barking was heard behind the group formed by the seamen and the passengers: the clear and joyful barking of a large dog. Everyone turned round precipitately, and what they saw chilled the hearts of the strongest.

Next to Naïni, whose was standing to one side with Azilis, an enormous Newfoundland was capering, and licking the Comtesse's hands. The beast could not be any other than the one they had just seen aboard the *Flying Dutchman*! The resemblance was perfect: the same size, the same color, the same silky and bushy coat. What was more, the identity of the two beasts was established logically by the fact that there had definitely been no dog on board before the appearance of the phantom ship.

Nevertheless, to salve his conscience, Schlacht went over to Azilis and said: "Is this Newfoundland yours, Madame?"

"No, Captain," the Comtesse replied.

"It seems to know you," the officer observed.

"That what astonishes me most of all," said Azilis. "My servant and I were just talking about the strange wave of cold that abruptly descended upon the ship when this handsome Newfoundland, emerging from who-knows-where, came to lick my hands and lavish the most touching caresses upon me."

"Emerging from you-don't-know-where?" cried the Captain. "So you didn't see it aboard the phantom brig?"

"What phantom brig are you talking about?" said Azilis, with a surprise that was certainly not feigned.

"What? You don't know? But you were definitely on deck!"

"Indeed, Captain—but you're talking in riddles, it seems, and I don't understand you."

She didn't see anything! thought the Captain, drawing away. *Nor did the Hindu, as his bewildered expression indicates well enough. It's futile to insist—but that only confirms my own observations. If it had been a mirage, the passenger and her servant would have witnessed the phenomenon, while an apparition might well not have been evident to everyone.*

Schlacht returned to his bridge, very thoughtfully, with his eyes moist and his mind confused, leaving his passengers to discuss the strange event to their hearts' content. *That's all right*, he concluded. *It's certainly the most astonishing and tragic adventure of my entire life, which has not been short of vicissitudes of every sort.* He sighed. *Poor, poor Krieger! He couldn't cope with the commotion, and that's a further proof that it really was a matter of the accursed vessel, for I never knew a fellow more skeptical than him, and it certainly required something more than a simple mirage to addle his brain like that and drive him to such a desperate act.*

With that, the Captain set his flag at half-mast and examined from afar, mistrustfully, the large Newfoundland dog that everyone aboard was avoiding, except for Azilis and Naïni.

IV. In the Midst of Mystery

A fortnight later, the Comtesse and the Hindu, who had disembarked the day before in Trieste, arrived safe and sound in Bordighera. Sâr Dubnotal was waiting for them in the drawing-room of the elegant villa that he had just acquired on the Strada Romana.

Having discovered the secret of the transmutation of metals and being able to exploit the pearl-producing oyster-beds off the coasts of Ceylon, the Great Psychagogue was so rich that he did not even know exactly how large his fortune was, and never hesitated before any prodigality.

On finding herself once again before her generous judge, Azilis de Tréguilly said to him in a tone of profound gratitude: "You have had mercy on me, Monsieur Severus, and I was unworthy of your forgiveness."

"Let's not speak of the past," he replied, gravely. "Men have absolved you, Comtesse. May God ratify their indulgent verdict the future be your element!"

"Where are my daughters?" she asked.

"You shall see them tomorrow. I wanted to avoid the stress of a further journey. They're at Ospedaletti, a pleasant winter resort situated a few leagues from Bordighera. I've rented a lodge for them and for you, where you can enjoy the tender joys of family life in peace. Naïni will take you, and I hope that everything will go well."

Without noticing the hint of anxiety that impinged upon the overman's voice, Azilis dissolved into emotional expressions of gratitude. Then, as she was very tired, she retired to the room that had been put at her disposal.

Immediately, Sâr Dubnotal turned to Naïni, who was patiently awaiting his orders. "Give me your report, my friend," he said, as he rang to summon his disciple Rudolph.

The gigantic servant let Rudolph in, then handed his Master the letter that the Captain of the yacht had given to him on behalf of Colonel Tedworth, in which the latter described the bizarre incident that had preceded Azilis' embarkation.

Sâr Dubnotal read the missive rapidly and said: "Have you read this, Naïni?"

"Yes, Master,"

"And what did you think of this business?"

"I feared, Master, that the Comtesse might suffer another crisis of the same sort on the way, which would have complicated my task considerably."

"That was not the case?"

"No, Master—fortunately."

The Great Psychagogue smiled. "So far as I can see, Tedworth didn't understand what happened at all," he said to Rudolph. "He's a valiant soldier, a man whom I can trust blindly, but he has no aptitude for psychognosis. I fully understand his amazement on seeing his captive refuse to leave and then, having become docile again, quit her cell of her own accord, after the combined efforts of six colossi had failed to extract her therefrom. There's nothing very mysterious in that for us, however. For a long time, Tedworth's reports have alerted me to the Comtesse's precarious mental state—her hallucinations and frightful nightmares. At first I thought it was a final rebellion of her conscience reproaching her for her crime, but certain details opened my eyes and I divined that it was not remorse that was tormenting Azilis thus."

"What was it then?" asked Rudolph, very interested.

"A *larva* or *lemur*," said the Great Psychagogue. "One of those miserable souls that carry all the base rancor and all the hatred they amassed on Earth into the Beyond, and which, instead of transforming themselves, spend their afterlife harassing humans."

"And whose was that infernal *larva*, Master?"

"Can't you guess?"

"Tserpchikopf's!" cried the disciple.

"Indeed. There is no other that had any interest in terrifying Azilis and preventing her from leaving my terrestrial purgatory. You know that he *larvae* of the damned are not satisfied until they have caused the ruination of their Earthly accomplices. Tserpchikopf's spirit seeks to drag Azilis into the abyss, and its fury knew no bounds when it learned that my intention was to restore the unfortunate woman's liberty. That's why the two phosphorescent eyes appeared to the Comtesse and why the poor woman offered an invincible resistance to her warders."

"A resistance that came to a sudden end, I'm told."

"Because I restored order," said the Great Psychagogue, tranquilly. "You'll recall, Rudolph, that I instructed Tedworth to embark his prisoner at a particular hour on a particular day."

"And when the moment came, you retired to the evocation room with one of your mediums. Yes, I remember that quite well, Master."

"The fact is that, already sensing the truth, I expected a difficult embarkation and wanted to lend my assistance."

"Psychically, Master?"

"Yes, Rudolph. Focusing all my psychic energy, I transported myself mentally to Redemption Island and I appeared to the Comtesse, whom I reassured and cured of her terrors, after chasing Tserpchikopf's *larva* away. The spell was immediately broken, and Azilis ceased to resist the warders."

"What a marvelous thing science is!" murmured the young disciple.

"Undoubtedly, Rudolph—and when it is in the service of Justice, it becomes the most precious gift that a human creature can receive from God. But God alone is really infallible, and Progress marches at a slow pace."

The Great Psychagogue remained thoughtful momentarily. "The enigma is elucidated, therefore," he went on, eventually. "Have you anything else to tell me, Naïni?"

"Yes indeed, Master," the Hindu replied. "I believe I should tell you about a strange event that took place during our voyage, which terrified our traveling companions, although the Comtesse and I saw nothing—or almost nothing—unusual."

"Go on," said Sâr Dubnotal, interestedly.

Naïni gathered his thoughts briefly, and then told the story of what had happened to the *Budapest*. He emphasized the fact that neither he nor the Comtesse had witnessed the phenomenon of the apparition of the *Flying Dutchman*, but that, on the other hand, they had suffered the drop in temperature along with everyone else, and that a black Newfoundland dog previously unseen on the ship had then appeared spontaneously and had attached itself to them.

"The *Flying Dutchman* actually collided with the *Budapest*?" exclaimed Sâr Dubnotal—who, for once, allowed his surprise to show.

"That's what all the passengers affirmed," Naïni replied, "but I repeat, Master, that I didn't see anything happen, and nor did the Comtesse."

"You both knew perfectly well, though, that something extraordinary had happened?"

"Yes, Master, for cold is unknown at that latitude, especially at that time of the year, and we were both literally chilled."

"The passengers also told you that the arrival of the phantom brig had been preceded by the abrupt descent of a fog?"

"It wasn't fog, Master, since that phenomenon was similarly imperceptible to me."

Sâr Dubnotal reflected for some time.

"Rudolph," he resumed, in a calm voice, "I know the story of the *Flying Dutchman* very well and I'm not at all of the opinion of the scientist Monsieur Granger—who, it seemed, claimed to explain the apparition of the phantom sailing-ship by solar refraction. The *Dutchman*, manned by a crew of *larvae*, really roams the seas, and many catastrophes, many shipwrecks and many disappearances of ships, the causes of which remain unknown, have been provoked by unexpected encounters with it. In addition, it is not given to everyone to see it, and there's nothing astonishing in the fact that Naïni and the Comtesse were unaware of its approach—but the phenomena that the Hindu has just described to me always occur in real instances of a collision with the *Flying Dutchman*."

"So you're convinced, Master?"

"Yes," Sâr Dubnotal replied, "except that I'm wondering how the phantom brig came to attack the steamer. Tell me, Naïni—what became of the black dog you mentioned?"

"That's another story, and a rather strange one," the Hindu said. "Throughout the remainder of the voyage, the dog caused the Comtesse and myself a great deal of annoyance because, as I told you, Master, it had immediately attached itself to us, and the other people aboard felt a mortal terror at the sight of it."

"They were sure that it really had come from the *Flying Dutchman*?"

"Absolutely sure. All those who had witnessed the maneuvers of the sailing-ship recognized the dog, whose presence they had observed on the bridge next to its Captain."

"Besides, it could only have come from there," observed Sâr Dubnotal, "since it had not been aboard the *Budapest* before."

"So everyone considered it to be an infernal creature," the Hindu went on, "and avoided it like the plague. After listening to everything that was said about the Newfoundland and hearing the complaints and fearful remarks of the crew and passengers, I was by no means tranquil myself and I would have preferred to be rid of it—but it lavished such obvious affection on the Comtesse, and she responded so quickly and so fully to its touching advances, that I could not bear to separate them."

"Azilis did not know where the Newfoundland had come from, then?"

"No, for I made sure that the terrifying stories that were beginning to circulate regarding her new companion did not reach her ears. The poor lady's health is so frail that a strong emotion, or too violent an alarm, might be fatal to her. In brief, Master, on due reflection, I thought it would be better to bring the dog here, in order that you might examine it and dispel the mystery that hangs over its origin."

"What!" said Sâr Dubnotal. "You brought it with you? It's here?"

"Yes, Master. It followed us meekly, and as we entered your house I left it in the courtyard with your own household pets."

Sâr Dubnotal leapt up from his chair. "I need to see it immediately," he said. "Follow me, Rudolph and Naïni. We're in the midst of a mystery, and I don't yet know what to think—but the Newfoundland will give me the key to the enigma, and my science is not all vanity."

IV. Initial Suspicions

The Great Psychagogue loved animals, and their instincts—which are, in some ways, superior to human intelligence—sometimes rendered him important services.

Among his favorite animals, the curlew Krak and the owl Kobe figured in the first rank. These intelligent birds, disciplined by long training, followed the Master almost everywhere. An aviary had been set up for them in the courtyard of the villa, in which Naïni had just given temporary shelter to the mysterious Newfoundland adopted by the Comtesse de Tréguilly in the circumstances just described.

This aviary, connected to the outbuildings of the residence, consisted of a sort of hut and a wire-netting enclosure.

When they arrived in the courtyard, Sâr Dubnotal, his disciple and his servant perceived, to their extreme surprise, that the Newfoundland, left by the Hindu in a state of good health, was no longer showing any sign of life. Its body, extended on the ground next to the wire-netting of the aviary, was as soft as flimsy cloth, and one might have thought that the flesh beneath its soot-colored pelt no longer had any skeleton or muscles to sustain it.

The curlew Krak, perched high up in the aviary on a bar provided for that purpose, was darting fearful glances in the direction of the dog. Its feathers were ruffled and it was whistling frantically, while the owl Kobe, perched alongside, remained silent.

"Master!" cried Naïni. "The dog is dead, Master!"

"A strange death, from what I can see," the Great Psychagogue replied. "What is this new enigma?"

Bending over the cadaver of the dog, he examined it attentively. "It's no more than a skin," he murmured. "Your Newfoundland, Naïni, was no ordinary dog. We knew that already, but we'd have great difficulty explaining its sudden end, if we weren't so well versed in the study of psychognosis."

Without ceasing to study the flaccid hide of the dog, but doing his best to reassure the frightened birds, the Great Psychagogue continued: "I've inculcated you with the principles of that sublime science, Rudolph, and you ought to have an inkling of what has happened. Do you recall that in the Celtic countries—in Scotland, Cornwall, Wales and Brittany—the souls of the wicked are thought to transform themselves, commonly, into black dogs. Perhaps that's not, as is generally believed, a legend. The Celts were more sensitive than other peoples to the supernatural."

"I do indeed recall that, Master…according to popular legend, certain Breton priests even had the power to dispatch these villainous souls to the abyss by throwing their stoles around their necks."

"Yes—that power, among others, was attributed not so long ago to the parish priest of Bégard commonly known as Tadig-Koz, and to those of Commana and Saint-Rivoal, parishes neighboring the marshes of Yeun-Elez, into which the suspect dogs were thrown, and which, the good folk believe, communicate directly with Hell.[30] But Master, might that not

---

[30] The *recteur* [parish priest] of Bégard whose nickname was Tadig-Koz ["little old father"] was Abbé Guillermic. The

be a mere survival of ancient Druidic beliefs regarding metempsychosis? Caesar, Lucan and several other ancient Roman writers and philosophers mentioned…"

"And what prevents that which was true in the days of Lucan and Caesar still being true today? Personally, I wouldn't be at all surprised if an infernal *larva* has been inhabiting the envelope of the black dog that lies at our feet for some time. I only hesitated to believe it because of the behavior of the dog. According to Naïni, it seemed so fond of its new mistress.

"Now, you know that Comte Jean never ceased to cherish his guilty spouse, even in the afterlife. Although that soul had no sin to expiate, I wondered whether it might not have been able, in order to get close to Azilis, to take on the appearance of a Newfoundland, embark on the *Flying Dutchman* and send the latter to ram the *Budapest*, in order to leap aboard the steamer.

"The instinctive affection of the dog for the Comtesse and its manifest desire not to leave her again renders my hypothesis quite plausible—but the animal's abrupt end gives me pause for thought, and I suspect there's a more ominous mystery."

"In that case, these suspicions will not be long delayed in assuming the character of certainty," Rudolph said, confidently.

The young disciple's remark cheered the Great Psychagogue up somewhat. "I admire your unbridled optimism and your absolute confidence in me," he said.

"I admire your supernatural genius even more, Master! The optimism for which you reproach me comes from that. You have given me such proofs of your power, and your wisdom is so profound, that it's entirely natural for me not to doubt the successful outcome of your researches."

---

marshes of Yeun-Elez were once host to a foul bog known as *Le Youdic*, whose methane emissions continually caught fire; hence its reputation as a hell-mouth.

"Let's leave it at that, if you will," said Sâr Dubnotal, whose extreme modesty was not very comfortable with that sort of praise. "Let's think about the problem, which seems to me, as it does to Naïni, strangle complicated. We need to find out whose *larva* it was that inhabited the body of the Newfoundland. I need to know that, Rudolph, and I shall."

Sâr Dubnotal prodded the skin of the dog with his foot. It really was the skin of a Newfoundland: a silky pelt of long dark hair, but empty, like those of animals that naturalists are wont to stuff.

"Throw that on the dung-heap, Naïni," he said. "When that's done, my curlew will doubtless calm down again."

The Hindu obeyed, while the two psychagogues left the aviary and the courtyard, without noticing the increasingly bizarre attitude of the two birds.

Instead of recovering its tranquility, Krak became even more agitated on the perch, and seemed to be shrinking away from the owl Kobe, with a horror mingled with terror. The latter, huddled at the extremity of the bar, was staring at it with its golden eyes. A diabolical flame sprang forth from the pupils of the nocturnal creature—whose eyelids, surprisingly enough, were not closed as they usually were by day.

Sâr Dubnotal and Rudolph did not return to the drawing-room. They called Annunciata Gianetti, the celebrated transalpine medium, and immediately went with her to the Green Room, also known as the evocation room, where the Master's occult experiments were undertaken.

"Annunciata," said the overman, "I desire to put a few questions to the spirit of Comte Jean de Tréguilly. It is with great regret that I trouble the rest of that poor soul, who has suffered so much, and you must offer him all my apologies, but it is important to shed some light on certain obscure matters, in the interests of Azilis, the deceased's still-beloved spouse."

As soon as the door was closed and the curtains drawn, the room—whose sober furnishings and wallpaper were green, hence its name—was immediately cast into deep darkness.

That darkness retained fugitive emerald glints, which permitted the discernment of the silhouettes of the two psychagogues and that of the medium—all three of whom had put on large robes of that emerald hue over their normal costumes.

Sitting down in armchairs, Sâr Dubnotal and his disciple did not move again. La Gianetti, picking up a little wand of black wood, groped her way to a table set in the middle of the room, let herself collapse on to a sofa set beside it, and patiently awaited the Master's orders.

"Pay attention, Annunciata!" the latter murmured, sketching a few rapid passes with his right hand, designed to provoke a state of trance, or psychic division, in the medium.

As if galvanized by an electrical discharge, the Italian woman stood up in front of the table, with her arm extended and her eyes closed.

In the silence of the hermetically-sealed room, her hoarse and urgent respiration was audible, alternating with a slight crackling sound, which could only be originating from the vibration of her nerves, as taut as a bowstring.

"Are you ready?" Sâr Dubnotal asked.

"Yes, Master," la Gianetti replied, in a voice that had changed completely: a disquieting, otherworldly voice.

"Good," murmured the Great Psychagogue. "Summon the Comte, and may God permit his soul to consent to enter into communication with you momentarily."

At these words, the medium, armed with her wand, tapped abruptly on the table-top, followed the first stroke with three lighter taps, and fell back on the sofa, inanimate and frozen, as if she were dead.

For a few seconds, there was nothing but silence and opaque darkness in the Green Room. Sitting in their armchairs, Sâr Dubnotal and Rudolph resembled statues. Their bodies were the mute slaves of their iron will, and they could do what they wished with them—especially the overman, who, by virtue of certain ascetic practices, had elevated his entire being far above vulgar sensation.

Suddenly, a sound more distinct and more bizarre than the crackling of the medium's nerves—a crystalline sound, simultaneously distant and close at hand, it seemed—rang out at the back of the room, like the mysterious chiming of a seraphic clock.

At the same time, a pale cloud—a sort of milky mist—rose from Annunciata's body, rose up slowly to the ceiling and condensed there, taking on the appearance of a fiery globe.

"The Comte's spirit!" murmured Sâr Dubnotal.

The two psychagogues watched the luminous ball attentively. It seemed to consist of a phosphorescent nucleus the size of a hen's egg, and a surrounding a halo of vapor.

"Annunciata!" Sâr Dubnotal resumed, while the fiery globe slowly descended from the ceiling and stopped above the table-top, floating in mid-air like an electric light-bulb.

La Gianetti abruptly got up from her recumbent position. "Master?"

"This really is the soul of Comte Jean de Tréguilly, isn't it?"

"Yes, Master."

"Ask him to grant us five minutes of conversation."

The medium, whose tragic face was illuminated by the light of the immaterial bulb, articulated painfully: "Comte Jean de Tréguilly, will you be generous enough to reply to my Master's questions, which he desires to ask you in the interests of your former spouse?"

The table, as if magnetized in response to the medium's question, seemed to be drawn toward the fire-ball. Its feet left the floor and a mysterious force sustained it in mid-air without any means of support—none, at least, that was visible.

Placing a hand on the edge of the suspended item of furniture, Annunciata appeared to be studying the nature of the tremors by which it was agitated. "Master," she said, then, translating the secret meaning of those oscillations into intelligible language, "the Comte de Tréguilly asks who you are and why you're interested in Azilis."

"He doesn't recognize me, then?" asked Sâr Dubnotal. "Hasten to inform him, Annunciata."

The medium struck the table again and said: "My master is Sâr Dubnotal, also known as Severus el Tebib, the Great Psychagogue."

An oscillation of the table-top, followed by a sequence of raps, was the immediate response of the item of furniture, the customary intermediary between the visible and the invisible.

"The acquaintance is made," stammered la Gianetti, who was already feeling the progressive diminution of her psychic fluid. "The spirit of the Comte knows who you are now, re-calls your role, excuses the disturbance you're inflicting upon him and consents to inform you to the extent that he can."

"Thank him for being so obliging, Annunciata, and ask him whether, in order to get closer to his widow, he has re-cently reincarnated himself within the flesh of a Newfound-land dog."

Very pale, la Gianetti drummed her wand precipitately, to which the table replied with a single rap.

"No," said the medium. "It wasn't Comte Jean that inha-bited the animal's body."

Sâr Dubnotal touched Rudolph's arm. "What did I tell you?" he said. "My initial hypothesis is worthless! Annuncia-ta, now ask the Comte whether he knows what did materialize itself in that form."

The medium transmitted the Great Psychagogue's ques-tion, and immediately received a long and important commu-nication from the interrogated soul, which she translated thus:

"Yes, Master, the Comte knows and did not hesitate to tell me what materialized itself in the Newfoundland's form. It was a *larva*, a *lemur*."

"Ah!" said the two psychagogues, in unison. "And did the Comte tell you the name of that *larva*, Annunciata?"

"Yes," stammered the medium. "Yes, Master, it was…oh!"

All of a sudden, to the amazement of the two psychago-gues, the Italian's voice caught in her throat. Dropping her wand, she twisted her arms frightfully, while the ball of fire gradually became paler and was extinguished, like the light of a chandelier that is no longer receiving an electric current.

Darkness—a black and sinister darkness—replaced the half-light that had reigned in the room.

Sâr Dubnotal and Rudolph could no longer make out the medium, who suddenly began uttering heart-rending screams.

"In Heaven's name, what's happening?" cried Rudolph.

"Pull those curtains that are masking the daylight, and I might be able to tell you," Sâr Dubnotal replied, in an anxious tone.

With one bound, he disciple was in the embrasure of a window. Drawn apart, the curtains let a flood of light into the Green Room.

What Rudolph saw caused him to utter a scream of terror.

Standing in front of Sâr Dubnotal, who rushed to help her, the Italian woman was scything the air with her stiff arms, foaming at the mouth like a hydrophobe and rolling her eyes, widened by the horrors of an abrupt and terrible agony.

"I'm dying!" she croaked. "Sâr...Master...help! Ah! Ah! Ah!"

"Great God!" said the young man, running to the Great Psychagogue, who was clutching the shuddering body of the medium to his broad bosom. "What's wrong with her, Master?"

"We'll find out sooner or later," Sâr Dubnotal relied. "But before we do anything else, Rudolph, let's carry her into my laboratory."

"Is she dead?" Rudolph stammered.

"Dead in human terms," said Sâr Dubnotal, coldly. "Dead for everyone, except for God and me."

V. In Which the Word Metempsychosis
Is Pronounced Again

The next day, Sâr Dubnotal having manifested the intention of spending the afternoon mediating, his disciple and his aides left him alone in the smoking-room, where he was accustomed to take his siesta.

On his orders, Naïni brought him a hookah, from which he took a few puffs, perfumed by their passage through rosewater, before asking: "Is the Comtesse de Tréguilly ready?"

"No, Master," the gigantic Hindu replied. "Not quite—but I don't think she'll be long."

"Poor woman!" Sâr Dubnotal murmured. "I doubt that she'll enjoy the joys that I promised her in peace, and that she'll have the good fortune to live for a long time in the company of her daughters. Her expiation, alas, has only just begun—but her repentance will render the ordeals she will have to undergo in the other world less painful. Without my intervention, they would have been terrible."

Sâr Dubnotal smoked in silence for a few moments and then, addressing the Hindu—who was awaiting his orders—he asked: "What were those frantic whistling sounds that were coming from the courtyard when I called you?"

"It was Krak who was whistling like that, Master. We don't know what's come over the bird since yesterday. Normally so tranquil, he continually goes back and forth within the aviary, screeching and beating his wings, throwing himself recklessly against the netting as if he wanted to escape."

"What about Kobe?" the Great Psychagogue asked.

"Kobe doesn't move, Master. That one remains isolated in a corner and seems tranquil. His companion's alarm, and the fuss the other bird kicks up in the vicinity, leave him indifferent. He's even gloomier than usual, and I think he might be ill."

"Might Kobe be suffering from a dangerous infection, which threatens the curlew, and whose seriousness the latter senses?"

"Perhaps, Master."

"Go fetch the owl," Sâr Dubnotal decided, abruptly having given the hookah back to the servant. "I need to examine the bird without further delay."

Naïni withdrew, and came back a few minutes later with the bird. "Master," he said, "you've divined the truth, for no sooner had I removed Kobe from the aviary than Krak became calm again. The owl is definitely ill."

"That's what I shall determine immediately," murmured Sâr Dubnotal. He made a sign instructing the Hindu to wait for a while, picked up the bird and began to subject him to a minute examination. By turns, he felt the owl's feet, wings, body and beak, without noticing anything abnormal. The owl allowed himself to be handled and did not seem at all inconvenienced by the particular attention to which he was subjected.

"That's bizarre," Sâr Dubnotal finished by up saying. "I've never seen Kobe in better health. If Krak is running away from the owl, it's not because Kobe's ill. On the other hand, the curlew's instinct is too reliable for him to be frightened without a reason."

Releasing the owl—which flew on to the table and settled down there, as if to go to sleep—the Great Psychagogue made a gesture of annoyance. "I'll take care of that later," he declared. "First I have to attend to a more pressing matter, which is to elucidate the mystery of the apparition of the *Flying Dutchman* and establish the identity of the *larva* that took refuge in the body of the Newfoundland brought back by Azilis. Naïni, you may go. I need to reflect—and besides, it's time to take the Comtesse to Ospedaletti, where her two daughters are awaiting her impatiently. Has Joseph been alerted?"

"Yes, Master; he's already sitting in the automobile."

"You'll be in Ospedaletti in half an hour. Stay with the Comtesse and her children for the rest of the day, in case they have need of you."

By the manner in which Sâr Dubnotal had pronounced these final words, the Hindu understood that his master was experiencing a certain anxiety. "Is the Comtesse in danger, Master?" he asked.

"Who can tell?" said the Great Psychagogue, evasively. "In life, must one not be ready for anything? Whatever happens, Naïni, I want you to watch over the Comtesse carefully."

"Have no fear, Master."

"And take Krak with you. The villa in which the Comtesse's children live is a good quarter of an hour from the nearest telegraph office, and Joseph's automobile might have an accident. Now, I want to be informed immediately as to the results of Azilis' meeting with her children. Whether the meeting goes well or badly, send me a dispatch by means of the curlew, which will get it to me in eight or ten minutes."

Being a strong bird, as we have said, and as swift as the wind, Krak sometimes served the Great Psychagogue as a messenger. The latter was able to correspond with his servant by means of thought-transmission, but preferred to use natural means whenever they were sufficient.

"Understood, Master," said Naïni, respectfully.

Having dismissed the Hindu, who left in the automobile shortly thereafter with Azilis and the curlew, Sâr Dubnotal sat down on the sofa. Grave anxiety was legible on his broad and noble forehead as he slipped into a profound reverie, with his eyelids half-closed.

Who was that dog? he asked himself, incessantly. *What* larva *incarnated itself within the animal in order to get close to Azilis and lavish such great affection upon her? I can't believe it was Tserpchikopf's, for if that were the case it's probable that, instead of getting into the Comtesse' good graces, the Newfoundland would have sought to harm her. It's most regrettable that my medium is no longer capable of revealing the name of the* larva. *My immediate intervention and energet-*

338

ic care has snatched Annunciata from the jaws of death, but the shock to which she was subjected, and the terrible nervous tension from which she had already been suffering for some time, prohibits me from asking her the slightest question before she's completely cured.

Sâr Dubnotal darted a distracted glance around the room. The owl, immobile on the table, seemed to be asleep. Through an open window, waves of fresh and pure sea air came into the smoking-room and bathed the overman's burning temples.

That's another mystery, he continued, *which needs to be clarified as soon as possible. The acute crisis that nearly carried Annunciata off did not have a natural cause. Taking advantage of my medium's trance, a hostile envious or jealous spirit—one of my enemies in the afterlife, or some demon—was able to take possession of Annunciata and provoke that terrible fit of hysteria. The spirit undoubtedly had an interest in preventing her from giving me the name of the* larva. *All these bizarre incidents have something disquieting about them, and it's high time that I found out what's behind them.*

Sâr Dubnotal took two or three reddish pills from a casket made of horn and amber.

"I hope," he said, as he raised them to his mouth, "that this small dose of hashish will put me right sufficiently to procure me the few hours of sleep that I desperately need. Psychic stress, the result of the constant mental tension to which I've been subject for several weeks, is preventing me from seeing clearly through the complications of the problem. If, as I suspect, an infernal *larva* was inhabiting the bodily envelope of the Newfoundland, how can I explain that, instead of trying to harm Azilis, the animal lavished marks of affection upon her?

"On the other hand, why did the Newfoundland cause such terror in the curlew while leaving the owl indifferent? Why, finally, did an anonymous demon attack my medium? Having tried in vain to cast light on these contradictory events, I can't connect them up and draw rational deductions from them that will set me on the right track. All that I know, or think I know, is that metempsychosis, or, at least the temporary incarnation of a spirit in a foreign body—possession, as the Church calls it—is playing a fundamental role in this business.

"Let's sleep on it, then, and pray to God that I wake up with a more lucid brain!"

Sâr Dubnotal set his head on a pile of cushions, stretched himself out comfortably on the soft sofa, closed his eyes and soon fell into a semi-somnolent state provoked by the rapid and powerful action of the soporific that he had just absorbed.

VI. The Sad End of a Guilty Woman

Meanwhile, Joseph's automobile was rolling rapidly along the road from Bordighera to Ospedaletti, carrying the Comtesse de Tréguilly and Sâr Dubnotal's manservant.

Azilis was not trying to hide the increasing anxiety that overwhelmed her at the imminent prospect of seeing her daughters again. She had been separated from Andrée and Jeanne for nearly 15 years. Might the children not have lost all memory of their mother during those 15 years?

Presumably not, since their tutor, the magnanimous psychagogue, had brought them up to respect her.

But what the Comtesse dreaded most of all, and what she was afraid of, was that some indiscretion might have been committed and that her daughters might know or suspect the truth.

"Naïni," she murmured, anxiously, "the closer we get to Ospedaletti, the more frightened I am."

"Frightened?" said the Hindu, in surprise. "Of what, or of whom, Madame la Comtesse?"

"Of everything. Especially my beloved daughters—who, instead of throwing themselves into my arms, might turn away from me in horror and disgust."

"Don't worry," said Naïni. "I assure you that Mademoiselles Andrée and Jeanne will be glad to see you, and that this will be the best day of their life—because it will give them back the mother that they love with all their heart."

"Will I have the strength to leave them in error?" sighed the repentant criminal. "How can I impose a mask of serenity upon myself, when frightful remorse is gnawing at my conscience?"

"You must," said the Hindu. "It's necessary that you seem happy, and that your daughters cannot suspect the sad thoughts that are disturbing you."

"I'd dearly like to chase those thoughts away when I see them," Azilis murmured, somberly, "but once again, will I have the strength? Oh, Naïni, Naïni, if you could read what is in my heart, you'd be frightened too. I wonder what got into me when, trampling my duties as a wife and a mother underfoot, I conceived the infamous project of getting rid of my father-in-law and my generous husband!"

"Your responsibility was considerably attenuated by the influence that Tserpchikopf exerted upon you, Madame la Comtesse. At least, my master Sâr Dubnotal has drawn that conclusion, since he was merciful enough to grant you your life, and has just set you at liberty."

"That's true. That great and mysterious man is as generous as he is perspicacious."

"Yes," said the Hindu. "Your role in these dolorous dramas was, after all, merely that of an instrument. The true criminal, Tserpchikopf, had you at his mercy by means of his hypnoptic passes. You no longer had free will, and were unfortunately destined passively to receive suggestions of the worst sort."

"May he be cursed in the next world as in this one!" cried the repentant sinner. "He has destroyed my happiness, ruined my life, racked my conscience with remorse. With every step I take, I seem to be trampling upon the bodies of the two Comtes. Oh, their blood is avenged! It has fallen back on my head! A red mist is always before my eyes."

There were a few seconds of tragic silence. They were drawing near to their destination. Leaning out of the window

341

of the fast-moving car, Azilis de Tréguilly could see the first houses of Ospedaletti at the end of the dusty road. "We're arriving!" she said. "Great God, How shall I withstand this ordeal?" She was trembling like a leaf, and drops of sweat were forming on her brow.

"Pull yourself together!" said Naïni. "Have courage, Comtesse!"

Vain objurgations! Torrents of tears sprang from the sad widow's eyes and ran down her pale and hollow cheeks.

Naïni began to get seriously anxious himself. Was something terrible about to happen? He asked himself that and, seeing her so distraught, so broken by emotion, he was about to tell Joseph to stop for a few moments in order for her to recover her spirits, when two joyful cries went up from the roadside.

The automobile slowed down, then came to a stop.

Naïni glanced out of the window and saw two big girls dressed entirely in white, who were running towards the automobile, as nimble as goats, waving handkerchiefs and giving every sign of excited delight.

It was Jeanne and Andrée. The Hindu recognized them at first glance. They had not had the patience to wait for their mother in Ospedaletti and had come to meet her, to satisfy their need to see her sooner.

"Mama! Dear Mama!" they cried, as they both precipitated themselves toward he window through which Azilis' head was visible.

At the sight of her daughters, the Comtesse had gone even paler. Suddenly, she was gripped by vertigo. Her eyes closed, and all the blood in her veins flowed back to her heart.

Just as Andrée, who had drawn ahead of her sister, was about to throw her arms around the poor woman's neck, she saw her slump backwards, inert, on the seat of the automobile.

Naïni only just had time to open his arms to catch her.

A great spasm twisted her entire body and, before the eyes of the two astounded children, the guilty woman who was Azilis de Tréguilly expired, murmuring: "Forgive me! Forgive me, my dear children! Ah! God is too good, since he has allowed me to see you before dying!"

VII. A Strange Combat

Under the action of the hashish, it was not long before a delightful numbness overwhelmed Sâr Dubnotal, who ended up falling asleep completely.

An hour went by.

On the table, the owl Kobe was still motionless, but the bird had opened his eyes, and his abnormally dilated pupils were burning like two jets of flame.

The Master Psychagogue did not move. An imperceptible flutter of wings could not draw him out of his profound sleep.

Kobe seemed to understand that, and took off, gliding over his master's head. The bird had undergone a frightful transformation. His claws were extended; his hooked beak was opening and closing incessantly, like a pair of pincers; and his wild eyes, fixed on Sâr Dubnotal's face, were still shining with a diabolical gleam.

Evidently, Kobe was preparing to descend upon the Great Psychagogue in order to pluck out his eyes. The owl's wings were already folding up, and the entire weight of his body was about to drop on Sâr Dubnotal, when a black shadow cut abruptly through the ray of sunlight that was dancing in the room.

Hurtling like an arrow, a bird with ash-grey plumage and a long curved beak had just come through the open window like a gust of wind.

It was Krak, the bearer of Naïni's dispatch.

At the sight of the other bird, the owl gave voice to a sinister ululation, to which the curlew replied with a shrill whistle.

Hovering momentarily in mid-air, the two birds seemed to be challenging one another. A mad rage shook them, and, with feathers ruffled, beaks threatening and claws extended, they looked like two duelists about to settle a supreme quarrel.

Suddenly, Kobe launched itself upon his adversary and, passing over the other bird like a streak of lightning, scored his back with its trenchant claws.

Although the attack had taken Krak by surprise, the latter did not take long to riposte. The curlew steadied himself, threw himself upon the owl in his turn, and struck Kobe such a blow with his beak that the owl fell on to the carpet of the smoking-room.

The valiant curlew placed himself between the owl and the sofa on which his master was asleep, seemingly resolved to defend him at all costs. Such was Krak's own distress, however, that he did not follow through with his offensive, and allowed Kobe to recover.

That did not take long. The owl gathered himself and leapt at Krak, and the combat recommenced, with more vigor and rage on either side than ever.

The two antagonists were almost the same size, but Kobe, being stouter than Krak and better equipped for combat at close quarters, would quickly have put an end to the other bird if the latter had been less agile. Nimbly, the curlew avoided the majority of the owl's attacks, while the blows he aimed at the owl rarely missed their target.

For a long quarter of an hour, the strange and dramatic duel of the two birds continued without respite.

Completely numbed by the effects of the hashish, Sâr Dubnotal heard nothing and saw nothing, while the owl and the curlew redoubled their efforts, fighting with the obstinacy of adversaries who know that their lives are at stake. Feathers were flying around the room, and the birds were losing blood from numerous wounds.

Already one-eyed and bent-legged—it will be recalled that the curlew had been wounded by a hunter in his youth—Krak almost lost his other eye several times, which would have put him at the owl's mercy. A charm seemed to be protecting his life, though. As if by a miracle, he avoided all the thrusts of the owl's beak and claws directed against his head, and continued to battle desperately for the salvation of his master, at whom Kobe launched himself savagely every time the curlew made as if to retreat.

Did Krak understand, instinctively, that the battle could not be further extended without imperiling Sâr Dubnotal? Releasing a furious whistle, it fell upon the owl, which was tiring at last by virtue of the lightning rapidity of his feints and ripostes.

Struck in the neck, Kobe fell on to the table, not to rise again. The curlew's pointed beak had literally impaled him, and the last drops of the owl's blood flowed from that mortal wound.

To avoid the claws of his agonized enemy, the valiant Krak prudently beat a retreat and went to perch on the shoulder of his master, who finally woke up.

Sâr Dubnotal could not understand what had happened. Astonished by the disorder that reigned in the room, he rubbed his eyes, wondering why Kobe was dying on the table and who had mistreated him so cruelly.

"Is that you, Krak?" he said, noticing that the curlew, perched on his shoulder, was in a pitiful state himself. He continued, pointing at Kobe: "Yes, it's you, scoundrel—and this is your work"

So saying, he got up in order to render assistance to the owl—but it was futile. Kobe had ceased to struggle. The spasms and frissons of the death-agony were no longer convulsing him. He was dead—well and truly dead, as proved by the rigidity of his legs, sticking up into the air. The strangest, most inconceivable and most frightful thing was, however, that his body exhaled a white mist, very similar to the fluid that constitutes the immaterial envelope of phantoms.

In fact, that pale mist gradually took on the appearance of a human body. It remained pale and transparent, but its contours became gradually more distinct, and an exclamation

345

sprang from the lips of the Great Psychagogue: "A spirit! The *larva* of a man!"

At this exclamation, the phantom disappeared, as if by magic, and Sâr Dubnotal could no longer see anything but the bloody and broken body of the owl.

"Poor Kobe!" he said, drawing nearer to the bird. "The avatar of that *larva* has cost you your life, and I regret it, for, if you have attacked Krak, as everything seems to indicate, it was that *larva* that drove you to do it." He caressed the other bird: "Are you back already, then, Krak?" he said. "If you've brought me word from Naïni, either you haven't lingered long on the road, or I've been asleep longer than I thought."

Sâr Dubnotal hastened to detach the minuscule tube of celluloid that the bird still wore around its neck, opened it and took out a slender roll of paper, which he unfolded swiftly.

It was indeed the expected message from the Hindu, and this is what it said:

Master,

The Comtesse's joy at the thought of seeing her children again was too much for her; she has just died suddenly, at the very moment of reaching Ospedaletti. I am staying here to notify the Italian authorities of her death. I hope that this formality will not hold us up for too long and that we will shortly be able to return to Bordighera, where Krak will already have brought you the sad news.

Naïni.

VIII. Astral Confrontation

Sâr Dubnotal had scarcely finished reading Naïni's dispatch when his keen ears heard an automobile coming into the courtyard of his villa. Hurriedly leaving the smoking-room, he went downstairs and saw Naïni and Joseph carrying the inanimate body of Azilis along the round-floor corridor.

"To the Green Room!" he said to them, greeting the mortal remains of the Comtesse with a slow and grave inclination of the head. "Lay Azilis de Tréguilly down on the table in the Green Room!"

Without saying a word, the two servants obeyed, and the Great Psychagogue followed them, after summoning Rudolph.

"Leave us, Joseph and Naïni," he said to the domestics. "We're going to conduct an experiment that has no relevance to you."

When the servants had gone, Sâr Dubnotal went to Azilis' body, sounded her chest, and said: "Death has done its work."

"Oh, Master, what a misadventure!"

"I almost anticipated it," the Great Psychagogue replied, "And I admit to you, Rudolph, that I shall not indulge in any futile lamentations regarding the death of the Comtesse. Think, in fact, of the situation the unfortunate woman was in—obliged to smile at the children of whom she had made orphans! Besides, Rudolph, this death might perhaps give me the key to the enigma that is tormenting me."

Sâr Dubnotal told his disciple about the duel to the death fought by the two birds, the owl's defeat, and the strange denouement that the strange battle had just produced.

"You didn't recognize the phantom, Master?" Rudolph asked.

"Yes and no," said the Great Psychagogue, evasively. "I certainly thought I recognized it, but I'm not sure, inasmuch as it vanished almost immediately. I'm thinking, therefore, of evoking the soul of Azilis."

What if Azilis doesn't know anything, Master?"

"Then I'll think again."

"Shall I summon a medium?"

"Yes, summon Rhoda Rooks—for la Gianetti is incapable of rendering me any service for the moment."

The disciple pressed a bell-push.

A few minutes went by.

Sâr Dubnotal, standing in front of Azilis' corpse, seemed to be lost in an abyss of reflection, and Rudolph did not dare make a move.

Finally, the door opened to reveal a rather tall woman whose thinness was frightening and who seemed more like a specter herself than a creature of flesh and blood. It was necessary not to judge by appearances, though, for Rhoda Rooks had an astonishing resilience and a psychic power well above the average.

She was not as marvelous a medium as Annunciata, and Sâr Dubnotal hardly ever employed her in his experiments in levitation, but she was very good at making the table speak, and even making spirits appear, to which she as far from antipathetic.

"Rhoda," said Sâr Dubnotal, "with your help, we're going to attempt a double evocation. I'd like to be able to confront the spirit of the Comtesse with a certain *larva*, which Azilis de Tréguilly undoubtedly did not know while she was alive, but whose identity might have been revealed to her since her death."

"At your orders, Master!" the American replied.

When all three of them had put on green robes and drawn the curtains over the windows, Sâr Dubnotal and Rudolph sat down in armchairs while the medium remained standing at the table.

Rhoda Rooks did not operate in the same manner as Annunciata. She did not use a wand, contenting herself with summoning the spirits by means of violent blows struck on the table with her fist, and then introducing them to the Master, who conversed with them directly.

As the soul of the Comtesse was not yet far distant from her body, Rhoda Rooks had no trouble in evoking it. Slowly, she ran her fleshless hands over the pale face of the dead woman, over the eyes that had closed forever, and over the lips that would be forever mute.

Mysterious passes were made, to the execution of which Sâr Dubnotal only had recourse in particularly grave circumstances, and incantations reminiscent of witchcraft. The method was brutal, but rarely failed; this time, once again, it was crowned with complete success.

As before, with the corpse of the owl, a mist the color of translucent alabaster detached itself from the body of the Comtesse like a long thin wisp of smoke. Instead of floating in the room, however, that mist went to deposit itself on the shiny surface of a large mirror, which Rudolph had abruptly unveiled by taking away the green rep cloth that ordinarily masked it. In consequence, a slightly blurred image—the vague silhouette of a woman—sketched itself upon the polished glass.

A slender torso, arms, and, finally, a head emerged from the vaporous cloud one after another, their outlines still indecisive. Even so, Sâr Dubnotal recognized the double of Azilis, rejuvenated and as beautiful as she had been in the early years of her marriage, before she had committed her crimes.

"It's her!" he murmured. "Introduce me to her, Rhoda."

The medium approached the glass and said: "Azilis de Tréguilly, my Master, the Conductor of Souls, desires to communicate with you directly."

At these words, there was a faint sound of silken wings in the half-light of the room. Detaching itself from the mirror, the phantom of the Comtesse came to take up a position in front of Sâr Dubnotal.

"Do you recognize me, Azilis?" the latter asked, not without emotion.

"Yes," the spirit murmured, in a strangely clear voice. "You are Severus el Tebib, the good genius to whom I owe my repentance of the sins I committed on Earth, the benefactor of my poor daughters, the man at whose service I shall remain eternally."

"In that case, Azilis, I hope that you will consent to answer I few important questions that I have to put to you."

"Speak, Severus!"

"Did your death have a natural cause?"

349

"Yes, I died struck down by excessive joy...before having completed my terrestrial penitence, alas!—which obliges me to continue it in the other life, until the purifying ordeal has washed the stains from my soul."

"Has God already imposed that ordeal upon you, Azilis?"

"Not yet, O Psychagogue—but it will soon begin."

"While waiting for it to begin, O suffering Soul, can you reveal the identity of the phantom which, shortly after your death, escaped from the body of my owl Kobe?"

"No," Azilis replied. "To my great regret, I cannot reveal that to you."

"You cannot, or you will not?"

"I don't know it myself," the spirit of the Comtesse said, more precisely, "and am thus unable to enlighten you—but you have numerous friends in the realm of the invisible who would like nothing better than to make up for my inability."

"I've already thought of having recourse to their clarification," Sâr Dubnotal replied, "And that's what I shall do, without delay. But don't go away, Azilis, for I shall have need of you shortly."

The apparition retreated as far as the back of the room, where it became immobile, like a statue of vaporous snow that has not yet crystallized.

An order from Sâr Dubnotal brought Rhoda Rooks back to the table where the terrestrial remains of Azilis lay. Transformed into an automaton, the medium struck the oak planks of the tabletop with her fist, and they split lengthwise. A sinister crepitation was followed by the fall of the cadaver on to the carpet, and in the place where it had been Sâr Dubnotal and Rudolph saw the immaterial form of a Hindu lying on the table.

"Ranijesti!" said Sâr Dubnotal.

"Yes," Rudolph confirmed. "It's him, Master! It's your best astral friend, your great tutelary spirit—the one whose collaboration has so often consented to guide you through the obscure labyrinths of the Beyond."

The faint emerald light that still reigned within the room took on an extraordinary mauve tint, and the white form became increasingly distinct. It was the double of Ranijesti, the famous yogi of Benares, who had had himself immured alive in a cellar in his native land in order to penetrate the arcane of the invisible.

The Hindu's double rose into the air above the table and floated there, then went to take up a position next to Azilis.

"Ranijesti, noble and pure Soul," the medium pronounced, "Will you come to the aid of Sâr Dubnotal."

"Always and forever," replied the sepulchral voice of the Hindu yogi.

"Can you see me, Ranijesti?" asked the overman.

"I see you, O Psychagogue! What do you want?"

"To converse with you about certain matters that intrigue me strangely, the solution of which persists in escaping me."

"Explain yourself, Sâr, my friend, and I will try to extract you from the impasse."

Succinctly and methodically, Sâr Dubnotal repeated Naïni's story. He recounted the mysterious collision of the Flying Dutchman and the Budapest, Azilis' return with the mysterious Newfoundland and the dog's bizarre death, which had been so closely followed by the no-less-bizarre duel between the owl and the curlew.

"I have not spared you any detail, O Ranijesti," concluded the Great Psychagogue, "for, in my opinion, all these singular events must stem from the same cause, and it's that cause that I beg you to let me know, if it does not escape even you."

"Do you not have a suspicion already?" the spirit asked, after a pause.

"Yes," said Sâr Dubnotal, dully. "I have a feeling that Tserpchikopf is no stranger to the events accompanying Azilis' return."

"You are not mistaken, O Psychagogue, for that perverse and wicked *larva* is the sole cause of the worries that preoccupy you."

"Tserpchikopf? So it was Tserpchikopf who incarnated himself in the body of the Newfoundland?" exclaimed Rudolph.

"Yes," said Sâr Dubnotal, "Although I don't know exactly why. In fact, Ranijesti, I begged you to watch over Azilis as over myself, and I know that you would not have allowed the *larva* of that villain to attack your protégée."

"In any case, he carefully refrained from attacking her," replied the phantom of the yogi. "On the contrary, he lavished all sorts of evidence of amity upon her, if you remember—although that, in actual fact, was nothing but a stratagem designed to deceive her and you, O Psychagogue. Since the day when you undertook to save his accomplice, Tserpchikopf has conceived a hatred against you that is not yet slaked. That hatred was exasperated by the fact that Azilis was to be set free. Knowing that he could not harm the unfortunate woman nor tempt her to ruination, Tserpchikopf set out to evade my vigilance and take revenge on you."

"Oh! I understand now! Thanks to you, Ranijesti, my eyes are open!" Abandoning the body of the dog, of which I had become suspicious, Tserpchikopf incarnated himself in that of my owl, which I was unable to suspect."

"That is correct, Psychagogue."

"That's why Krak suddenly began to avoid Kobe like the plague."

"And why Kobe almost blinded you while you slept!"

"What!" cried Sâr Dubnotal. "The wretch…"

"…Had only passed through all these avatars to reach that point," said the yogi. "Knowing that he could not end your life, he sought to render your existence odious by plucking out your eyes. Yes, my friend, those were the reprisals he intended to exact from you!"

"Then I owe my salvation to Krak?"

"To Krak and your humble servant," said the yogi's double, smiling. "Just as Tserpchikopf incarnated himself in the owl, I incarnated myself temporarily in the body of your curlew, in order to save you."

"And the Soul of the Just vanquished the *larva* of the Wicked!" said Sâr Dubnotal, prey to a sharp emotion.

"Yes, my friend; it is vanquished forever."

"Infamous Tserpchikopf!" Rudolph stammered. "Is it possible to imagine a viler and more odious vengeance? How can a being freed from his corporeal prison render himself guilty of such outrages?"

"Because death does not relieve the souls of the damned of their terrestrial defects," Sâr Dubnotal replied, gravely. "Divine mercy does not extend to them. Other souls slowly purify themselves, but they remain prisoners of evil forever."

"You speak wisely, my brother," said Ranijesti. "However, I repeat that, so far as you are concerned, the *larva* of Tserpchikopf will cease to pursue you with its posthumous hatred."

"God knows that I do not doubt your word, Ranijesti. Nevertheless, I would be glad to receive that assurance from Tserpchikopf's own lips His *larva* has never consented to respond to the evocation of any of my mediums, and I have never been able to talk to it."

"That will no longer be the case in future," the yogi affirmed. "Your medium has only to summon it, and it will immediately present itself to you."

"Summon it, then, Rhoda!" Sâr Dubnotal ordered. "My keenest desire was to bring the spirits of Tserpchikopf and Azilis into confrontation and to arrange things so that the one would henceforth be prevented from harming us by the other. Azilis is already at the stage of remission. Her spirit, if it pleases God, might watch over that of Tserpchikopf and prevent him from doing evil."

Rhoda Rooks rapped on the tale and, at the same moment, another phantom—the pale specter of a man—emerged from the crack opened up in the tabletop. An iridescent mist enveloped it, and the only part of it that could be clearly made out was its eyes: two magnetic eyes, like those that Azilis had once seen shining in her cell on Redemption Island.

"Tserpchikopf!"

"Severus el Tebib!"

The two exclamations overlapped, the one sharp, launched by the Great Psychagogue, and the other dull and hoarse, as if stifled by rage and shame.

The spirit of Azilis and Ranijesti's double came to take up positions to either side of Tserpchikopf's *larva*, and the immaterial trio came closer to the two men.

"Do you regret your crimes, Tserpchikopf?" said Sâr Dubnotal.

"No!" replied the *larva*, grimly.

"So your hatred will never be appeased?"

"Never! I am damned!"

"What! You will seek to harm me again?"

"I would like to, but I shall not be able to."

"Why?"

"Because Evil is henceforth impotent against Good."

"You recognize that, but will not try to amend yourself?"

"I cannot."

"Keep trying. You have eternity before you in which to appease divine wrath."

"Eternity!" sighed the criminal soul, lugubriously. "That's a long time, Mortal—alas! But even eternity cannot wash away my sins."

"In that case," said the Great Psychagogue, "nothing remains for me to do but place you in the care of Azilis." Turning to the phantom of the repentant woman, he said: "Do you understand, Azilis, the service that we are asking of you?"

"Yes," stammered Azilis. "I am to be the guardian of this *larva*, and I am to prevent him from doing harm."

"And I shall continue to observe both of you and to watch over my terrestrial brother," said Ranijesti.

"Thank you, O most beautiful of Souls!" replied Severus el Tebib.

Immediately, the three phantoms faded away into a purple and gold cloud that fell from the ceiling of the Green Room, while Azilis' cadaver resumed its place on the table and the curtains, drawing back of their own accord, allowed daylight into the room again.

Epilogue to the Tserpchikopf Affair

The soul of Azilis did not fail to keep its word. It still remains by Tserpchikopf's side, bathing it and dominating it with its effluvia. Since then, Sâr Dubnotal has no longer had to occupy himself with that blood-thirsty *larva*, except to reassure humans frightened by the persistence of its apparitions.

Tserpchikopf is in fact, condemned to haunt the places that were the theater of his crimes, and Azilis accompanies him everywhere. On the anniversaries of the pseudo-boyar's crimes, on the stroke of midnight, two shades can be seen gliding through the skies of Paris, Trez-Hir, Tunis, Marseilles and London, tightly intertwined. That astral couple is formed by Tserpchikopf and Azilis.

As for the Comtesse de Tréguilly's daughters, they were grieved to learn of their mother's death, but they still do not know what she did, and their innocent lips only pronounce her name in order to bless it.

THE END

BLACK COAT PRESS

M. Allain & P. Souvestre. *The Daughter of Fantômas*
Anicet-Bourgeois. *Rocambole*
Guy d'Armen. *Doc Ardan: The City of Gold and Lepers*
Aloysius Bertrand. *Gaspard de la Nuit*
A. Bisson & G. Livet. *Nick Carter vs. Fantômas*
Félix Bodin. *The Novel of the Future*
Comte de Chousy. *Ignis: The Central Fire*
Lucien Dabril. *Rocambole*
V. Darlay & H. de Gorsse. *Lupin vs. Holmes: The Stage Play*
C.I. Defontenay. *Star (Psi Cassiopeia)*
Charles Derennes: *The People of the Pole*
Harry Dickson. *The Heir of Dracula*
Sâr Dubnotal. *Sâr Dubnotal vs. Jack the Ripper*
Alexandre Dumas. *The Return of Lord Ruthven*
J.-C. Dunyach. *The Night Orchid: Conan Doyle in Toulouse*
J.-C. Dunyach. *The Thieves of Silence*
Paul Féval: *Anne of the Isles*
Paul Féval. *The Blackcoats: The Companions of the Treasure*
Paul Féval. *The Blackcoats: The Invisible Weapon*
Paul Féval. *The Blackcoats: The Parisian Jungle*
Paul Féval. *The Blackcoats: 'Salem Street*
Paul Féval. *Captain Phantom*
Paul Féval. *Gentlemen of the Night*
Paul Féval. *John Devil*
Paul Féval. *Knightshade*
Paul Féval. *Revenants*
Paul Féval. *Vampire City*
Paul Féval. *The Vampire Countess*
Paul Féval. *The Wandering Jew's Daughter*
Paul Féval, *fils. Felifax, the Tiger-Man*
Emile Gaboriau. *Monsieur Lecoq*
Arnould Galopin. *Doctor Omega*
V. Hugo, Foucher & Meurice. *The Hunchback of Notre-Dame*
O. Joncquel & Theo Varlet. *The Martian Epic*
Jean de La Hire. *Enter the Nyctalope*
Jean de La Hire. *The Nyctalope on Mars*
Jean de La Hire. *The Nyctalope vs. Lucifer*
Steve Leadley. *Sherlock Holmes - The Circle of Blood*
Maurice Leblanc. *Lupin vs. Holmes: The Hollow Needle*

Maurice Leblanc. *Lupin vs. Holmes: The Blonde Phantom*
G. Le Faure & H. de Graffigny. *The Extraordinary Adventures of a Russian Scientist Across the Solar System* (2 vols.)
Gustave Le Rouge. *The Vampires of Mars*
Jules Lermina. *Panic in Paris*
Gaston Leroux. *Chéri-Bibi*
Gaston Leroux. *The Phantom of the Opera*
Gaston Leroux. *Rouletabille & the Mystery of the Yellow Room*
Jean-Marc Lofficier. *The Katrina Protocol*
Jean-Marc & Randy Lofficier. *Edgar Allan Poe on Mars*
Jean-Marc & Randy Lofficier. *Robonocchio*
Lofficier. *Tales of the Shadowmen 1: The Modern Babylon*
Lofficier. *Tales of the Shadowmen 2: Gentlemen of the Night*
Lofficier. *Tales of the Shadowmen 3: Danse Macabre*
Lofficier. *Tales of the Shadowmen 4: Lords of Terror*
Lofficier. *Tales of the Shadowmen 5: The Vampires of Paris*
Lofficier. *Tales of the Shadowmen 6: Grand Guignol*
G. Marot & L. Pericaud. *Nick Carter vs. Jack the Ripper*
Xavier Mauméjean. *The League of Heroes*
William Patrick Maynard. *The Terror of Fu Manchu*
Frank J. Morlock. *Sherlock Holmes: The Grand Horizontals*
Marie Nizet. *Captain Vampire*
C. Nodier, Beraud & Toussaint-Merle. *Frankenstein*
Charles Nodier. *Lord Ruthven the Vampire*
Henri de Parville. *An Inhabitant of the Planet Mars*
John William Polidori. *Lord Ruthven the Vampire*
P.-A. Ponson du Terrail. *The Vampire and the Devil's Son*
Albert Robida. *The Clock of the Centuries*
Eugène Scribe. *Lord Ruthven the Vampire*
Brian Stableford. *The Germans on Venus*
Brian Stableford. *News from the Moon*
Brian Stableford. *The New Faust at the Tragicomique*
Brian Stableford. *The Shadow of Frankenstein*
Brian Stableford. *Sherlock Holmes - The Vampires of Eternity*
Brian Stableford. *The Stones of Camelot*
Brian Stableford. *The Wayward Muse*
Villiers de l'Isle-Adam. *The Scaffold*
Villiers de l'Isle-Adam. *The Vampire Soul*
Philippe Ward. *Artahe: The Legacy of Jules de Grandin*

P. de Wattyne & Y. Walter. *Sherlock Holmes vs. Fantômas*
David White. *Fantômas in America*

Non-Fiction:
S. R. Bissette. Blur (Vols. 1-5)
S.R. Bissette. Green Mountain Cinema
Jean-Marc & Randy Lofficier. Shadowmen (2 vols.)
Randy Lofficier. Over Here

Art Books:
Randy Lofficier & Raven Okeefe. *If Your Possum Go Daylight*
Jean-Pierre Normand. *Science Fiction Illustrations*
Raven OKeefe. *Raven's Li'l Critters*
Daniele Serra. *Illusions*

Screenplays:
Mike Baron. *The Iron Triangle*
Emma Bull & Will Shetterly. *Nightspeeder*
Emma Bull & Will Shetterly. *War for the Oaks*
Gerry Conway & Roy Thomas. *Doc Dynamo*
Steve Englehart. *Majorca*
James Hudnall. *Devastator*
Jean-Marc & Randy Lofficier. *Despair*
Jean-Marc & Randy Lofficier. *Royal Flush*
Andrew Paquette. *Peripheral Vision*
Roy Thomas. *Rivers of Time*

Comics:
CLASH
Kabur
Phenix
Strangers: Homicron
Strangers: Jaydee
Strangers: Starlock
Wampus
Zembla